SHERLOCK HOLMES

THE MISSING YEARS: TIMBUKTU

VASUDEV MURTHY

JAICO PUBLISHING HOUSE

Ahmedabad Bangalore Chennai
Delhi Hyderabad Kolkata Mumbai

Published by Jaico Publishing House
A-2 Jash Chambers, 7-A Sir Phirozshah Mehta Road
Fort, Mumbai - 400 001
jaicopub@jaicobooks.com
www.jaicobooks.com

Published in arrangement with
c/o, Baror International Inc.
Armonk, New York, USA

To be sold only in India, Bangladesh, Bhutan,
Pakistan, Nepal, Sri Lanka and the Maldives.

SHERLOCK HOLMES
THE MISSING YEARS: TIMBUKTU
ISBN 978-93-86348-80-7

First Jaico Impression: 2017

Printed by
Trinity Academy For Corporate Training Limited, Mumbai

Remembering Ruby
A little child who went away too soon

"O thou who goest to Gao, turn aside from thy path to breathe my name in Timbuctoo. Bear thither the greeting of an exile who sighs for the soil on which his friends and family reside. Console my near and dear ones for the deaths of their lords, who have been entombed."

—*Ahmed Baba*

Foreword

Sir Arthur Conan Doyle wrote sixty stories about Sherlock Holmes.

Actually that isn't quite true. There are also the two neat, subtle little self-parodies: "The Field Bazaar," written to help raise funds for the Edinburgh University Cricket Club, and "How Watson Learned the Trick," Conan Doyle's contribution to the Library of Queen Mary's Dolls' House—but the accepted canon consists of just the sixty tales.

For many admirers sixty is not enough. Long before the last stories appeared in *The Strand Magazine*, devotees had begun to extrapolate and expand upon the life and career of the great detective.

Today, thanks to the expiry of the original copyright in almost every country and a concatenation of circumstances and events that could hardly have been predicted in the author's lifetime—varied and immensely popular dramatic presentations of Holmes and Watson, technological progress that's made publication of almost anything not only possible but easy, the scientific miracle that enables a document to be composed and read anywhere in the world without ever having been written on paper—Conan Doyle's sixty stories are vastly outnumbered by the ones from other hands.

Those are what we call *pastiche*, a word defined in part by the *Oxford English Dictionary* as a "literary or other work of art composed in the style of a known author." And there is an awful lot of Holmesian pastiche.

It would also be true to say that there is a lot of awful Holmesian pastiche. Quantity tends to obscure quality, which is unfortunate, because over the years some excellent new adventures have appeared. Novels worth seeking out include *The Seven-per-cent Solution* by Nicholas Meyer, *Dust and Shadow* by Lyndsay Faye, *The Quallsford Inheritance* by Lloyd Biggle Jr., *A Slight Trick of the Mind* by Mitch Cullin, *The Case of the Raleigh Legacy* by L B Greenwood, *Art in the Blood* by Bonnie MacBird, and *Sherlock Holmes: The Missing Years—Japan* by Vasudev Murthy.

Those "missing years," of course, are the ones between the unobserved duel on the ledge at Reichenbach in 1891 and the detective's return to London in 1894. In Doyle's "The Empty House," Dr. Watson gives us Holmes' own account of his activities during that time—or, at least, what purports to be Holmes' own account.

"I travelled for two years in Tibet, therefore, and amused myself by visiting Lhassa, and spending some days with the head lama. You may have read of the remarkable explorations of a Norwegian named Sigerson, but I am sure that it never occurred to you that you were receiving news of your friend. I then passed through Persia, looked in at Mecca, and paid a short but interesting visit to the Khalifa at Khartoum, the results of which I have communicated to the Foreign Office. Returning to France, I spent some months in a research into the coal-tar derivatives, which I conducted in a laboratory at Montpellier, in the south of France."

There are those who doubt that that's what really happened. There are those who doubt the official story of the fight at Reichenbach Falls, and such suspicions may be valid, given the number of errors, contradictions and obfuscations in Watson's published chronicles. *Sherlock Holmes: The Missing Years—Japan* is a witty, learned and desperately exciting alternative.

The book you're now about to read, *Sherlock Holmes: The Missing Years—Timbuktu*, is neither a sequel nor a prequel, but an alternative to the alternative. Inspired by that mention of a visit to Khartoum, Mr. Murthy has imagined* the meeting with the Khalifa, the extraordinary events and perilous journeys that preceded it, and the amazing events that followed.

Come with us—Holmes, Watson and their little party—to Rome, to Tangier, south through the Sahara to Timbuktu, and then across the desert to Khartoum. It's a dangerous venture, but I think you'll enjoy it!

Roger Johnson, BSI
Editor: *The Sherlock Holmes Journal*
July 2015

---

* Sherlock Holmes considered the faculty of imagination to be essential in his own work. In the Silver Blaze case he told Dr. Watson: "Inspector Gregory, to whom the case has been committed, is an extremely competent officer. Were he but gifted with imagination he might rise to great heights in his profession."

By way of introduction...

In perusing my extensive notes, I find that the adventures in Timbuktu of my friend, the eminent consulting detective Sherlock Holmes, stand out for their extraordinary complexity and cultural richness. And yet, it has been necessary to keep the matter utterly secret all this time, though for reasons outside some associated diplomatic sensitivities. The reader will soon understand why.

I have faithfully—and, I believe, accurately—documented over three hundred situations where Holmes' dexterity made all the difference, often in matters involving life and death. That is an interesting turn of phrase I have stumbled upon while writing, because this particular chronicle addresses that aspect of the human experience. Concepts like God, reincarnation, souls, and so on present difficulties to the logical mind. Yet religion thrives, with the mass of humanity believing that the universe is under the control of a benign power, who demands obedience, placation, and worship in many odd and sophisticated ways.

It is admirable that modern education frowns on what cannot be tested and verified. This is necessary for the vast majority of our sciences. I can hardly imagine my patients being satisfied with vague and dramatic pronunciations of appeals to spirits for healing if they were to seek the alleviating of a stomachache, for example. And yet such is the case in many parts of the world untouched by modern medicine and its principles. Men and women would rather pray to unseen temperamental spirits, who must be addressed *just so,* rather than accept the products of scrupulous scientific inquiry that are repeatable and validated by peer review.

No, this story[1] is not about magic. Sherlock Holmes was always contemptuous of the black arts, demonstrating to me more than once, with chemicals and logic, how a clever man could take advantage of the credulity of thousands. It can also be argued that what we know today may be a fraction of all that really exists, and therefore, when confronted with entirely new situations, we may not have a ready explanation that science accepts. The use of the telephone in large parts of the civilized world is endemic; we may lift the phone and ask an operator to place a call to someone many hundreds of miles away and have a conversation. While the entire principle of telephony is based on scientific logic involving magnetism and electricity, perhaps a hundred years ago we might have summarily dismissed the possibility of speaking to another person in such a manner through copper wires. In fact, had someone even suggested this, execution might have followed in certain countries where allegations of witchcraft invariably end badly for the dilettante inventor. The world is indeed moving forward. Who can say how we shall be communicating a hundred years from now? Perhaps we will not need wires or even operators.

But I digress.

What followed after the events at Reichenbach Falls has been debated extensively. Many theories were propounded by members of an excitable public seeking satisfactory closure. Some said Sherlock Holmes had spent the period in Japan assisting the Emperor Meiji. Others insisted that he had spent time in a monastery in Tibet as some kind of advisor to the Dalai Lama. Many swore that Holmes had been sighted in the United States, providing confidential counsel to the President. I listened to these fanciful theories and refused to be provoked to comment. I held back even when charlatans claiming to have conclusive information about Holmes' secret life as an undertaker in Edinburgh—which they would part with for a fee—tried to swindle members of the public with the guarantee of a personal meeting. It is painful for me to state how remarkably gullible the average citizen is. So convinced is he of a particular viewpoint that he reacts with righteous indignation if any other theory—nay, even the truth!—is advanced. This is true of religion, too, the reader will agree, in which indoctrination from an early age renders the mind incapable of even considering

[1] Many have remarked that this is one of the most extraordinary pieces of writing they have yet encountered.

an alternative viewpoint. Indeed, it once happened that a devout reader almost assaulted me in London, claiming that my entire body of work could be considered heretical because I had had the temerity to state that one or more stories were, in hindsight, entirely false. He spoke of "The Canon," and made much of it, and called me an imposter. Yes, me, Dr. John Watson.

But the passage of time and the need to clarify certain matters has now made it necessary for me to place before you the truth. Our unusual journey through the Sahara Desert to the ancient city of Timbuktu and then to the lower Nile Valley needs to be brought forward so that the uncomfortable questions raised in Parliament recently are put to rest, specifically with regard to the meeting we had with the khalifa in Khartoum, the details of which Holmes conveyed in a confidential note to the Foreign Office. Unfortunately, the Vatican has refused to confirm or deny the related events and claims, leaving us with no alternative but to put the matter before the public and appeal to its sense of discernment. My solicitors are prepared to respond to any legal challenge from allegedly affected parties, but we suspect that eventuality is extremely unlikely, given the embarrassment that may result.

I have, as you might expect, carefully masked some names and changed dates and locations in order to prevent the eruption of an unintentional international crisis. I am pleased to say that Mycroft Holmes, very likely the most profound thinker of our times and deeply influential at the Home Office, returned my manuscript with only an exclamation mark noted on the first page, which I took as a compliment for my diligent work. Sherlock Holmes, too, gave me his tacit approval, albeit with a sardonic smile. He has lately been consumed by the energies required to produce a series of monographs that were a direct consequence of our remarkable experiences. I am not assisting him in this exercise, as I have never been enamoured of monographs.

It is a truism that men are the same everywhere. If there is a shortcut available to acquiring wealth and power, and settling scores, and if their value systems permit and they think no one is looking, they will use that shortcut with little regard for how their actions might impact others. The regrettably bloodthirsty public relishes horrendous crimes followed by the apprehending of the perpetrators. My published stories of Sherlock Holmes have been popular for that reason; they appeal to the reader's sense of righteousness and the need for a noble closure. Yet we have kept away from the public a very large number of cases that have to do with thwarting of intent. Just under the surface of awareness lurk motivated men and women with unspeakable evil in their hearts, seeking to destroy people, institutions, and nations. Had it not been for the highly developed logical mind of Holmes, I can say with certainty, many families and nations would have been grievously—and permanently—maimed in many ways. There is, I am sorry to say, no "market" for such tales, to use the odious word employed in a letter to me by my editor in the United States of America, a country driven by endless excitement, the boundless pursuit of lucre at the cost of every civil courtesy that one man may extend to another, and an unfortunate celebration of decadence.

This book that you have chosen to acquire, thereby demonstrating the finest of literary tastes[2] and the highest of intelligence, is a chronicle of the period between the (false) story of the demise of Sherlock Holmes at Reichenbach Falls and his supposed miraculous reappearance in the enticingly titled story "The Empty House." In this book, you will observe how the world has shrunk: China, India, Sudan, Egypt, Morocco, Italy, and Mali have all been woven together with the invisible threads of human endeavour through the passage of time. History, geography, culture, music, and—regrettably, perhaps—crime will find a place in subsequent pages. The magnificent, incandescent presence of Sherlock Holmes permeates each page of this chronicle.

John H. Watson M.D.
London
26th May 1909

---

[2] A Swedish gentleman, Alfred Nobel, invited me to Paris for a private discussion on the matter in November 1895. Unfortunately, pressing matters pertaining to the confounding disappearance of the Earl of Gloucester's wife detained Holmes and me, leading to a misunderstanding. I understand he subsequently set up a much-coveted prize for the literary arts and, I am told, referred specifically to me as one of his inspirations and the obvious winner. I may clarify that had I been nominated, I would have declined. I affirm that I never wrote the chronicles for recognition or acclaim. A newly evolving term "best-seller" typifies, I regret to say, an insecure author's constant need to seek validation of his efforts by assuming that unthinking social behaviour (akin to the behaviour of lemmings) translates to a positive certification.

A Visitor from Italy

"Ah Watson! A merry affair there at Norwich! The constabulary in ferment, I see!"

"Indeed, Holmes. Would you call it merry, though? Six murders in two months! And not a clue in sight! One wonders why the authorities have not reached out to you yet!"

"Frankly, Watson, I would prefer they did not. The answer is so obvious that I would not wish to embarrass them. However, if it pleases you, and since the loss of life is a regrettable matter, perhaps you could send a wire to the inspector in charge—Cowley?—to interview Lazarus Smith, the village blacksmith, who very kindly took them to the scene of the crime in the second case. Ask them to inspect the attic. They are wasting their time talking to Donahue. Being Irish and ugly is not a crime."

"Yes, Holmes," I said, making a note.

I was visiting Holmes after a long interval. Consequent to my marriage, our meetings had become infrequent but were always warm. My wife was away on a visit to Glasgow and I had taken the liberty of travelling to London to meet him and attend to sundry business.

We had spent the better part of the day talking about past cases and discussing the eventual fates of many notables. The bitter January cold had seeped inside our room, and we moved a few inches closer to the fireplace that Mrs. Hudson had so thoughtfully prepared. Outside, the fog swirled and I could hardly imagine that anyone would be foolhardy enough to walk about, risking life and limb. It was not an evening for profitable crime. Holmes was stretched languidly across the sofa, violin resting carelessly on his left thigh and his right leg dangling on the floor. He was leafing through a copy of *Debrett's Peerage*.

"Well, well, I see that the Duke of Beaufort studied classics at Oxford in 1875. I happen to know that he was almost rusticated for suspected plagiarism. And at about the same time, the Earl of Breadalbane played cricket there and was challenged for unsportsmanlike conduct. Two very different personalities, Watson, but both with some claim to a common experience at the same moment in time. *Debrett's* says nothing about their scandals! The world is filled with strange people, eh, Watson?"

Before I could respond, he flung a wire toward me.

"What do you make of this, Watson?"

I looked at it.

WHY WOULD ANYONE BE INTERESTED IN THIS PARCHMENT? THE BRITISH AMBASSADOR IN ROME SUGGESTED I MEET YOU URGENTLY ON A MATTER OF UTMOST SENSITIVITY. 1030 PM TONIGHT. GRAZIE. ANTONIO ROZZI. VENICE

"An Italian travelling all the way from Venice to meet you, Holmes? Very flattering."

"It must be very sensitive for him not to find it prudent to write. Something has happened that has made him abandon his routine tasks. He seems to be a man given to objectivity. A historian, I would wager, given the reference to a parchment. Ah, the time draws near! A carriage just outside, Watson."

We heard the creaks of a carriage and the shuffling and snorting of horses, as they settled outside 221B Baker Street. In a few moments, we heard the sounds of someone taking the stairs quickly. Shortly, there was a polite knock.

I opened the door.

The man opposite was about my height, though stout. He was clean-shaven, bald, with luxurious sideburns, and immaculately dressed. He looked quite English. He stooped a little, was about fifty-five years old, and carried a valise.

He bowed.

"Signore Holmes? I am Antonio Rozzi from Venice." His accent was distinct.

"No, I am Dr. John Watson. Do come in."

I helped him with his overcoat, while Holmes watched.

"I apologize for this late meeting," said Antonio Rozzi, bowing to Holmes. "I had no choice."

"You reached London this afternoon. There must have been something of interest at the British Museum that detained you for a few hours. But do sit down."

Signore Rozzi gasped. "*Che cosa*! You are quite right, Signore Holmes! I visited a friend at the Chinese antiquities section. But how did you know?" He seated himself heavily on a chair, catching his breath, valise in hand.

Holmes shrugged. "The wire was sent from the Post Office at Great Russell Street at about three in the afternoon. I would expect a historian from the continent to visit the Museum first, practically as a religious duty."

"*Si, si*!" exclaimed Signore Rozzi. "That is so!"

"And how may we help you, Signore Rozzi?"

"Ah, Signore Holmes, a very strange situation! I met your Ambassador at Rome, Lord Dufferin, and he said that you were the best person to help me. A most vexing matter, I am afraid, *si*. Extremely confidential, if I may say."

Holmes nodded. "Please proceed. Everything remains within these four walls."

Signore Rozzi looked relieved and began.

"I am the chief conservator of the Venice Museum, Signore Holmes. We have a highly unusual situation and need your advice."

Holmes listened patiently.

"Have you read the Bible, Signore Holmes?" Signore Rozzi leaned across and peered intently at Holmes.

"As a matter of academic interest, yes. I am not a believer per se, but the book is entertaining and has its merits."

"In what language was it written, do you know?"

"Yes, originally in Hebrew, Aramaic, and Greek."

Signore Rozzi sat back, beaming. '*Superbo*! Very rare, Signore Holmes, for anyone to know this, very rare!"

He opened his valise with great deliberation and carefully removed a document. "I would like to show you something sensitive." He placed it on the table and invited us to come closer.

It was a dull brown parchment with unusual faded markings. Some were in red and some were in black. Holmes examined it carefully against the light.

"Where is the other half?"

"Signore Holmes, you are clever! *Si*, this is the left half of a manuscript. The right half is missing. And it has always been missing since this came into our possession shortly after the death of Marco Polo in the year 1324."

"The script is perhaps Aramaic, since you touched upon the matter of the Bible. The parchment looks old. And, wait, the indentations on the paper seem to indicate the words were embossed in some way and then coloured."

"*Si! Si!* How correct you are! Someone has taken an impression of the text from a surface and then coloured it. Which means it is a copy."

"This manuscript is about two thousand five hundred years old, we think, pre-dating Christ. But the script is, surprisingly, not ancient Aramaic. It is not even related, as far as I know. It is Meroitic, which, sadly, I cannot read, but which I know originated in the Nile Valley. Indeed, there are very few scholars who can read that script. This is the reason I visited the British Museum to meet Signore James Conway, who is such a scholar, and can read Meroitic with some effort. However, he was not available, so I shall be meeting him tomorrow."

Holmes peered intently at the manuscript. "There seems to be some kind of a map at the bottom, perhaps. And only half of it."

"Correct! We think so, too."

"And how may I help you? Surely this is not a treasure hunt."

"It is much more than that, Signore Holmes." Signore Rozzi looked grave. "About two months ago, I started receiving strange notes in Arabic, which I happen to be able to read. Here is one. They are almost all identical."

بـقاوعلا ةءجاوم كيلع الا و روفـلا ىلع رخالا فـصنلا دعأ - ١

"And this means…?"

"Return the other half immediately or face consequences."

"To what address?"

"A post box in Casablanca, Morocco."

"I see. And the reference is to this manuscript?"

"*Si*, we believe so now, but we did not know about this until a month ago.

"You see, Signore Holmes and Dottore Watson, we get many anonymous letters at the museum. People are fascinated by history and often believe that some object truly belongs to them. They ask for its return, claiming it belonged to an ancestor. We routinely ignore such letters."

"I see."

"But a month ago, we had an attempted burglary in the Chinese antiquities section. An alert security guard foiled the attempt and challenged the intruder, who stabbed him. The guard described the intruder as having Arabic features. Most unfortunately, the guard passed away the next day because of his injuries.

"When I examined the antiquities, I found that everything was in order, except for the section that contained old manuscripts. We have thousands, and most of them are of unknown origin. They are often trivial—books of accounts or a journal of a ship's voyage. It appeared that the intruder had just started looking through them when he was surprised. However, while going through the manuscripts, I found this parchment. And I stopped."

"A parchment with Meroitic inscriptions in the Chinese manuscripts library?"

"Yes, it was very surprising. But then again, it was not, because they were in the papers bequeathed to us by Marco Polo."

"The great traveller," nodded Holmes. "Well, yes, he did travel to China and would have brought back many articles of interest, including manuscripts, picked up along the way."

"That is correct, Signore Holmes. The matter became a bit clearer when we saw that there was a note in the hand of Marco Polo with this parchment. Here it is." He took out something from the valise and spread it on the table. The three of us gathered around to look at it.

"It is in Old French, so let me translate it for you."

He read the manuscript in a halting voice:

> *Many come to me, as I lie dying, asking me to proclaim that my account of my travels to China is a falsehood. I have not done so. Indeed, I have not revealed even half of what I know to Rustichello da Pisa, when we were in prison together in Genoa, since the haughty citizens of Venice have no regard for anything that goes against what they think is the truth. Let them mock at me. I go to the Heavenly Father with a clear conscience.*
>
> *Oh, our ignorance! Only travel will erase it, but how can I insist?*
>
> *I beg my descendants to guard this document with their lives. It has value beyond money.*
>
> *I left the court of the great Kublai Khan with immense sadness. The Khan himself wept, for I was like a son to him, and he, to me, was like my father. He asked me to take anything I wished from his Kingdom, a generous offer that we accepted in small amounts. Yes, gold, paper, gunpowder, vases—these were his gifts. You know, perhaps, that I was escorting a princess from his court to Hormuz in Persia to be wed, but I spent time in his ancient and large library in his capital Xanadu seeking books, for they have great*

and everlasting wisdom, and I felt that they would have permanent value.

The many books which you see, along with this letter, are from his library, and reflect his infinite generosity to me and the Catholic Church.

I found a strange copper sheet in a dark corner of his library and became curious. It had peculiar inscriptions etched on it—they were neither in Chinese nor in any other language that I was familiar with. It looked very pleasing, though out of place in the library. How is it that such a copper sheet was found in the library of Kublai Khan of China? No one had any idea as to its origin or value. I sought permission to take it because my interest was piqued. The Great Khan agreed, as he could not find any use for it. For safety, I made a print of the copper sheet by pressing a sheet of paper down and then colouring the indentations created by the etches. I thus created a paper manuscript.

After the parting about which I have written, I sat down in the ship that we had boarded at Zaitun and tried to translate the manuscript. It was impossible, as I had no knowledge of this peculiar script. And yet, somehow, I felt uneasy. It was as if the letters were appealing to be read and understood.

Weeks later, we docked at the port of Calicut in India where I befriended the Zamorin of Calicut, who welcomed me with great honour. We became good friends very soon and he gave me additional gifts and mourned with me for the shipmates I had lost on the way.

He introduced me to some priests of the Syrian Catholic church who seemed knowledgeable about ancient languages. Since I was concerned about the contents, I was cautious, and gave only tiny bits of the letter to them to translate, which they attempted to do with enthusiasm, employing guesswork and experience. I then pieced the document together as best as I could.

As I learned how to read the faint letters and understand the words, I felt their impact. I will not tell you now what it was.

I took a decision to safeguard this manuscript in an unusual way for I was afraid of what would happen if someone with evil in his heart were to read it, fully understand it, and act on it. And so I tore the manuscript in two and requested that the Zamorin keep half of it in his custody, saying that it was a letter guaranteeing safety to those who wished to meet me in Venice. The Zamorin kept it carefully without asking questions and said that he would wait for someone to claim the letter someday.

I left directly for Persia. I had memorized the contents of the manuscript, of course, and chanted them to myself quietly as my ship bore west. My head was full of dark, angry clouds and confusion. In a moment of extreme fear, I flung the copper sheet into the sea, as though it were on fire. I instantly regretted my action, but of course, it was too late.

We reached Hormuz, and then you know the rest.

Keep this letter with the manuscript, for everyone's safety. It is too valuable to be destroyed and yet too dangerous to be completed. Let us pray that mankind does not find the other half. It will bring infinite misery, though many will believe, foolishly, that it will be the opposite.

Marco Polo
Citizen of Venice

I was flabbergasted by this peculiar story. We sat in silence absorbing the words.

Holmes puffed at his pipe and said nothing, waiting for our visitor to continue. We could hear the beat constable just outside.

"We feel convinced, Signore Holmes, that the attempted burglary pertained to this document."

"What would you like me to do?"asked Holmes, after some reflection.

"Visit Venice with me and help us to understand the matter better."

Holmes shook his head. "We are working with conjectures. And my current engagements will not permit a trip. Why can your police not assist?"

"They lack the scientific approach, Signore Holmes. More importantly, we think this requires secrecy and if we were to go to the local police, we cannot say with certainty that the matter would not become widely known, resulting in new complications. And we want to understand the mystery. Why is someone so interested in this parchment?"

"Why can you not get this document translated? Would that not help, even if partially?"

"Yes, it would. This is why I visited the British Museum, as I said. And I shall do so again tomorrow. However, we think your involvement is needed. The Catholic Church worked closely with Marco Polo and sent some sepulchral oil to the Khan on his request; that is an interesting story I could tell you about some day. Marco Polo was buried in the Church of San Lorenzo in Venice but his body was lost. Father Agnelli of that church is very knowledgeable about him. The Patriarch of Venice has expressly asked for your involvement after he consulted the Pope, though I must add that the decision was opposed internally at the Vatican. Though there are ancient Aramaic and demotic scholars in Rome, who could have perhaps translated the Meroitic, it was felt that the matter must be kept very confidential, which is why I have brought it here. This may have ramifications beyond murder and a simple translation."

"What kind of ramifications, I wonder. Hmm. Perhaps I should think about it. Shall we meet again at eight tomorrow evening after you consult your friend?"

"S*i, si!* Let us hear what he has to say."

With that, Signore Rozzi stood up, placed the documents back into his valise, bowed, and left the room quietly.

"Very interesting, Holmes," I remarked.

"Indeed, no clear case, but an atmosphere of history and mystery. Well, let us wait until tomorrow. Meanwhile, *Debrett's* beckons!"

And with that, Holmes sank back into his sofa and was shortly lost in the vagaries of British royal lineage.

The Museum

At breakfast the next morning I was surprised to see a somewhat subdued Holmes.

"A bad night, Holmes? Perhaps another perspective to the Norwich case? Or the recent letter from the Home Secretary seeking your views on the forgery case?"

"No," said Holmes, slowly. "The strange case of Signore Rozzi. I was too dismissive, I think. There have been cases with much less information to go on that I took up with greater vigour. Well, I see that we have an eager visitor."

We heard someone quickly bounding up the steps. A young urchin burst in without the courtesy of knocking.

I stood up, outraged.

Holmes merely smiled and waved me down with his right hand. "Yes, Wiggins? You have something of importance?"

"Yes sir, Mr. Holmes, sir! It's not a clue, sir, but I know you like me to tell you if I hear something unusual, sir!" He was panting and sweating.

"Go on, Wiggins. You'll get your shilling."

"Seems like something's going to happen in Great Russell, Mr. Holmes! The talk is that someone big—I don't know from which gang, sir—is having the museum watched, sir!"

"Any idea why, Wiggins?" Holmes was suddenly alert and he leaned forward, his eyes on the boy.

"I heard the name Conway, Mr. Holmes, sir, but I don't know. I saw two men with funny hats, sir, and they might have something to do with it. They were asking about Conway, sir!"

"Describe the hats, Wiggins."

"Kind of like a flowerpot but upside down, sir. Reddish, like. And a thread running down from the top, Mr. Holmes, sir!"

Holmes sprang across to the bookshelf and pulled out his recent acquisition, the Ninth Edition of the *Encyclopaedia Britannica*. He leafed through the pages until he came to what he was looking for.

"This, Wiggins?" he gestured.

"Yes, Mr. Holmes, sir. That's what they were. I've seen these hats before, sir, but there was something about the men that made me look at them closely! I think they had daggers, sir, but I'm not sure."

"Excellent, Wiggins, excellent! Here's your shilling! Make sure you keep a watch and don't let the men out of your sight."

"Yes sir, Mr. Holmes, sir!"

Wiggins left in the same noisy manner as he had arrived.

"Always pays to have a few people on the ground, eh, Watson? A sharp lad there. Trained him to notice the unusual and bring it to my attention." Holmes was quite pleased.

"The museum again, Holmes? A coincidence?"

Holmes shook his head. "No. Coincidences are for the romantic. I think Signore Rozzi will soon confirm a connection. I hope he is safe."

"What was it you showed Wiggins, Holmes?" I asked.

"Images of hats, Watson. And Wiggins picked a fez, also called the *tarboosh*, one that Arabs from North Africa and Turkey usually wear."

"Silly of the men to wear something that would help to mark them out. But habit makes us blind."

"Well said, Watson, but you are possibly unaware that there are many Arabs in London who visit on business. That hat is not unusual. It is only Wiggins' powers of observation that helped him pick up details. A lad with a promising future, Watson."

"I wonder now, however, if someone I know is involved… no, no, that is farfetched. Or perhaps I have too little to go on." Holmes suddenly looked thoughtful.

"Whom do you refer to, Holmes?" I was intrigued.

"It was just a passing thought, Watson. A matter of no consequence. Disregard my comment. We shall just wait for Signore Rozzi to return."

Holmes thereafter busied himself with his seven percent cocaine solution, annoying me to the extreme. He rolled up his sleeve and injected a vein carefully. I demonstrated forbearance and avoided comment.

He also examined his correspondence and was soon exasperated.

"Really, Watson, sometimes I wonder if we are dealing with children. The absurd problems of the Danish and Spanish royalty…tut…do their juvenile indiscretions warrant convoluted and pompous diplomatic manoeuvring and agonizing? Are my services required to hold their hands, or to deal with the torment of the common citizen and his desire to live a peaceful life, without the presence of violence and depravity? Sometimes I have half a mind to simply decline their entreaties and let the entire world become acquainted with what goes on behind the silks, brocades, and fancy crowns. Bah!"

I knew he was not looking for a response. I listened and noticed with great concern his wan countenance, and his forearm punctured with needle pricks.

Precisely at eight, Signore Rozzi presented himself at our door. He seemed slightly disturbed.

"Were you waylaid as you travelled here, Signore Rozzi?" asked Holmes, eyeing our visitor with concern.

"*Sì*! That is so! How did you know?" gasped our visitor.

"The frayed shirt sleeve and the dust on your shoes are conclusive, sir. You would not intentionally attend a formal meeting in such condition. In fact, I was almost expecting that you would not be in a position to keep your appointment."

Signore Rozzi stared at Holmes, the blood leaving his face. "You are a wizard, *si*, a wizard! It is so, Signore Holmes. As I was boarding the hansom outside the museum, two men rushed across the road and tried to abduct me. However, I sensed their approach and was able to escape after striking them. The driver was alert and he moved the cab the moment I jumped inside. They did not pursue us."

"Did you see them?"

"It was dark. I could not see them clearly. London is quite unsafe, *mamma mia*!"

"As is Rome, Signore Rozzi," responded Holmes, dryly. "The world is changing. Crime is everywhere. In this case, however, I had a feeling this might happen."

"*Vero*? Why?"

"I know that you were being watched."

"But why?"

"Because you have something or know something important. I think it is the parchment, whose significance is unclear to me. I see seven—no, eight—different possibilities. No doubt you will enlighten us and will prove one of them correct. Please do proceed."

"I visited my friend Signore James Conway this morning, as you know. He is very knowledgeable about Semitic languages, especially the classical ones. I must tell you, Signori, that Meroitic as a language became extinct after the Byzantine era, but was common much before the arrival of Jesus Christ. There are many variants, of course, and this parchment's alphabet is from one of them. I knew all this before I came here, but Signore Conway was likely to be the best person to help. It also happens that he has a reputation of being a practical scholar, by which I mean that he travels a lot to correlate theory with facts."

Holmes nodded.

"When I showed the parchment to Signore Conway, he was very excited. He held it against the light and exclaimed many times. At last, he turned toward me, his face flushed with excitement.

"'Do you know what you have, Signore Rozzi?' he asked me.

"'No,' I said. 'But it seems very old and valuable. And there is a map.'

"'This is not Aramaic. It is likely Meroitic or a variation of Old Nubian. A Nilo-Saharan Nubian language! A very rare document indeed!'

"'See this 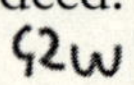 and this slightly clearer one 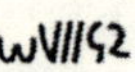.

"'The first is a reference to the God Ra and the second is, I think, to Osiris. But I am guessing, and need time. This is a script that's been a mystery for most scholars. We do not have something like the Rosetta Stone[3] to help us, so it is all conjecture and intelligent guesswork. Fascinating, fascinating!'

"Signore Conway's eyes were bright with excitement and he was positively dancing with joy. 'I think—*I hope*—we have a beautiful poem! A wonderful poem or a chant! Wonderful! It could be some form of chant, because I see that there is alliteration. I think this is Osiris, here. And I think it has a connection to a place indicated in the map. Some kind of funerary chant, perhaps? Remarkable!'

"How do you know it is a chant?" I inquired.

"He said, 'Because Meroitic was written from right to left, like Hebrew and Arabic, and there appears to be alliteration, and we have the left half. I do not know for certain, as I am not an expert. What we have are the ends of sentences. But the letters are unclear and I do not recognize most of them, which is not surprising.'

"Signore Conway paused then. 'I can *guess* some words. *abundant, water, soul, light, life*...But I need time. And of course, without the other half, how do we know what this is? Let me remind you that we may be able to pronounce the words, but we may never know what they mean. I am amazed that this

[3] From the desk of the chief archaeologist at Poisoned Pen Press: In 1963, Dr. Nicholas Millet, curator of the Egyptian department at the Royal Ontario Museum, did uncover something in the Nile Valley called the Adda stone, which was helpful but not conclusive.

manuscript was found in Peking and brought back by Marco Polo! How did it even reach China? How wonderful, Signore Rozzi!'

"'*Si!'* I said, 'You are right! This is a great treasure! But why would someone want it suddenly and be prepared to use a knife?'

"'Of that, I have no idea. Do you wish to leave this in my safekeeping?'

"I hesitated. 'No, Signore Conway. I do not have permission from the Patriarch. But I have made a copy for you. Will it help you?'

"He was disappointed.

"'I understand. Well. I think I will need at least three months to come to a conclusion and I do not know if I have the knowledge for it. But I shall try. Can you come again in April? Say the twentieth?'

"'Of course!' I answered.

"Then we discussed other areas of research and passed the day pleasantly. Thereafter, we had an early supper at the museum and I left to visit you. That is when the incident happened."

Holmes was lost in thought.

"Intriguing. Written threats in Arabic from Morocco. A case of bodily assault, possibly by Arabs. A murdered museum guard in Venice. Half of a parchment written in Old Nubian or Meroitic. A letter in French by Marco Polo. And a report from Wiggins about rumours in the London underworld," Holmes murmured.

Signore Rozzi looked bewildered. "Wiggins? Arabs? What do you mean, Signore Holmes?"

"I am reasonably sure you were attacked by Arabs, Signore Rozzi. And my sources have already told me that you are being looked at with interest. It could be because you have the parchment. Or there could be some other reason."

"Should I leave this parchment with you then, Signore Holmes?"

"I thought the Patriarch did not give you permission to leave it with anyone."

"No, he has given me permission to leave the parchment *only* with you, on the explicit order of the Pope."

"Why is the Pope interested, I wonder. Well then, that probably explains it. These things cannot be kept secret. An indiscreet word here and there and clever people conclude that a man is travelling to visit the well-known detective Sherlock Holmes in London with the encouragement of the Pope and the British Ambassador."

Holmes smiled. "Do leave it with me, by all means, though I decline to guarantee its safety. It is you who must now be careful. I recommend you take the eleven o'clock overnight ship from Dover to the continent and then proceed to Venice. In case you hear from Mr. Conway, do let me know."

"I agree. Thank you."

Signore Rozzi handed over his valise, bowed and left.

Holmes and I were silent for a good ten minutes.

"A noteworthy case, Watson," he said. "And yet, I can presently make nothing of it. Someone wants this parchment. He probably has the other half. There is some secret here that is of relevance to even the Pope. The script is very difficult to decipher. Men wearing fezzes have already been observed by Wiggins and were seen at the museum in Venice, too. Intriguing. Music may provide the answer."

Holmes turned to his violin and began playing. Strangely enough, it was an Arabic tune. I had no idea that Holmes was acquainted with that kind of music.

In a few days, the aforementioned events retreated from our minds and Holmes busied himself with issues pertaining to the Scandinavian question and the brutal Charing Cross murders. The latter was relatively straightforward to unravel, though it needed patience, which Holmes had in abundance. The former was more complex, and Holmes was forced to consult his brother Mycroft more than once at the Diogenes Club. I returned to my home, leaving Holmes to the ministrations of Mrs. Hudson.

In a later account, I have spoken about the unusual behaviour of Sherlock Holmes in the period between the events previously described and up to the accident at Reichenbach Falls. When he visited me, I was shocked by the transformation. He had become a bundle of nerves, had lost weight, and was altogether not himself. He spoke about being afraid of bodily harm and encouraged me to travel with him to Europe with no specific destination in mind. It happened that my wife was again on a brief holiday with her sister and so I was able to oblige my friend's odd request. We travelled to Paris and then to Switzerland.

That was the first time he spoke of Professor Moriarty.

He described him in great detail, as a master criminal, a spider at the centre of a web responsible for crime everywhere, but always impossible to specifically charge. Holmes expressed respect for the professor's intelligence, and I listened in silence, slightly disturbed. You may wish to read about those events in detail in my publicly told story "The Final Problem," in which I speak of our travels to Europe and the purported disaster at Reichenbach.

The events that shook the public in May 1891 are still fresh in my mind. The reports of Holmes' fatal plunge down the Falls were greeted by the public with shock and consternation. A much-loved figure had been lost in the most alarming manner at the hands of a master criminal. The world despaired—how could evil be allowed to triumph over a man as beloved as Sherlock Holmes?

Yet Holmes had left behind, at Reichenbach, a courteous letter, perhaps hoping to soothe the outraged sentiments of the law-abiding citizen, and to console me.

My Dear Watson,

I write these few lines through the courtesy of Mr. Moriarty, who awaits my convenience for the final discussion of those questions which lie between us. He has been giving me a sketch of the methods by which he avoided the English police and kept himself informed of our movements.

They certainly confirm the very high opinion I had formed of his abilities. I am pleased to think that I shall be able to free society from any further effects of his presence, though I fear that it is at a cost that will give pain to my friends, and especially, my dear Watson, to you.

I have already explained to you, however, that my career had in any case reached its crisis, and that no possible conclusion to it could be more congenial to me than this. Indeed, if I may make a full confession to you, I was quite convinced that the letter from Meringa was a hoax, and I allowed you to depart on that errand under the persuasion that some development of this sort would follow. Tell Inspector Patterson that the papers he needs to convict the gang are in pigeonhole M., done up in a blue envelope and inscribed "Moriarty." I made every disposition of my property before leaving England and handed it to my brother Mycroft.

Pray give my greetings to Mrs. Watson, and believe me to be, my dear fellow

Very sincerely yours,

Sherlock Holmes

I believed—and there was clear evidence—that Holmes and Professor Moriarty had fallen off the cliff and met an unfortunate end in the furious waters of the falls. The signs of a bitter scuffle, the letter he had left behind—there could be no doubt.

I was subsequently interviewed by several newspapers of repute. I met dozens of grieving devotees of the great man, and his friends at the French Sûreté and at Scotland Yard. The unfortunate matter took several months to settle down.

I swore to myself to keep Holmes' memory alive. I organized his papers and personal effects and kept his violin aside with great reverence. My wife aided me in what was to us a sacred task. We had lost a remarkable friend and human being, who embodied so many of the qualities that define excellence in human endeavour.

I owe the public an apology.

It is time to reveal that Holmes had not died.

My story was written in ignorance.

◇◇◇

In May 1893, about two years to the day after the events of Reichenbach Falls, I received a letter in a familiar script.

The envelope was stamped Tangier, Morocco, but the handwriting stirred memories. I knew no one there, and yet…

I opened the envelope carefully. And inside was a brief letter from Sherlock Holmes.

April 19, 1893

My Dear Watson,

This letter will undoubtedly come as a surprise, though I shall hope it will be a pleasant one.

I am about to embark on an important journey. I cannot do so without you by my side. Much depends on the success of this mission across unfamiliar and hostile terrain. I am not in a position to explain more.

I have enclosed a ticket for passage from Liverpool to Tangier via Gibraltar on a ship by Compania Transatlantica for the 15th of May. The journey may not be comfortable but it will prepare you, it is my hope, for a much longer and more arduous journey.

When you disembark at Tangier, ask for Mehdi Benbouchta at the Casa Barata souk (market) and introduce yourself by name. The password, should he ask you for one, is Rihla. He will bring you to me.

I would certainly appreciate the accompanying transport of my violin.

Very sincerely yours,

Sherlock Holmes
Oasis of Tafilalt
Eastern Morocco

A letter from Haji Ibn Batuta to his son

Bismillah ar-rahman ar-rahim

This letter, my son, should have been given to you by a member of the Guardians of the Letter, two families that I have sworn to secrecy and will help you on an important mission.

I have spent my life travelling and perhaps I have travelled far more than any man ever has or will. To see so much and to learn so much—verily, I have been blessed by Allah. How many can say they have visited Mecca seven times? How many have been to China, Andalusia, India, and Mali?

I have described everything, as far as I could remember, in *Tuhfat al-Nuzzar fi Ghara'ib al-Amsar wa-'Aja'ib al-Asfar*[4], which others call *Al-Rihla* (الرحلة) ("The Travels"). I beseech you, my son, to ensure that your sons read my words and become pious and humble. The customs and languages of the people whom Allah has created are all different, and must therefore be respected, even if we lack understanding. I may not have

4 A Gift to Those Who Contemplate the Wonders of Cities and the Marvels of Travelling

liked, for instance, the behaviour of the black cannibals near Timbuktu, who smeared themselves with the blood of their victims before prostrating in front of Sultan Mansa Sulayman. Yet, as a traveller, though a Qadi, I had to keep within some boundaries, as I had learned at a cost in my early days as a traveller in India, when I was somewhat brash.

For what I have seen everywhere in the world, my son, has been a desire to live long. Allah has granted us an exact number of breaths. But we, in our greed, ask for more. Death is the only thing that seems to truly bind together everyone everywhere in the world.

In all lands, I have seen this greed, my son. In Damascus, in Sind, in Yemen, in Kathay, in Serendip—no one truly believes he will die, and is therefore unprepared. Each hopes for some secret to be revealed. No matter how unhappy, no matter how poor, no matter how lonely—all beings hope to live forever. I must tell you this strange tale, because I am now too aged to find what is missing and solve a mystery as old as man.

As you know, and as I have said in *Al-Rihla*, I left the court of the moody Mohammad Bin Tughlaq in Delhi on a mission to China, and came to the west coast of India after many difficulties. From Khambhat in Guzzerat and down Kambay and Honnavar, I finally came to Calicut. And there again, as you know, I had many occasions to visit, marry, and to suffer setbacks and become wealthy. None can say what Allah would have us experience. How often have I been robbed and assaulted and how often have wealth and fortune smiled on me again.

During a particular period, while I waited for the winds to die down, I sought and received the friendship of the Zamorin. He was a good man and was interested in my travels. We spent many an hour talking about various matters of astronomy, mathematics, botany, and the scriptures. And at some point, he confided in me.

"Haji, God has been kind to send you to me. I have learned much from your wisdom."

"Allah alone decides who should meet whom and for what purpose," I responded with a bow.

"I feel that you are the messenger that my father had told me about."

"What do you mean?" I asked, puzzled.

"Wait here," said he, smiling, and he went inside his private room and emerged shortly thereafter, carrying something covered with Chinese silk.

During my father's time, Haji, there was another famous explorer who visited Calicut. He was not a Haji. He was from beyond Persia, perhaps from Rome or Greece. He visited us while returning from China. My father told me he was a wise man, sent by the Chinese emperor on a mission. He had with him a princess whom he was to take safely to Persia to be wed. As you see, there are many Chinese junks that visit us here. Visits by royalty do happen. I know that you plan to visit China once the winds die down.

This man's name was Marco Polo, according to my father. One fine day, Haji, he visited my father with a strange request. He said that he had with him half of an important document that he wished to have my father keep safely. "There are secrets here," he said, "and I trust only you in this world to keep this manuscript, waiting for the right man to come and claim it."

"Who will he be?" asked my father.

"You or your son will know him. It is destiny. If he brings this to Venice, the city where I live, he will have riches beyond his wildest dreams once he demands and receives the other half of the document. I only beg you to be careful in deciding who that person ought to be."

My father could never refuse any request, and without further questioning, he accepted this document—yes, this one in your hands—and enjoined his guards to keep it with his own most valuable possessions. He ordered that anyone who opened the package without his permission should be put to death immediately.

And as time moved forward relentlessly, Marco Polo went away and my father died. The story was kept alive for a while, but was forgotten, like other stories. It is only after I met you, Haji, that I remembered it, and the very fact that the story came back to my memory is a sign that you must be that person.

I therefore request that you take this with you. It belongs to you and we have only been custodians. Go in fair winds, and when you reach this place, Venice, meet the descendants of Marco Polo and claim what is yours.

I accepted his gift humbly, though I was quite unsure about what it was. I kept it aside and we continued our discussions.

Finally, it was time for me to travel to China, which I did. Those matters I have described in Al-Rihla. Read it again and again and learn about the world, my son. Remember that even the Prophet had enjoined us to seek knowledge, if even as far away as in China. If you can, travel. If you cannot, read Al-Rihla.

I travelled first to Chittagong, which I did not much care for, though I was happy with the slave girl I purchased there. I also met a holy man who could see into the future, quite like the Qadi in Alexandria and Sheikh Al-Murshidi, and who was at least one hundred and fifty years old. I learned there that some men had indeed conquered time, difficult as it might be to believe.

I was repelled by the customs and practices of the heathen Chinese. They eat pigs and dogs and their conduct is, on the whole, not to my liking. I travelled to Peking, too, to meet the descendants of Kublai Khan. Along the way, I heard stories again of this man, Marco Polo.

While in China, I suffered from a period of sickness. I stayed in bed in Quanzhou and prepared to return to my homeland. I learned that a ship was soon to set out to Sumatra and I resolved to travel on that ship. But while I lay gathering my strength I decided to open the package that the Zamorin had gifted to me.

I saw immediately that it was much older than most things I had encountered. I could not read the language, though I thought that some of the letters looked familiar. But I could certainly tell that I had with me half of a map, for at the bottom were unmistakable signs. I felt sure it was a map to some treasure, and it occurred to me that if I found the left half (I had the right half), I could indeed see the entire map. I would need to learn what the words meant, of course, but I felt sure that would be possible. It must be an extraordinary treasure, something beyond gold and gems. But what?

I returned to Morocco through Yemen and Persia, the story of which you will find in Al-Rihla, so carefully written by Ibn Juzayy. I had no wish to return to Delhi and meet the unpredictable Mohammad Bin Tuglaq, who could shower me with gold coins or have me sawn in half, depending entirely upon his mood. But shortly thereafter, I travelled southward. For me, who has travelled so far, it is impossible to stay at home. I have always said, never travel the same road twice.

I travelled on the Niger River[5] and had many strange experiences, with unusual people. I travelled initially with a group of merchants from Sijilmasa, though we went our separate ways later. The salt mines at the Taghaza oasis and the hippopotami in the river, the wise men and the barbarians—the experiences again demonstrated that there is no end to strangeness in this world. I finally reached Mali. The date of my arrival at Mali was 14th Jumada I, 753.

As a Qadi, I was able to enjoin many to be true to Islam. With others I failed. However, I was always given respect, and I gave manuscripts that I had brought with me to many libraries along the way. I saw that the people of Mali respected learning

---

[5] In the *Rihla*, Ibn Batuta surprisingly mistakes the Niger river for the Nile

and forced their sons to memorize the Quran, as well as books of law and other matters, by chaining them cruelly. In some places, I was surprised to see small rooms hollowed out of the huge baobab trees, and there certain valuable manuscripts were stored. When the people seek knowledge, the job of the Qadi becomes easier, even if all the customs, such as the nakedness of women, are not to one's liking.

As you also know, I fell sick during this period when I ate some yams that had been cooked carelessly. I resolved to return to Fez, but could not do so easily. There was also some rumour gathering speed that the Black Plague was impending. I had seen its effect in Damascus and was aware of how quickly the disease could kill thousands. In Damascus, the Jews, Christians, and Muslims had all come together to pray to God, but yet the plague had swept through the city. Further, Mansa Sulayman, the King, was not as strong as his brother, and Negro tribes from the southwest were in a state of tension with him. If I fell into the wrong hands, I would be killed, without a doubt, as they are suspicious of white Arabs.

Under the circumstances, I resolved to travel quickly and so, as was the local custom, buried my own most valuable manuscripts at the Sankore Mosque of Timbuktu, built by Musa I, hoping to come back later and claim them. I gave instructions to the learned Negro Qadi of the mosque to hold my manuscripts for my return. And I left Mali via Gao in haste on 22nd Muharram of the year 754. It was a marvellous return journey, though some parts were again very arduous.

Alas, it seems clear now that it will not be possible for me to return to Timbuktu. My time is approaching fast, and while I have acted and recorded my travels in detail, my age and health will not allow me to undertake another journey in the desert.

I tell you this, my son, because the half-manuscript I was given by the Zamorin of Calicut is also amongst those that I left behind in Timbuktu. My understanding of the document was increased after years of studying it and seeking guidance from other scholars and Qadis who knew the language of the infidels. I am sure it is safe because the people there respect learning and books, and will not destroy any documents even if they do not understand them. They are very proud of being black and look down upon us for being white and raw, but at the same time, their respect for learning exceeds their ignorance. If you have a book, it is considered more valuable than gold, and you may also know that there is so much gold in Mali, no one thinks about it. Yet, surprisingly, the location of the gold mines is kept secret. Did you know, my son, that the King of Mali, Mansa Sulayman, is the younger brother of the fabled emperor Mansa Musa, who went to Mecca with thousands of citizens, slaves, and wives through Cairo? Mansa Musa gave away enormous amounts of gold to everyone along the way and returned empty-handed, though not perturbed, because he brought back with him scholars and books, declaring them to be of greater value. I pray that you too are gifted with such wisdom. The designs of some of the mosques in Timbuktu are the result of the blessed knowledge of the architects he brought back with him from Mecca.

At the library of the Sankore Mosque, I have read many books such as the astronomy commentary by Muhammad bin Sa'īd bin Yaḥya al-Sūsī al-Marghitī, *The Ethical Treatment of Animals* by Ismā'īl bin Bāba bin Sīdi Muhammad al-Ntishāi" ī, and *The Principles of Jurisprudence* by `Abd al-Qādir bin `Abd al-Karīm al-Wardīghī al-Khayrānī al-Shafshāwnī. All knowledge is welcomed in Timbuktu. It is a remarkable place, truly blessed by Allah.

Go forth then, my son, and as soon as you can, take a caravan to the Sankore Mosque of Timbuktu in Mali, and find the manuscript quickly. It came into my hands by accident but left them because of carelessness and haste. Prevail upon the Qadi there to hand over my books and manuscripts to you.

Find, too, the other half in Venice and thereafter find the treasure that is promised. Take the help of the Guardians of the Letter. They live only for you and for this noble purpose.

Abū ʿAbd al-Lāh Muhammad ibn ʿAbd al-Lāh l-Lawātī ṭ-Ṭanǧī ibn Baṭūṭah

19 Safar 770 A.H.

Journey to Venice and the Vatican

X

Sherlock Holmes had commented bitterly and often upon the propensity of the public to demand, in the first instance, tales of apparently extreme evil, almost as an appetizer, to be then followed in the next instance by a sequence of highly logical steps that ensnared the perpetrator. This was a matter of some wearying significance for a chronicler like me, for whom the onerous task of detailing the activities of a very great man must involve objectivity and attention to detail rather than distraction by the hysterical demands of a shallow public that can only be satisfied by bloodshed in a book.

Yet, the fact is that the cases involving such depravity were few and far between. For the most part, the cases involved attending to a quirk in human behaviour and smoothing of a misunderstanding, which if not addressed quickly, could likely become a more serious matter. Avoiding a catastrophe was more satisfying intellectually than running about looking for men or women who committed a grievous act and thought they could get away with it. That is the reason that Holmes avoided interacting with the public as far as possible and let me write the stories that won him so much admiration. He would read my drafts with amused contempt, offering an occasional correction or suggestion. But he refused to be drawn into a dialogue with the public, of whom he had a poor opinion.

I mentioned that Holmes did not die at Reichenbach. I shall now elaborate.

I have listened to many theories on what happened at the Falls. All seem compelling. I could not disagree with any idea advanced because, after all, there was no sign of Holmes for months. There was the letter and there were the clear signs of a scuffle at the edge.

A single point has always been overlooked: there were no witnesses.

Let me go back to the time when Signore Rozzi came to meet us in January. Holmes had asked him to return to Venice and to let him know if Conway had anything new to say. I had returned to my home and did not meet Holmes again till later in April when he came to visit me and persuaded me to travel with him to Switzerland. That is when he spoke of Moriarty.

As we travelled to the continent, Holmes spoke in a subdued voice.

"Watson, we have not spoken lately of the affair of Signore Rozzi. Let me remind you that Wiggins had observed two Arabs watching the museum. He felt that someone had ordered the watch, but could not provide a name. Were you aware, Watson, that Conway had been set upon very badly a few days ago?"

"No!" I gasped. "I do not recall reading about it in *The Times*!"

"For good reason, Watson. Please do not assume that if something does not appear in *The Times* it has not happened at all! Since when is that paper the final word on any matter?"

He continued. "I specifically told Lestrade to arrange that the press would be in the dark. I am convinced that Moriarty is involved and it has to do with the half-parchment. My suspicion is that Moriarty has even more specific information on the possible nature of the parchment than we do, and was waiting for Conway to finish his inquiry and extract the meaning as best as he could.

"Note two things. One, that Conway was using a copy of the parchment, while the original is with me. And two, that Moriarty possibly concluded that it was best for him to have an expert do the work for him before he acquired the translation. Once he was done, Conway was of no consequence. So the attempt at murder, which went awry. Why? Because I had told Wiggins to guard Conway. I had also visited Conway very discreetly in early April and had a productive conversation with him. I happen to be well acquainted with his brother, so an introduction was not a problem. He had translated the half-manuscript to the best of his ability, yes, but on my request had deliberately introduced a couple of errors as a safeguard, just in case inimical forces felt the need to act. The errors would have considerably confused the reader. The copy was indeed stolen when Conway was attacked. But he had the good sense to keep the real translation elsewhere and he gave it to me. And as it happens, he had received a letter from Signore Rozzi at about the same time, saying he was indisposed and therefore not in a position to travel to London for the meeting scheduled for the twentieth.

"Yes, the time has come to travel to deal with Professor Moriarty, Watson, particularly given the broad hints that Conway, in his limited knowledge, could give me about the contents."

"But what of the contents, Holmes?" I had asked, my curiosity aroused.

Holmes shook his head. "In case we get the other half and are able to translate it, the entire meaning is likely to take us into another realm of understanding of the laws of physics, Watson. I will not burden you with sensitive information that would put you at risk."

The public knows the "facts" about the events leading to the grim battle at the edge of the Reichenbach Falls. Since Holmes had not confided in me, I too was taken in by the evidence as it was, and came to the conclusion that I had lost my friend forever. This matter greatly exercised me and caused me profound sorrow for an extended period.

Much later, Holmes told me that he had already written the famous "good-bye letter," which he placed on a ledge, prior to arriving at the falls. He thereafter arranged for further evidence of a scuffle. He left the area before I could return but not before he attracted the attention of Professor Moriarty, who chased him. But Holmes had a significant advantage and he vanished into the mountains, from where he watched me and other rescuers arrive at the falls and arrive at an incorrect conclusion. Professor Moriarty obviously hid, too. Holmes had managed to shake him off.

Then he hiked his way across the border to Italy, touching little villages along the way. The Alps were very remote in any case, an ideal refuge. He reached Lugano, Bergamo, Verona, and then Venice after several days, travelling incognito.

When he reached Venice, Holmes disguised himself as a stout professor, claiming to be visiting from Grenoble. He feared, rightly, that Moriarty was on the lookout. The reach of the man was extraordinary and it would be only a slight exaggeration to say that everything and everyone was somehow connected by a thread back to him.

Holmes went to the Venice Museum.

At the main desk, he asked in French if he could visit Signore Antonio Rozzi. "I am Professor Olivier Picart from Grenoble," he said.

The two guards looked at each other. Finally one spoke.

"Monsieur, we are sorry, you cannot meet Signore Rozzi."

"Perhaps he is busy. Would you oblige me by taking my card and asking when I might visit him? I have a message from his friend Professor Charpentier at Grenoble."

"I am sorry, Monsieur, it is impossible."

"But why?"

"Because, Monsieur, Signore Rozzi is dead."

Holmes was shocked and showed it.

"What? Dead? When?"

"Just two days ago, Monsieur. He was murdered in his office in the evening. If you wish I will find out if you can see Signore Batista, who used to work as his deputy."

"Merci."

A guard departed and came back in a few minutes, asking Holmes to accompany him. They went through a couple of long rooms with high ceilings and plenty of exhibits, and then they turned a corner into a rather secluded and quiet alcove. The guard knocked on one of the doors and pushed it open.

Signore Batista was at his desk, a pale, short, middle-aged man with black hair, obviously still in the throes of shock. He was slim and wore a gray jacket over a white shirt. He was unremarkable except for his rather large ears.

Sherlock Holmes stepped in and extended a hand. "Signore Batista, I am Professor Olivier Picart from Grenoble."

"Professor Picart, welcome. I am Vincenzo Batista. I was the assistant to Antonio Rozzi. Please sit down."

"I am very sorry. The guard told me. This is very bad news. As you would say, *Tragico*! *Tragico*!"

"S*i*," sighed *Signore* Batista. "*Tragico*! It is unfortunate, very unfortunate. But how can I help you, Professor Picart?"

"I am visiting Italy on holiday. His friend Professor Charpentier at Grenoble asked me to visit the museum and convey his regards."

"Ah, I thank you. The name is not familiar, but then Signore Rozzi was well travelled and knew many people. His special interest was the preservation of ancient manuscripts."

"That is right. And Professor Charpentier has a similar strong interest. In fact, he has a particular interest in Marco Polo."

Signore Batista clicked his tongue in mild irritation. "Ah yes, he is very popular, Marco Polo. Everything in Venice is named after him! Everything happens under the shadow of his great name, *si*. Signore Rozzi himself was a specialist on Marco Polo and wrote many monographs on various aspects of Marco Polo's travels."

"Indeed? Professor Charpentier mentioned to me that Signore Rozzi had visited him in January while travelling to London and hoped to do so again in April. But he did not visit him, and so Professor Charpentier was worried. He asked me to inquire and conveyed his best wishes."

"He had not been keeping well for some time. I was worried about him. He did not rest at all and seemed to be worried about something. But I did not expect him to be murdered."

"How did it happen? What do the polizia say?"

"Someone hit him violently on the head in his office," Signore Batista gestured to show the blow. "Over the past several weeks, he was busy trying to translate some ancient documents. It is not clear if anything was stolen, say the *polizia*. We have lost a great scholar, *si*."

"Is it possible for me to visit his office with you? I would like to pay my respects to him there, if possible. Professor Charpentier was a great admirer, and I would like to tell him I visited his office."

"*Si*. I have the key. Let us go." Signore Batista stood up from behind his desk and walked around it. They then walked across the hall to the late Signore Rozzi's office. He turned the key and they entered.

The room had been severely disturbed.

Papers and books were strewn everywhere. It seemed like a storm had passed through the room.

Signore Batista exclaimed with shock. "*Santo Cielo*! What is this? This is not how it was when we removed the body and locked the room! Someone has visited again!"

Holmes sprang across the room. It was clear that the intruder had come in through the window that faced the road outside. It was a very easy task for a professional burglar.

"What did he have of valuc, Signore Batista?"

"He was just a scholar. He had manuscripts that he would borrow from the archives for detailed study. Then he would return them. There was nothing else. I cannot understand why someone would do this!"

"What was he studying recently?"

"The Old Nubian and Meroitic scripts. He did not discuss the matter with me. but that was not unusual. It is not necessary to share all aspects of one's research all the time. For that matter, he did not know the details of my own research, either. I have a vague idea that he visited the patriarch of the Catholic Church here in Venice a few times in connection with a new manuscript. But I have been occupied by other matters and did not pay attention."

"Did you have any books on that subject?" asked Holmes.

"*Si*. And I see that they are here." He waved his hands in an expansive gesture. "So that was not what the thief wanted! And what possible value could they have anyway?"

Holmes walked around the room. He knew quite well what the burglar had been looking for. And he had it with him!

"Should we call the *polizia*?" he asked.

Signore Batista snorted in exasperation. "Our *polizia*? They are useless! Useless! Let them find the murderer; that is enough! But they are fools!"

His opinion of the abilities of the local constabulary was clear.

"Anything else unusual here, Signore Batista?"

"Hmm, I see a map of Africa here, perhaps nothing unusual. Except that he has marked a few places, do you see?"

Holmes looked at the map along with Signore Batista. "Yes, he has marked Tangier, Cairo, Khartoum, Gao, Timbuktu…I wonder what it means. And what do these markings suggest?"

Signore Batista shrugged. "I have no idea. Was he planning to travel there? I doubt it. He was not a strong man and could not have survived the journey. I just cannot understand it! The markings are probably Old Nubian or Aramaic, I do not know. It is not my field of research."

"Would you have any objection if I took the map to Professor Charpentier at Grenoble? Perhaps he could express a view, given his knowledge of Signore Rozzi's recent research."

"I have no objection. It is just a standard map of Africa. You may take it. We have hundreds of them."

But not one with these places so conveniently marked, thought Holmes, as he carefully folded the map and put it in his pocket.

"Shall we lock the windows and door?"

"Yes, and I shall ask our polizia friends to walk about outside. They cannot be bothered! They would prefer to sleep all day, crime or no crime! We had one such incident in the museum in January when a guard was killed. But the killer was never found."

"What happened?"

"Someone tried to steal something from the Chinese antiquities section and was surprised by the guard before he could proceed. However, he managed to wound the guard fatally. And now looking at the murder of Signore Rozzi, I would not be surprised if people wondered whether this were a museum or a house of criminals! Two murders in less than a year! In a museum of all places! *Cielo*!"

"By the way, did Antonio Rozzi smoke?"

"No. Why do you ask?"

Holmes bent down and picked up a cigarette butt. He carefully collected a small amount of residual ash. He also sniffed.

"Something distinctive...when did I last come across this..." he murmured softly. "The cigarette ash...hmm ..."

As they walked back to his office, Holmes asked Signore Batista about the manner in which Signore Rozzi had been set upon.

"A blow to the head."

"Which side?"

"His left side." Signore Batista pointed at his own head at the place of impact.

"Did he fall forward or backward?"

"Hmm. Yes. On his desk. Blood was all over his papers. There are a few spots on that map, too."

"Professor Charpentier had mentioned casually that Signore Rozzi had been receiving anonymous letters."

"We all do. We ignore them most of the time." Signore Batista rolled his eyes.

"I shall take leave then. Professor Charpentier will be greatly saddened by this news. I sincerely hope the perpetrators are apprehended."

Holmes bid good-bye to Signore Batista and left the museum. He spent some time with the guards making a few inquiries. He also asked them for directions to the Church of San Lorenzo.

He sat on a wrought-iron seat in a nearby park for about half an hour looking over the map, trying to commit to memory the names of the towns that the late Signore Rozzi had written.

Then he went to the Church of San Lorenzo, one of the oldest in Venice.

It was late. A quiet evening mass was on. Holmes went inside and sat discreetly in the last row, waiting for the mass to conclude and the worshippers to leave. The church was certainly very old and grand, though not large by the standards of others he had seen.

The last of the worshippers had left and Holmes slowly walked up to the priest who was busy cleaning up and bidding good-bye to an altar boy.

"Father Agnelli?"

"S*i*. And you are…?"

"Professor Olivier Picart from Grenoble. I have just come from the museum."

Father Agnelli looked up sharply.

"I see. And how may I help you?"

"May we sit down?

"Yes."

They walked together to the side of the church where there were a couple of chairs.

"A beautiful church. Very old, I imagine."

"Yes. Possibly thirteen hundred years old, but rebuilt a few times."

"You knew Signore Rozzi."

"Yes. We were close friends."

"I met him on his trip to France and England," said Holmes.

"I guessed. And I think you are not Olivier Picart but Mr. Sherlock Holmes."

"Correct. Thank you."

"Antonio told me about you."

Father Agnelli was an unsmiling, heavyset man, about sixty with white hair and rimless spectacles. He looked at Holmes for a long moment.

"His funeral will be held in a few days. I am greatly saddened by his violent death. But somehow, I was not surprised. When I saw the manuscript and read the notes in Arabic, I knew it was of great importance. I took him to meet the patriarch of Venice who then took Antonio to Rome to meet the Pope. I will tell you whatever you would like to know. Please ask."

"First, be assured that the manuscript—or rather, the half—is safe."

"Good."

"The translation is with me, but those hostile to us also seek it."

"I am again not surprised. I know it is of great importance. I had warned Antonio. He did not listen. Well, at least he did not travel to London a second time. I told him to avoid travel. So he wrote to his friend in April saying he was unwell. He hoped to get the translation through the hands of someone else. Even though you have it now, it is too late." Father Agnelli sighed and looked dejected.

"What can you tell me about the parchment?"

"I am not sure I know much, but I can certainly guess it is of great importance. Come, let us take a stroll outside and I will show you something."

It was not yet dark. We walked through the lawns and past many headstones of long departed Venetians. We stopped at a plain, unmarked one.

"Some people think this is where Marco Polo is buried."

"Is he?"

"He was buried at the church, yes. We have records. But his body vanished during a period of renovation. In 1592. We like to believe he is here. But who really knows? Some say he is buried in Spain!"

"However, the point is, we take all matters pertaining to Marco Polo with utmost seriousness. He was the ambassador of the Pope, in a manner of speaking, to the court of Kublai Khan. He was judged to be an individual with great credibility with the Catholic Church, even though some records seem to show otherwise, as concerns his relationship with the citizens of Venice. He himself despaired of the ignorance of his fellow men. But let us remember that that was a different time and we must be forgiving."

"Of course."

"Therefore," continued Father Agnelli, "even if *we* do not understand the nature of that manuscript, we, by default, believe it must be of great importance, since Marco Polo said so in his letter, which was with the parchment. The Pope was informed, and he took the advice of the prefect of the archives, and determined that it was of paramount importance that the entire manuscript be put together, fully absorbed, and then hidden away in the archives, where we store many thousands of very sensitive parchments, as you can guess.

"It is my belief that Antonio was very close to determining the meaning of the words. The language is dead, he said, and he could only pronounce some of the words but did not fully know their meaning. This parchment was before the time of Christ and originated in the lower Nile Valley, he said. He was the expert, not I, and I know he had the virtue of patience."

"I see."

Father Agnelli leaned forward. "Yet, when he received those anonymous notes in Arabic, I became alarmed. It was easy to conclude that it was somehow related to the parchment. But what triggered this sudden interest almost six hundred years after the death of Marco Polo? Something had happened somewhere.

"My belief is that the other half of the parchment has been discovered, perhaps by chance, and those in possession have come to an independent conclusion about the matter. Perhaps it is of great spiritual significance. Whatever the case, they are prepared to kill. We think it could be Arabs from the Maghreb, specifically Morocco, but that is based only on superficial evidence.

"That is why the Pope, after consulting his aides, asked your ambassador in Rome, whom he knows well, to suggest the name of an individual who could take care of this problem in a discreet manner. We sent Antonio to meet you and ask you to come to Rome, which you did not, as you could not."

Father Agnelli sat back abruptly. He was suddenly bathed in sunlight that emerged from behind some trees and onto the bench where we sat. Then he extended his arm and touched Holmes gently on his shoulder.

"Stay in our monastery tonight as our guest," he said. "Let us leave for Rome tomorrow morning."

◇◇◇

Father Agnelli and Holmes travelled to Rome the next morning after having sent advance word that they were to be expected. The journey was uneventful, with both men not inclined to converse. Holmes had managed to get a copy of an English newspaper published in Italy that spoke of his deeply regretted passage at Reichenbach.

◇◇◇

Holmes and Father Agnelli were welcomed at the Vatican with great respect by the Pope's secretary. Pope Leo XIII was anxious to meet Holmes, they were told, and so they were quickly escorted to his official chambers where he sat on a comfortable chair with armrests. On an adjacent chair sat another priest.

The Pope had achieved some renown for his forward thinking and was considered liberal and approachable. He greeted Holmes warmly, while Father Agnelli bowed and kissed his hand.

"I welcome you, Mr. Holmes. You are famous here, did you know?"

Holmes bowed in acknowledgement. "I thank you."

"This is the prefect of the Vatican Secret Archives, Father Agostino Ciasca. He is very knowledgeable about what we have in the archives and has some opinion about the matter, though he has been hesitant about bringing in outside experts."

Holmes bowed briefly in the direction of the other priest, a man of short stature with intense eyes.

"I have also invited the British ambassador to join us. He should be here very shortly."

Lord Dufferin was ushered in at that point and after a round of pleasantries, Father Agnelli raised the issue.

"Your Holiness, we have suffered the loss of the eminent scholar Antonio Rozzi two days ago at the museum."

"Very tragic." The Pope closed his eyes and mouthed a prayer.

"We think the time for action has come and seek your advice."

"What is your view of the parchment, Your Holiness?" asked Holmes, coming quickly to the point.

"It predates Christ and is from the lower Nile Valley and the Nubian Kingdom, I am told," responded the Pope. "But I am not an expert. It may be best for us to listen to the views of Father Agostino Ciasca. He is a good storyteller!"

"Please."

"Before I answer your question, Signore Holmes," said Father Ciasca in an unusually gentle and melodious voice, "I must give you a little background. We have many thousands of parchments in the archives. They are not really secret—they are simply the property of the Pope and are private. It is not possible for us to know the details of everything we have. While the vast majority of documents were added after the eighth century, from the time of Pope Innocent III, there are several that are preserved simply because they are old. A few may be innocuous documents about commerce or letters from one person to another or letters of appointment. Or they may be incantations, spells, procedures for worship, procedures for exorcisms, and so on. Unless you have all the time in the world, there is no possibility of reading all that exists in the archives. We do merely two things: one, work on preservation and cataloguing, and two: guide scholars to the specific manuscripts they seek, without necessarily having an idea of the meaning of what lies within."

"I see."

"It follows that the documents we possess are often in languages that are rare or even dead. Aramaic, Hebrew, Meroitic, Greek—ah, there are so many! And, as I have mentioned, many predate Christ. Please understand that we distinguish between customs and religious thought. If you wish to follow a train of inquiry on practically any field of human endeavour, it is entirely possible to do so here, though it is true that the popes of the past were principally occupied with theological issues.

"Many are surprised that documents about China are in the archives. But there were travellers even before Marco Polo. However, none had his flair for capturing the details of his travels and did not wish to think beyond their trip. Objects have moved between civilizations across thousands of miles. Therefore our archives also have material from China, which may or may not have theological significance. Similarly, we have material in Arabic, too—I myself am considered a scholar in Arabic.

"Perhaps you are aware that Christianity flourished in Abyssinia much before it reached Europe. The language in which the Bible was first written was a combination of Greek, Hebrew, and Aramaic, which I think you know. Biblical history, parables, stories...many have their origin in the Nile Valley. Let us also remember that many myths referred to magic, which included physical phenomena not adequately understood at that time. We have been guilty of mistreatment of scientists and we are making amends."

The Pope clicked his tongue and nodded in solemn agreement.

"With the spread of Islam, an entirely new dimension of documents started entering the archives. Whether of the Crusades, the depredations wreaked by the Ottoman Turks in Bulgaria and Romania, the question of the Armenian Church, Constantinople, the Moors in Andalusia—ah, there is much to find, provided you know what you seek!

"Again this should not be a surprise. What, after all, separates us from Africa? Just a modest body of water that we call the Mediterranean Sea. It is inconceivable that people could have been insular simply because of the sea. There was trade, there were raids and conquests, and there was the exchange of theological thought. You certainly know this. It is simply that we do not think about this every day and therefore find the very question something unusual. So we have parchments in Arabic as well, and they are of great value, too.

"Let us come to the point of this discussion. In our archives, there are several parchments that use veiled language to convey ideas and thoughts. In some, you will find spells to deal with ghosts, demons, the devil, et cetera. There are procedures for exorcisms. I am not discussing the theological questions here; merely stating what lies in the archives, of which I am the custodian."

Holmes nodded.

"The question of eternal life has occupied the thinking of many scholars since the dawn of time. Why do people want to live forever? There can be a number of reasons. To continue to do good, to continue to do evil, to earn more and more, a fear of death, a desire to enjoy the pleasures of life...Who can say why? Yet it consumes everyone. Many people would give all their wealth to attain immortality."

The Pope interrupted. "We understand this desire but we do not approve of it. The meaning of eternal life, as far as we are concerned, is to be embraced by the Holy Ghost. To live a pure life is of greater value than to somehow evade the state of death."

"Yes, Your Holiness," Holmes concurred. "There is really nothing logical about wishing to be alive forever. It is too great a burden from any point of view."

Father Ciasca leaned forward in his chair. "We see that the bodies of some of our saints do not fall to corruption because of their holiness, but that does not mean we are evading death. It is impossible. Many cultures, Signore Holmes, have attempted to embalm their rulers so that they may enjoy the afterlife. Egypt is particularly famous for that, as you know. They were quite obsessed by the idea of immortality and may have gone to extreme lengths. And obviously, the efforts would have been ongoing for centuries. It is natural to expect that many alleged spells and incantations and formulas were spoken of that guaranteed immortality. If you have an interest in Egyptian history, you will likely be satisfied by what you find in our archives, Signore Holmes.

"But let us now look at our own interest in this matter. Marco Polo, his father, and his uncle, travelled to China with the oil from the lamp in the Church of the Holy Sepulchre in Jerusalem that Kublai Khan had asked for. The Khan was fascinated with Catholicism and wanted a hundred priests to educate his people. The new Pope, Gregory X, was unable to oblige. He sent two priests, but even those two returned in fear after noticing the grim situation in Armenia. The Poli were truly brave and unusual persons and the Church is grateful to them. The correspondence regarding this matter is in the archives.

"In the year 1323, in a private conversation that he had with the Pope John XXII, which the Pope recorded, the ageing Marco Polo claimed that the parchment bore an incantation that guaranteed eternal life, provided it was performed in the right manner at a particular spot in the Nile Valley. Unfortunately he did not recall the map and was also sketchy with details as he was, by then, rather feeble. Some say his memory was already eroding. Further, he did not bring the parchment with him to Rome from Venice, so it seemed like mere hearsay and the natural ramblings of an old man. The Pope merely recorded the matter. Marco Polo died shortly thereafter and everything was forgotten.

"But when Father Agnelli here arrived with the patriarch of Venice and the historian Antonio Rozzi, he showed us the parchment and my interest was piqued. I checked the archives for documents of that period out of curiosity, and found that note about the meeting from Pope John XXII. I realized that there was something more to the matter. I informed the Pope—his Holiness here—who advised the severest confidentiality and then called Lord Dufferin for his advice."

"And I suggested that you, Mr. Holmes, be consulted," said Lord Dufferin, smiling. "I know you, of course, in the context of the Sumatra question and the rather vexing issue of the Manitoba land surveys."

Holmes nodded imperceptibly but did not respond.

"I believe," interjected Father Agnelli, "that the reason why this matter has suddenly come up is because someone has possession of the other half and has come to a conclusion similar to ours. They would like what we have. This is what I have told Signore Holmes."

"I agree," nodded Father Ciasca. "The fact that the guards noticed a possibly Arab burglar and you too have observed men wearing fezzes, and the notes in Arabic, which I have read, suggest that someone in the Maghreb has the other half. The handwriting suggests a Moroccan influence."

He continued. "I have read about your alleged death at Reichenbach Falls. I dismissed it immediately, as did Lord Dufferin, as being a most convenient conclusion. I somehow sensed that you were seeking anonymity and would reach us soon. And that is what you have done. We think this helps us, provided you are willing, of course."

"And what specifically do you have in mind?" inquired Holmes, his eyes closed.

"If you agree, we can keep you safely at the Roman Catholic Prefecture of Tangier in Morocco while you conduct your own investigations into the matter. You will be, of course, more than adequately compensated. The task is quite simple—find the other half of the manuscript and bring it back to us. If it falls into the wrong hands, think of the consequences."

"I see," said Holmes, his fingertips together, his brows furrowed, and his eyes on the ground. "But I certainly wonder, Father Ciasca, what you would do with it. Would not possessing the entire document, if that were possible, create a new problem? And if the other claimant is genuine, why should he not equally be entitled to acquire this half?"

The Pope and Father Ciasca glanced at each other.

"A perspective we acknowledge. I can only say that if we assume that the parchment came into the hands of Marco Polo first, with the permission of Kublai Khan, then he must be the rightful owner. We have no evidence to the contrary. Since he went to China on a mission that had our explicit blessings, we feel that whatever he found belongs to us in some way. Further, given the violence involved thus far, and since the other party has not found it necessary to approach us formally and peacefully for the other half, his intentions are likely malevolent. I suspect that a very powerful entity is behind this and he is willing to go any extent to get it back. He has possibly employed all his resources in Europe toward that end. That means you may be safer in Morocco than Europe."

"I agree," said Lord Dufferin. "On our part, we can keep the matter completely under wraps and will continue with the story that you are dead. You can correspond with me through the Tangier prefecture, though we have a diplomatic presence there. The fewer persons you know the better. "

"I accept," Holmes agreed. "There is no way to determine how long I shall be in Morocco and whether I will even find the manuscript. Let us agree on two or three years."

"I have made arrangements for your departure tonight in the escort of one of my assistants. The prefecture in Tangier will provide you with rooms and an allowance. You will go as Father Andrzej Bąkiewicz, the new official in charge of accounts at the prefecture. You are Polish and know little of Italian. That would be useful because the present bishop at Tangier is a Belgian, Hubert Landel, who generally keeps to himself. Would that be acceptable? Even the head of the prefecture will not be made aware of your real identity."

"Yes, that would be acceptable."

"I have prepared the documents for your appointment. You will be briefed about other details by my assistant in about an hour."

The meeting was over.

Holmes bowed to the Pope and to Father Ciasca. The Pope blessed him and Father Agnelli in turn.

As they stepped out of the Vatican, Lord Dufferin pulled Sherlock Holmes to one side. "Eternal life be damned, Holmes! Keep an eye out for the French in West Africa! We need your eyes and ears there to tell us what the French are doing. They've been colonizing West Africa and creating difficulties for us. Dahomey, Mali, Morocco, Algeria, Tunisia—a bit too much, I say! Well, we've been sloppy too! Send me a note from time to time if you pick up some useful information, would you? You have a gift, my man! Here's my card, just in case you run into trouble."

"You would like me to spy for you, Your Lordship?"

"Yes! Find that mysterious parchment, by all means. But if you find something else, why not? And by the way, your brother Mycroft is in the know and he approves. Good day, 'Father Bąkiewicz.'" He rolled his eyes, smiled, tipped his hat, and left.

Father Agnelli came out slowly.

"I do not know when I shall meet you again, Signore Holmes. I wish you good luck. For the memory of my good friend, Antonio Rozzi, I pray that you will find what you seek."

The two shook hands. Father Agnelli turned slowly and departed.

A smiling young man appeared at Holmes side. "I am Giovanni. Father Ciasca's assistant. I shall now take you to the guest rooms to help you prepare for the journey."

In Paris, an old man rocked slowly in a chair. His eyes were closed for a very long time. Perhaps two hours.

Suddenly, they opened wide.

In absolute comprehension.

Tangier

Travel the world and then live in Tangier

In the words of "Father Andrzej Bąkiewicz":

Giovanni, Father Ciasca's assistant, was an intelligent and cheerful young man of about twenty-five summers. I gathered his role was to provide protection and take care of administrative details.

Some twenty-four hours after my meeting with the Pope, we were on a ship from Naples to Tangier. I spent time in quiet reflection. I really had no idea what to expect. I would have to do everything on my own and there was to be no one in Morocco to help me. What was I looking for? A parchment that would guarantee eternal life? Poppycock! I was amused but could see no harm in the diversion. In any case, a murder had indeed occurred and ambassadors, Popes, and other important individuals were relying on me. I hoped I had given Professor Moriarty the slip.

Giovanni did not know my real identity and believed I was indeed Father Bąkiewicz from Warsaw. He travelled regularly between Rome and the prefectures along the Mediterranean Rim.

We spoke little, with language being the principal and convenient barrier. The sea was calm and the ship comfortable, and we reached Tangier soon enough, after a brief halt at Sardinha. I felt the breeze go through my hair while the sun beat down on us. The sea was a brilliant blue. I had half a mind to ask for paints.

But every few minutes, my mind went to the half-manuscript in my personal effects. Who wrote it? Why? How did it reach China? What was so important about it that Marco Polo felt the need to tear it vertically and leave half in the city of Calicut in distant India? Had someone since picked it up and understood its importance? Where was that person? Was I escaping from him or nearing him? Was the fact that the script of the notes been in an Arabic style suggesting Moroccan influence enough reason for me to travel to this country?

Bishop Landel had graciously come to receive me, having been sent a wire earlier by Father Ciasca. He spoke English quite well and there was no problem in communication. He was a taciturn individual preferring his own company and would spend hours together in prayer, which suited me, since I spent none.

Tangier was a beautiful town with colour and charm. White and blue were the recurring motifs. I saw all kinds of people at the harbour—Arabs, Europeans, Negroes, and a group of people with blue robes, who I later discovered were called Tuaregs. The men were veiled—but with sharp confidence in their eyes. They were to be my lifeline later. These veils were called *tagelmust*, I learned, and were very central to their heritage and personal identity.

"And how is Father Ciasca?" Bishop Landel asked, as we walked together.

"He seemed in good health."

"A gifted scholar. Lost in books but very alert. Have you known him long?" Bishop Landel asked casually.

"No. I travel rarely to Italy. This is a new assignment so I was asked to visit the Vatican to learn more about the duties. But I am sure I will learn more from you."

"Our flock is quite small and our properties modest. There will be little to do except taking care of our creditors, sending reports to the Holy See periodically, and managing the accounts."

"I hope to do these to your satisfaction, Father."

"I used to know Bishop Józef Glemp in Warsaw once. I wonder what became of him."

"I had heard he was well. When did you come here, Father?"

"Two years ago. I like the place. There is peace and quiet, though it may not seem so, looking at the crowd here." He waved his hand at the noisy market that we were passing.

He showed me to my rooms and made me feel quite comfortable. I had an attendant Abu, who took care of various odd jobs in the church, including cleaning the living quarters and cooking for the small number of residents. Father Landel explained my duties, and in a few days, we had settled into a routine of minimal though courteous contact. The books were quite in order and did not seem to present any challenge. I sent Father Ciasca a brief note that I had arrived in Tangier and thanked him for the courtesies extended.

I decided to learn about the city as a first step and stepped out at the first available opportunity, perhaps a week after I landed at Tangier.

The city was typically Mediterranean. Cobbled sidewalks, a glorious blue sky, and charming buildings all in white. Despite the bustling markets, the place was quite clean. I was vaguely reminded of Barcelona, and I was pleased to know that artists often frequented Tangier.

The prefecture in Tangier was quite central in the town and everything looked very pleasant. I decided to let my legs take me wherever they felt like going. It felt liberating to walk anonymously in a foreign city. Nevertheless, I took care to wear my habit and make slight changes to my gait. One can never slack.

Two Tuareg men walked by, and I smiled and nodded at them. Their faces being covered, I could only see their eyes, but they smiled in return and bowed slightly and moved on. Elsewhere

I saw a simple whitewashed mosque set against the blue sea. It was really quite delightful.

I turned in and out of narrow, uncrowded lanes. The white-washed houses were all set close together and men and women peered down from the iron-grilled balconies. There was an atmosphere of friendliness, which cannot be explained. It was in the smiles and eyes of the people. The signs were in French: Rue Faquih Abadi, Rue Ben Abdessadak, Rue Ibn Batouta. I liked the sound of the last street and I decided to explore further.

At the end of the tiny street, I saw a small white structure with a sign in French: *Tambeau Ibn Batouta*. The Tomb of Ibn Batuta.

It really meant nothing, but curiosity got the better of me, and I stopped a man passing by and asked him in French if he knew someone who could tell me about the tomb.

He pointed to a house, like any other, and replied in French. "Go there and ask for Haji Ahmad Bouabid. He is an old man who knows all about Ibn Batuta."

I did as suggested, enjoying the little adventure, and knocked on a door.

"*Entather, entather!*" someone shouted from within in Arabic.

The door opened. An old, bearded, slightly bent man peered out with rheumy eyes. He sized me up.

"Monsieur Haji Ahmad Bouabid?" I inquired.

"Yes. Come in, come in!" he responded in French, which surprised me for a moment, till I realized that everyone in Morocco, including old men, spoke French.

I stepped into a tiny room with a low ceiling. I had to bend and squeeze in. The smell of coffee and cardamom hung heavy. On the walls were various Arabic inscriptions that I assumed were from the Quran.

Haji Ahmad Bouabid gestured to me and I sat down gratefully—though awkwardly—on a thick rug on the floor after introducing myself as Father Andrzej Bąkiewicz, newly arrived in Tangier.

"I visited Roma when I was a young man," said Haji Ahmad Bouabid, smiling with the recollection. "I am happy to see you.

You must have coffee." He shouted out something in Arabic and in a few moments, a smiling young man with a fez on his head came in, bowing repeatedly, and poured some thick black coffee into tiny cups. On a plate were dates and nuts. I had my first introduction to Arab hospitality at the home of Haji Ahmad Bouabid.

"I liked the tomb outside. A man in the street told me that you knew everything about the tomb and the man buried there. Can you tell me about it?" I asked, sipping the extremely bitter coffee.

"Ibn Batuta? You do not know? He is a very famous traveller of the world! They say that he visited China, India, Yemen, Mecca, Mali—we are very proud of him. Perhaps I am his descendant! Here he is buried!"

His pride was evident, but I was none the wiser. I waited for him to tell me more; it sounded interesting.

"He was a Qadi, a religious scholar. He travelled from Tangier to Cairo, Constantinople, Damascus, Mecca, Medina, and Sanaa. And wherever he went he was treated with great respect. He wrote a great book called *Al-Rihla*, which means *The Travels*. Never before and never after will there be a traveller like Ibn Batuta. And he lies just fifty feet away from us!" he chuckled.

"I see. Very interesting. Where else did he travel?"

"Oh you must read the book! You can get a copy in French in any bookstore in Tangier. How do you like the dates?"

"Their quality is exceptional." I nibbled slowly, savouring the unusual sweetness.

Haji Ahmad Bouabid immediately shouted out, and the same young man came back with a huge plate of dates and more coffee. I understood that the Arabs took hospitality very seriously.

"He travelled to India and China too. And finally, his last trip was to Mali where he visited the town of Timbuktu."

My ears went up when I heard the mention of Timbuktu. I had seen it marked on Signore Rozzi's map.

"Timbuktu? When was this?"

"It is difficult to give exact dates. But I see that your interest is genuine. Let me get a book and give you correct information." He again shouted and the boy rushed in with a very old book, almost in tatters and placed it in front of him.

"This is the "*Al-Rihla*" in Arabic," he beamed. He turned some pages.

"Yes, he was born in—let me see—your Christian year, 1304! Then he travelled from Tangier in 1325, yes, 1325! He went to Mecca seven times! Seven times! I see that he visited Delhi in India in, perhaps, hmm…1334. He did not like the king, Mohammad Bin Tughlaq, who was mad, ha ha! Then he went to the Maldives. He reached China in, let me see, 1345, yes, yes! Then he came back through India, Persia, and Syria. In Damascus, he escaped the Black Plague. Then he returned to Tangier. Ah, he was not satisfied! No, not at all! He crossed the sea again and went to Andalusia and Valencia, and again he had many adventures. Then he returned to Tangier. In 1351, he travelled to Mali to the city of Timbuktu, a city of gold! Great adventure! Great adventure! Then he finally came back to rest in 1354. The king asked him to stay behind, and he dictated his story to Ibn Juzayy. So *Al-Rihla* was actually written by Ibn Juzayy, while listening to Ibn Batuta! Is it not interesting?" Haji Ahmad Bouabid was positively beside himself with joy. He must have repeated the story a thousand times but still found it fascinating.

"Wonderful story! Thank you! And when did he pass away?" I gestured outside at the tomb.

"I will tell you. 1369, I think. Yes."

"How fortunate to live so close to the tomb of such a great man!" I said, finding it prudent to join in my host's happiness.

"Here, here, I have a map, come and see," he beckoned and I clambered across the floor on all fours. He smoothened out a very old map of the world. It was grimy and torn at many places, with coffee stains and many markings. But it was clear enough.

"Here you see? This is Tangier. Now we see how he travelled to Cairo, Damascus, Medina, Mecca, Sanaa, then we see Persia,

Delhi, and then he came down to Calicut, then Maldives, then here Chittagong—"

I stopped him. "Calicut, did you say?"

"Yes. Very famous place for trading. He visited Calicut many times, yes many times!"

"Exactly when?"

"I think 1341. I am not sure, but he speaks well of Calicut in *Al-Rihla* and he says that it was a very rich and wonderful city. You must read the book!"

"Oh I must!" I said. I recalled that Marco Polo had died in 1324 when Ibn Batuta was about twenty. And both had travelled to Calicut in the span of some fifty years! Surely…

"I see you are very interested in Ibn Batuta! I am very happy" said Haji Ahmad Bouabid, beaming. He shouted again and the smiling young boy rushed in with fresh supplies of coffee and dates. "Have some, and then let me show you the tomb!"

I stood up with some difficulty and emerged into the street to bright sunshine and fresh air. Haji Ahmad Bouabid followed me and we walked across to the tomb.

He described various aspects of the tomb, the inscriptions, the shape, the angles, the directions, the scrolls on the walls and so on.

"His mother is also buried in Tangier. I can show it to you someday if you like Monsieur!" he said.

"I would be very happy," I said. "You must be so proud of Ibn Batuta."

"Oh yes! There are many people who love him! There are secret societies too!"

I was intrigued.

"There are men who swear to safeguard the secrets of Ibn Batuta! Many in Tangier!"

"What secrets?"

"How can I tell you? Then it would not be a secret!"

We had a hearty laugh, and, as it happens with two men who laugh at the same joke at the same time, became closer in seconds.

I invited him to the Catholic prefecture church to continue our discussion. He knew the place, and promised to come at seven-thirty p.m. "I will bring you more information about Ibn Batuta!" he said proudly. "These days so many people are showing interest in him. A few months ago, there was a man who came from India to inquire. I wonder what happened to him."

I knew I was on the edge of discovering something.

I picked up a copy of the English translation of *Al-Rihla* from a bookstore along the way. I also bought the latest copy of *The Times*, which was from two days prior. There was continued debate on the tragic death of Sherlock Holmes at Reichenbach Falls and an interview with my good friend Dr. John Watson, whose affinity for hyperbole, I noticed with amusement, seemed to increase with each interview.

◇◇◇

At about a quarter to eight, Haji Ahmad Bouabid reached the church and I escorted him to my accommodation inside. My rooms were quite spacious, but did not, quite obviously, have the warm and cosy feeling I had enjoyed at the Haji's home. I had consulted the cook and he prepared mint tea and a few Moroccan delicacies such as aubergine fritters and brochettes for my guest.

"You must say '*As-Salaam-Alaikum*' when you meet someone in an Arab country, Father Bąkiewicz!" advised a smiling Haji Bouabid, as we settled down.

"I certainly shall! Thank you for your suggestion!"

"And when someone says '*As-Salaam-Alaikum*' to you first, you must respond '*Wa-Alaikum-Salaam.*'"

I practised a couple of times to the delight of Haji Bouabid.

"Excellent! A wise traveller knows that he must learn the customs of the land! Ibn Batuta would have been happy with you!

"Look, I have got you a gift. This is a French translation of *Al-Rihla*!"

I was gratified and expressed my appreciation. I glanced through the book in Haji Bouabid's presence. I did not find it necessary to share with him that I already had a copy in English that I had started reading.

"I also got you a new map and I have written the dates of his travels to various cities as well!" said my new friend.

"That is very generous of you!"

"Not at all! We are proud of Ibn Batuta and wish to spread his story around the world!" Haji Bouabid beamed.

"Admirable! Tell me, Haji Bouabid, did Ibn Batuta have a son?"

Haji Bouabid laughed uproariously. "A son? Ah, he must have had many! Wherever he went, he married someone and divorced her! Who can say how many descendants he now has?"

"What about here in Morocco?"

"I am aware that he had one son in Tangier, who died early. He was very fond of him. After that, we have no idea."

"You say 'we.'"

"Yes, I belong to a group of people who study *Al-Rihla* and propagate his story. Of course, we know many things about him which we cannot share!" His eyes twinkled.

He saw my disappointment. "Ah, do not feel sad! Study the book and ask me questions! If your interest continues, I can take you with me to attend a meeting of my group."

"What is your group called?" I asked.

He hesitated. "Well, I am not supposed to tell you. But since you are a man of God, I can do so without fear. We call ourselves the Ibn Batuta Society of Tangier. My society's objectives are purely academic. We have no religious or social desire. We just wish to ensure that Ibn Batuta's memory is honoured.

"You see, *Al-Rihla* is only the publicly known chronicles of Ibn Batuta. A young man, Ibn Juzayy, was appointed by the king to be Ibn Batuta's secretary and take notes of all his stories. He certainly took many notes and did not include everything in *Al-Rihla*. There may have been many reasons. Perhaps Ibn Batuta wanted to see the notes and reconfirm what he had said in certain matters. Perhaps Ibn Batuta decided against including the material. Maybe he felt he would like to write another book to add to *Al-Rihla*. But I am talking too much. I shall give you one month to read and understand *Al-Rihla,* and we shall talk about this again."

"I agree, Haji Bouabid. I know very little. But I am interested." I put down my coffee cup carefully.

"Recently, many people have shown interest in the matter, Father. That is nice! This is a town of tourists and most of the interest is limited. It is sad that people are not interested in reading and learning about history." He clicked his tongue. "Therefore I am very glad to have met you."

My senses were on alert.

"Will you help me to learn Arabic, Haji Bouabid?" I asked.

He was delighted. "Of course, of course! I am very happy. If you learn, you can read *Al-Rihla* in Arabic! But it will take time and patience!"

"I have both in abundance," I said.

And so for the next several weeks, I started learning the language and practising. I explored Tangier on foot and dropped by little museums and mosques. Very soon, I was quite familiar with the town.

One morning, Bishop Landel complimented me on my efforts, quite unexpectedly.

"I see that you are trying your best to assimilate. That is a very good thing. I do not see that in many priests."

"I like this place and the people. They seem very friendly and helpful. That can be useful for the church's efforts too."

"That is right. By the way, I will have a guest today from the continent. So I will not be able to meet you to review the accounts as we had planned. Can we do so tomorrow?"

"Of course! Is he from the Holy See?"

"No. He comes with a letter of introduction from my brother in Brussels. Someone called Colonel Sebastian Moran. He sounds like an Englishman. Now I wonder why he wishes to meet me. What can I do for him?"

◇◇◇

I broached the topic of Ibn Batuta again the next time I met Haji Bouabid.

"Such a wonderful book, *Al-Rihla*! I am so grateful that you introduced him to me. I almost feel as though I travelled the world with him! I must have read the book ten times now!"

"I am very happy that you have liked the book. Yes, many people express similar feelings about it!" Haji Bouabid smiled.

I probed further. "Did you say that Ibn Juzayy had many notes that were not included in *Al-Rihla*"?

"Yes, Father, yes! That is what scholars believe. I do, too."

"Why did he not include them?"

"You see, Ibn Batuta dictated to Ibn Juzayy for a very, very long time. It is inconceivable that anyone could maintain the same energy and keep the same routine for so long. If you look at the later chapters of *Al-Rihla*, you will observe that the flow has changed. Ibn Batuta compressed many events in single sentences and small paragraphs. In fact, some of what he says is actually wrong and suggests carelessness or some desire to finish as soon as possible. We think there are many possibilities. Shall we go and visit my friend Abdelaziz El-Kahina? He can tell you more about this."

We visited Abdelaziz El-Kahina, who was an old friend of Haji Bouabid and lived fairly close by. The gentleman was younger and quite strongly built. While he was helpful and spoke in detail, he kept looking at me in a queer way and twirled his moustache constantly. A lesser man would have become nervous.

We sipped mint tea at a café outside. It was a beautiful day.

"Yes, it is true," said Abdelaziz. "Ibn Batuta got restless after a while and did not give as much attention to the last part of his dictation to Ibn Juzayy. We really do not have proof he went up the Volga or that he visited Sanaa. He did not really write anything down while he was travelling and much came from his memory. And in some cases, he probably thought that it simply made sense to copy material from the work of others who may have written in far greater details. And look at his description of China! For such an important destination, he has written very little! Almost nothing! So the quality of those sections is not very reliable. We accept it."

"Why did he do that? I read that the king had given him Ibn Juzayy to capture all details for as long as he wished."

"We think there are some possibilities. One, Ibn Batuta was impatient and accelerated his dictation to stop the activity. Perhaps he lost his enthusiasm. Perhaps he was already restless and wanted to travel again and the king refused to give him permission."

"Possible," said I.

"Two, he did tell Ibn Juzayy everything in great detail but considered some sections 'drafts' and proposed to revisit the sections later and maybe write an addendum. He did not, ultimately, for some unknown reason. In the meanwhile, Ibn Juzayy suddenly passed away after the publication of *Al-Rihla* and Ibn Batuta continued with his duties as a Qadi. Perhaps there are some drafts here and there, who can say."

Abdelaziz El-Kahina looked elsewhere when he spoke and I realized he was hiding something.

He spoke to Haji Bouabid in Arabic in a low undertone. He was unaware that I had already picked up some Arabic in three months.

"Should I continue?"

"Yes, don't worry. He is a good man." Haji Bouabid made some deprecating gestures and urged him on.

Abdelaziz El-Kahina continued slowly. "Three, he halted the dictation for a while and sent Ibn Juzayy on a mission to verify facts. He then resumed the dictation. He was unhappy about the results of Ibn Juzayy's mission."

I raised a quizzical eyebrow.

Haji Bouabid laughed at length. "Father, do not be confused. These are things that happened hundreds of years ago! They are only of academic interest!"

"But how is the third different from the first? Where is the proof that Ibn Juzayy went on a mission and Ibn Batuta was unhappy with the results? "

Abdelaziz El-Kahina sat back heavily and adjusted his fez.

"Since Haji Bouabid is vouching for you, I can reveal a few things. But in case I find you have used this information in an incorrect way, I will have to order your death."

I nodded. "My interest is purely academic. I am a man of God. I do not seek to profit from this information. I can only give you my word as a great admirer of Ibn Batuta. You do not have to tell me anything if you prefer not."

He smiled in a satisfied way. "Very well. Let me then correct the information you have read in your books.

"We have Ibn Juzayy's notes. Some in the Moroccan archives and some with local families, like mine. I do not know why it happened. But here is the story.

"In those days frequent marrying and divorcing was routine. Ibn Batuta had relations with a number of women, some wives and some concubines. He therefore had many children, most of whom he did not know—because he did not get the time to live with them.

"There were two sons in particular that he was very fond of. One lived here in Tangier and one in Maldives. When he returned from his travels, he found that his son in Tangier had passed away. He was griefstricken.

"But his thoughts went to his son in the Maldives. Strangely we do not have his name but since Ibn Batuta was well known there, it probably did not matter. So to simply say that one was looking for the son of Ibn Batuta was perhaps enough.

"In any case, Ibn Batuta dictated a letter addressed to his son in the Maldives to Ibn Juzayy, asking him to come immediately to Tangier and be with him in his old age. He was overcome with emotion and asked Ibn Juzayy to take the letter and travel to the Maldives. The king gave a six-month leave of absence and Ibn Juzayy reached the Maldives very rapidly. He was able to find that son and handed over the letter. We do not know its actual contents.

"Unfortunately, the son, while happy to receive the letter and desirous of travelling back to Tangier with Ibn Juzayy, became fatally ill, possibly with malaria. Ibn Juzayy left Maldives with a heavy heart and returned to give Ibn Batuta the sad news. Ibn Batuta reacted predictably and became very depressed. He lost interest in the *Al-Rihla* project but continued the dictation in a mechanical way, perhaps deliberately adding misinformation. He was no longer interested in life. *Al-Rihla* was published in 1355. And in 1357, the young scholar, Ibn Juzayy himself passed away.

"However, before Ibn Juzayy left, he had extracted a promise from Ibn Batuta's dying son, who was an adult then, and had a young son, that he would ensure that the directive in the letter would be honoured by some subsequent generation. So he left the letter behind. Ibn Batuta waited for more than thirteen years and then passed away in 1369.

"Now in Morocco, you should know that, just like us, there are many who are very possessive about the heritage of Ibn Batuta. For example, many enemies of Ibn Batuta have accused him of being a liar. We disagree very strongly. We believe that we must defend his honour and do whatever is needed to keep his memory exalted. We do it with scholarship, reading, writing, and debating. But others have more zeal.

"In 1368, Ibn Batuta formed a secret society. Its name I cannot tell you. You can guess what the objective was. Ibn Batuta felt that there was some unfinished business tied to the letter and swore the men to complete secrecy. They were to pass on the secret to their descendants and would wait for something to happen."

"What would that be?"

Abdelaziz El-Kahina paused. Then he said, very slowly, in a low voice, "The arrival of the descendant of Ibn Batuta."

"I see. Very, very interesting."

"Generations have passed waiting and waiting. The members know, roughly, what the letter contains. And they believe that they are obliged to help Ibn Batuta's descendant—whoever arrives with the letter in Tangier—to fulfil the promise within the letter.

"It may seem like a fruitless wait. But several months ago, something happened.

"A young man arrived from India. Much like you, he made inquiries about the Tomb of Ibn Batuta. And Haji Bouabid here extended his courtesy to him as well.

"But when he asked specifically for the secret society, our friend brought him to me. I know many people and often assist them in an informal way. That is why I was contacted.

"Suffice to say that I was soon convinced that this man was indeed the descendant. He had the letter. He had the seal. He had some very old coins. His Arabic was not very good, but he could read and write. He actually produced a letter in Ibn Batuta's hand asking him to search for the secret society.

"I introduced him to a member of the society, who happens to live nearby. They tested him and were convinced that his ancestor was indeed Ibn Batuta. I was told bluntly that any further interest from me was not welcome and there were things to be done. They thanked me, of course. After that, everyone disappeared. It is almost as if nothing happened. My friend vanished. As did the Indian.

"I was happy to be part of a historic moment. Now I wonder what the letter's revelations mean. Is it about wealth? Is it magic? We have no idea. But we learn not to get involved.

"I hope this satisfies you."

I listened to this fascinating narrative carefully. I did not interrupt Abdelaziz El-Kahina.

Haji Bouabid spoke with restrained passion. "We are possibly witnesses to history. The smallest thing is ordained by Allah. Even our meeting, Father, is Allah's will."

I bowed in appreciation. "Yes, thank you. You have been very trusting."

We asked for some more tea.

The writings of the descendant of Ibn Batuta

My name is Thalassery Vatoot Mohammad Koya and I am a descendant of the great traveller Ibn Batuta.

How do I know?

I shall explain.

There was always a story in my family that we were somehow related to a famous traveller whose name was Ibn Batuta, and that we had moved to Thalassery in India from Maldives several hundred years ago. All families have such interesting stories about famous ancestors. We did not know much more, except that he was from a country beyond Misr (Egypt) and had visited the Maldives during his trips and that we were his descendants. There was no real proof. My father was a little fairer than most and his nose was very sharp, but that hardly meant anything. It was a nice story that amused us and we would tease our relatives that the Vatoots were actually wealthy Arabs. We boasted that Vatoot was just a corruption of Batuta and this pleased us. But no one really knew who he was.

My father was a merchant of spices in Thalassery and only minimally literate. It was expected that I would follow in his footsteps and become a cinnamon merchant, and I was quite happy to do so.

But my father made a mistake.

He sent me to a local school.

In his view, merchants ought to know a little more than basic arithmetic. I believe he was right. But his intention and how it affected me diverged.

I learned how to read and write and I appreciated these gifts with more passion than learning simple mathematics, which was not a problem either. But a tiny school in a remote town on the Malabar Coast could hardly satisfy my needs, other than the kindness of a teacher, who gave me books to read. There was no library. I picked up Malayalam, some basic English, and Arabic, the last from the madrassa in the town where all Muslim boys were expected to learn how to read the Quran. But learning from rote, while necessary, was not enough.

But what is a boy to do? I was forced to suppress my desires and continued in the traditional way, working to understand my father's business and supporting my family. There was an unspoken belief in our business community that only excessively rich men and fools spent time reading, and I, not having the right kind of friends and encouragement, slowly regressed into the daily routine of cinnamon trading and continued our traditional, timeless business and the routine of life. But I did have one indulgence—every Sunday, I would have an English newspaper delivered. It came all the way from Bombay and would be a week old. It helped me develop my reading skills in English, though I could not speak it, since I had no one to speak with.

And, as happens to all families all over the world, the final moments arrived, when first my mother and then my father passed away, one after the other during the course of a year.

As my father held my hand on his death bed, he asked me to come close. I bent my face and he spoke softly in my ears.

"As my father whispered to me, I now do the same. There is a wooden chest under this bed. It is yours. It is important. Very important. It is your heritage. It should always continue in the family."

Then he breathed his last.

I buried him beside my mother in the rich soil of the Malabar under the cinnamon trees that had sustained them. I spent some time alone, allowing my tears to flow and fall on the graves of my parents. And then I went back home, as head of the family, to continue life and attend to my responsibilities.

One evening, perhaps a week after I buried my father, I sat down and went through the papers of my family that my father had kept away from me. It was not intentional. He was not very well read and did not have a sense of history. As far as he was concerned, there was nothing worth trying to read and understand, except matters pertaining to spices.

Outside, the winds had gathered speed. A storm was approaching and I could already hear the rumble of clouds moving in. The coconut fronds were in a state of agitation and scraping against each other. Coconuts were likely to fall overnight because of the furious winds.

My wife, who was expecting our first child, was busy cooking in the kitchen and my younger, unmarried sister was with her.

It was a large non-descript wooden chest, clearly old, that I had pulled out from under my father's bed. I opened it and turned it over. It held various papers, cowrie shells, some silk cloth, some old copper coins, a couple of dead cockroaches, dust, some beads, two account books—all these fell out. I looked through them carefully and cleaned the chest and each item.

I could tell that there were very old account books, perhaps belonging to my great-grandfather or even before him. The Malayalam script was a little different. A brief note referred to the Maldives and some references to those who had been given credit. "Abu Baker—sixty sacks of coconuts. Ibrahim Koya—forty sacks of coconuts" and so on.

I untied a dirty, stained cloth bundle, which seemed to contain something heavy. I gasped when I saw that it had many heavy gold coins with Arabic inscriptions. I could tell that each was worth a lot and I was surprised that it never occurred to my father to open it out of just curiosity. I then realized—and my eyes clouded with tears—that my father probably had opened them but had obeyed his father's instructions to pass them on to me, and had tied the cloth back again. The value of the gold coins was not in the coins themselves but in the caress of all those in the family who, through the generations, had touched them.

Then I saw a small packet covered in Chinese silk. My interest was piqued just by looking at it. I opened the bundle and took out a very fragile piece of paper. It had yellowed and was brittle. Rough handling would have destroyed it in seconds.

It was a letter in a very traditional Arabic script, which I, fortunately, could read. It was to me, from a distance of more than twenty generations. My father was probably unable to read it and decided to leave it for a subsequent generation. That was clear, even to a man such as I, who had limited exposure to the world outside. I felt the dust and breath of men from hundreds of years prior, as I opened the document.

Bismillah ar-rahman ar-rahim

My dear son whom I have only seen once.

The love of a father for his son is of great power. I am in you and you too shall have sons and continue my name. It is a selfish love, it is true. Yet, why are we here on earth, sent by Allah, if not to love and to belong?

I am now at death's door and I wish to see you one last time. I had many wives and many children, but you are special. Because destiny wished for me to travel and see the world, I could not spend time with you. But be assured that I thought of you with every breath. I wondered how you took your first steps. I wondered how you lost your first tooth. I hoped that you memorized the Quran and grew up to be of good character, to be relied upon by strangers at times of need, to be loved by all and to be healthy and prosperous. I believe in all sincerity that this has indeed happened.

I must tell you, dear son, that I wish to meet you not for sentiment alone. You must come to claim a great inheritance. I have sent Ibn Juzayy personally to bring you to me. If Allah wills, you will return with him.

But it has occurred to me that it might not be possible for some reason, in which case he is to leave this letter behind to be claimed by your sons or theirs.

If Ibn Juzayy is forced to leave the letter behind and it falls in the hands of your son or his, then he must travel to Tangier as soon as possible. For this expense, I have also sent twenty gold coins with Ibn Juzayy.

Once your son comes to Tangier, he must exercise good judgment and search carefully for someone who has heard of the Guardians of the Letter. The Guardians are two families whom I have sworn to secrecy and paid handsomely. They are to wait for your son for as many generations as necessary. When the son arrives in Tangier, the Guardians are required to take charge of his affairs, give him a more detailed letter that I wrote two days ago and handed over to them, and get both pieces of a certain document—one from Venice and the other from the Sankore Mosque in Timbuktu. Do not worry if this confuses you. The Guardians know exactly what is to be done and will help your son. But they will do nothing till someone hands over this letter. They will wait—for as many hundred years as needed.

But of course, I hope that you will return with Ibn Juzayy and my eyes will be comforted before I close them for eternity.

Abū ʻAbd al-Lāh Muhammad ibn ʻAbd al-Lāh l-Lawātī
ṭ-Ṭanǧī ibn Baṭūṭah
21 Safar 770 A.H.

I sat back in silence. Outside, the rain beat down furiously. Lightning flashed and thunder shook the walls of my house. I took it as an auspicious sign.

I understood that I was expected to travel to a city called Tangier, seek out the Guardians of the Letter, understand the Letter and claim an important inheritance.

I thought about the matter long after a silent dinner with my wife and sister, who knew better than to converse with me when I was preoccupied.

I slept on my father's bed that night, looking through the window at the pounding rain. I did not extinguish the oil lamps. The flames flickered and I saw on the walls the silhouette of my illustrious predecessor,

Haji Ibn Batuta, as he travelled on camels and horses through the world. Perhaps he had a turban, perhaps he had robes. Was he short or tall? Whom had he met on his travels? How did it happen that he visited the Maldives? Why was his son unable to return with Ibn Juzayy? What was this mysterious letter? What was this inheritance? Why was it so important that two entire families had created a veil of secrecy around the matter and were waiting patiently, generation after generation, for someone to come?

Yes, I had to go to Tangier immediately and solve this mystery and bring peace to many.

The next morning, I called my wife and sister to my room. In a few words, I explained to them that I intended to embark on a trip with no immediate clarity on when I would return. I handed over the running of my business to my sister, who was a reliable and sensible woman. I asked my wife to be brave and manage the birth of our child on her own and to travel to her mother's village nearby if she so wished. I reviewed my finances and ensured that both of them were clear about my debtors and creditors, whom I visited the next day.

I also handed over five of the gold coins to my sister in case of an emergency. I promised to send more whenever I could.

Neither protested, understanding that I was on an important mission, which had to do with our family's honour. They helped me pack and organize my effects. It was agreed that they were to tell others that I had travelled to Delhi and Lucknow in the north of India, seeking new trade, and that I would be back in three or four months. I was fortunate that both had presence of mind, and were mature; I have a loathing for hysterical women.

In a few days, I bid good-bye to my wife and sister and travelled to Cochin, and then boarded a ship to Bombay. From there, after learning the location of Tangier, I decided to take a ship to Liverpool via Gibraltar. From Gibraltar, I was to take another ship to Tangier.

The journey passed without incident. It was my first sea voyage but I did not suffer from sea sickness, to the surprise of my fellow passengers. I did not have to wait long at Bombay and chose not to get off at Aden, Jeddah, or Alexandria.

The salty tang in the air seemed extremely familiar. Not the familiar air on the Malabar Coast, but the one in the high seas. Memories, voyages, grief, excitement—yes, these were the additional flavours that I could sense in the air. And yet, I wondered, how? Had

I awakened a long-dormant memory within my blood, the memory of my ancestor, Ibn Batuta?

And after several days, I landed at Tangier and took in a long breath of the same air that he had breathed.

My spoken Arabic was poor but I was able to manage. I found dwellings, helped by another traveller on the Gibraltar-Tangier ship, and rested for a day.

Then I walked about the beautiful city.

I was unused to such bright skies and the warm sun. It was not very humid either. I obviously stood out because of my darker and differently coloured skin, but the citizens seemed very easy-going and did not ask questions. It was a colourful place with people from all parts of the world, it seemed. I was possibly the only person from India.

I made very casual inquiries about Ibn Batuta and was happy to see that everyone had heard of him and seemed proud of him. I was ashamed that I knew next to nothing about this great man. I picked up an Arabic copy of the Rihla, promising to read all about him as soon as possible.

I stumbled upon my ancestor's grave, quite by chance, on a road named after him.

I stood silently outside. My mind was a blank and yet I felt overcome by waves of emotion. This man had waited for me for five hundred years and had even paid for my visit from a small coastal town in India. And he was not done—he wished to give me more. But what of?

It was a pleasant and deserted street. The houses were whitewashed and the contrast with the brilliant blue sky made the whole setting quite cheerful. Ibn Batuta was fortunate to spend eternity under a warm sun.

I looked about. An old bearded man with a fez was sitting outside his house in the sun, on a rocking chair. He was peering at me quite intently.

I walked across and greeted him in halting Arabic.

He nodded, continuing to look at me closely. He waved me toward another chair close by. He called out in Arabic and in a minute, a young man came out of the house and, smiling, placed in front of me a tray with coffee, dates, and pistachios.

We sat in silence. The old man had stopped sipping coffee and rocking on his chair. He was staring at me, unblinking.

"Where have you come from?" he asked very slowly, so that I could understand his Arabic.

"India," I replied.

"Why?"

"To visit this tomb," I said, gesturing. "Can you tell me about Ibn Batuta?"

"Of course. He is Morocco's greatest gift to the world. He travelled the world and wrote about it. He visited India too. Delhi, Calicut, and the Maldives."

"I am from near Calicut."

"I see."

He sipped coffee again, his eyes staring at me over the rim of the cup.

"Many people visit this tomb. Some with a purpose. Some without one. What brought you here?"

"There is a legend in our family about Ibn Batuta. I came to find out more." I drank some coffee.

"Can you help me?" I then blurted. Perhaps unwisely, but then he was an old man and I did not think he would harm me. And I had to start somewhere.

"How can I help you?"

"Are there any groups of people who swear by Ibn Batuta?"

"Many. I belong to one. We study the Rihla."

"Is it a secret group?"

"No. It is not. But I know of secret groups. Is that who you seek?"

"Perhaps. Is there any that was concerned with his trip to the Maldives?"

The old man put down his cup and stared at me again.

"Who are you, really?"

"My name is Thalassery Vatoot Mohammad Koya and I am a spice merchant from India."

"Then why the Maldives?"

"Because my family was originally from there. It is not far from Calicut"

"I see."

The old man became silent, twirling his moustache gently.

"Where are you staying?" he asked.

I mentioned the place and he nodded in acknowledgment.

"I will bring a friend there in two hours. He may be able to help. Is that fine?"

I nodded. "Thank you."

"Come, let me show you the tomb of your ancestor." The old man gathered himself to rise.

It took me a moment to register what he had said.

I glanced up when his words hit home, but he was already looking elsewhere.

He introduced himself as Haji Ahmad Bouabid. We walked across to the tomb. We entered the little room and he showed me inscriptions on the wall and on the tomb itself. It was rather small. Haji Ahmad Bouabid summarized Ibn Batuta's life in a few minutes and explained that he had passed away in 1368 or 1369. The story that has lingered through the centuries was that he died pining for a beloved son in the Maldives.

He did not look at me.

We exited the room and shook hands.

"I shall be there in two hours. Go carefully. God be with you, my son."

I walked back to my room, after eating something at a roadside café. I thought about my experience. In a few short weeks, I, a cinnamon merchant from Thalassery, had ended up sitting at a little French café in Tangier in Morocco. How extraordinary life is!

And I had seen the tomb of the man to whom I owed my very existence.

At the appointed hour, Haji Ahmad Bouabid arrived with a friend. He was younger and looked very stern and formidable. Tall, well-built, and with a thick black moustache, I could sense that it would be wise to be on his side in any dispute.

They removed their fezzes as they came into my room.

"This is Abdelaziz El-Kahina, my friend. He may be the person who can help you. And this is Mohammad Koya."

I bowed. I felt a little scared. I myself was short and slim and could not handle a physical attack.

"Don't worry. He is here to guard you," Haji Bouabid smiled, sensing my nervousness.

"Speak, Abdelaziz," he gestured.

"I am a member of a society that keeps the memory of Haji Ibn Batuta alive. What is your interest, Koya?"

"I wish to meet someone who knows about his visit to the Maldives," I said, coming straight to the point.

"Why?"

"We moved from the Maldives to India several generations ago. There was a story in our family that we may be related to Ibn Batuta."

Abdelaziz snorted. "Many people say that. Do you have anything that can be called proof?"

"I don't know if this is proof. But here is a coin that I am told was given to my ancestor by Ibn Batuta," I proffered one of the gold coins that I had got with me.

Haji Bouabid and Abdelaziz stared long at the coin in my open palm, their eyes growing wider by the second and their faces losing colour.

"Where did you get that?" Haji Bouabid asked, hoarsely.

"I told you. It has always been with us. My father died a month ago. I found it in his personal effects and understood from some papers that it has always been in our family and we are not supposed to give it away. I came to Tangier to find out more."

"Do you seek anyone in particular?"

"Haji, I feel you know what I am looking for. My knowledge is very poor. I can always go back and continue my life as a spice trader." I was surprised by my confidence.

"Have you heard of the Guardians of the Letter?" Abdelaziz asked keenly.

"Yes. But I have no idea who they are and what their purpose is."

"How do you know about them?"

"I have seen a letter suggesting I travel to Tangier and meet them. I do not know anything further."

"Do you have the letter?" asked Abdelaziz.

"Yes."

"May I see it?"

"Would you show it?" I looked at Abdelaziz steadily, with a confidence I did not feel within.

"Hmm. Your point is reasonable. I do not belong to the Guardians of the Letter. They are very dangerous people. But I can take you to them immediately, if you like."

I agreed. In half an hour, we were ready to go.

"We must travel to the outskirts of Tangier to the house of one of the Guardians of the Letter. You are safe with me. Haji Bouabid cannot come as they do not know him."

Haji Bouabid again blessed me and waved as we set out on horseback, which I was not used to and found uncomfortable. Abdelaziz was silent but his presence was strong. After Haji Bouabid's reassurance, I felt better. But it was a strange feeling, to be on a horse for the first time in my life, trotting gently on the cobblestoned paths in little bylanes in Tangier.

We travelled for at least an hour and a half and had left the city limits of Tangier. The countryside was quite beautiful, with no one on the pathway that Abdelaziz seemed to know well. I was becoming uncomfortable.

We turned a corner beyond a large thicket of palm trees and came to the entrance of a small farm. Abdelaziz stopped and help me dismount. We walked down a narrow path and reached a modest house. Two children were playing outside. They rushed into the house shouting when they saw us approaching. A tall, strongly built and stern man stepped out, studying us as we walked toward him.

Abdelaziz greeted him and the man nodded.

As we approached, I saw that he was almost twice my size, in both height and girth. He looked down at me with cold eyes.

"As-Salaam-Alaikum," I said.

"Wa aleikum salam," he replied, without enthusiasm.

"Koya, this is Boughaid Arroub. I will tell you about him inside."

We walked inside. Boughaid Arroub shooed away the children. An attendant brought in the ubiquitous coffee, dates, and pistachios.

"Koya is from India. His family is from the Maldives."

Boughaid Arroub halted for the briefest of moments. He looked at me.

"What do you want, Koya?"

"Koya has come here on my suggestion," interjected Abdelaziz. "He may be the one, the one you seek. But you have to decide."

"He? Why do you think so?"

"Koya, show him the coin."

I did so. Boughaid Arroub stirred with some more interest. I handed it over to him to examine. He did so, studying it from all angles. "This coin is genuine. It is at least five hundred years old. It may have belonged to someone in Morocco." He handed the coin back to me. There was a new respect in his voice.

"Koya is searching for someone," said Abdelaziz, looking meaningfully at Boughaid Arroub.

"I am searching for the Guardians of the Letter," I said, without skipping a beat.

Boughaid Arroub continued sipping his coffee.

"Step outside, Abdelaziz," he snapped. Abdelaziz went outside quickly.

"When did you arrive in Tangier?" Boughaid Arroub asked me at length, his tone quite normal.

"Two days ago."

"What do you know about the Guardians of the Letter? But first, where did you hear about them?"

"In India. I read about them in my father's papers after he died. I have been asked to meet the Guardians to complete a certain desire of Ibn Batuta."

Boughaid Arroub rose abruptly and walked across to the opposite wall where there were a number of swords hanging. He removed one from its sheath and returned.

"In case I feel you are lying about anything, I will kill you," he said, in a cold and even voice. His eyes flashed, quite in contrast.

"There is no reason why I should come all the way to a foreign land where I know no one if I am possessed by a lie," I said with a calmness that was different from the terror I felt within. "I have a letter, you can read it," I added. "If the letter is a lie, do what you choose." I took out from within my dress the letter which Ibn Batuta had written to his son and delivered to him through the hands of Ibn Juzayy.

Boughaid Arroub took the letter from my hand and opened it carefully.

The transformation was remarkable.

His eyes opened wide and the stern and grim jaw loosened. His hands shook and his face turned pale.

"It is he! It is he who we have waited for! For so long! Yes, it is he, it is he!" he broke out into a babble, his hands shaking. "The time has come!" He fell on his knees, throwing the sword away and kissed my hands repeatedly, tears in his eyes.

"Forgive me, O Master, forgive me! I had no idea! We have waited for more than five hundred years for this moment! We have lived only for this moment! My father, my grandfather, and all those before them from the time of the great Ibn Batuta—we have waited and waited! For you, the great son of the greatest of all of Morocco's sons, Ibn Batuta! Welcome to my humble home!" The man wept, completely overcome.

I could not say anything. I, Thalassery Vatoot Mohammad Koya, a cinnamon merchant from a small town on the Malabar coast, was suddenly being celebrated as the venerated descendant of Ibn Batuta.

"Boughaid! Please! I am here for your friendship and for your help. I am not your master! Please!"

"You do not know what you say, Master! I and my family have been waiting for hundreds of years for this very moment! Everything will become clear very soon! Please wait."

Boughaid Arroub collected his emotions and sat down again, opposite me, gaping, his face tear-stained and very mobile. He shouted out and attendants came in, in a great rush, replacing the coffee and dates with more coffee and dates and a variety of dry fruits. The cups were of Chinese porcelain, it now seemed, and the hospitality had climbed to the highest level. I was extremely embarrassed. My poor Arabic did not allow me to express my gratitude adequately.

Abdelaziz whispered in my ear: "Koya, try to understand this: the Guardians of the Letter were specially appointed by Ibn Batuta. They have a letter for you which they have kept carefully for all these years. Each generation has been sworn to secrecy and their only task has been to wait and wait, to fulfil the promise their forefathers made to Ibn Batuta. It is a very big moment for them. Boughaid needs to think about what to do next."

In a few minutes, Boughaid's breathing became calmer.

"O Master, did you not know about Ibn Batuta before? Did you not know you were the descendant of one of the greatest men who ever walked this earth?" he asked me, his voice still quavering.

"No. My forefathers were not literate and we knew little. My father died last month and I discovered these papers. I decided to come here to find out more. I met Haji Bouabid and he introduced me to Abdelaziz and now I am here."

"Remarkable, remarkable! God is great! We have been waiting for so long for you. And you had no idea!"

"I do not know what the letter contains."

"Neither do we, O Master. But it does not matter. It was a promise that Ibn Batuta took from our forefathers and we have been sworn to uphold the promise forever. It is the reason we live. And die. About one hundred years ago, someone tried to get the letter from us by pretending to be Ibn Batuta's descendant. But we found he was lying. He was killed. We tore him apart limb from limb, my grandfather said."

"I see," I said. I was shaking inside. "What should we do now?" I asked, presently.

"You must come with me to Casablanca. That is where the other members—the Guardians—are. And that is where the letter is. We must hand it over to you. Then you must command us to do as you wish after you read and understand the letter. The role of Abdelaziz is over. He is not a Guardian. He is not to know anything further after this. If he reveals the incidents of today, he and his entire family will be slaughtered. He knows this quite well."

Abdelaziz was brought in and reminded, very sternly, about what was expected of him.

"My job is to simply help you. I know nothing further. I do not wish to know anything further."

"When should we go to Casablanca?" I asked Boughaid.

"Right away, Master. Give me an hour. I will assemble the camels and provisions and we can leave.

"We shall be there in two or three days. It is a long journey. I know there is a caravan leaving soon from Tangier. We shall join them."

And so, I, Thalassery Vatoot Mohammad Koya, shortly found myself on a camel, travelling in a caravan, protected by Boughaid Arroub, who called me his Master and who himself was one of the Guardians of the Letter. I bid good-bye to Abdelaziz and never saw him again.

The journey was long and arduous for me. But for the rest, in a caravan of some forty camels and a few hardy horses, it was quite normal. I got opportunities to improve my Arabic but I avoided speaking about why I was travelling to Casablanca. Boughaid Arroub was always hovering about me and he made it clear in many ways that I was an important dignitary who should be given the utmost respect and regard. The caravan was managed by a number of veiled men with blue turbans who I learned were Tuaregs, very prominent nomads of the desert.

The heat of the sun was unlike what I had experienced before in the Malabar. And the pleasant warmth of Tangier soon disappeared, replaced with an oppressive heat that left me gasping. My eyes clouded over and I found it difficult to even think. Boughaid Arroub kept a close watch on me and made sure we stopped after every hour so that I could rest. This delayed the caravan, obviously.

The Tuaregs found my distress slightly amusing and occasionally laughed as I gasped in the shade created by a camel.

I asked Boughaid Arroub why they were laughing.

"They are saying that the poor man – you, O Master – thinks this is hot. Let him travel from Sijilmasa to Timbuktu and he will know what heat is."

"Where are these places, Boughaid?"

"Sijilmasa is not far from Tangier. It is the gateway to the Sahara desert, O Master. From there, one travels down on old caravan routes in the desert to Mali, which is a famous country. The journey is extremely dangerous. But your illustrious predecessor, Haji Ibn Batuta travelled to Mali and back in the most oppressive conditions. Timbuktu is a famous city in Mali, noted for its mosques and centres for learning."

"We may have to travel to Timbuktu, Boughaid. Do you recall it was mentioned briefly in the letter I showed you?"

"Yes, O Master. You are right. Perhaps the letter you are going to receive from the Guardians will tell us more."

"Yes," I said, getting up, dusting off the sand from my clothes and climbing back on the saddle of my camel. The caravan resumed.

And by and by, we reached Casablanca. It was a very pretty town, in some ways similar to Tangier. But it was sunnier. The wind from the ocean kept things comfortable, and I was relieved that the journey had ended.

Boughaid and I reached the house of someone who he said had the letter in his safekeeping. It was a sprawling mansion, with a very large garden. There was a large tent in the middle, which, as I guessed correctly, was where the refreshments were kept.

Boughaid had already sent word to them and some others, and so, by the time we reached the house, there were a good ten or fifteen men waiting to greet us. All had very fierce countenances and all were armed. We assembled in the open area but very close to an open French window where an old man was sitting at a desk and watching.

Boughaid greeted them and introduced me. He spoke a dialect I could not follow, but I observed all of them listening very carefully and nodding, and looking at me again and again. He then showed the group – starting with the old man - the gold coin and then the letter.

It was enough. The entire group became hysterical and went on their knees, hailing me as their master, with tears in their eyes. The old man was bent at his desk, sobbing.

Fawning over me, they escorted me first to the tent to ply me with drinks and refreshments of every variety. Then they took me to a guest room where they had a steaming bath ready, with all kinds of oils and soaps. After I was done, I was presented a set of brand new clothes, which seemed to be of very fine cotton. They competed to show their devotion to me, a man who was completely ignorant of their reason for existing barely a month ago! I did not know what to say or do, so I smiled and said thank you many times.

"O Master, you see how important this occasion is. They never thought that their mission would be accomplished in their lifetime! All our forefathers prayed that they should have the honour of fulfilling the mission of the Guardians, but their prayers went unanswered. And now, without warning, we are the chosen ones! It is a very emotional moment for all of us!

"And now let me introduce you formally to the keeper of the letter. His name is Khalid Ibn Ziyad. He has been sitting at the window listening to all this. He is old and has problems walking. But he has understood everything and looks forward to meeting you."

I went in my new cotton dress to meet Ibn Ziyad. He must have been in his late eighties. He was very frail. When I entered with Boughaid, he made feverish attempts to stand up, speaking continuously. Then he tried to kneel down and kiss my hand. I insisted that he sit down. It was very awkward for me.

Only the three of us were in the room, with the other Guardians outside.

Ibn Ziyad spoke in his dialect to Boughaid who translated. "O Master, he wishes to know if your journey from India was comfortable."

"Yes, by the will of Allah, it was. Thank you."

They looked very pleased with my response.

"He is very happy. He wishes you to know that his life's mission has ended today, now that he has met you, the descendant of Ibn Batuta."

"Please tell him I am very fortunate to have met him."

"He wishes to know if you have a son."

They looked at me eagerly.

"No, my wife is expecting a baby soon. But I do not know if it will be a boy or a girl."

"He prays that the first child will be a boy and that you will have many more." The old man's eyes were sparkling with new energy.

"Thank you."

"He asks if you would like to see the letter, O Master."

"Yes, if it is not difficult for him."

"No, it is with him."

Ibn Zayid produced a stylish box from his desk. He then unclasped a necklace from around his neck and removed a key from it. Then he turned the key in the box after which he opened the top. In the chamber was a parchment - the secret letter - which we looked at silently and in awe.

"He has worn that key on his neck since he was fifteen years old, O Master. His father placed it there just before he died," said Boughaid. "That box has never been opened since the commissioning of the task to the Guardians of the Letter. That means it has now been opened after about 523 years. The lock worked! It is a miracle."

Ibn Zayid held up the box and presented it to me in an elaborate way, looking down at the floor, his body heaving and trembling with emotion.

"O Master, I, Khalid Ibn Zayid, the head of the Guardians of the Letter, now fulfil the task given to me by my forefather, who received orders from the great Haji Ibn Batuta," he said, his voice faltering and cracking. I accepted the box and put it on the table.

They expected me to open the letter and read it and give them further instructions. I opened the parchment and read the contents quietly first, as best as I could. The letter spoke of Marco Polo, China, the half-letter handed to Ibn Batuta that was now at Sankore Mosque in Timbuktu, the other half in Venice and so on.

I then read out the letter to Khalid Ibn Zayid and Boughaid.

They sat and listened in stunned silence. They asked me to repeat a few points once again and further discussed the nuances of whatever they had heard.

"O Master. While a very important task is now over for us, a far greater task must start immediately. We believe that we have to do the following.

"Retrieve the half parchment from Venice. It belongs to you. Retrieve the other half that Ibn Batuta left behind in the Sankore Mosque when he left Timbuktu in a hurry. Once we assemble the parchment, we must act on it. Perhaps the answer is in the parchment. Who can say?"

"I agree. But how do we begin? And where?"

Ibn Zayid spoke in a high querulous voice suddenly and Boughaid pacified him with many smiles.

"He says you must rest. You must leave the planning to us because that is the duty of the Guardians.

By tomorrow morning, we shall be ready with the plan. But you must rest, O Master. You have come from such a distance!"

And with those words, our meeting came to an end. I was taken to a lavish room where I slept on a large bed with elaborate silks and plush pillows. I slept for many hours, dreaming of accompanying Ibn Batuta on his adventures.

The next day, I entered the room of Ibn Zayid with Bughaid. Ibn Zayid again made an attempt to kneel and kiss my hand, but I respectfully declined.

"O Master, we seek your permission to set forth on the plan."

"Please go ahead. What do you propose to do?"

"We shall send four of our men to Europe to retrieve the half-manuscript. It will take time because we have to determine exactly where it might be. Venice has been mentioned. But it may be elsewhere. We must coax the owner of the parchment to give it to us. Either free or for money. If not, we shall use force."

"How will you find out?"

"The Guardians always maintained a network for any eventuality. In Europe, there is a famous man, Professor Moriarty. We shall take his help. He knows everyone and everything. He will help us, of that we are sure. We have helped him in many other situations in Morocco. Recently, we have been spying for the French for him. You would not be aware of the politics of this region."

"Very well."

"Meanwhile, we shall prepare to travel to Timbuktu immediately after getting the first half from Venice."

"Why not travel immediately?"

"We must travel with you and the half-parchment. It may be necessary to show it to someone in Timbuktu. We do not know. Also, the trip to Timbuktu is long. While in the desert, we cannot contact anyone in case anything were to happen or we were to receive some news that requires us to change our plans."

"I see. Therefore, what do you recommend?"

"We recommend, O Master, that you stay here. We shall create detailed plans right away and keep you and Ibn Zayid informed."

I stayed in the luxurious mansion in Casablanca for several weeks. I received many interesting pieces of information from time to time.

1. A Guardian went to Venice and made inquiries. He strongly believed that the parchment was in the museum, perhaps unknown to the curator, simply because Marco Polo had donated all his papers to them.

2. The curator was then asked by letters to return the half-manuscript in his possession. However, he ignored the letters.

3. An attempt was made to burgle the Venice museum. The Guardian who made the attempt felt sure that the half-manuscript was in the museum because he was able to glance at something in the Chinese section that looked suspicious. But before he could examine the matter further, he was surprised by a guard. In the scuffle, an alarm was raised and the guard was severely wounded. He had to escape. He said that he became doubly sure because the curator and the priest of a famous church travelled the next day to Rome to meet the Pope. Immediately thereafter, the curator travelled to meet a detective in London and to consult a famous friend in the British Museum.

4. Two Guardians attempted to kidnap the curator in London but failed.

5. They found that the curator had given a copy of the document to an expert in the British Museum who promised to do something, and then explain the matter to the curator. However, when two Guardians attempted to acquire the copy and his translation, the expert burnt both while battling them. He was seriously injured but survived.

6. They again tried to get the half-manuscript from the curator once he returned to Venice but discovered that he had already been killed. His room was searched thoroughly in any case.

The half-manuscript was not found, suggesting that he had handed over the document to someone, possibly in London.

7. The detective in London disappeared in Switzerland. We suspect he has the document, the original half-manuscript.

8. They do not know where the detective is. There was a rumour that he went to the Vatican again, but we could not confirm it.

I was finding it very difficult to understand all this. I was, after all, a humble merchant, suddenly immersed in a very complicated matter. Even though I was not personally involved in these acts, the strict instructions of my forefather five hundred years ago were resulting in all kinds of things happening even today!

I asked Boughaid if there was some way in which I could send my wife and sister some money for them to sustain themselves. He told me that Ibn Batuta had not only set up the Guardians of the Letter but had also kept aside some money for his descendants.

"This mansion, O Master, belongs to you. We are mere custodians and have been so all along. And we have kept accounts very carefully for you. I request you to check and ask us any question you feel like. I can arrange for a thousand gold coins to be sent to India immediately, if it is your wish."

I was not sure how to react. I could only stammer, "Please do," as I silently thanked my benefactor, Haji Ibn Batuta.

Tangier and Holmes

Holmes always had the ability to surprise me in the most unusual ways. The letter from Tangier was just the most recent. For some time, my head swam with the realization that he was alive, while all this time I had been labouring under an illusion that he was no longer with us. As I reflected and traced back events, I realized that it was not particularly surprising that he was in Morocco. No doubt the issue of the half-manuscript parchment was still unresolved.

I consulted Mary on the matter and was delighted to receive her wholehearted acquiescence. "A man like Sherlock Holmes does not simply fall over a ledge at a waterfall and die, John. I never believed that ridiculous story. How gullible people are! I am not surprised he is in Morocco. I would have equally well expected him to be in America, India, Japan, or Australia."

"Would you like to come with me?" I asked.

"No. I would come in Mr. Holmes' way. I shall wait for you to return from your adventures. I hope you do solve the mystery of the manuscripts."

I had confided to her about the mysterious matters in London during her countryside sojourn in 1891.

And so, as planned, I set out to Gibraltar. A short sail later, the ship docked at Tangier. I looked at the approaching town with pleasure. The blue sky, the whitewashed buildings, the gulls in the harbour, the colourful clothes of the inhabitants—it was a refreshing change from the drabness of Liverpool and London.

I walked down the gangplank from the ship, and asked a customs officer for suggestions for lodging. He named a few places quite close by.

"Where is the Casa Barat, my dear sir?"

"Not very far. It is a rather unremarkable market. Very few visitors go there. But you may get some cheap bargains. It is actually on the way to the hotels I suggested."

I left my baggage at the cloakroom at the port and strolled down to the *souk*, enjoying the sunny weather. In a few minutes, I reached Casa Barat, which seemed a noisy place full of confusion. I walked in, and avoided all the merchants who tried their best to attract my attention.

At a quieter garment store, I saw an old man sitting with his back to the wall. He watched me approach. I nodded, as did he.

"English?" I asked.

"Yes."

"May I know where I can find Mehdi Benbouchta?"

"Mehdi Benbouchta?"

"Yes."

"Hmm. Please continue down. Look for a shop selling hats—fezzes. You will find him there. Just six or seven shops down."

"Thank you."

He nodded.

I found the shop and asked the young man there, who was busy arranging fezzes on display, if he could direct me to Mehdi Benbouchta. He looked at me for a moment and responded.

"Yes, I am Mehdi Benbouchta. How may I help you?"

"I was asked to meet you to take me to my friend."

"His name?"

"Sherlock Holmes."

"What is the password, please?"

"Rihla."

"Thank you. I shall take you to him. Half an hour away. I must bring my grandfather with me."

He went into a room behind the shop and came out with a stooping, very old Moroccan man. He must have been at least eighty years old and seemed to be blind with cataract.

"Good afternoon, my dear sir," he said in accented English, in a high-pitched quavering voice.

"Good afternoon. Are you Mehdi Benbouchta's grandfather?" I asked.

"Yes, I am. He is a good boy. Is there anything I can do for you? Do you wish to buy some dates or perhaps a fez?"

I did not think there was anything he could have done for me. "No, thank you."

"Mehdi has many friends. Too many," he grumbled, putting on his fez and adjusting his prayer beads, as his grandson appeared with a bag and a cloak.

"Indeed?" I responded politely.

"Some are dangerous. Some are lazy. I tell him to be careful. But who listens to an old man?" He started grumbling in Arabic.

We started walking out of the souk. Mehdi very kindly supported his grandfather, who leaned heavily on his right shoulder as he struggled along.

"Can he walk the distance?" I whispered to Mehdi.

"Oh, yes. Don't worry."

We crossed a little road and walked very slowly for another twenty minutes.

"My knees. They are paining. Also my back. And I have difficulty seeing. Old age problems," grumbled the old man, quite unhappy about the situation.

"One must take care with diet and exercise."

He broke out in a flurry of Arabic, which I thankfully did not understand. Mehdi listened patiently, while letting his grandfather rest even more heavily on his broad shoulders.

We reached a nondescript building in a little alley.

"Mr. Holmes is here," said Mehdi. "Let us go up to the second floor."

"Second floor? Won't that be too much for your grandfather?" I remonstrated.

"Not at all! They are good friends and meet every day!" grinned Mehdi.

I could hardly imagine Holmes being taken by the querulous old man and becoming "good friends," but then again, his tastes were unpredictable.

We walked up, step by step, with Mehdi's grandfather huffing and puffing and muttering in Arabic under his breath, while holding on to his young grandson's shoulder.

We entered a spacious and well-appointed room.

"This is where Mr. Holmes lives," said Mehdi.

"It seems comfortable. But where is he?"

"Right here, my dear Watson," came a familiar, confident voice behind me.

I turned.

Mehdi's grandfather had miraculously straightened out. His face had become younger. Gone were the wrinkles and the cataract eyes. And standing in front of me was that dearly loved, familiar face.

I was speechless.

"Holmes!" I cried, finally.

Mehdi held me as I tottered.

Holmes, too, had stepped forward quickly and helped ease me into a chair.

"This is impossible, Holmes!" I cried, stupefied. "It was you all along!"

And then I fainted.

When I came to, Holmes and the young man were hovering anxiously above me, fanning me and sprinkling water on my face.

"Watson, my apologies, my dear fellow! I could never have guessed you would be so severely affected! It was just a little joke!"

I got up slowly and sat back in the chair. I looked long and deep at my old friend, back from the dead. The sharp features, the intelligence, the alertness—yes, it was him. There was no doubt about it. Sherlock Holmes was alive and well and with me in Tangier.

Mehdi returned with coffee and some dates, insisting that I have them to regain my strength.

"What is going on here in Tangier, Holmes? Why were you dressed up like an old Moroccan? "

"I shall explain everything, Watson. First, let me introduce you to my good friend Mehdi, whom you have already met. He will be helping us prepare for a long journey."

Mehdi bowed. "I am an assistant to Mr. Holmes' friend, Mr. Said aṣ-Ṣabār, a prominent lawyer in Morocco. I travel with him sometimes between Tangier and London. I hail from Casablanca and that shop belongs to my family.

"And now I must leave and return to my family shop. If you authorize me, I shall have your luggage picked up from the cloakroom at the port office. Please stay here as my guest."

"Thank you." I gave Mehdi the details he needed and he left Holmes and me together.

"And will you now tell me how it is that you are alive while the rest of the world labours under the delusion that you are not?"

"All in good time, Watson. It was easier than you could imagine. But at the moment, we are seized of a larger problem." Holmes took a chair and leaned back, after taking out his pipe and slowly refilling it.

"Concerning the manuscript?"

"Yes."

Sherlock Holmes told me about his escape from Reichenbach and his subsequent visit to Venice and Rome and how it came about that he managed to find a position in Tangier as a representative of the Pope. He was as comfortable in the Vatican as a renowned detective as he was in an old grimy market in Tangier as a grumbling old grandfather. And now he was masquerading in Tangier as "Father Andrzej Bąkiewicz," with the explicit permission of the Pope, in order to find a parchment of unknown origin and import!

"In brief, Watson, I was thus far comfortable at the prefecture rooms in Tangier, though I was taken aback when Colonel Sebastian Moran paid a visit. Bishop Landel is a rather uninspiring representative of the Vatican at this outpost but there are deeper waters.

"When I heard that he was visiting, I felt my room would be searched. But on my return that evening, I found nothing disturbed. I have a hunch, but not much more. I may have to take a leave of absence in case you and I have to travel shortly, which I think is a strong likelihood.

"This is a complex place, Watson. If you are prepared to accept people as they seem to be, all is well. But then if you probe deeper, you discover unusual relationships that transcend even time. I have reason to believe, Watson, that the missing piece of the puzzle, someone who has triggered this entire chain of events, is in Morocco. But first tell me, my good fellow, how is your health?"

"I think I have never felt better, Holmes. The sunshine and clean air here are quite bracing."

"Hmm. Will you be up to crossing the Sahara with me, Watson?"

"Absolutely, Holmes. You must decide, knowing this place better than I do, whether I would be a hindrance or an aid."

"I would not have called you if I felt you might create an unnecessary twist. There is no one I would trust more, Watson. But I wished to hear it from you."

I was quite touched. "I hope to assist in whatever capacity you deem fit, Holmes."

"I did inspect the road to Sijilmasa and I am confident we will be fine. That is where I wrote my letter to you, from the oasis there." Holmes had an admirable knack for going into details. Planning, he had once said, wins half the battle.

He continued. "Let us get into the details of preparation. Please consult Mehdi on the most common ailments that a desert traveller might experience. And the relevant medications needed. Then please prepare for a journey of at least a month, likely more, in the most hostile terrain."

"Yes, Holmes."

"And read this book," Holmes tossed something across.

I examined the book, which was the English translation of something called the *Rihla.* "I appreciate your interest in the classical literature of this country, Holmes. But is this the time for it?"

"If ever there was a time to read the *Rihla*, Watson, it is now. Everything here is related to Ibn Batuta. Please read every page and absorb it completely. This man defines Moroccan identity as no one else. Whatever we have experienced and will experience is connected to his legacy. And a word of caution. Under no circumstances should you ask anyone if they have heard of the Guardians of the Letter. This is the secret group that is behind the attempted thefts, the murders, and assaults in Europe. Unfortunately, they take their job very seriously; they have a duty that has been handed down over five hundred years and they will do anything to fulfil it. They are absolute fanatics. If they hear of anyone asking about them, they go to violent extremes."

"Do you have the half-manuscript, Holmes?" I inquired.

"Yes, it is safe. Our task is to determine where the other half is. I think I know, but we shall need help."

"Where is it?"

"It is in—"

We were interrupted by the sound of hurried footsteps outside our door. Holmes slipped his hand into his pocket—I presume he had a revolver.

It was Mehdi and he had arrived with my bags and Holmes' violin.

"Here you are, Dr. Watson," said Mehdi, handing over the bags.

"Thank you."

He turned toward Holmes. "We should leave immediately, Mr. Holmes."

Sherlock Holmes raised his right eyebrow. Mehdi's agitation was noticeable.

"I understand that some men, likely the Guardians, visited the prefecture church a few days ago and were asking for you.

As we had feared, the news about a Father saving the life of a Tuareg and apprehending a magistrate has spread rapidly. I am sure they heard about it and want to find out who you are. They are intelligent people."

"In other words, we need to leave for Timbuktu immediately."

"Yes. I have no doubt they will follow you. The sooner you leave, the better. Hasso Ag Akotey and his group are in any case almost ready to leave. I have three horses outside. Shall we go?"

In a few minutes, after Holmes transformed into Father Andrzej Bąkiewicz and I took on the guise of a Moroccan wearing a traditional *jalaba*, we were racing at a clip across Tangier and to the east. I had an opportunity to take in the sights of the pleasant city of Tangier with the backdrop of the Mediterranean and, in the far distance, the Atlas Mountains.

We finally reached an open field where quite a large number of Tuaregs had assembled. It was a sea of indigo, black, and white—a pleasant sight.

"These are the Ahaggar Tuaregs," Mehdi informed us. "They are traditionally from the south of Algeria and Mali, but spend a lot of time in the border areas between Morocco and Algeria. That man there is the chief that Sherlock Holmes saved. Hasso Ag Akotey."

Mehdi hailed one of the older Tuaregs, who made for an impressive figure. Tall, with a weather-beaten face and piercing eyes, his veil—*tagelmust*—made him an imposing figure at the centre of a group of men with swords.

We went into a tent. Holmes surprised me by speaking brokenly but confidently in a local language, which he later told me was *Tamasheq*.[6] He had picked it up over the past few weeks. Holmes had a great facility for languages. He later wrote a monograph about the secret language of the Inadan

---

[6] I was surprised to know that some Tuaregs preferred to be called *Kel Tamasheq*, meaning "those who speak Tamasheq""

blacksmith Tuaregs, which seemed about as arcane a subject as I could imagine.[7]

Mehdi and Holmes convinced the Tuaregs to leave immediately. They worked out a plan. I had hoped to spend a few days in Morocco, but it was not to be.

---

[7] He said he proposed to present a paper to the Royal Society and had received some agreeable comments, from the review committee, though I may reassure you that I did not make similar comments, having no interest in this eminently forgettable matter.

Holmes and the Tuaregs

Note by Dr. John Watson: I have recreated the scenes here after extensive interviews with Holmes, a Moroccan lawyer (now deceased), and Hasso Ag Akotey. I have preferred to use their voices. I showed each of them what I had written, and all agreed that I had captured their statements accurately.

In the voice of Sherlock Holmes

I, Father Andrzej Bąkiewicz, walked about the narrow streets of Tangier. The sun snaked its way in between the buildings. The breeze from the Mediterranean was cool and bracing. It was another perfect day.

"Never before have I had a student with such passion," exclaimed Haji Bouabid. "You come every single day! You study for two hours! You ask questions, you push yourself, you work at home! You wish to learn calligraphy! We are now speaking in Arabic, not in French, in just five months! Wonderful! At this speed, you will soon be an Arabic scholar!"

"A grand and wonderful language, Haji! I wish I had learned it earlier. But never mind. Regret is pointless. There is so much to read and learn!" I skimmed the pages of another book—this time on the fundamentals of astronomy—that Haji Bouabid had retrieved for me. "When I return to Roma, I shall write a monograph on Arabic calligraphy."[8]

That evening, after an enjoyable Arabic class with Haji Bouabid, I stopped at a café for a cup of coffee and to think. I had received a coded telegram from Lestrade on the nexus between Professor Moriarty and the Guardians. They had apprehended an intruder at the Royal Archives at Windsor Castle in London but he simply refused to talk, though he had alluded to some "Guardians" to whom he was duty-bound to deliver results. The issue seemed messy—frost between France and England on the issue of colonial designs in Africa. The Guardians were active in Europe, searching for the half-manuscript and me.

But I was not as perturbed by that as the fact that my sixth sense was telling me that Professor Moriarty was likely to connect various dots and conclude that I was in Tangier; it would need just one slip from my side. Like me, he too found guesswork and conjecture in all matters undesirable. Unless there is a basis, it is positively absurd to guess.

I imagined Professor Moriarty thinking in silence: What is Holmes' current preoccupation?

> *The finding of a rare document of great value, about which I have been notified by my Moroccan comrades, the Guardians of the Letter.*
>
> Has his body been found?
>
> *No.*
>
> Then why are people talking about Holmes in the past tense?

---

[8] Once again, we see Holmes' perplexing desire for immortality by producing monograph after monograph on various (rather inconsequential) aspects of the human experience.

Because they are fools who like excitement and do not stop to think. Like readers of crime fiction who want daggers, blood, and the revelation of secrets on every page instead of quiet intelligence.

What was he likely to have done had he wished to escape?

Head for safety in a direction opposite to Meirengen.

What was the country closest to Reichenbach?

Italy.

Which city made sense for someone like him to go to pursue his objective?

Venice.

Why had he disappeared so completely from sight in Europe?

Because he was no longer in Europe and had left the continent.

Where would he find safety?

Very likely in Morocco, right under the noses of the Guardians, who were busy focusing on Europe.

I had no doubt that this was likely to have been the train of thought in the mind of Professor Moriarty, though the last answer would probably emerge sooner rather than later. This was the possible reason for the unexpected arrival of Colonel Moran—first to meet the Guardians and then to initiate the search, using the relatively safe confines of the prefecture church. My disguise was good enough to pass muster, but not for very long. The average person is not as stupid as we think, and can actually apply his intelligence when asked to concentrate. I probably had, at best, a few months to finish my task. I had to find a way to travel to the Sankore Mosque in Timbuktu.

My attention was distracted by a commotion nearby.

Three French gendarmes were dragging a Tuareg man along the road. He seemed to have been beaten quite severely; blood poured from wounds on his head. His *tagelmust* had been torn off. Behind them, a few more gendarmes were keeping a small crowd of noisy Tuaregs at bay with guns. Many voices were raised. Everyone seated at the café fled inside, not wanting to get involved. I remained seated and watched the little procession pass by.

One of the gendarmes stopped by, momentarily, close to where I was seated on the pavement. I asked him what the problem was.

"We have just arrested someone for the murder of a Frenchman. A dirty Tuareg! Of course, he says he is innocent! Dogs!" He spat.

The angry gendarme walked on, holding back the small crowd of agitated men.

In a few minutes, the uproar abated and the crowd disappeared. The other customers who had fled inside the café came out cautiously. I tried to resume my coffee, but I no longer felt the need. I took out my pipe, filled it with tobacco and began smoking.

I was approached by one of the customers, an older Moroccan wearing western attire, who asked me politely in French if I could tell him what had happened.

I explained as best as I could.

He spoke, but now in English. "And what, sir, is Mr. Sherlock Holmes doing in a café in Tangier?"

I was quite taken aback.

"I beg your pardon?" I said, pretending to be puzzled.

"You are Sherlock Holmes, the famous detective. I am sure of it!" the man smiled. "My name is Said aṣ-Ṣabār[9] and I am a lawyer here. Here is my card, sir. I travel often to London for

---

[9] I have masked the real name because there are important diplomatic sensitivities involved.

certain legal matters and visit my colleagues at Lincoln's Inn. How can a frequent visitor to London be unaware of Sherlock Holmes and his distinctive nose and pipe? You do look different, though. Perhaps you are in disguise. I quite understand and—"

The matter had gone too far in a very few sentences. I raised an eyebrow.

He was perceptive to understand that this was hardly a matter to be discussed at a roadside café, and stopped abruptly, his eyes suddenly expressionless.

"You are mistaken, sir. I am Father Andrzej Bąkiewicz from the Catholic Prefecture. I would be pleased if you dropped by for some tea at your convenience," I said, bowing.

Mr. aṣ-Ṣabār understood and he too bowed. I walked back quickly to the prefecture, annoyed by the incident.

My friend, Dr. John Watson, interviewed Hasso Ag Akotey during the journey to Timbuktu and recreated the subsequent story. It is better that you read it without my interpretive bias.

In the voice of Hasso Ag Akotey

I am Hasso Ag Akotey, the chief of a group of Ahaggar Tuaregs.

We spend our lives in what you call the Sahara, and what we call the Tinariwen. The Tinariwen is sacred—it supports us, it gives us our culture, our language, our music. We respect it. You see sand, you see heat, you see death, you see waste and desolation. What a pity. But we see life, we hear music, and we listen to the stories that the dead, whom we never name, sing from their graves. They sing stories of men and women who were born here, travelled across the desert, to Bamako, Timbuktu, Tindouf, Tamanrasset—oh, how fortunate we are, to travel, to move, to visit—and not to be tied to the earth!

And we travel on our camels to visit the grave of our great Queen, the Mother of us all, Tin Hanan, in the Ahaggar Mountains. It is sacred for us. She gave us life, she gave us our identity, she gave us our language, Kel Tamasheq.

It is difficult, Englishman, for you to understand us and our ways. Your people and the French think we are strange and savage. We, too, find it difficult to understand you and your odd customs. Yet a strong friendship has been created and we are happy, because of the goodness of your companion, Mr. Sherlock Holmes, who we thought was a Christian priest for a long time.

Just as you have a king, we have an *amenokal*, whose name is Aytarel ag Muhammad Biskra. I meet him sometimes. I think he is presently somewhere near Abalessa. If we go there, we shall meet him.

No doubt you think that the veil we wear and the way we wear it are unusual. It is our tradition. It has practical use in the hot desert but also has cultural meaning and protects us from spirits. By the way Sherlock Holmes ties his *tagelmust* it seems that he was probably a Tuareg once upon a time. What? You do not believe in spirits? That is very strange indeed. Perhaps we shall soon convince you. Please believe me. There are many spirits in the Tinariwen. Some good, some bad.

Where are we actually from? I just told you. Our mother was Tin Hanan. She was originally from Morocco but now she lies in her grave in the Ahaggar Mountains, at Abalessa, not far from Tamanrasset. We remember her with great fondness and regard. I hope you, too, will visit her with us.

Yes, you wished to know why we have so much respect for Mr. Sherlock Holmes. The simple reason is that he saved my life. The act of saving my life also meant that the honour of my tribe was preserved. We are indebted to him.

Let me tell you what happened, though I am sure that he has told you the same story but from a different window, where the light shines in a different way.

Our usual camp is on the eastern outskirts of Tangier, which by itself is not a very large town. I was sitting outside my *ahaket*—tent—with Amedras, Wararni, and Amayas—yes, the same men you see sitting together next to the fire over there—talking to another friend, Hasso, who had just come from Rabat. Yes, we both have the same name. That was in fact the simple root of a much more serious problem.

"You have come alone. What has happened?" I asked Hasso.

"A Frenchman was found killed. Many people came to see the body lying in a ditch, including my friend Ziri and I. Some gendarmeries came to check. A Frenchman accused me of being the murderer. We became quite agitated. I escaped from the scene during the chaos and came here for safety. Had I been caught, I would have been killed for sure."

Amayas shook his head "Yes, you would have been killed. They would pretend to have a trial since they think they are very civilized."

"Of course. We are nothing to them."

"I heard six of the Kel Owey were killed recently near Fez."

"How dare the French treat the Amazighs like this? How long should we tolerate these foreigners?" Amayas was angry. He is hot-blooded and does not know when to hold back his words. Young men are invariably impractical and consumed by feelings of invulnerability.

"They have guns. We do not. It is simple," I sighed.

As we discussed our plight, we heard some loud shouting from the edge of our camp. Men were shouting, women were screaming, and some guns were fired, too. We looked in the direction and saw a large group of armed French gendarmes burst into the camp.

"Who is Hasso?" shouted their leader, striding toward us, glaring.

I stood up. "I am Hasso," I said. That was the truth.

He strode up and grabbed me roughly.

"Filthy Tuareg!" he yelled in French, which I understood. "Worthless scum! I am arresting you for the murder of Jacques Pétain in Rabat! This will be the end of you! Dog!"

He and some other gendarmes then hit and kicked me very brutally. I tried to protest but to no avail. I understood immediately that it was a case of mistaken identity, but in any case, it was my duty as their leader to protect my fellow Tuaregs.

I was soon bleeding from many wounds all over my body. I did try to stop them, but they were too many. Soon, I lost consciousness for a few minutes.

Someone splashed some water on my face. The gendarmes had torn away my *tagelmust*, a deeply insulting act for any Tuareg, as you know. They pulled me up and dragged me away, with the other gendarmes keeping my men at a distance. Then I was taken through a few roads of Tangier to their jail. I was thrown into a dark cell, where I once again lost consciousness.

I learned later that as I was being dragged to the jail, we passed a café where Mr. Sherlock Holmes, whom we called The Father, was seated, enjoying a cup of coffee. And so was a very important lawyer, Said aṣ-Ṣabār. I knew neither at that point.

God is great. He connected two important persons with me and with each other at just the right time.

When I awoke, I found myself with a terrible headache. I had many bruises and my ribs felt sore.

The next few days were unpleasant. The gendarmes delighted in insulting me and torturing me in many ways—look at my arm, this is where they used their cigarette butts. They wanted me to confess to the murder of a man I had never even seen. How could I do that? Would you have, Dr. Watson? We have learned how to withstand extreme pain.

Somehow, it seems that word spread about my detention. They could not have easily killed me, I suppose, because I was too well known and people had seen me being taken away and dragged through a road. In any case, there is a lot of tension here with the Frenchmen and they have to pretend to give the accused a trial because they claim they are civilized, while we are not. The French are everywhere now—in Mali, in Algeria, in Bornu.[10] And everyone hates them. It is good you are not a Frenchman!

One morning, the jailor came to my cell with another man, who introduced himself as a lawyer. He was, in fact, the famous lawyer, Said aṣ-Ṣabār, who had seen the incident. He is

---

[10] At that time, a territory part of French Equatorial Africa and later, Chad.

also involved in the struggle for Morocco's freedom against the colonial designs of France and Spain.[11]

The guard brought in a chair on which the man sat. I continued sitting on the floor. We conversed in Arabic, since Said aṣ-Ṣabār was not a Tuareg and could not speak Tamasheq fluently.

He introduced himself. "I am here to help you," he said.

One must be suspicious of help that comes unasked.

"How will you do that? I think they are getting ready to execute me."

"Tell me the truth. Then I shall think of a way."

I told him what happened.

"So the other Hasso knows about it but you won't give the gendarmes his name."

"Yes," I replied.

"They may guillotine you if they find you guilty. They say they have proof."

"I do not know what happened. I was not there."

"Can you find out?" he asked.

I refused. "No. I will not help the Frenchmen. I would rather die. I will not be a traitor."

"They say that the Frenchman was buying vegetables at a market in Rabat when you attacked him."

"I do not know since I was not in Rabat. What else do they say?"

"That you took away his horse and fled. You were identified by several witnesses. Your height and weight were described. The assailant was called Hasso."

"I was not there. They are speaking of the other Hasso. But I cannot believe he committed the crime, either. The story is not complete."

Said aṣ-Ṣabār wrote down many things in a book he had brought with him.

---

[11] The Melila War of 1893 proved deeply damaging to the Rif tribes of Northern Morocco, who fought against the Spanish.

He sat quietly for a while, thinking about the matter. Then he got up.

"I must think and I must consult someone else. Be brave. They cannot do anything now that I am your lawyer. I know this inspector and I shall ask him to be kind to you."

"How did you become my lawyer? I am poor. I cannot pay you."

"For us to become free of the French, all patriots must help each other and stop thinking of their tribes. I have chosen to assist those who are accused of crimes against the French." He spoke with great sincerity.

"I belong to no country. You know that. The Tuaregs belong to the Tinariwen. We are from the Haggar Mountains, many weeks from here."

He smiled. "I know," he said. He then pressed my hand and left.

The gendarmes were no longer violent with me. I sat crouched in a dark corner of my filthy cell for long hours. The heat inside a closed room is much worse than the heat of the desert. So I suffered. There was no toilet, and very little water in a mud pot. I thought of my family, my tribe, my camels, my music, and the Tinariwen. I wondered if I had lost them forever.

Then two days later, abruptly, the inspector opened my cell. With him was Said aṣ-Ṣabār, who was smiling.

"You have been released."

"Why so?" I was careful not to betray emotion.

"I shall tell you later. Come."

I wound my *tagelmust* tightly and walked out.

◇◇◇

The account of the Moroccan lawyer and freedom fighter Said aṣ-Ṣabār

I visited the Catholic prefecture church immediately after my interview with Hasso, and presented my card, requesting that I be allowed to meet Father Andrzej Bąkiewicz. I was soon escorted to his modest room by a suspicious servant.

"I wished to see you, Father Andrzej Bąkiewicz, on an important matter that I believe only you can resolve," I said, bowing.

"I shall make every attempt, if it is in my ability."

We sat down and 'Father Bąkiewicz' took out his pipe to give his attention to my narrative.

"I see that you have just visited the police station. And you have postponed your meetings with your clients. The matter must be quite pressing."

I was utterly amazed. "Absolutely right! But how did you guess? I never told you!"

"I do not guess, sir. It is an irrational vanity. It is too early in the day for the court to have opened, yet you are formally dressed and have come in holding files. The pen I see on your breast pocket is at an angle suggesting you must have already used it this morning; you have not screwed the cap well suggesting recent, hurried use. I deduce that you have met someone at the police station, interviewed him, and then arrived here. Further, most lawyers would meet their clients at this time, but you are here instead of your chambers. *Ergo*, you must have requested your clients to come again."

"Ah, yes, a simple deduction. You are quite right."

"Logic is always considered simple," observed Father Bąkiewicz with a thin smile. "Please proceed."

"A most peculiar case. I am a lawyer and represent the man who you saw being dragged along the road outside the café where we were. I am unable to prove his innocence, though I am convinced of it. I thought of you since you had seen this man."

"Ah, the Tuareg man. I wondered what happened to him."

"Here are the facts, as my client has told me.

"About ten days ago, a Frenchman, Jacques Pétain, was reported to have assaulted a Tuareg man near Rabat. He had too much to drink and possibly misbehaved with some Tuareg women, too. He was accompanied by two other Frenchmen who behaved similarly, except that they did not touch any woman.

"This man, Jacques Pétain, had a colourful past. I have checked and found that he already had a reputation for violence and general debauchery. The other two, Alain Beaumier and Henri Toussaint had no such reputation.

"Pétain snatched away the Tuareg's *takouba*—his dagger—and threatened the people assembled there. Then he went away. On a complaint by the people, however, he was apprehended by the gendarmeries and brought before a magistrate. The magistrate, also a Frenchman, gave him a warning and let him off.

"A day later, he was found dead in a ditch. The takouba he had stolen the previous evening was in his back—he had been stabbed. There was considerable commotion and the two Frenchmen who had been seen with him earlier brought in the gendarmeries. They insisted that one of the Tuareg onlookers—Hasso—had possibly killed him. It was essentially their word—as Frenchmen—against a Tuareg. Hasso denied it, and in the melee, he escaped on a horse that, unfortunately, had been used previously by Pétain.

"Hasso was followed over the course of a chase of a couple of days, to Hasso Ag Akotey's camp east of Tangier. Unfortunately, there is a slight physical resemblance, too, and the wrong Hasso was apprehended for a crime that the other Hasso had been falsely accused of."

"And how can you be so sure that the first Hasso did *not* commit the crime?" Father Bąkiewicz asked.

"At the moment, it is his word and he insists. His story does not vary. He avers that he was merely passing by when the commotion broke out over the discovered body. He admits that he knew Pétain but only as someone who lived in the neighbourhood. He had no dealings with him.

"Now we come to the strange part of the story. First, tucked in Pétain's pocket was a slip of paper. I was able to persuade the inspector to let me borrow it for a while. I wanted to show it to you. Please take a look."

I showed Father Bąkiewicz the slip of paper.

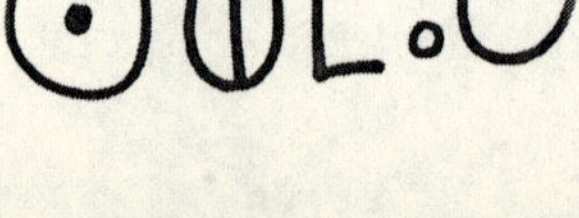

He held the slip of paper very carefully at the edges. Then he looked at it against the light for a few minutes, and nodded.

"Very interesting. Now what do these symbols mean?"

"This script is Tifinagh, used often by Tuaregs for their language Tamasheq. The word is *shimar*, which means rebellion."

"The police infer that this was placed in Pétain's pocket by a Tuareg—Hasso—as a message to the French. There is a political crisis here, as you know."

"I see something more," observed Father Bąkiewicz. "But pray continue."

I hesitated. "There was a crucifix in the other pocket."

Holmes raised an eyebrow.

I continued. "Not unusual, true, and may be irrelevant. But what was unusual was the type of crucifix. Here is a drawing.

Now I am a Mussalman, and cannot claim to know much about crucifixes, but I had never seen this before. Since you are here as a Father at a Catholic church for some reason, I felt you were likely to know. Again, it may have no significance."

"Well, we do not know yet, but it is good to look at everything."

"I have sought a meeting with the magistrate to discuss the matter. He is to decide when the court will formally proceed. They are currently framing charges."

"When is this meeting? What is his name?" asked Father Bąkiewicz.

"His name is Alain Favreau. We have to meet him the day after tomorrow at nine in the morning."

"Hmm. That does not give us much time. But let us think carefully."

Father Bąkiewicz walked about in his room for several minutes, frowning, his head bent. He suddenly halted in mid-stride.

He asked for the scrap of paper again. "Do you think I can keep this till the evening?"

"It will be difficult. Can you try to return it by the late afternoon? I shall come again."

"There is a strong possibility that I would have made significant progress by then. Four o'clock is fine."

I then left.

The issue of the occupation of my country by the French and Spanish is a matter of deep despair and anger for us. Our own selfish countrymen are to be blamed for not being united enough. We worry more about our tribes' interests than our country. The outsiders exploit our weaknesses, set us against each other, and finally treat us like dirt. It was obvious to me that the missing Hasso was framed while Hasso Ag Akotey, who had nothing to do with the matter, was caught.

I was hopeful that this man, Sherlock Holmes, would help. But I could not see how. I have not yet understood why he calls himself Father Bąkiewicz. But that is his business.

I returned at four p.m. after attending to my work. Father Bąkiewicz was waiting.

"I think I am on the verge of coming to a conclusion. But I needed two matters sorted out. I visited the library of this church and I know now what the unusual crucifix means. However, I cannot determine its meaning to this case until we do a background check. This is what I want you to find out from your sources."

He handed over a piece of paper on which he had scribbled a few words. I looked at it, glanced up at Father Bąkiewicz, and nodded. "I may be able to get this information."

"I also went to the market earlier and was able to find something of great interest," Father Bąkiewicz said. "The case may close rapidly if we meet the magistrate."

Two days later, we reached the office of the magistrate where we had been given an audience for about twenty minutes. In the meanwhile, I had been able to extract the information that

Father Bąkiewicz sought. He was very pleased with what I had discovered, and nodded.

"Though I would otherwise have preferred not to meet the magistrate and call attention upon myself, I have no choice. Justice must be done," he said.

We entered the magistrate's chambers at precisely nine a.m. I had asked the gendarme inspector friend I knew to accompany us. The respected magistrate was seated and he waved us down to the chairs across the table. He was busy writing.

"Good morning. Please sit. Let me finish writing these last couple of lines," he said curtly.

He was a handsome man, perhaps in his late fifties, but clearly fit and alert.

Father Bąkiewicz sat quietly in his chair.

The magistrate was finally done. He put down his pen and leaned back in his chair, surveying us with expressionless eyes.

"Yes, gentlemen, how may I help you? Father, a great honour to have you here. You are at the prefecture, are you not? I think I have seen you there on my rare Sunday visits. How is it that you are with this man? And you are Inspector Lachapelle, if my memory serves me right."

"I happened to meet him at a café and became acquainted. He has promised to show me some old manuscripts. I am just accompanying him at the moment."

"Ah, I see. And the inspector?"

"I am here because Said aṣ-Ṣabār requested me to come. He is Hasso Ag Akotey's lawyer and the accused is in the jail of my police station."

Favreu was satisfied.

Father Bąkiewicz spoke. "A fine poster, Monsieur Favreu," he said, gesturing to the far wall. "One of the principles I so admire about France."

Favreu looked puzzled and turned his head. "What do you refer to? Ah, you mean *Liberté, Égalité, Fraternité.* Yes. A constant reminder that we are all equal in the eyes of the law."

"Most commendable, and a principle most worthy of emulation by all. Where are you from, Monsieur Favreu?" Father Bąkiewicz asked with a gentle smile.

Favreu was surprised by the unexpected question. "What? Oh, from the south of France."

"Specifically where?"

"The village of Béziers in the Languedoc region."

"Lang—?"

"Languedoc. It is a small province. Not many people know of it."

"I am very interested in geography. Could you write down the name?"

"Certainly." Favreu scribbled the name on a sheet of paper and handed it over to Father Bąkiewicz, who examined it.

"Ah, LANG-uedoc! I see!" exclaimed Father Bąkiewicz. "The land of the Cathars!"

Favreu was suddenly on guard. He sat upright.

"It once was, true. Few know this." His eyes were wary.

"Well?" Favreu raised a quizzical eyebrow at me.

"We would like to discuss the case of my client Hasso Ag Akotey," I said. "We believe he is innocent."

"Yes, yes, they are all innocent! Poor Tuaregs, misunderstood heroes of the desert!" sneered the magistrate, a representative of the grand majesty of France. "Please come up with something original. The police appear to have made a clear case! Yes?" He looked at the Inspector, who nodded briefly in assent.

"If I may ask, what is the case?" asked Father Bąkiewicz mildly.

"A Tuareg dagger was used."

"Anyone could have used it," observed Father Bąkiewicz. "Was it seen being used?"

"A slip of paper was found with threatening words in Tifinagh."

"Incriminating, but not serious. It could have been placed there by persons unknown. Is it in the handwriting of the suspect?"

"The suspect fled the scene, stealing the horse of the victim. An innocent man does not flee!"

"Running away is not a crime. He may have panicked. Stealing is a crime, yes. But you are charging him with murder. Did anyone actually see him commit the murder?"

Alain Favreu stared long and hard at Father Bąkiewicz.

"Why are you so interested in this man?" he asked.

"As a matter of principle, I believe in the goodness of men. I have not heard anything incriminating yet. May I ask when you first met Pétain?"

"What? That was a few weeks ago, when he was brought before me for disorderly behaviour."

"Yet, that is odd. He, too, was from Béziers, was he not? I would have thought that everyone knew each other from such a small village."

The colour drained from Alain Favreu's face.

He brought himself back to his former self with some effort. "Gentlemen, I have an appointment now. Please excuse me."

Father Bąkiewicz did not stir, and spoke in a low and cold voice. "Pétain was a Cathar, an Albigensian, was he not? Yes, he was. And you belong to a secret Cistercian denomination that still hunts down the Cathars, six hundred years after their massacre. When will this hatred cease, I wonder."

"This—this is an—an outrage!" sputtered the magistrate, sitting back in his chair.

"Not really. This was not a perfect murder. It is a clumsy one committed by someone who believes his power will help him get away with anything. A magistrate retains a strong leaning toward the loathsome objective of his secret Cistercian society. He spots a Cathar from his village in France brought before him for the minor misdemeanour of drunkenness. He—or someone he assigns—kills him with a Tuareg dagger, leaves a slip of paper with Tifinagh writing in the victim's pocket—really, not very clever, but a classic red herring, nevertheless—and gets a passing Tuareg blamed, counting on the fact that the police would be glad to believe the story, given the current political situation here, and his own personal standing. But you did not notice the Cathar cross, which was mistaken for a crucifix by everyone, in his other pocket. It is actually the Cross of Toulouse, and very few people are likely to have known that. Were you saying to yourself, like your Cistercian abbot hero, Arnaud Amaury, "*Caedite eos. Novit enim Dominus qui sunt eius*!"[12]

"You cannot prove this! This is calumny!" Favreu's voice was hoarse.

"Indeed? It will be difficult for you to throw a respectable Catholic priest in Tangier in jail on a whim. I have more than enough evidence to have you arrested. It was rather careless of you to write that Tifinagh message on expensive Ibérico water-marked paper, a sample of which you just gave me and which is identical to the other paper. I checked with the purveyor of stationery goods in Tangier and he confirmed that this specific kind of paper was recently purchased by you. Overconfidence, my dear sir, overconfidence! I recommend you issue an order for the immediate release of Monsieur Hasso Ag Akotey. He is quite innocent. Was it you? Or did you ask one of the other French-men to act on your behalf? Will you arrest yourself on suspicion, perhaps, given the poster you proudly put on your wall?"

Father Bąkiewicz stood up. "I say this often, my dear sir: *Once you eliminate the impossible, whatever remains, no matter how improbable, must be the truth.* Good day."

He walked out of the office, leaving me and the inspector with the magistrate.

I looked at both of them. They did not look at me in the eye.

"I would like to have my client released," I said.

The strong and energetic magistrate had been reduced to a mere shell of a man in less than fifteen minutes by the words of a priest sitting across the table. I could never have imagined such a situation.

---

[12] *Kill them all. God will know his own!* – This most sobering perspective expressed in other ways through history by those who deem their religious affiliations to be absolute and final. The reader is requested to reflect on the matter and visit a library for additional details of this particular deplorable incident that marked the mass murder of the Cathars.

Inspector Lachapelle stood up silently. We both left the magistrate's office. Soon we reached the police station. And about half an hour later, Hasso Ag Akotey was a free man.

I told Hasso Ag Akotey what had happened, though he did not fully understand the nuances of the Catholic currents of southern France. But he understood that Father Bąkiewicz had saved his life and challenged a magistrate. As far as he was concerned, he was in eternal debt to the Father.[13] [14] [15]

◇◇◇

Once again, in the words of Hasso Ag Akotey, as related to me.

My life was saved by a brave man who had never met me and who was responsible for putting a French magistrate in jail. Had I not been witness to what happened, I would have dismissed such a story as being ridiculous. Someone told me that, many months later, the magistrate was actually arrested and sent away

---

[13] A note from Dr. John Watson: I discussed this extremely strange event with Holmes years later. He was, he said, quite exasperated and fascinated—at the same time—by how enmities come down through the centuries. "If the peculiar undying loyalty of the Guardians we came across to Ibn Batuta was remarkable, so was the zealous desire of this man of Cistercian roots to erase any sign of the Cathars—the *Perfecti*—almost 700 years after the grim events of the Languedoc, spurred by Pope Innocent III. I wonder how many more men the magistrate quietly eliminated as he discovered their religious views were incongruent to his. And we look down upon the 'savage and primitive' beliefs of those elsewhere in the world, eh Watson?"

[14] Said aṣ-Ṣabār died mysteriously shortly after his discussion with me. The French apparently kidnapped him and executed him, though they claimed that he had taken his own life. Inquiries with my friends at the Sûreté drew a blank; let us remember that those were troubled times in northwest Africa. It may seem that he has a cameo role in this story, but his fortuitous appearance made a profound difference to the chain of events; it gave true meaning to the word "serendipity." We deeply regret his demise.

[15] My American editor had not heard of the word mentioned in the previous footnote. I was not surprised.

to a French colony called Suriname where convicts live in the most deplorable conditions and finally die an agonizing death from fever, starvation, and exhaustion. A magistrate being sent to jail!

After my release, I went to the prefecture church to meet this Father. I was not allowed inside by the guard because I am a Tuareg. Such insults are nothing new, so I was not disheartened. Luckily Father Bąkiewicz came outside and allowed me to come in. He even served me tea. He is indeed a man of God, though somehow different. He does not talk about the value of virtue. He demonstrates it in quiet ways.

Rarely have I met a man of such intelligence and compassion. I made it my duty to be of service to him in any capacity. I invited him to visit us and he promised to do so.

The next day, Father Bąkiewicz did visit us and we had a grand celebration. We sang and danced in happiness. Several goats and even a camel were slaughtered in his honour, but I observed that he ate meat sparingly and was really more interested in our music. Though he had no knowledge of Tamasheq, he expressed a desire to learn. Many visitors say that out of respect, but few actually take the time to learn our language.

But Father Bąkiewicz was different. The very next day, he came to see me again and reiterated a desire to learn our language and our music.

I was willing to begin the process. But as we stood in a circle, laughing and talking, an old woman pushed her way in. We respectfully gave way. She peered at Father Bąkiewicz carefully and suddenly smiled. She insisted on becoming his teacher instead. And very soon, we saw the strange sight of a Catholic priest sitting on the sand practising words and phrases, taught directly from the old woman. He picked up simple words and sentences rapidly, and through some games and puzzles, learned our Tifinagh script. In a few weeks, he could speak easily without halting, though of course, he is unfamiliar with our customs and traditions and made many unintentional, amusing errors.

After several weeks, Father Bąkiewicz asked me for my help in travelling to Timbuktu very soon, saying that his life was in great danger and he was being pursued. He spoke to me about a strange gang of bandits, whose name I had never heard. He wished to pay me for my efforts, though I refused. He did pay for many things quietly, without telling me. He is a man of great honour.

"It will be very hot and you will suffer since you have never travelled before," I warned him.

"I must travel in the Tinariwen. Much is at stake," he said. "A dear friend is due any day now from Europe. I would like to leave very shortly after he arrives. I have quietly arranged for him to land at Tangier and then travel here."

We planned the journey carefully, and fixed a date. We chose those who would accompany us, the food and water we would take, weapons, and so on. A journey at peak summer through the Tinariwen is only for fools or for those with skill and stamina who prepare well.

As planned, he brought you one day, and we moved immediately. By this time, I had been made aware of the identity of the pursuers—the Guardians of the Letter, is what they arrogantly called themselves. But I knew of them in a different way, and I was aware they were nothing but bandits. We would have to be very careful.

I found you, Dr. Watson, a strange but gentle man. I was not sure if you would be able to handle the rigours of the Tinariwen, especially since you had just arrived from a much cooler place. But Father Bąkiewicz assured me that you could and, moreover, he said that you were very important for the mission. In addition, you were a *tanesmegal*—a doctor— and perhaps your presence would be helpful. When I look back, I am glad I agreed.

We set out for Timbuktu. Father Bąkiewicz was in a great hurry. As for us, we were to travel again across that which has made us, the Tinariwen. And how can I explain the joy of returning to the Ahaggar Mountains and once again feeling the presence of Tin Hanan, the beloved Mother of us all?

A conversation reported to Said aṣ-Ṣabār:

The mint tea was excellent at the roadside café. A group of Moroccans were scanning the newspapers and enjoying the pleasant morning sun.

"Said aṣ-Ṣabār must be admired. He is growing to be a leader, someone who will fight for the Berbers without fear."

"But we must be careful. The French are capable of anything. And they particularly do not like their people to be exposed or ridiculed."

"This case has helped all of us feel united, we must grant."

"Yes, that is quite true. The Father from the prefecture apparently played a very important role, though Said aṣ-Ṣabār has received the credit." He slammed his cup heavily on the saucer, drawing a glare from a passing waiter.

"Yes, that is what I heard. It appears his thinking was simple but sharp and he unearthed something that Said aṣ-Ṣabār would not have known by himself about some point of history regarding the Roman Catholics in France."

"Is that so? But why would he be willing to get involved? After all, most of the French are Catholics. It is really difficult to be heard in this noise, my friends!"

"Yes. Well, for one, he is not French, I hear."

"Is that so?" The group looked at the speaker with new interest.

"Yes, though I do not know where he is from. By the way, isn't it time for this menu to be changed? Why do we come here?"

"Waiter, some more tea! Why the delay?"

"Sometimes I feel the service here is deteriorating," the speaker grumbled, lowering his voice.

"Ah! I know who you mean! I have seen this man walking about town. He speaks Arabic well and minds his own business. He does not try to talk about religion."

"A smart man, if so. It would be arrogance to try to convert us. Especially since ours is the true religion anyway."

Everyone nodded. Elsewhere, some crockery crashed and an acrimonious argument began.

"I wonder if he is a priest at all. Something does not seem to be right."

"Could he be a spy? Waiter! Here please!"

"Anything is possible. How could a priest from another country help in freeing a Tuareg and getting a Frenchman suspended from his job? Why would he?"

"I have heard that he never conducts services in his own church."

"Very strange. Could it be that he is not really a Father?"

"But if he is a spy, whom is he spying for and why?"

"Strange are the ways of these foreigners. Ah, more tea, finally! Excellent!"

Two tables away, a man listened carefully. He sat motionless for several minutes. Then he got up, paid at the counter and left. His plans had abruptly changed.

He was now to travel to Casablanca immediately.

◇◇◇

"The news that you have brought us is interesting. Our friend in Paris should know."

"The Moroccan lawyer was assisted by a Catholic priest? We can easily get the lawyer to talk."

"I do not recommend that. He is influential even in these troubled times. Let us move carefully and not react spontaneously. Let us check to see who this man is."

◇◇◇

The following came to our attention much later through sources:

"Interesting. We made some enquiries at the church, and also elsewhere in Tangier. He arrived several months ago. He does not conduct any Christian ceremony. He is some kind of accountant at the prefecture. He visits that old man, Haji Ahmad Bouabid, near the tomb of Ibn Batuta and learns Arabic! The Haji has no other information about this man except that he is a sincere student. However, in the initial days, he did express some interest in Ibn Batuta, but perhaps not more than any tourist."

"Our advisor in Paris is certain this is the man. Our contact, Colonel Sebastian Moran, confirmed it when he called today."

"Why are we waiting then? Months have been wasted searching for the man in Europe and he has been right here!"

"He has been busy meeting Tuaregs too, recently, I hear. There too, he has tried to learn how to speak Tamasheq."

"Why has he not left for Timbuktu yet, then?"

"Perhaps he was preparing, who can say?"

"Yes, that may explain his desire to learn Arabic and Tamasheq."

"Our advisor in Paris has also sent us the English copy of a half-manuscript which was stolen from a London museum. Let us prepare to travel. Inform the Master from India that we may leave for Timbuktu shortly. Write to Paris if we should do that."

The return wire a week later was to the point.

DO NOT WASTE ANY MORE TIME. GO.

The new caravan started from Tangier a week after we had left.

"Master, we shall look after you, do not worry," bowed one of the Guardians.

"I have never experienced such heat. It must be even worse along the way!" Thalassery Vatoot Mohammad Koya was concerned.

Months had passed. He had been treated like a king. Money had been sent to his wife and sister but they must have wondered what had happened to him. He was homesick. He missed the sands and coconut trees of the Malabar. People were communicating with others in Paris and London. They were coming and going. It was easy to see that everyone was frustrated.

Now, it suddenly looked like things would move. Excitement swept the band as arrangements to travel from Casablanca to Timbuktu were made at a feverish pace. And very shortly, a caravan of twenty motivated Guardians, accompanied by some

Tuareg guides, was observed to be getting ready to set off for Fez, Sijilmasa, Taghaza, and Timbuktu.

Hasso Ag Akotey had arranged for a much smaller messenger caravan to travel behind us to warn of any new development. This caravan left Tangier barely a day or two ahead of the Guardians.

I travelled alone on that ancient path, onward to Taghaza
Caressed endlessly by the restless sands
That held the memories of a thousand caravans
I sang the tunes I had heard from my grandmother
She watched from the night sky
The ghosts of the Tinariwen hummed with me
I was no longer alone

The Sahara

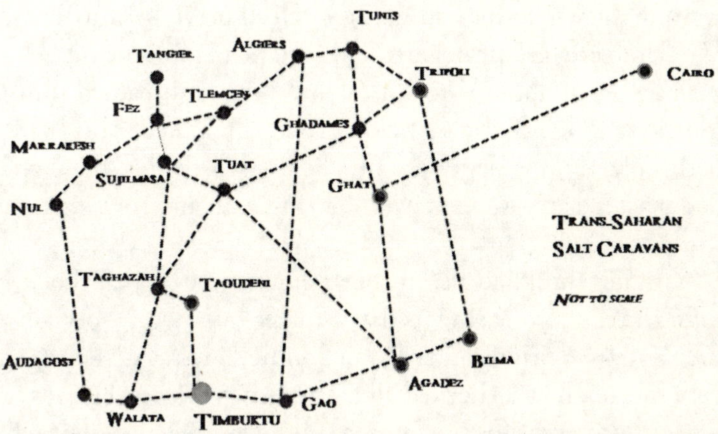

Holmes had done his planning brilliantly, as might be expected.

He sent me ahead with Mehdi to the city of Fez, and joined me a day later after bidding a quick good-bye to Bishop Landel in Tangier, with the story that he proposed to see the city of Fez and then Casablanca and then return. Bishop Landel did not show his surprise; he was used to managing his own affairs perhaps, and had not found the presence of Holmes very necessary. The recent visit of the Guardians inquiring about Father Bąkiewicz had also unnerved him. The sooner Holmes left, as far as he was concerned, the better.

He said that the plan seemed agreeable. "I have not seen either city, Father Bąkiewicz, even though I have been here for a few years. You certainly have quite the spirit of adventure in you!" he remarked. "That must be the secret to your youthfulness!"

Holmes met me in Fez, and Mehdi returned to Casablanca. He took with him a message from Holmes to be passed on to Lestrade. He also promised to keep watch on the movements of the Guardians and ensure that word was sent ahead in case events escalated.

We travelled over the rugged Atlas Mountains on mules for a couple of days with another group of travellers and finally reached the ancient town of Sijilmasa in the oasis of Tafilalt late in the evening. Hasso Ag Akotey, our Tuareg friend, was patiently waiting there with his comrades as agreed previously in Tangier. We slept early as our departure was to be before sunrise.

We rose at about three in the morning and readied for our journey and left Sijilmasa before dawn as planned. The Tuaregs had probably not slept very much; I observed that the camels had been fed and watered overnight, and all our provisions were loaded.

Holmes and I had already been shown how to wear the *tagelmust* and the accoutrements that a Tuareg must wear especially in preparation for a long and arduous journey. Hasso Ag Akotey was very thorough and checked all matters many times. He was not just our protector for the purpose of the journey; he knew what it would take to travel across the Sahara. The slightest carelessness would kill not just us but endanger the lives of everyone. Travelling between known oases was a timed activity, contrary to the apparent lassitude observed. Calculations needed to be made about the weight the camels could carry, which included food, water, live goats strapped to the side of the camel, and so on. A delay caused by carelessness or overconfidence meant death, especially of camels, who were sometimes valued more than men.

The *tagelmust* was no longer a matter of a disguise; it was a very practical garment, needed to counter the endless sand that swirled about us. The chief, Hasso Ag Akotey, also applied some kind of oil to our faces to protect us from the sun and to make us look like authentic Tuaregs. We were warned that banditry was still common and staying together at all times was our only guarantee of personal safety. "This is not the time to discover how brave and tough we are as individuals. We shall survive only if we are together. We fully expect to battle a few bandits and perhaps lose a few of our group. Our weapons are sharp and tested. Since we are a large caravan, we may not face a problem. But who can say? We must always be very careful," said he.

I was apprehensive about travelling on a camel but we had no real choice. I was shown my beast and was assured its temperament was even and he would follow the rest quietly. Holmes' strong personality allowed him to control his larger camel easily. We were told that his camel had travelled on the trade routes many times and could possibly cross the Sahara without human intervention. Mine was travelling for only the second time.

Our caravan was of a modest size and completely Tuareg in composition, except for the two of us. There were perhaps about thirty five camels and some thirty men. Many Tuaregs preferred walking for short distances when they could, I learned, to avoid sleep and a consequent drop in alertness, and so some camels carried only goods to trade.

We slipped away gently into the desert in one long line. Holmes and I were somewhere in the middle with Hasso behind me. The caravan was silent. An onlooker could be forgiven for calling the sight ghostly. We proceeded to the east and soon observed the first rays of the rising sun. The silhouettes of the veiled and turbaned Tuaregs in front of me, moving to the rhythm of their camel's walk was quite charming and picturesque. The silence was punctuated by the sounds of the noisy exhalation of the camels and the swish of their hooves through the sand. The effect was hypnotic.

The Tuaregs began to sing a song softly using the implicit cadence of the caravan. The melody was quite lovely and blended perfectly with the rolling sand dunes. I was familiar with the concept of men singing together while performing certain tasks, having witnessed sea shanties with Holmes at the London Dockyards. This was done to bond together as a group and to relieve tedium.

But there was a difference here, and an elegance that was captivating. The tune began at the head of the caravan and rolled back toward the end. The man at the head would sing a line and the next person picked it up and so on. Because of the veil we all wore over most of our face and mouth, the words were muffled and indistinct. The collective effect was wonderful. In spite of myself, and not knowing the language, I soon found it pleasurable to join the singing. It made the journey bearable, given that I had never before ridden a camel. The tune was probably more than a thousand years old, and was important to keep the nomads focused especially on long walks through the blazing sun. The Tuaregs were not able to translate the tune to my satisfaction and understanding, but I decided to express it as my imagination interpreted. It had to do with the grave of their legendary Queen Tin Hanan in Abalessa, deep in the Sahara desert. She was, I understood, the originator of the Tuareg culture.

Where do you journey?
Abalessa, Abalessa, Abalessa...
I must go to Abalessa
Blessed camel, take me there
Whom do you seek in
Abalessa, Abalessa, Abalessa?
She who is our blessed mother,
blessed mother of us all
What is her name, this
blessed mother, blessed mother, blessed mother?
What is her name, this blessed mother?
She is called Queen Tin Hanan
How will you know that you have found her
when you come to Abalessa...
How will you know that you have found
the Queen you are seeking, Tin Hanan?
We shall find her with our music

With our music, with our music...
She will hear our blessed music,
And her voice will lead us home
What will you do once you have found her,
When you come to Abalessa?
Shed our tears of joy and sadness
for our mother, at her grave

The caravan turned south at some point and we came to a small oasis where we stopped. At this point Hasso helped us dismount and we ate our first meal of the day. We sat together as a group and they conversed in their language about the path ahead, how the sands were likely to be, which camel would need extra attention and so on. We had a heavy meal of millets, sour curds, and some mutton.

"What is our next destination?" asked Holmes.

"The salt mines and oasis of Taghaza. It will take us about twenty-five days if we move quickly and conditions are favourable. Remember that we are in peak summer. Even we think many times before travelling this time of year." Hasso was quite matter of fact.

We were soon on our way.

The sun was high above in the clear blue sky. Suddenly the heat became oppressive. The winds had picked up a little and biting hot sand blew across our path. The camels carried on unperturbed, but the men had stopped singing, conserving their energies. I followed the lead of others and adjusted my *tagelmust* very carefully. No part of my skin was to be exposed, except my eyes. And yet, because of my inexperience, sand entered my garments. Soon I was in acute discomfort, scratching and moving about on my saddle. I thought of asking that we stop, but held back, fearing that I would cause delays. I was able to manage well soon, but I was already feeling quite exhausted. After a few hours, the caravan stopped and we dismounted. We were not at an oasis, but at some place with a few rough buildings. It appeared that travelling at this time of the year and at this time of the day was dangerous. We were to stop till the heat from the late afternoon sun was bearable and then restart. The Tuaregs understood these nuances of desert travel exceedingly well.

I came down from my saddle, in some distress because of the novelty of the experience.

Holmes looked every inch a Tuareg. His sharp features and commanding presence had already marked him as a natural leader and everyone crowded around him for no particular reason. His ability to tie the veil perfectly also helped.

"Not a pleasant experience, Watson," he observed. "We have passed a few hours but I understand we are already delayed because of the unexpected desert wind that we encountered. I do not know if the Guardians are behind us. I rule nothing out. It is unfair to expose our Tuareg friends to dangers, but they are our only guarantee of safety."

"How will we know if the Guardians are behind us, Holmes?"

"I think the idea is to have Mehdi send another small caravan slightly ahead of the Guardians once it becomes clear that they are chasing us. The situation is grave and unpredictable. Travelling across the Sahara in peak summer is a foolhardy adventure for men like you and me. If we are in such a terrible condition after just a few hours, I cannot imagine our fate for the next twenty five days! And then again from Taghaza to Timbuktu for about the same number of days! Tut! We must find strength in our heads first! I shall count on you to keep me mentally engaged, my good fellow!"

I drank some water while the animals were also given some, though not too much. We began again at about four o'clock.

The dunes along the way became more pronounced. The wind had dropped but sand still shifted gently everywhere. For a long stretch, I saw not a single date palm, not even some miserable acacia shrubs that the camels are so fond of. And on that stretch, along the way, we saw the skeletons of two camels. Someone ahead of us pointed to the east and when we looked carefully, after shielding our eyes, we could see the bleached skeleton of a man at the edge of a sand dune. How he must have suffered in the heat, with thirst, sand, and flies, poor man!

"By the looks of it, a recent fatality, Watson," said Holmes, turning back toward me. "What might have been his story? A confused search for water is what I would guess. A deeply regrettable matter.

"That reminds me, Watson, you were to entertain me by talking of our adventures in an altogether more convivial past."

And so I recounted, for Holmes' amusement, many of the adventures we had been on together. We had a good laugh over the absurdity of the Brittany cottage mystery. We were annoyed again by how we had been tricked by the Czar's cousin in Munich. We regretted the boat tragedy in Copenhagen, an entirely avoidable eventuality; if only the Duke of Manchester had bothered to read Holmes' letter a day earlier! We talked about the shocking cases of the Speckled Band and the Red Headed League. And the Scandal in Bohemia, of course!

"The machinations of man, Watson, are beyond the realm of imagination." Holmes' muffled voice was heard from behind his indigo *tagelmust.* "Even now, we are working hard to thwart diabolical plans. We are completely cut off from civilization, moving slowly through the endless Sahara desert, with no guarantee that we will reach our destination and get our hands on the manuscript. We have only each other, Watson, to remind us of a different life, when we smoked quietly in the evenings at Baker Street."

"What of Professor Moriarty, Holmes?" I asked.

"I have no doubt he has guessed that we have taken a caravan across the Sahara to Timbuktu. We are safe only because of remoteness. Danger actually escalates as we near Timbuktu. Will someone be lying in wait for us? I understand that the region is extremely volatile in any case."

He raised an eyebrow. "By the way, Watson, what of the readers of your tales?"

"You are sorely missed, Holmes. The atmosphere was positively funereal across the country after the Reichenbach episode."

Holmes laughed scornfully. "Bah! A hysterical group of barely literate lemmings, Watson! Easily excited by tales of bloodshed and the application of common sense. The insanity of modern civilization, Watson—people thirsting for violence and horror but only on the pages of a book or newspaper! They think, I am sure, that you and I are perpetually engulfed in a miasma of crime and punishment. This is entirely your fault, Watson, for allowing your sensibilities to be compromised by the need to pander to a immature mob. I would be quite happy with just my violin. Now I am sure you plan to write about this very episode, am I right?"

"Of course, Holmes! Why ever not? Surely this remarkable tale must be known to the civilized world! But you do me a grave injustice by claiming that my work is read by common men with limited intelligence! These men and women positively adore you and wish you well, Holmes!"

"I disagree, Watson. However, I am now obliged to make this story as exciting as possible so that every page of your forthcoming book reeks of gore, illegality, blackmail, murder, and diplomatic intrigue. Most vexing indeed, most vexing! A profoundly juvenile citizenry! These are the times when the private preferences of my brother Mycroft seem so attractive. Imagine the pleasures of sitting quietly at the Diogenes Club, not having to worry about public opinion! Well, I have made my bed and have to lie in it. Meanwhile, I can watch your amusing literary efforts, filled with astonishing exaggerations!"

By and by, the soporific effect of the movement of the camel combined with the intense heat, the swirling sands and the monotonous landscape caused us to cease talking. We were barely awake, but the ingenious saddles kept us secure.

The baking heat was beyond belief. It hit us relentlessly from all sides. For someone like me, who had seen action in Afghanistan and still had a Jezail bullet throbbing within, pain and suffering were no strangers. Yet the tropical heat I experienced in the land of the Balochs and in Sind was nothing compared to the unrelenting waves of hot air, the pinpricks of heated sand,

and the uncomfortable jerking sway of my camel taking its toll on my back.

I have only a bare recollection of how the day ended. I was barely conscious. Somehow, the sun set slowly in the west, and the head of the caravan finally stopped at a tiny oasis. Holmes and Hasso came up to my camel and made it sit down so that they could help me. My distress was acute and obvious.

The Tuaregs collected dry fronds of date palms and added some charcoal. Soon a roaring fire took form in the middle of the oasis. Some in the group began cooking. Others went from camel to camel, brushing and cleaning them first and then feeding and watering them. They examined the hooves of all of them, searching for sores or anything else that might cause them discomfort. They did all this before they themselves ate.

Many Tuaregs came to see me and offered suggestions on how I could massage my legs to bring back some comfort. I felt better after walking about the oasis for a while. I washed my face in the brackish water at a spring there and felt a new man.

The sun had set and, as if by magic, the heat vanished, to be replaced by a steadily increasing cold. The Tuaregs passed around their *taguella* bread with a heavy sauce, millet porridge, and goat cheese. Then a few of them took out *tambours,* their traditional instruments, and began singing. The entire group sang and clapped their hands. I must confess that I thoroughly enjoyed their energetic music though I did not understand a word.[16] The atmosphere was most cordial and cheerful.

Hasso Ag Akotey asked Holmes if he would play the violin for them. I had quite forgotten that he was carrying it with him. It occurred to me that the sensitive violin must have endured heat it was not accustomed to. But on the contrary, when Holmes applied bow to string, the sounds that emerged were of the highest timbre. Holmes, with his keen ear, had already picked up a

---

[16] I must add that Holmes expressed a desire to write a monograph about the music of the Tuaregs. His habit of writing definitive monographs on every possible subject for the consumption of unknown scholars in tightly knit circles invariably irritated.

few Tuareg melodies, and he played a vigorous fiddle while our friends accompanied him with clapping and their own instruments. Holmes had again demonstrated his ability to assimilate into any group with ease. Admiration for him in the group increased even more. I was proud of him.

Who could have imagined that Sherlock Holmes, still considered dearly departed, and I, Dr. John Watson, would be part of a tribal entertainment event in the middle of the Sahara desert, miles from civilization, enjoying music under a wonderful clear sky with thousands of stars, and camels, peacefully chewing the cud, looking on?

The cold of the desert had increased quickly. The same *tagelmust* and other garments that were necessary to keep away heat and sand during the day were equally effective in keeping us warm at night. We slept in the open under the night sky, with thick blankets. I was exhausted. I had no idea when I slept.

At this point, I must pause to remind the reader of something important. I am a chronicler of the activities of my esteemed friend, Sherlock Holmes.

When the Strand took it upon themselves to start publishing my reminiscences, they very successfully created a set of loyal readers who developed a piercing respect for Holmes. But alas, due to the whims of the editors, my original work was often tampered with. Many details and recollections were struck out because of the belief that readers only sought vivid descriptions of crimes and how Holmes foiled the designs of unpleasant men. As a result of such conditioning, readers forgot that Holmes himself was quite contemptuous of the modern citizen's vicarious delight in bloodshed and mayhem. He was the finest gentleman, preferring to untangle rather than brutally excise. If not for his skill in communicating with many wayward young men in a certain strata, London would today have been a wilderness with a reputation for excessive crime. To expect Holmes and myself to be forever immersed in the fog of crime and provide the morbid citizenry with an endless stream of stories celebrating blood and depravity is unfair. Attention must be drawn to his scholarship, his love for music, and his unfortunate interest in cocaine. Perhaps it is a fruitless hope.

Nevertheless, I have spent time including the details of a memorable trip through the Sahara. I decline, as a matter of principle, to simply blank out the journey and string together an absurd collection of events specific to crime. Should you find this position to be not of your liking, I may suggest the following options:

1. *Destroy the book in a suitable manner,*
2. *Return the book to your bookseller and request a refund, or*
3. *Write to the editor of Poisoned Pen Press expressing your anguish about the deplorable lowering in standards that you have been forced to endure in the course of your perusal of the book.*

If you are, as I am certain, an individual of high intelligence, I seek your indulgence, and request you to continue your voyage within the confines of these pages.

I now return to my main narrative.

When I awoke, I noticed the quiet bustle about me. The Tuaregs had been readying for the journey and had most courteously allowed me to sleep a little more, out of consideration for my condition.

Hasso suggested that I keep a packet of kola nuts with me for the journey. They were, he said, useful to ward off sleep and to concentrate. I kept some in one of the folds of my dress. I had already started developing a facility for putting on the *tagelmust* in an efficient way, and soon, our caravan was on its way in the darkness.

Holmes and I discussed the situation of which our friends were not entirely aware.

"The Tuaregs are in conflict with the French, Watson. The possibility of a confrontation can never be ruled out. If two Englishmen are found in a Tuareg group, everyone will be in trouble. We must extricate ourselves from their company after we finish our task at the Sankore Mosque. While I have told them I propose to return with them, it would be wiser to find some other means. After studying the map, a new plan has occurred to me. I shall discuss it with you at some point."

"Is the manuscript safe, Holmes?"

"Oh yes, Watson." Holmes smiled sardonically.

I did not inquire further.

And so the days passed, with the caravan covering set distances according to a plan. The heat was oppressive but after a couple of days, I was able to adjust. I became quite addicted to the kola nuts, which Holmes too found useful, given that he had no recourse to his other, far more lethal cocaine addiction.

I lost count of the days. At one of the oases, when I sought to ask Hasso how much further we had to travel to get to Taghaza, he merely replied "soon." Then he smiled and observed, "It is not Tangier."

Along the way, a couple of the Tuaregs suffered from heat-related maladies including bad stomachs. I had followed Holmes' suggestion and was well equipped with medicines. The Tuaregs had their own traditional medicine, of course, but were curious about what I had to offer. As it happened, Epsom salts and Bicarbonate of soda worked very well and the ill travellers were very grateful for my attentions.

The quality of water at a particular oasis was a matter of some concern, and we were advised to avoid drinking it. Further along from that oasis, we saw evidence of the effect of a lack of water and the most searing heat. A caravan of four camels had come to an unfortunate end recently. The bleached bones of the camels and the skeletons of the two unfortunate travellers caused me great distress. Such scenes were apparently quite common along the path.

"This happens when you become *trop confiant*—overconfident," said one of the Tuaregs, who knew a little French. "You cannot master the desert. A grain of sand is more powerful than your strongest camel."

"How do you suppose they died?" I asked him.

"By overloading the camels or not taking enough water. Or not planning the journey. Who can say?" he shrugged, adjusting his *tagelmust*.

Twenty-five days passed in a haze of intense heat, biting cold, music, sandstorms and disorientation. Occasionally, I lost all sensitivity to the passage of time. It was just a never ending sway, the grunts of camels, the occasional cry from one of the caravan drivers. Stopping, eating, restarting: one day merged into another. I found it difficult to believe that we were on one of the most important trade paths in the history of human endeavour, where tons of goods had travelled north to south, and south to north.

We finally reached Taghaza.

We dismounted at one of the traditional points and looked around. It seemed a most uninspiring town, with just a handful of buildings and a few palm trees.

"We shall stay here for about three days," announced Hasso Ag Akotey, after conferring with his men. "The conditions have been very harsh and the animals need rest. As do the men."

"How far is Timbuktu from here?" inquired Holmes.

"Perhaps a few days less than the journey thus far. Who can say?" He was in no hurry. He had travelled on this route more than one hundred times, he said, but each journey was different. The desert dictates our speed, he said, and no emergency would make him travel faster than what the desert permitted. The price to pay for violating the rules was unacceptable.

At Taghaza, we met many more Tuaregs. Some were travelling north, back to Sijilmasa. Others were like us, halting for a few days before continuing to Timbuktu. We observed that there were certain differences in the way they tied their *tagelmusts*. This had to do with their tribal affiliations, we were informed.

At this crossroads, it was possible to go in the direction of Iwatlan in Mauritania or to Timbuktu, which was our destination. Ghana's reputation for gold was known, but our objective was something presumably of greater value, a mysterious half-manuscript hidden somewhere in the ancient Sankore Mosque.

Taghaza was a disappointment, even if it was an important transit point. Commerce was still driven by salt mines, though much less so, and we saw a few camels carrying large slabs of salt from the salt mines and from a larger mine at a place called Taoudenni. Since it was peak summer, activity was not as intense. Sadly, we saw many slaves as well. Slavery was common and accepted, by both master and the slave, and no one thought much about it. Our British values would not have found application and resonance here and we wisely kept our counsel. The slaves worked the mines under deplorable conditions and invariably died young, we gathered. I saw two of them pass by. They happened to glance at me and we looked at each other for several moments. Perhaps he saw freedom in my eyes. And I saw a man who was more or less dead, simply lurching from day to day in absolute dull hopelessness, with death being the only relief he could look forward to. I do not think he craved freedom, which to him was an unimaginable prospect. I averted my eyes.

The buildings were constructed with large slabs of salt and some were covered with the skins of camels, goats, and gazelles. The whole experience was unsettling. A town full of travellers. Salt mines. Slaves. Brackish water. And, to add to our misery, endless swarms of flies! Nothing had perhaps changed since Ibn Batuta had travelled here and made a note of all this in the *Rihla*.

The Tuaregs replenished their supplies, rested their camels and freshened them. We noticed that there was now a greater variety in dates and fruits available. Already, the faint suggestions of the lush tropics were visible, brought to Taghaza by caravans from the south.

One evening, Holmes shared with me his daring plan. I was stupefied.

◇◇◇

We continued from Taghaza. The journey to Timbuktu was expected to take about three weeks and the conditions were slightly better, we were informed by travellers from the south.

This was true to a certain extent. The effect of the Niger River, still very far away, was gradually seen, and the sands merged into a darker, brown soil. The flora changed too, with the occasional acacia and mimosa tree. The availability of water remained unpredictable except where we saw baobab trees, which were always a sign of fresh water.

On a particular day, as we set out, Hasso asked us to be extremely careful and keep awake. "Eat more kola nuts today," he said. "There are Djinn here and they find persons in caravans who are sleepy and take over their thoughts. Such men lose their minds. They see things in the desert that do not exist and no one can convince them otherwise. This is the most dangerous part of our journey. It is not the heat that worries me. It is the Djinn."

We noticed that the dunes were particularly restive that day and the winds brief, intense and, on the whole, quite unpredictable. The camels were agitated and had to be controlled with greater effort than earlier. This continued for a good forty miles. Once, a few of us were sure we heard music beyond some dunes, but Hasso warned us not to investigate. "These are the tricks of the Djinn. Do not be swayed," he said grimly.

There were no visible caravan routes as the sand shifted constantly. The leader was very experienced and quite knowledgeable about this section, but had planned his journey using the North Star as a reference, a practice common across numerous cultures.

"Watson, the man ahead of me says that many Djinn here are the ghosts of water-bearers, who died, having gone mad with the heat, waiting for caravans," Holmes remarked, turning in his saddle to address me at the rear.

"A most regrettable matter, Holmes. I am not one to believe in ghosts but heat and disorientation can certainly stimulate a fertile mind."

"Yes, quite so, Watson. And the shifting sand dunes remind me of our good friend in Paris, Professor Moriarty. Here one moment, there the next, leaving no trace behind. The only way to tackle him is to be like our friend Hasso—rejecting distractions and being clear about the destination. I find the analogy most helpful."

At a place where the dunes suddenly disappeared, replaced by a completely flat stretch, we saw what appeared to be a huge caravan in the far distance, heading slowly to the east. It glittered brightly.

"That must be a caravan of gold," shouted a Tuareg excitedly, pointing.

"Fool! It does not exist," said Hasso sharply. "It does not exist! It is an illusion. It is the work of Djinn!"

The caravan abruptly vanished, and we then saw a beautiful lake and palm trees to the south west.

"That too does not exist, do not be tempted," Hasso urged us on. "If you travel there, you will die. Look at those skeletons at the top of that dune. Those are not illusions."

We passed the forty miles with great difficulty.

Each day was as punishing as the one before. The sun did not relent. One or two of the camels developed problems in their hooves, which slowed the caravan. Their loads were redistributed and that took a little time.

Along the way, at a small, lush oasis with several massive and curious baobab trees where we rested, we had an unfortunate encounter with a snake, which resulted in the death of a young Tuareg. The boy was a cheerful lad who had a talent for singing. He made the mistake on sitting on a rotting log of wood without checking to see if it was hollow. A viper emerged, bit the young man, and went on its way. He did not realize he had been bitten till it was too late. Neither I nor one of the Tuaregs who knew about snake bites could save him. We were grief-stricken.

He was buried near the oasis amidst great sorrow. The caravan continued, considerably subdued. And yet their philosophical perspective of life and death in the harsh Sahara helped the Tuaregs deal with the tragedy with greater equanimity than what I might have thought possible. They sang a slow and beautiful dirge as they left the oasis.

That was the only unfortunate incident we experienced. We had no knowledge of the passage of time, even though we adjusted our movements to travel early, stop for some four hours at about eleven o'clock when the sun was at its merciless high and then travel again till about nine o'clock. Any other plan would have been foolhardy to the utmost.

And then one day, sometime in the later evening, Hasso announced that we would be reaching the famous city of Timbuktu in about an hour. Everyone in the caravan cheered.

At the outskirts of the town, we came to a halt at a resting place for travellers, called *Abaradiou.* The tall and muscular Negro attendants there took charge of our camels and goods in a familiar way while we celebrated our arrival at Timbuktu after the most arduous journey that either Holmes or I had ever experienced. It had taken us fifty-five days during the hottest period of the year across unimaginably cruel and inhospitable terrain. After resting in the straw huts of the *Abaradiou*, the Tuaregs proposed to set up a camp.

"You look authentically Tuareg, Holmes," I remarked jocularly.

"That must change soon," he responded curtly, his mind already on the pressing matter ahead of us.

His Arabic and Tamasheq had already improved substantially over the course of the several weeks. His innate confidence allowed him to experiment with languages without worrying about making mistakes.

The mud brick architecture of Timbuktu was quite fascinating. Without modern bricks and stone, builders had constructed edifices with mud and wood that had, I understood, lasted for centuries. This was one of the most important towns of Africa, the confluence of trade passages across the continent and from the Atlantic, Mediterranean, and Red seas. I learned later that there was another town called Djenne to the south west with similarly rich history and architecture.

For now, we were happy to have reached our destination. I, Dr. John Watson, who had once seen action in Afghanistan and hoped to spend a quiet retirement reading books, had managed to cross the Sahara and reach a city I had never dreamed I would ever see in my lifetime!

But my intense friend had no time for architecture and history. His was a single-minded pursuit and everything, if not relevant, was dismissed. For once, I wished he would consider writing a monograph about the town.[17]

Holmes made a few inquiries about the location of the Sankore Mosque, which was fortuitously very close by. He also asked about the political climate in the city, and he received ambiguous replies. The French were indeed everywhere, including near the Sankore Mosque. There was a general air of tension for no specific reason. The country's political situation was unstable after the final collapse of the Toucouleur Empire. The Tuaregs were generally perceived as restive and difficult, and not in the good books of the French.

Firm decisions had to be made.

After a satisfying dinner, Holmes spent time looking over various documents. Prominent was a map of Africa that he had procured from the Venice Museum.

It had once been the property of the late Antonio Rozzi.

---

[17] Many years later, Holmes did indeed write a monograph, "The properties of the mud bricks employed in the construction of buildings in the historical city of Timbuktu," in which he dwelt at length on the characteristics, composition, and methods used to make the bricks. He presented the monograph at the Royal Society, and was much feted. Elsewhere, brickbats might have been employed.

Who is the father of Timbuktu? The Tuaregs.
Who is the mother of Timbuktu? The city of Djenne.

Timbuktu—The Sankore Mosque

Salt comes from the north, gold from the south,
and silver from the country of the white men,
but the word of God and the treasures of wisdom
are only to be found in Timbuktu.

The loyal reader who has followed the exploits of Sherlock Holmes over the years would not fault my assertion that he was a man of action.

Unlike his brother Mycroft, who roamed the world while sitting in a couch at the Diogenes Club, Holmes was in favour of decisive and firm movement. There was no question of idling. Everything he did, including playing the violin, starving himself, and even injecting himself with cocaine, was driven by a specific objective. For instance, he believed firmly that drug helped him to think clearly, a matter where I strongly disagreed.

During the months Holmes had been alone in Tangier, masquerading as Father Andrzej Bąkiewicz, he had achieved many objectives. I shall list them.

He had learned about the existence of the secret society, the Guardians of the Letter. In spite of their grand name, the Guardians had actually degenerated into a group of criminals with international connections. This was not surprising, as such fanatical groups invariably lost their moorings over a period of time and found recourse in crime to keep alive a mystique about them, and to thrive.

Sherlock Holmes had become very familiar with the *Rihla* and become a great favourite of Haji Bouabid. During this time, he made sure he did not pass any remark that could be misconstrued, and avoided asking questions about Timbuktu or the son in the Maldives. He could now speak and read Arabic quite well.

He read about the Sankore Mosque and its enchanting history. He looked at the various journeys that Ibn Batuta had taken and looked at many convincing permutations for the possibilities he had in mind.

He had become fast friends with the elders of the Ahaggar Tuaregs who happened to be in the Tangier area. After his services to their clan in the matter of saving Hasso Ag Akotey, the Ahaggar Tuaregs had sworn their undying and eternal loyalty to him. He continued to delight them by seeking to learn their language in an earnest and methodical way and by going deep into their history and culture, with specific references to their revered Queen Tin Hanan and their wonderful music.

He kept in sporadic touch with Father Ciasca at the Vatican. He was informed that there were no further attempts to burgle the Venice Museum. Perhaps the Arabs had concluded that the parchment was no longer there. But there were a spate of attempted burglaries at other museums—the Louvre in Paris, the Madrid Prado, another in Brussels, and elsewhere. There seemed to be a grim desperation. Lestrade too confirmed, via a coded telegram, that historical archives were being targeted. Security had been tightened and a few attempts had been thwarted. The hand of Professor Moriarty was also suspected, but as usual, there was never any direct evidence. A Professor of Mathematics from Lyons at the Louvre. A soldier just back from Nairobi visiting his sister in Munich. An army physician newly returned from Poona on vacation in Antwerp. Why had they shown a remarkable interest in the archives and exhibits? Holmes knew immediately, but kept his counsel. He had listed at least eighty-six ways in which Professor Moriarty would make attempts to ease his agents into the museums.

Lestrade also warned him that despite the warmth between Scotland Yard and the Sûreté, diplomatic tensions were on the rise. The French wanted to consolidate their position in North and West Africa. The Foreign Office had suddenly woken up, and confabulations were on at the highest levels. There was awareness of Sherlock Holmes' presence somewhere in Africa and there was some hope that he could be a source of information. This displeased Holmes, as he was not interested in undertaking such skulduggery as a formal agent of any government.

But Holmes was surprised when Lestrade hinted that he was possibly being watched. By whom, he wondered, and proceeded to take immediate action. It did not take long to suspect that the man-servant at his apartment, responsible for his maintenance, was also passing on information to Bishop Landel.

To test his hypothesis, Holmes made very casual remarks while Abu was in the room. The remark often came back in discussions with Bishop Landel. And he set up a few mechanisms to be triggered quietly if his personal effects were being searched. A broken thread, a carelessly placed sock, a few coins on the floor in his bedroom—each was a means to determine mischief.

"I am going for a walk to the sea front, Abu," he said one day. "It is a nice evening. I may just decide to eat outside. Do not prepare dinner unless I return."

"Yes, Father," said the attendant obsequiously.

Holmes slipped out of the gates and walked to the end of the road where the church's compound ended and turned left into the street, ensuring that whoever was watching him was convinced that he was gone.

Then he let himself in through a small breach in the far wall. He prowled through the lawn under the shade of the trees and let himself into the church again through a side door. It was a Thursday evening and only Bishop Landel and Abu were inside the prefecture.

Holmes stood behind the drapes in Bishop Landel's office after slipping in noiselessly through the open French windows. The Bishop was at his desk, some thirty feet away in a very spacious room.

After a long wait, Abu walked in.

"Well?"

"Yes, Father. He has gone for a walk."

"Did you check his room?"

"Yes, Father. Nothing, except his notebook where he practices Arabic. He has been doing quite a lot of that."

"Where did he go yesterday?"

"To meet his Arabic teacher again, Haji Bouabid. And before that, he went to meet his Tuareg friends in the east of the town."

"Why this interest in the Tuaregs?"

"I do not know yet, Master. One Tuareg even visited him briefly, but I was listening outside and the conversation was formal. This was possibly because of that case he got involved with. He said something about their music too. The Tuaregs are not trustworthy. We Arabs do not like them. And they do not get along with the French, especially the gendarmes."

"Keep a watch. I need to keep the French government informed of anything the Tuaregs are planning to do. If Father Andrzej Bąkiewicz works for our enemies, it would be helpful to watch his interaction with the Tuaregs carefully."

"Yes, Father."

Abu left the room.

Bishop Landel spent another twenty minutes, writing a few notes. Then he left, closing the French windows barely four feet away from where Holmes was hiding, and then the door to the office.

Holmes waited for a short while and then quietly went across to the table. He looked carefully at what Bishop Landel had written, and reviewed other correspondence.

In half an hour, it was clear.

Bishop Landel was a French spy apart from being a holy man deputed by the Vatican to minister to the Tangier flock.

And Sherlock Holmes was under suspicion for being a British agent, masquerading as Father Andrzej Bąkiewicz.

Holmes did not mind that as much, since this was not quite true, and as far as he could tell, he had not been in any extreme situation where such a conclusion could be arrived at. He wondered how this inference had been reached. Was there a spy in Father Ciasca's office in the Vatican? But would not such a mole be more concerned about the matter of the parchment rather than the squabbles between the French and the British? Oh yes, it was Lord Dufferin. That made sense. Had Lord Dufferin leaked the matter deliberately or inadvertently?

Holmes shrugged and let himself out of the prefecture gently. He was soon on the street and he completed his planned outing as indicated to Abu.

◇◇◇

The long months of learning Arabic allowed him to look at new possibilities in his inquiries. He had managed to read the *Rihla* several times and worked hard to form a bond with the Tuaregs in a respectful way. He had studied the mannerisms and inflections of the Tuaregs. And when the events described earlier about his confrontation with the French magistrate over the attempted framing of the Tuareg chief, with the accompanying news that the Guardians of the Letter were looking for him, caused his presence in disguise to be compromised, Holmes took rapid decisions. He asked the Tuaregs to help us travel to Timbuktu. He did not reveal his mission, though he gave broad hints that his life was in danger. He also spoke about his admiration for the Tuareg's culture and how he hoped to visit the tomb of Queen Tin Hanan in Abalessa. The Tuaregs agreed readily, and as you have read in the previous section, did indeed succeed in taking Holmes and me across to Mali.

After resting a night at the *abaradiou* on the outskirts of Timbuktu, Holmes and I went on a tour of the city, assuring Hasso that we would be back soon. At a safe distance, Holmes discarded his Tuareg robes and transformed into an old Uzbek merchant from Bukhara and named himself Yaqub Beg.

"You are now my deaf and dumb slave Morteza, Watson."

"Indeed, Holmes? This comes as a surprise."

"This is the reason I asked for you to come to Tangier, Watson. We must now slip away from the Tuaregs for their own safety and visit the Sankore Mosque to find the parchment. The reason for the new disguise will be evident shortly. Time is of the essence."

I donned clothing befitting a slave. Holmes told me to be very deferential, stay a good five feet behind and always look at the ground. "I shall be introducing you as my deaf and dumb slave, Watson, since your knowledge of Arabic is negligible. Therefore take care that you do not react to sharp and loud sounds. Please carry my personal effects, which I hope you will agree, are minimal, except perhaps for the bulk of the violin. In any case we have left the violin behind at the *Abaradiou*."

"Yes, Master," I said, as humbly as I could.

In a few minutes, Holmes and I were walking toward the Sankore Mosque. My new Uzbek master made me quite cognisant of my status as a slave, ensuring I walked slowly behind, while he himself strode forward masterfully, surveying the city.

We found the mosque quite easily toward the north of the town and were pleased. The old mud walls were still standing, bolstered by more recent brick facades. The annual summer restoration of the mud walls had just concluded, we gathered from some overheard remarks. The architecture was most distinctive, with a pyramidal minaret supported by wooden beams. Hundreds of students milled about noisily streaming in and out of the doors. It certainly had an aura of academia and age about it.

Holmes asked an official-looking Negro who was walking about if he could meet the administrator of the Mosque.

"Why do you wish to meet him?" he asked, appraising us carefully.

"I have come from a distant land with a letter for him."

"Come, I shall take you to the *marabouts*," said he.

Holmes and I were escorted inside. We reached a simple mud building which we inferred was where the administrators were to be found.

We entered a room with high ceilings and elaborate drapes. On the wall were Arabic inscriptions of various kinds. Three men were seated on the floor on thick rugs, smoking hookahs and talking. Fans woven with reeds hung down from the ceiling and they were operated by slaves sitting inconspicuously in niches in the wall, pulling ropes constantly.

Holmes bowed, and I followed his example.

"As-Salaam-Alaikum."

"*Wa-Alaikum-Salaam*," the men replied in unison. All wore white with turbans. All were strongly built Negros of varying age. They were a splendid sight.

"My name is Yaqub Beg and I am a merchant from Bukhara. This is my slave Morteza."

"Bukhara? Wonderful! Wonderful! Welcome to Sankore Mosque, my friend. My name is Haji Ahmad Al-Kaburi. I am the Imam of the Sankore Mosque. These are my friends Haji Toumani Kouyate and Haji Mohammad Yahya Wangari, Professors of Law at the Madrassah. Please sit down."

We did as bid, though Holmes indicated with a subtle gesture I should sit quite a distance away.

"What can I do for you, my friend?" asked Haji Ahmad Al-Kaburi in a warm manner. He was of a jovial disposition with friendly eyes and was quite heavy.

"The Imam at the Juma Masjid in Bukhara has sent these special dried fruits to you. You will not find them anywhere else in the world. Please accept them." Holmes handed over a small packet after bowing elaborately. I had no idea where and when he had picked up such a packet. His resourcefulness was remarkable.

The three men were delighted.

"Ah, thank you! We are so grateful."

"How does the Imam in Bukhara know of us?"

"Who does not know of the Sankore Mosque in the lands of Islam?" Yaqub Beg said dramatically. "The light of your wisdom and knowledge shines across the world, O Hajis!"

The men were even more flattered.

"Please forgive my poor Arabic," said Yaqub Beg apologetically. "The language of the Uzbeks is different and we do not speak Arabic often. With your guidance and Allah's will, I shall improve."

"All of us can speak French well. We can converse in that language. You are our first visitor from Bukhara, as far as I know," said Haji Al-Kaburi. He clapped his hands and two slaves were summoned. He spoke to them sharply, and shortly, tea and dates were brought in. They served me separately (and rather rudely, slamming down a plate in front of me) as I was a slave, and moved me to a niche in the wall, which had, possibly accidentally, a soft carpet for my comfort.

"When did you come to Timbuktu, Yaqub Beg?" asked Toumani Kouyate, reaching for some dates.

"Only last night. I came from Morocco with a group of Tuaregs."

"Ah, a long and difficult journey! You must be praised! But be careful of the Tuaregs. Some of them cannot be trusted. They are often cheats and murderers."

"So far, I have not faced any problem with them, but thank you for your advice. I shall be careful. And I do not feel any fatigue. When I saw the Sankore Mosque, it was like a dream that had come true. Praise be to Allah!"

"Do you have a place to stay? And when do you go back?"

"Yes, I do. I am staying with the Tuaregs at the *abaradiou*. I shall perhaps leave in a week. This time I hope to visit Yaounde and then return. But after Morocco, I hope to visit Mecca and Medina before returning to Bukhara."

"A noble goal, indeed! Tell me about your slave," said Haji Al-Kaburi, gesturing in my direction. Everyone turned to examine me.

"He is from some tribe in Persia. I purchased him in Tabriz many years ago. He is deaf and dumb. That can be quite useful sometimes."

Everyone laughed uproariously at my expense. Since I was deaf, I did not react and continued looking downwards.

"He is very loyal and helps me with my accounts," said Yaqub Beg, helping himself to a date.

"Oh? What do you do?"

"I am a trader, Hajis. Mostly of carpets and sometimes spices."

"What brings you here to Timbuktu?" asked Haji Al-Kaburi.

"I was looking for trading opportunities. I proposed to come back next year if I find that the products of Bukhara and Samarkand are of value here. I would like your opinion about the dried fruits I have brought for you."

"Ah these are Turkish apricots, I think. I once ate them in Gaza," remarked Toumani Kouyate, chewing with deliberation.

"And those are a rare variety of pistachios, Qadis. I hope you find their quality to your satisfaction." Yaqub Beg remarked modestly.

"These are wonderful! Excellent! We thank you!"

Yaqub Beg quickly established a cordial friendship with the three *marabouts*. I, on the other hand, given my new status, failed to form any meaningful bonds.

Toumani Kouyate and Mohammad Yahya excused themselves as they were needed in classrooms. That was convenient for Holmes.

Yaqub Beg edged forward toward Haji Al-Kaburi.

"Haji, you are a great man of God. I ask for your forgiveness before I ask you my questions, just in case they are not appropriate. I am not a scholar like you and do not understand many things, including the art of speaking with care and respect."

"Certainly, Yaqub Beg. We are an old and famous madrassah. Perhaps we do not know the ways of the world. But he who comes with a clean heart to Sankore and asks questions may easily get answers, Insha Allah."

"I search for a treasure in your library," said Yaqub Beg.

"I shall be happy to take you there myself and help you find that treasure."

"I know I shall not find it easily."

Haji Al-Kaburi looked puzzled. "Why do you say that? You have not seen the library yet. There are thousands and thousands of manuscripts. We even have a rare copy of the *Tarikh Al-Sudan* and so much more. What do you seek? We can certainly try to help you." Haji Al-Kaburi looked surprised.

Yaqub Beg hesitated and then spoke slowly. "Haji, my real name is Yaqub Beg Batuta."

Haji Al-Kaburi was startled. "What? Are you a descendant of Haji Ibn Batuta?"

"Yes."

"Ah! That may explain your fairness and features. You do not look like any Uzbek I have seen before, though I have not seen many. But how do you know you are from him?"

"I know because the story was told to me by my grandfather. And the story of his visit to Bukhara is in *Al-Rihla.*"

"You may be right, Yaqub. Let me refresh my memory." He clapped his hands and asked a slave to bring him a copy of *Al-Rihla.* It arrived shortly. He thumbed through it and found what he was looking for.

"Ah! Yes! It is true that Ibn Batuta visited Samarkhand, Bukhara, and Termez. And many more. Yes, I now recall. I am not as knowledgeable about Ibn Batuta as my friends. In fact, Toumani Kouyate possibly knows more. Shall I call him?"

Yaqub Beg raised a restraining hand. "No Haji. Hear me out. I know the *Al-Rihla* quite well and, to be frank, it is not Ibn Batuta that I have come to discuss."

"But it is such an honour, Yaqub Beg! The descendant of Ibn Batuta visiting the Sankore Mosque after more than five hundred years! It is cause for celebration! I must call the scholars in the area for a discussion of *Al-Rihla* at the very least!" Haji Al-Kaburi was quite excited.

"Yes, Haji. I am greatly honoured. But I pray once again that you understand why I am here. Once you do, I will have no objection if you wish to call the scholars. After all, I am just an ignorant merchant, while Ibn Batuta was a Qadi."

"Tell me what you wish to know."

Yaqub Beg Batuta requested Haji Al-Kaburi to ask his slaves to provide me with food and drink, which he readily agreed to do.

"You are a good man, Yaqub Beg. Very few care about their slaves, especially a deaf, dumb, and rather ugly one with little obvious value. Many would have put such a slave to death a long time ago."

Yaqub Beg sighed. "I have occasionally thought about it, Haji. I may do so at some point in the future. But for now, he is useful."

"Continue then, Yaqub Beg." Haji Al-Kaburi leaned forward, his brow furrowed, quite puzzled by the tenor of the conversation.

"Haji, the story is that Ibn Batuta travelled to Uzbekistan with a slave girl he purchased somewhere in the land of the emotional Seljuks. She claimed she was originally from Tabriz in Persia. He brought her to Uzbekistan where he stayed for some time. He left Uzbekistan and moved on toward India, but he left his concubine behind as she was carrying. A male child was born and adopted by the Sultan, Uzbeg Khan, who gave him to a friend to nurture. We are descendants of that son of Ibn Batuta, and we continue to marry women from Persia. That is why we look different, perhaps, though we consider ourselves Uzbek."

"A remarkable story. Now what is wrong with your slave? He seems to be swaying."

"Let me correct him," said Yaqub Beg, rising angrily from the floor.

I stopped laughing and became still again. Yaqub Beg sat down slowly, glaring at me, and resumed his narrative.

"Alas, Haji, we preferred the life of merchants instead of the life of scholars. It is late in my life but I hope my son becomes a Qadi and becomes worthy of your respect."

"We respect everyone, Yaqub Beg." He hailed a slave curtly and asked for more tea and dates.

"I have found a letter, Haji, which was always considered priceless and very important for our family. I wish to read it to you. But before I do that, could you confirm to me that Ibn Batuta indeed visited the Sankore Mosque?"

"Certainly, Yaqub Beg. Al-Rihla is one possible proof. But there is stronger proof. Haji Toumani Kouyate will tell us specifically. In Timbuktu, there is a great tradition of storing manuscripts in metal and wooden chests under the desert sands. Whatever documents are not used often, we store in these metal chests and bury them. It is safe. We know where all our buried documents are kept. There is an index that Toumani Kouyate has. The records of important visitors to the mosque were kept, as far as I know. I am quite sure there is a record of Ibn Batuta's visit somewhere. It is probably an insignificant point. But if I recall, the Sankore Mosque was being rebuilt at that time—was it in AH 752 perhaps? Who can say if the record keepers were consistent at that time? That opens a new line of thought!"

"Let us continue this discussion further at lunch time. Come with me. Toumani Kouyate will certainly join us. You can leave your slave behind."

To my horror, Holmes did just that and I was left in my niche in the wall. The heat had become intense. The other slaves seemed in a better condition, and once Haji Al-Kaburi and "Yaqub Beg" left the building, they too disappeared, leaving me in a hot room with still air.

After some time, some slaves summoned me to their area and bade me sit down with them. Then they placed a plate with a huge mound of some camel meat—only slightly cooked— rice, porridge, and a paste of yam and something else. It was the most deplorable and unappetizing meal I have yet encountered, with clotted blood dripping off the plate and on to the floor, but I was hungry and needed my strength. I closed my eyes, held my breath and ate a little. Then I washed it down with water. I missed my Yorkshire pudding and bacon. It was a pity that the wonderful, refined cuisine of the English had not yet found favour in this land.

I was then escorted back to my niche in the wall of the office of Haji Al-Kaburi to wait for the return of my old friend, "Yaqub Beg Batuta," whom I knew so well from our adventures together in London and elsewhere at a time when I was not a slave but a free man.

◇◇◇

The account of Sherlock Holmes, in the guise of Yaqub Beg Batuta, an Uzbek merchant

I walked with Haji Al-Kaburi to another large room where a number of others had started assembling for an early lunch, as was the custom. Al-Kaburi introduced me to many as his guest from Uzbekistan. He hailed Toumani Kouyate and the three of us sat on a thick carpet together as slaves came by to serve us. The fare was interesting, though challenging to an epicurean perhaps. Goat meat, goat cheese, camel meat, millet, yam, fruits, and so on. It was expected that I would eat this alien fare constantly.

"Toumani Kouyate, Yaqub Beg is an interesting guest. You may be able to answer his questions."

"Yes, we rarely get visitors from Uzbekistan at Sankore." Toumani Kouyate bit into some salted mutton.

"Do you know who he really is?" smiled Al-Kaburi.

"I only know him as Yaqub Beg." His lack of interest was obvious.

"His real name is Yaqub Beg Batuta, Toumani Kouyate!"

Toumani Kouyate stopped eating and stared at me.

"Is that so?"

"I believe it is the case. I hope to convince you."

"But you are not a Qadi."

"No. We are descendants of Ibn Batuta in a different way. He brought a concubine from Tabriz to Uzbekistan. When he left, she was carrying and he left her behind. We are descendants of the son she gave birth to."

"A very interesting story." He paused for a few moments. "But I do not recall reading about Ibn Batuta's son in Bukhara in the *Al-Rihla*."

"It would not have been possible, Toumani Kouyate, because Ibn Batuta did not return and therefore never knew for a fact that he had a son."

Toumani Kouyate looked sceptical. "Then what proof do you have that you are indeed a descendant? Anyone could have made up such a story."

"I would not dare to do so at such a holy place, Toumani Kouyate. But I understand your point. I have proof.

"I have with me a letter that the dying Ibn Batuta sent to Uzbeg Khan from Tangier. Uzbeg Khan handed it over to the son when he became an adult. In our family tradition, it was hoped that if a male child had the resources, he would visit Timbuktu and present this letter to the custodians of the Sankore Mosque. I am the first such person who could afford to travel such a distance. But I would like to show that letter to you in Haji Al-Kaburi's room because it is an old and delicate parchment and I would not like to show it while eating."

Toumani Kouyate continued to look sceptical. Al-Kaburi smiled at me and shook his head slightly. We then changed the topic and I asked the two about the students, the curriculum, the faculty and so on.

We returned to Al-Kaburi's room, where I found Watson sitting quietly in his assigned niche. I was most impressed by his forbearance. I had not anticipated that he would be so obedient a slave.

We sat down on the carpet and the conversation resumed.

◇◇◇

Haji Al-Kaburi repeated Yaqub Beg Batuta's question about the storage of manuscripts to Toumani Kouyate.

"Yes, Yaqub Beg, we have thousands of scrolls and books," said Toumani Kouyate. "Most are of immense value. They must be protected from the sun, air, and moisture. In any case, there is only a small set of books and manuscripts used by scholars again and again. Therefore, it is wise for us to store most of the documents in metal and wooden boxes underground. We take them out when necessary. This method is absolutely safe. The documents are dry and cool in the sand and there is no possibility of insects destroying them. And of course, there is no rain in Timbuktu."

"Very admirable," said Yaqub Beg Batuta, nibbling at a date. "But we are equally sensible about indexing them. We have a complete list of what lies below and can retrieve anything we need. Such retrieval happens rarely these days—perhaps once a month. It depends on what the scholar wants. There is no restriction.

"But why do you ask?" Toumani Kouyate asked keenly.

From my niche in the wall, I could sense acute scepticism.

"Toumani Kouyate, as I mentioned, I am a descendant of Ibn Batuta. I do not expect you to believe me. However, I would like to show you a letter that Ibn Batuta sent from Tangier to King Uzbeg Khan, who in turn gave it to Ibn Batuta's son when he grew up. I have no reason to believe he lied."

Yaqub Beg Batuta took out a soft leather bag from within the folds of his dress. He took out what appeared to be a parchment, quite similar to the half-manuscript of Marco Polo. He gave it to Haji Al-Kaburi, who took it eagerly but carefully.

"Toumani Kouyate! Look at this! Let me read it!"

O Great Sultan Uzbeg Khan.

I salute your memory as one of the greatest Emperors the world has seen. In all my travels, no ruler has impressed me with his kindness, generosity and wisdom as you did.

I am now at death's door and am sending this letter to you in the safe hands of my friend. I recall that I had left behind my concubine when she was heavy with child and you had very kindly agreed to make sure the child, if a boy, would carry my name and be treated respectfully.

Advise my son, if son there is, to take this letter with your seal and travel to Timbuktu. Ask him to present it at the Sankore Mosque and request the documents that I gave the Imam for safekeeping. He promised me that he would keep my books and letters safely till I returned. These are the only gifts I have for my son, but in all families these are important treasures for the sons to preserve and hold dear.

Abū'Abd al-Lāh Muhammad ibn 'Abd al-Lāh l-Lawātī ṭ-Ṭanǧī ibn Baṭūṭah

19 Safar 770 A.H.

The letter did indeed have an elaborate seal. It was of the Sultan Uzbeg Khan.

Toumani Kouyate's face changed. He seemed quite impressed and less sceptical. He read the letter again and seemed to be thinking of something. I guessed it was the date. Then he nodded; the date seemed right. The parchment looked genuine and so was the handwriting and language.

Then he set the letter aside and was again lost in thought. Had he guessed the letter was a brilliant forgery?

"Ibn Batuta travelled last to Mali. Yes, it is possible he left his documents here. I can find out easily. But why would he have not mentioned his son in Bukhara in Al-Rihla?"

Al-Kaburi was exasperated. "How could he, Haji? He left before the child was born and never returned. The letter also says "if a boy." Perhaps he was taking a chance that he had a son in Bukhara. He mentions in *Al-Rihla* that his son in Morocco had passed away."

Toumani Kouyate nodded reluctantly. "Yes, that is possible, I agree. Yes." He paused. "Shall I then check my records and find out if Ibn Batuta left behind something?"

"I would be very grateful," bowed Yaqub Beg Batuta. "May I return in the evening?"

"Yes you may. But if we find it, it would take us a day to retrieve those documents. The hidden library is vast."

Toumani Kouyate said suddenly. "And I am a little surprised you do not look like an Uzbek." His tone was sharp.

"I already asked him about that, Toumani Kouyate," said Al-Kaburi, now slightly irritated. "It appears that the concubine was possibly from Tabriz in Persia. And he says the family has always sought brides from Persia since then. Let us believe him. We have no reason not to."

Toumani Kouyate nodded, again reluctantly. The meeting dispersed. I was reclaimed by my master, who bid a warm good-bye to Al-Kaburi and a slightly less effusive one to Toumani Kouyate. It was agreed that they would meet again at about five in the evening.

Timbuktu—The Manuscript

"Books sell very well there (in Timbuktu), and a greater profit is to be made out of them than out of any other merchandise."
—Leo Africanus

We returned to the *abaradiou*, with me following at an appropriate distance. Holmes spoke in a low voice.

"A fine performance there, Watson. Please continue for a while till I advise you. It is possible that we are being followed. Toumani Kouyate is certainly suspicious and will try to verify our story as best as he can. I must think."

I followed silently and deferentially, as we walked through the narrow streets of Timbuktu, with mud houses lined on both side.

Hasso and his fellow Tuaregs were waiting for us anxiously.

"Where were you, my friend?" he cried. "We thought you had been kidnapped or were lost. And why have you changed your dress? Where is your *tagelmust*?" He seemed slightly offended.

"We thought it would be an excellent adventure to explore Timbuktu and try on a new dress, Hasso. We went to the Sankore Mosque, as you and I had discussed earlier. We ate some local fare. The Tuareg food is certainly more appetizing!"

We sat down with Hasso and his friends, who had pitched tents close to the *abaradiou*. The afternoon stretched out, with the blazing sun refusing to relent. Holmes and Hasso conversed quietly in a corner. I thought philosophically about the advantages and disadvantages of being a deaf and dumb slave. What is the need to speak at all, I wondered. And far better to listen to oneself rather than the noise of others. Better to be Holmes' slave than someone else's, I thought, and certainly not Al-Kaburi, who might put me to death with little notice. Would my wife be disturbed to know that I, Dr. John Watson, was now a slave in Timbuktu? I drifted away to sleep.

At about four o'clock, Holmes woke me up and we set out to Sankore Mosque.

We reached the charming mosque and went to Al-Kaburi's room. Toumani Kouyate was already there and had brought along several manuscripts.

"Yaqub Beg, I am searching for the entries."

"I am sorry for the trouble," replied Yaqub Beg Batuta.

"We should have the answer soon."

He examined many parchments closely, rejecting them one after the other. He finally found one that seemed promising.

"AH 752, yes, there is a possibility here. I had suspected that the entries at that time were not very detailed, so we see much fewer. And many were destroyed during times of war, of course."

He exclaimed. "Ah! There is an entry by the Imam of that time! Let me read."

He mumbled to himself as he read the entry. The suspense was intense, even to me, who was just an object against the wall.

"This says that the traveller, Qadi Ibn Batuta, has expressed the need to leave Timbuktu for Gao and then to Morocco as quickly as possible. He proposes to come back next year. To lighten his burden, he has asked us to store his books. We prefer not to store the personal papers of others and take responsibility, especially for those not related to scholarship. But we decided to make an exception this time as Ibn Batuta was a renowned scholar and had also made a generous donation to Sankore Madrassah. He handed over an iron and wood box which we buried toward the back wall of the mosque."

"Has the location been mentioned?" asked Al-Kaburi eagerly.

"Yes, though not in the specific way we do these days."

"It simply says…hmm, "a foot away from the third column at the North." Shall we take a look? I had planned to do this tomorrow, but perhaps we can start now."

We stood up, and I was curtly summoned to start digging. But an amused Toumani Kouyate took pity on me and suggested that their younger and stronger slaves handle the matter. All of us travelled to the back end of the mosque, which was some distance away. We went to the north boundary wall and identified the third column.

The slaves began digging with crow bars, shovels, and other implements while everyone else watched.

The sun was milder and the sand yielded easily. The job progressed fast. But after a couple of hours, nothing had been found except pieces of an old pot.

Our disappointment was evident. Had we made a mistake?

Yaqub Beg, Toumani Kouyate, and Al-Kaburi returned slowly to the room, heads bent, thinking deeply.

As slaves dispensed tea and dates, Al-Kaburi mused.

"How strange! It seems odd and unnecessary to have someone give incorrect directions."

"It is possible that the box was discovered and stolen years ago. It is not impossible. In 1591, this mosque was attacked and ravaged," mused Toumani Kouyate.

Yaqub Beg stood up and walked around the room in ferment, his head bowed and his hands clasped behind him. The other two were startled by this display of energy.

"Perhaps it is too much to expect a mosque built in 1325 to be in exactly the same condition after all these years," Yaqub Beg mused. "What could have changed?"

"What makes you think this mosque was built in 1325?" asked Al-Kaburi, astonished. "Yes, the very first mosque was built in about 988 with a donation by a wealthy Mandinka woman. And then there were many changes. As a recognized mosque and madrassah it is true that it was re-established about

1325. But technically this mosque was rebuilt by El-Agib in 1582 after being destroyed earlier, based on measurements that he had taken with a rope of the Kaaba during his pilgrimage there. Then there were many restorations in 1709, 1710, and 1732. So you see, it has not been a building with no changes!"

Yaqub Beg Batuta spun around, his eyes flashing.

"What specific changes do you know of, Haji?"

"As I said, I know that the mosque was expanded and redesigned to the exact dimension of the Kaaba by Imam El-Agib in 1582. That means that the mosque area effectively doubled in size."

"Did it expand equally in all directions?" asked Yaqub Beg keenly.

"A good question, a good question" said Toumani Kouyate slowly, thinking. "I think the answer is that it expanded in three directions. The front was kept as is, though the *mighrab* was demolished and rebuilt too."

Comprehension dawned, and his face cleared. "Ah! I understand what you are saying!"

"Do you have a map of the old mosque floor plan?"

"I can find it. That will be easier to find as it would be part of the administrative records. Give me an hour."

Within twenty minutes, Toumani Kouyate was back, his excitement evident. "Yes, I have the plan."

"I do not understand all this," said the bewildered Imam, Al-Kaburi.

"Haji, what Yaqub Beg Batuta is saying is that the directions provided in our records refer to the old mosque, not the newly built one. All we have to determine is where the wall was before the mosque was expanded!" explained Toumani Kouyate.

"Excellent! A very intelligent man, Batuta!" exclaimed Al-Kaburi, delighted.

"This did not occur to me earlier because we have never searched for documents before the 1582 re-construction," Toumani Kouyate said, slightly defensively.

"But it is almost dark now. Much as I would be happy to be of assistance, I must leave for prayers. And further, we need light. If you wish, we can begin digging early. Say at seven in the morning? I can rearrange my classes."

"Thank you, Haji. That seems possible."

"Meanwhile, I suggest you look at the other two mosques in Timbuktu. They are very grand—the Djinguereber Ber and Sidi Yahia."

"I shall follow your advice, Haji." Yaqub Beg Batuta bowed.

"Batuta, if we find the box, I would be very happy for you. It would be a historic moment for us." Al-Kaburi was very excited. "I have prepared a box for you to take back to your Tuareg camp. Your slave will carry it for you."

He beckoned and I went up quietly to him. Other slaves lifted a rather large and unwieldy wooden box and tried to place it on my head. It was clear immediately that I had neither the strength nor the skill needed to carry the box. Everyone present laughed loudly at my plight, but Al-Kaburi took pity on me and assigned two slaves to carry it for us.

"I cannot understand why you are so fond of this weak slave, Yaqub Beg! Ibn Batuta would have been disappointed in your choice!" chortled Al-Kaburi, his body shaking with amusement. "I shall be happy to present you with a younger and stronger slave, if you like."

Yaqub Beg Batuta laughed. "Ah well, he has his uses, Haji! Thank you for this. We shall be back early tomorrow."

With that, we left the mud-walled Sankore Mosque and returned to our camp. There was a feeling of accomplishment, but we were tense, too. Toumani Kouyate had thawed but who knew if he might change his mind.

The slaves accompanied us, walking with me while Yaqub Beg Batuta walked the streets of Timbuktu, admiring the other mosques.

We reached Hasso's camp. He was standing at the entrance of his tent, waiting for us. Though his face was covered with his *tagelmust*, it was clear that he was tense. His eyes were unsmiling.

The slaves placed the wooden box full of food on the carpet and departed. The Tuaregs opened it and shared camel meat and cheese. We had some too. The taste was again extremely alien and disturbing, but I persevered. Who knew when we would sample the cuisine of England again?

We waited for Hasso to speak. He came up to us.

"We will have to leave Timbuktu soon." His eyes betrayed grim concern.

"Why?"

"We have received news that the Guardians are only a few days journey behind us. It is expected that they will reach Timbuktu quite soon. And you can be sure that the Guardians will visit the Sankore Mosque immediately. If you finish by then by God's grace, we must escape. Otherwise we shall be in trouble. If there is a confrontation, the gendarmes will arrest us first as we are Tuaregs."

Hasso had barely finished speaking when there was a disturbance just outside the tents.

A Tuareg rushed in and spoke in an urgent undertone to Hasso, whose eyes widened.

"French gendarmes. Are they looking for you? Thank God you are not wearing our clothes! Remember to pretend to be who you say you are!"

Six French gendarmes and a number of Malinese policemen rushed in with revolvers and rifles. The inspector, a formidable looking Frenchman, pushed a few Tuaregs about, shouting in broken Tamasheq.

"Who is your chief? Where have you come from? Speak up!"

Hasso identified himself and walked across.

"I am Hasso Ag Akotey. I am the chief." He spoke with authority.

"Come outside! I have questions for you!"

Hasso was dragged away roughly by the policemen. They stood at a distance from the rest of us.

"When did you come?"

"Yesterday," replied Hasso.

"Lying to me, dirty Tuareg? If you are, I can do many things to you!"

"I am not lying," Hasso said quietly.

"Where have you come from?"

"Fez, Sijilmasa, Taghaza."

"Who travels at this time of the year?"

"Sometimes we do. We plan to visit the mosques here and then go to Abalessa."

"How many in the caravan?"

"Twenty nine. One died of a snake bite. We buried him on the way."

"Only Tuaregs in the caravan?"

"Yes."

"Who are those two men?" asked the Inspector, pointing at Holmes and me.

"They are Uzbeks. Yaqub Beg and Morteza. They came from Iwatlan yesterday and asked for shelter. We know nothing about them."

"Call them here!" shouted the Inspector.

Holmes and I walked across. Holmes smiled pleasantly. I continued as a slave.

"You are?"

"Yaqub Beg. This is my slave Morteza. He is deaf and dumb."

"Where are you from?"

"Bukhara in Uzbekistan."

"And where are you going?"

"Possibly Yaounde."

"Can you speak French?"

"A little, sire. I picked it up during my travels."

Bon, alors parlons en français plutôt qu'en arabe. Qu'est-ce qui vous amène à Tombouctou?[18]

Je suis un commerçant, Monsieur. Je me suis rendu de Gibraltar à Tanger, puis à Rabat, Casablanca et le long de la côte de

---

[18] "Good, then let us speak in French instead of Arabic. What brings you to Timbuktu?"

Mauritanie. Nous avons ensuite atteint Iwatlan et sommes arrivés hier ici à Tombouctou. Nous sommes venus pour visiter les mosquées et rechercher des occasions d'affaires.[19]

Avez-vous des preuves de votre histoire?[20]

Des preuves? Voyons voir. Oui, voici quelques pièces de monnaie de l'Ouzbékistan. Puis voici un livre que j'ai acheté à Istanboul, en route pour Tanger. Et voici encore une lettre de l'imam de la Jama Masjid à Boukhara; il s'agit d'une lettre de présentation à l'imam de la mosquée de Djenné. Et voici enfin une lettre de l'imam de Boukhara à son ami, l'imam de Yaoundé.[21]

The inspector examined the papers, and asked about me. He did not wait for an answer. The police team left abruptly.

Hasso and Holmes looked at each other and nodded imperceptibly. Hasso heaved a sigh of relief, turned to his Tuaregs and left.

Holmes looked at me.

"A routine check. Luck has favoured us, Watson. Or should I say, Morteza? No, no, do not say a word, let us rest."

In perusing my notes, I see that Holmes and I were acutely aware that the day was to be crucial in more ways than one. Bereft of cocaine and any other stimulant, and in a strange and exotic land with no recourse to the majesty of the law in case of a crisis, Holmes was, for the first time that I could recall, particularly nervous. He did not sleep well and walked about outside in the

---

[19] "I am a merchant, sire. I travelled from Gibraltar to Tangier, Rabat, Casablanca, and then along Mauritania. We then reached Iwatlan and came here yesterday to Timbuktu. We have come to visit the mosques and look for trading opportunities."

[20] "Any proof of your story?"

[21] "Proof? Let me see. Yes, here are some coins from Uzbekistan. Then here is a book I purchased in Istanbul on my way to Tangier. And here is a letter from the Imam of the Juma Masjid in Bukhara—it is a letter of introduction to the Imam of the Djenne mosque. And here is a letter from the Imam in Bukhara to his friend, the Imam at Yaounde."

open and cold air, muttering to himself. He woke Hasso, and the two of them were engaged in a long and intense discussion. I knew Holmes' methods. He often did not involve me in certain matters because he did not want to compromise my safety, which would happen if I were aware of specific details.

It was clear to me that the day would be very significant. The news that the Guardians of the Letter would likely arrive on the morrow was unpleasant and unnerving. They were ruthless people, guarding someone they believed was Ibn Batuta's descendant from India. They had a deep-rooted and exaggerated sense of loyalty to him and would brook no opposition. While they had the fake copy of the half-manuscript that Holmes had so cleverly created to throw them off, they were certain to visit the Sankore Mosque and demand access to Ibn Batuta's documents. They would likely create an ugly situation if it were discovered that someone else had only lately acquired them and disappeared. We could add the administrators of Sankore Mosque and French gendarmes to the list of those who were looking for us. That was on the assumption that our own plan worked smoothly and we escaped.

The next morning, Holmes and I presented ourselves at the Sankore Mosque. It was still cool and the religious school was already humming with activities, with boys of all ages rushing about. I could hear collective recitation of the Quran from a building as I walked by.

Toumani Kouyate and Al-Kaburi were already waiting. Yaqub had told me that it was critical that we exhibited patience and not convey the fact that we knew every minute was important. If everything went well, we hoped to be lucky, take the box and leave Timbuktu. Holmes told me that he had informed Hasso to convey to everyone that we should plan to return the same way, via Taghaza. The Tuaregs were getting ready for another long journey. They had exchanged their tired camels with others. These camels would reach Fez in due course in the possession of related Tuaregs.

Yaqub Beg greeted the two men, who reciprocated. Both seemed cheerful. A small team of slaves had been assembled.

"Come, Yaqub Beg Batuta! Let me show you the plan!" cried Al-Kaburi, waving at Holmes. His excitement was contagious.

They pored over an old parchment, while I sat again in the niche reserved for me, Morteza, the deaf and dumb slave of Yaqub Beg Batuta, accidentally of Bukhara but originally from London.

"The old wall was broken down and a new one was built where it stands now. I have calculated the distance and I believe the old wall is here"—he indicated the place on the map. "This spot is quite close to this building. Let us begin right away!"

We stepped out of the building and the slaves started digging with vigour. The sand this time was somewhat harder to breach because it was on a well-trodden path. But the team carried on. Curious onlookers were shooed away.

After about an hour, with the pit easily about ten feet deep and about six feet across, nothing had yet been found. Toumani Kouyate was puzzled.

"Was it stolen? Or have I miscalculated?" he frowned, scratching his chin.

"May I look at the entry again?" inquired Yaqub Beg.

"Yes."

Yaqub Beg looked carefully again at the entry and thought for a moment.

"When we looked at the North side earlier, why did we choose the area on the right? Why not the left?"

"Because the area on the left had a building built there. We cannot dig there. We could not have destroyed a building."

"But now, since we are digging in the area of the old wall, the new place to dig may not have a building!" exclaimed Holmes-Batuta.

"Very correct!" said Abdurrehman, who had converted from an antagonist to an admirer of his Uzbek visitor.

The three again pored over the map and agreed on the new location.

The team rushed there with the slaves. Work began again. Sand flew in the air and the sounds of digging took over.

In about fifteen minutes, the first signs of success were seen. The diggers had encountered something hard. As they removed sand from what appeared to be a metal box, another digger hit another object a few feet away.

In a few more minutes, it became clear that the team had hit not one but a number of metal boxes. Excitement grew in both the slaves and the onlookers. Which box was Ibn Batuta's?

Al-Kaburi counted the metal boxes as they were lifted up to the surface. All were made of iron and wood and were of a modest size. They had tiny latches but no locks. Due to the lack of moisture, there was very little rust. The boxes were taken to Al-Kaburi's room where the sand was removed with a soft cloth. And finally, the three looked at the nine boxes on the little table in the room.

Yaqub Beg asked Toumani Kouyate how he hoped to determine which box belonged to Ibn Batuta.

"I already know," said Toumani Kouyate with a smile. "Can you not guess? What do you expect he would have engraved on the box? His own name, of course. Except that he has taken care to write out his complete name instead of simply Ibn Batuta."

"This is the box," he said, pointing at a nondescript metal box of average size. You can see that he or someone else has painted out his name. Look carefully, it is in red and the colour has faded."

ابو عبدالله محمد بن عبد الله بن محمد اللواتي الطنجي ابن بطوطة

"*Abu Abdullah Muhammad Ibn Abdullah Al Lawati Al Tanji Ibn Batuta,*" he pronounced softly, rolling each syllable on his tongue. "Yes, this is the box he entrusted to us to keep for you, Yaqub Beg Batuta. This is your heritage."

He handed over the metal box to Al-Kaburi. "Now it is up to you, Haji."

Haji Al-Kaburi held the box with reverence and looked at it from various angles.

"Now Yaqub Beg Batuta, we would like to give it to you. But we have a condition. A request."

My heart stopped.

"Of course!" said Yaqub Beg Batuta.

"Once you read what is within, will you tell us about it? If the matter is not about the family, can you copy it for us?"

The request was made with great humility. Yaqub Beg was taken aback.

"Of course, Haji. This is my property, true. But it belongs to mankind as well. Once I read it and understand it, I will start the process of copying it. It has been here for hundreds of years and it should continue in some way for eternity."

Al-Kaburi handed over the box. "Do you not want to open it?" he beamed.

The air hung heavy with anticipation.

Yaqub Beg Batuta slowly opened the box. It was stuffed with many manuscripts.

He withdrew several manuscripts from it from it and leafed over them one by one. He took out something at random and asked Toumani Kouyate if he would do him the honour of reading it out first. Abdurrehman and Al-Kaburi examined the manuscript.

"This is not a letter, Yaqub Beg. It is just a list of purchases from the Timbuktu market, perhaps before he set out for Gao and Morocco.

Two bags of millets
Six goats
Various vegetables
Ten bags of dates
Ten lengths of cloth

And so on.

"It is in the handwriting of a very great man."

Toumani Kouyate was moved by the moment. He handed the list back to Yaqub Beg wordlessly.

The clock was ticking.

Yaqub Beg was silent, overcome by emotion.

"I must pay the Sankore Mosque for this. I must repay you," he said in a breaking voice.

The other men protested vehemently.

"No, no, we have done our duty! Do not insult us by paying us!"

"We must thank you for this opportunity!"

"Once I return to Bukhara, I will send something appropriate on behalf of my family," said Yaqub Beg, with tears in his eyes.

"I would like you to leave your slave behind. I have taken a fancy to him, though I see that he is entirely useless," Al-Kaburi chortled. His body shook with delight as he looked at me, sitting quietly on a rug in my assigned niche.

Yaqub Beg was startled, as was I. It was an awkward moment. Would he leave me behind to spend the rest of my life in a niche in the wall of Sankore Mosque in Timbuktu, fanning Haji Al-Kaburi?

Yaqub Beg responded with equanimity. "A very reasonable request. I shall oblige. Once I reach Bukhara, I shall have Morteza teach another slave how to work with my accounts and then send him back. He will be with you in about eight months, In sha' Allah.

"Now, Hajis, I leave for Yaounde. Perhaps I shall take a ship back to Tangier from there and then to Istanbul."

The other men agreed that it was an excellent plan, though they made loud protestations about our imminent departure. Yaqub Beg also extracted a promise from both men that they would visit Bukhara soon as his guests, a suggestion that received a favourable and enthusiastic response, especially since they were told that their expenses would be reimbursed.

All along, the other slaves had been plying the three men with tea and dates. It was finally time to leave.

With great ceremony, Yaqub Beg Batuta left the beautiful Sankore Mosque, with me walking behind. Yaqub Beg gestured to me to carry the metal box for him, as it would not have been appropriate for a man of his stature to carry anything himself when there was a slave available. Since Tuaregs were common in

Timbuktu, the silent attentions of Hasso Ag Akotey and a few of his friends were not noticed. We were quite safe.

We walked back to our Tuareg camp. We entered the tent and Yaqub Beg was transformed into the Holmes I knew so well. With extraordinary speed, he quickly changed into his Tuareg dress, complete with the *tagelmust* while other Tuaregs helped me do the same efficiently.

"The chase is on, Watson! Every minute counts. We must leave immediately!"

"Are you sure you have what you needed, Holmes?"

"Absolutely sure! The half-manuscript parchment was there. I saw it and took it out from the box without their seeing it while I distracted Toumani Kouyate and Al-Kaburi with another document—what was it?—ah, a list of purchases from the market! Sleight of hand. It is in my pocket. I was unsure if they would part with the box as easily as they actually did, and I planned accordingly. Now I possess both parts. Getting it has been easy. But getting out of Timbuktu and back to London will be difficult. I fully expect that the Guardians will reach this very campsite very soon. There will be violence if we are here. I will write a brief letter to our friends in the Holy See informing them of our travel plans and then we leave."

In a few minutes, the letter was written, sealed in an envelope and handed over to Hasso to post in Timbuktu as soon as he could. Holmes' meticulous planning over the previous days had resulted in the entire caravan setting off in minutes. There were no delays.

"Has everyone outside the camp been informed that we are headed back to Taghaza?" he asked Hasso.

"Yes. Now as per the actual plan, you will travel to the Joliba—the Niger River—with these two men on horseback and board a boat to Gao. We shall go due east in our caravan toward Abalessa, as per the story we told the gendarmes. We shall meet you at Gao. If we do not reach Gao by this time tomorrow, it will mean that we have been caught. Hand over this paper to the Tuaregs you meet. They will guide you. Godspeed, my friend!"

Holmes and I set out on horseback to the Niger River, a few miles south of Timbuktu, to begin the next phase. We possibly now possessed the secret to eternal life, but at the moment, we were very concerned with avoiding almost certain death.

The caravan dispersed, moving through the streets of Timbuktu, due east.

◇◇◇

A day later, twenty Guardians of the Letter, armed with weapons of all kind, arrived at the deserted campsite.

In the middle of the group was the exalted descendant of Ibn Batuta, Thalassery Vatoot Mohammad Koya, citizen of the British Empire, most recently of Calicut, returned to lay claim to his inheritance.

Travelling on the Niger

Take me home, O Joliba, take me home
Flow gently, O Joliba, flow gently
I play your songs on the n'Goni, O Joliba
The fish swim by my boat, O Joliba
How tired I am, O Joliba, how tired I am
Take me home O Joliba, take me home

Holmes and I quickly reached the smaller port of Djitafe on the banks of the Niger River, passing the French Fort Bonnier to our left. We skipped Kabara and other larger ports that also serviced Timbuktu. Hasso had arranged for a large *pirogue* to be ready with provisions. Two local Tuaregs were waiting for us with a Fulani boatman and his young teenage son. They helped us off our horses and on to the boat with our precious possessions. It must have been quite a sight—five men in a hurry on the bank. What could possibly be the rush?

And soon, we were off, praying that the Joliba would take us swiftly to Gao where we hoped the other Tuaregs would wait for us. I was still unsure how we would finally escape.

The river was picturesque and most appealing. We were at the edge of the desert and yet there were many reminders of the tropics as well. Stretches of the desert were interspersed with fields and occasional remote mud houses. On the south were forests, some of them dense. At some points, huge trees bent heavy boughs into the river. Many wild animals sat in the shade or were at the banks, seeking water. We saw a group of hippopotamus and were told by the boatman that they were extremely dangerous animals, much more so than lions or elephants. And often, we saw gnarled logs of wood floating about that we soon recognized as crocodiles, waiting for gazelles or zebras to drop their guard and walk close to the water. The trees were full of a variety of monkeys and their cries punctuated the air. Geese, herons, kingfishers, egrets, ospreys, and storks were everywhere. My friends at the Natural History Museum in London would have been most gratified, I reflected.

When I put my hand in the river to feel the current, the boatman shook his head and smiled, and conveyed that there was every possibility of a crocodile snapping at my hands. I presumed that a mishap in the river meant certain death, and I resolved to be still.

"I must write a monograph on the fauna of the Niger River when we return to Westminster, Watson. I believe the Natural History Society would receive it with considerable warmth," mused Holmes, now puffing his pipe and watching the scene, after adjusting his veil, as though he were casually reviewing a copy of the *Debrett's Peerage*. The boatman must have been rather surprised to see a Tuareg smoking a pipe.

I did not react. I found Holmes' views on monographs to be irrelevant and even baffling at a time when crocodiles were swimming by lazily viewing us as a light afternoon snack. I adjusted my *tagelmust*, irritated.

We sat in the middle of the boat, with one Tuareg in front and the other behind us. The boatman was strong and experienced and since we were going downriver, he simply steered the boat, using the current to his advantage. He sang and hummed along the way while his young son, at the forward end, who must not have been more than twelve years old, played an interesting native instrument called the *n'Goni* with verve and enthusiasm. One of the Tuaregs produced a drum called the *tende* and joined in the music. It helped us calm down and enjoy the ride. We were perhaps fortunate that there were no other boats, it being mid-day, a time for siestas. Though it was the dry season, the rains had been plentiful earlier in the year and so the boat ride was possible.

Holmes conversed with the Tuaregs in broken Tamasheq.

"Do you live here?"

"Yes, near Gao."

"How do you know Hasso?"

"He is our uncle. You are his friends. So you are our friends." He smiled.

"And we know how you helped our brothers in Morocco."

"Can anyone stop us before Gao?" inquired Holmes.

"We shall only stop at familiar villages. We are quite safe from here till at least Gao. We shall be in the care of the Kel Gossi, a Tuareg tribe of that area."

"Do you know this boatman?"

"Yes, do not worry. He is an old Fulani friend," the boatman reassured Holmes.

"How long will it take?"

"We may have to halt at sunset at a small village along the way. If we start again at dawn we should be there quickly."

Holmes was satisfied, and sat back in his wooden seat, in a familiar posture recalling our tête-à-têtes at 221B Baker Street, a world away.

"Ah, Watson, an idyllic journey, would you not concede? A trifle warmer than London perhaps, but this interlude allows us to rest and collect our thoughts. I will show you the complete parchment when we reach a position of safety. I have already committed its contents to memory, in the event we are overtaken by forces beyond our control. I hope Hasso is able to avoid trouble and reach Gao. We have had a charmed life thus far. I expected trouble at Sankore Mosque, but we were lucky. We must leave the influence of Timbuktu as soon as possible."

"Rather than return the same way as we entered, you believe we should go east, Holmes? From what I have gathered, it is extremely dangerous in addition to having an inhospitable climate." I was very surprised.

"Those are the precise reasons why I brought our Tuareg friends along and why going east is what anyone else will not believe we could consider, Watson."

"If you had not taken the trouble to learn Arabic and Tamasheq in Tangier, the result might have been considerably different, Holmes. I must compliment you."

"You flatter me, Watson, my dear fellow. Planning is everything, Watson, everything!"

Shortly thereafter, with the sounds of the chattering of monkeys and the gentle splash of water providing an agreeable soporific symphony, I fell asleep.

When I woke after a half hour, I found Holmes with an open map of Africa that he had borrowed from the office of the late Antonio Rozzi, considering various options.

"Ah, Watson, a pleasant nap, it would seem. I fear that the Guardians, after some initial inquiries, may conclude quite correctly that we are likely to go east toward Gao. They are not Tuaregs and do not have connections in various tribes.

"For now, Watson, let us take the time to enjoy the finer things in life, such as the wonderful music of Mali, instead of confirming the stereotype of stuffy Englishmen who have no idea how to enjoy themselves. Try to sing wildly, Watson, without a care in the world, without wondering if you are in tune or not and whether your actions would invite disapproving comments and censure! Look at how well the Tuaregs enjoy themselves. And look at that young, smiling boy with his n'Goni! Is he worried about Eton and Cambridge and a club where he will waste hours together looking pompous? No! We have much to learn from them, Watson!"

I demurred. "Yes, Holmes. It will be difficult to dance on this boat, with crocodiles looking on, but I shall follow your advice at the opportune time."

Holmes muttered something under his breath, which I could not understand because of the *tagelmust.*[22]

"Would you recommend I write a monograph on the architecture of the Sankore Mosque or the salt mines at Taghaza or the music of the Tuaregs, Watson?" he asked. "Or perhaps all three?"

"Holmes, I find it alarming that at this time, when we are likely chased by men armed to the teeth, who look forward to our death, you are considering the production of monographs! Can this matter not wait?"

Holmes sighed. "Watson, you certainly are from England."

"And so are you." I was puzzled. "But how is that relevant now, Holmes?"

"If only you knew, Watson, if only you knew," Holmes puffed at his pipe, looking away.

Time passed on the boat, with the natives occasionally using tobacco as a stimulant. The taciturn natives have extraordinary powers of endurance, I must confess, and go on paddling or steering for hours on end without rest or refreshment. They would occasionally exclaim "*Tara! Tara! Bosos*!", a refrain to encourage everyone to push on. The colour of the river seemed to change relentlessly, sometimes blue, sometimes black, sometimes grey. It was never still.

The flow and depth of the Niger between Bamako toward the west of Mali and through the rest of the country past Timbuktu and Gao was erratic. During the dry season, entire stretches of the river bottom were exposed to the hot sun and people would grow vegetables there. Only expert boatmen would know which stream of the mighty Niger to take. But when the volume of water increased, it was an entirely different story. It was a most charming river with its own personality. The Thames, I must reluctantly admit, does not possess such colour; it is a civilized river—though rather anaemic— for a civilized people.

It seems perhaps the right time to make a few, brief observations of the people and the countryside which we passed on

[22] It could not possibly have been "This man is so constipated."

our boat. The objective of this book is not to constantly feed the appetite of the reader of *The Strand* who hungers for death, danger, and destruction on every page of a book. The wide variety of human endeavour must be acknowledged graciously, even if they are entirely alien to our thinking. Though the advanced thinking of the European is not in doubt, the character of the natives of the region deserves mention. The reader will benefit by being aware of peoples and cultures. Humility is a hallmark of our civilization, after all.

We passed by little villages where the women folk were busy washing clothes and attending to their household tasks. Most did not wear anything above their waists while holding on to their infants. There was no shyness—the embarrassment was only ours. A wave from Holmes or me would invariably get a smiling response. "*Annisagai!*" or good day was our passport to a friendly passage and goodwill. As a physician, I would easily see that the bloated stomachs of the young children splashing at the banks were often a sign of a constitutional ailment caused by a nutritional anomaly. But who would have gleaned that from their wide and innocent smiles and cheerful shouts?

The many tribes and ethnic groups that swirl in circles of varying radii around Timbuktu, and certainly along the Niger, are usually minimally Islamic in their religious affiliation. However, they continue to worship spirits and ghosts, and interpret events and the future based on, for example, the sounds of animals. The griot storytellers and historians are in demand and greatly respected for their knowledge. The observance of the tenets of Islam seemed to diffuse as the distance from Timbuktu increased.

All this is true of the Tuaregs, too, who selectively follow the precepts of Islam, but continue age-old traditions such as insisting that women not be veiled.

Witchcraft continues to be accepted without question and a witch-doctor is trusted implicitly, a matter that might raise the eyebrows of our finest physicians at Harley Street, products of the rational science that is at the foundation of the advanced European civilization.

Holmes was lost in thought, looking east as the boat moved along the Niger.

"Watson, there are two matters that I must tell you about. One, that we shall get off at Bourem instead of Gao. Hasso is aware of this. Only he and I know this. If he has passed through Timbuktu unscathed, he should be arriving at Bourem very soon. We deliberately spoke of going to Gao because it seems like a likely destination for anyone travelling to Yaounde, from where we could presumably find a way to travel to Europe, though of course, one of the large ports in the Niger Coast Protectorate is a more logical choice.

"I have studied the map of this region carefully with Hasso. If anyone is in pursuit, they can hope to cut us off by crossing the Niger at the point where we began our travels on this boat. Then they can dash east and reach Gao very quickly. Therefore, we decided that getting off at Bourem is best. From there, we travel east to Kidal, race across the desert to Abalessa and proceed east. Our objective now, broadly speaking, is to travel carefully through the French and uncharted territories, Watson, and reach Khartoum. From there, we must find the lost valley in the lower Nile and complete our journey. I expect it will take us at least two months, Hasso has made excellent arrangements and we shall be relieved of the heat of the desert once we pass Gao."

I was dismayed. "Why Sudan, Holmes? Would that not delay our return to the Vatican?"

"Ah, but are we returning to the Vatican, Watson? Why should we?"

"But if you have successfully collected both parts of the manuscript, that concludes the mission!" I cried out.

"Does it, indeed, Watson? No. I have thought about the matter. The Vatican has no obvious right over this valuable piece of knowledge. It belongs to mankind. It is inconceivable that we should come all this way and not travel to the place marked in the map. There we ought to verify the facts. That was my second point."

I was considerably chagrined by this change in plan. I had imagined that this adventure was at its logical end, provided we were able to slip away from the Guardians.

"And to answer your unspoken question, Watson, I have already made arrangements to recompense the Vatican for its expenses made toward my welfare all this time. I am not a crook."

"I—I never meant to imply—," I stammered in embarrassment.

"Think nothing of it, Watson. "

At Bourem, where we finally got off the boat, we were met by other Tuaregs who were also waiting for Hasso Ag Akotey to arrive. Holmes showed one of the senior Tuaregs a slip of paper in Hasso's hand.

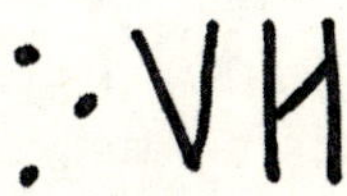

"What is that, Holmes?"

"I believe it reads 'Kidal' in Tifinagh, which is where they are to take us, perhaps, in case Hasso is unable to reach this place."

While we waited, we were entertained by some griots who sang songs describing the history of the land, including the great feats of the Songhay kings, of wars where they always emerged victorious. Holmes took notes and engaged in long conversations with them using the Tuaregs as interpreters.

I was content to walk along the banks of the Niger, admiring the raw charm of the flora and fauna. I walked very close to a large rock python, and only knew about it after one of the Tuaregs called out excitedly and drew my attention to it.

In a few hours, we spotted a caravan approaching from the west. Yes, it was Hasso Ag Akotey and his group! There was a sense of relief amongst us as greetings were exchanged.

The news was not encouraging. "The Guardians are certainly chasing us and hoping to intercept us at Gao. They have guns too. The matter could be quite serious. We must leave immediately for Kidal." Hasso was tense but clear about what to do next.

Without much ado, we continued our journey north east to Kidal. The caravan now consisted of about fifteen, with a few of the original group having returned toward Tangier in the original bid to confuse our pursuers.

◇◇◇

The report of Omar Al-Bidisi, a senior Guardian of the Letter. It was found as a diary entry on his person many months later.

The journey from Tangier to Timbuktu had been very stressful for our master. He had no experience travelling long distances on camels in such hot and dry conditions. As we raced after the Tuaregs who were with the Father, we were constantly held back by his problems. We had started a week after them, but a week is not much. Our group was small but agile, and there was a possibility that we could catch up especially because their caravan was twice as large. Unfortunately, the Master pulled us back unintentionally.

He could not handle the sand and heat for long periods and we had to stop after every two hours. Alas, he found his camel uncomfortable. The food did not agree with him quite often. He frequently panted for long periods in the heat and even became unconscious once near Taghaza. We were very concerned and thought we would lose him. He was eventually revived, and then we wondered momentarily if it might not be better to return to Morocco. But we really had no choice. The mission was clear. To catch the Father, kill him and his companions if necessary, and retrieve the missing part of the manuscript. This was the command of our leader, as well our advisor in Paris. Once both parts of the manuscript were safely in the hands of the Master, we would take him back to Tangier. We hoped to then serve him for the rest of our lives.

But he was otherwise cheerful and kept us happy with his stories about the strange people of India. We had some vague idea about the Hindus, but his description of their peculiar religious beliefs was confounding. We sometimes laughed loudly when he talked about their many gods and the strange things they would do to idols. The fact that they cremated their dead was quite horrifying. It had indeed been mentioned in *Al-Rihla,* as someone reminded us. The great Ibn Batuta had been right, after all.

The Master also talked about the heavy rains, their unimaginable vegetables and languages. He had brought some spices with him which he generously gave to all of us. Even though we had spent several months in his mansion in Casablanca, we had not known this side of him. Truly, it is said that only when you travel with a man do you really know him.

He said that the journey across the desert seemed, somehow, seemed familiar. Perhaps the memories of Ibn Batuta were within him, and he could sense the presence of that great man who must have walked on the very same path hundreds of years ago.

We were attacked by a group of bandits shortly after Taghaza. They probably thought we were merchants. They had not known who we were, and within half an hour we had killed three of them and sent the others away. We captured one and took him with us to Timbuktu to alert us of other possible bandit groups who might be waiting to ambush us. Once we reached Timbuktu, we killed him. Despite our difficulties, we had managed to move quickly and completed the journey in about fifty days, which was slightly better than most other journeys over this path.

When we reached Timbuktu, we heard at the *abaradiou* that the group ahead of us had left just a day earlier. Some said a few had returned to Tangier and others said they had gone east. The situation in Timbuktu was not good, with the French harassing travellers and strangers at random, and other political forces active. We were advised to finish whatever work we had come for and leave Timbuktu as soon as possible.

The Master, Boughaid Arroub, and I proceeded to the Sankore Mosque. After some initial inquiries, we were escorted in to meet the Imam, whose name was Haji Al-Kaburi. We bowed low as we entered.

"I welcome you to Timbuktu and to our madrassah. How can we help you, travellers?" The Imam was very polite and gracious.

"We have just arrived from Tangier, Haji, and have a matter to discuss." Boughaid Arroub bowed respectfully.

"That is a coincidence! We just had a visitor from Tangier, though he was from Uzbekistan. We feel happy when so many visitors come here. First, I must insist that you have some refreshments!" The Haji called out to a slave, and within a few minutes we were seated on thick rugs, drinking mint tea.

"Haji, we are on an important mission. Our Master here is from India and has come all the way to meet you."

Haji Al-Kaburi was very pleased. He beamed. "All the way from India? Al-Hind! Wonderful! Wonderful! Our madrassah's fame has spread so far! And what is your name sir?" he said, beaming at the Master.

"My name is Thalassery Vatoot Mohammad Koya and I am a descendant of the great traveller Ibn Batuta," said the Master in his accented Arabic.

Haji Al-Kaburi put his cup of tea down abruptly, spilling some on his spotless white dress. "What?"

The Master repeated what he had just said.

The Haji stared at us. His mouth was open and his eyes were wide, displaying immense shock and confusion.

"I—I—don't know what to s-say," he stammered after several minutes.

"Wait, let me call my colleagues," he finally said, struggling to find words. He called out to some slaves asking them to get Haji Toumani Kouyate and Haji Mohammad Yahya Wangari. He was told that they were teaching.

"Tell them it is very urgent. They must come immediately!" His tone was quite vehement.

While we waited, Haji Al-Kaburi continued looking at us in a strange way. None of us spoke. We felt uneasy and nervous. The atmosphere was tense. We looked at the walls, the drapes, the floor, and the windows.

In a few minutes, both the Hajis rushed in, perplexed by the unusual summons.

Haji Al-Kaburi asked them to sit. He was very nervous. Both looked surprised to see him in such a state.

Then he asked the Master to introduce himself to the two new Hajis.

"My name is Thalassery Vatoot Mohammad Koya and I am a descendant of the great traveller Ibn Batuta," said the Master, bowing low.

The reaction from both the Hajis was identical to the one previous. They were completely taken aback. They looked at each other. One of them spoke. "We are very surprised."

He paused. "We have only the day before said good-bye to another descendant of the late Ibn Batuta!"

It was our turn to be surprised.

"How is that possible, Hajis? We have a letter of introduction!"

"And so did he. Please show the letter to us."

We handed it over and all three read the letter carefully. Then they again looked at each other. They put the letter on a small table.

"Well, you will have to excuse our confusion," said Haji Toumani Kouyate, agitated. "Over the past few days, we met another man who said he, too, was the descendant of Ibn Batuta. He, too, had a letter of introduction that seemed genuine."

"Can you please describe him?" asked Boughaid Arroub, leaning forward.

"He was tall, quite slim, a slightly hooked nose, sharp features. He spoke broken Arabic and said he was from Uzbekistan."

We looked at each other and nodded. He was certainly referring to Father Bąkiewicz, the man we were pursuing.

"And he said he was a descendant of Ibn Batuta?"

"Yes. As I mentioned, he had brought with him a letter of introduction."

"May we see it?"

"Certainly. Let me go and get it." Haji Al-Kaburi got up from his seat with the help of his slaves. He walked to a room at the back, trembling noticeably. In a few minutes, he returned with some papers and sat down again. He looked at his colleagues, seemingly to get their approval for what he was about to do. They nodded.

"Here is the letter," he said, offering it to us.

The three of us looked at the letter with the seal of Osman Beg. The letter looked authentic. Anyone could have been fooled. I could sense it was a brilliant forgery—the script, the folds, the smudges, the dirt, the delicate nature of the paper itself, the seal—someone had taken a lot of trouble. The matter was very serious.

"This is a forgery, Hajis. We have no information of the existence of a son in Uzbekistan who might have had a descendant."

"A forgery? Well, you may be right, but how do we know who *you* are?"

"What exactly did this man do here, Hajis?" inquired Boughaid Arroub, ignoring the question.

"Unless we know who you are, there is no need for us to give you any information," snapped the definitely upset Haji Toumani Kouyate, taking back the letter from Boughaid Arroub.

"We have a letter of introduction."

"And so did this man Yaqub Beg Batuta. He had a letter of introduction, too, and he said the very same thing to prove that he was a descendant."

"Have you read *Al-Rihla,* Haji?"

"Yes."

"Was there a mention of a child in the Maldives?"

"Implicitly, perhaps, I think so."

"Was there a mention of one in Uzbekistan?"

"Not that I can recall."

"Well?"

Haji Toumani Kouyate was getting more and more annoyed. "This is not an examination. Yaqub Beg Batuta convinced us about this seeming gap. I do not know why we are having this talk. I see four possibilities. One, that he told us the truth and you are liars. Two—"

"We are NOT liars!" Boughaid Arroub shouted. He was upset and tried to get onto his feet. The Master and I restrained him and pulled him down.

Haji Toumani Kouyate continued. "Two, that *he* was a liar and we were cheated—though cheated of what is the question since we did not and even now have no idea of the value of what was inside. It was not our business. And therefore, that you are telling us the truth."

"Yes, clearly!"

"Three, that both of you—you and Yaqub Beg—are liars. Or, four, that both of you are telling us the truth, and perhaps both, this man and Yaqub Beg, are descendants! That is quite possible because it is quite unlikely that anyone but the descendants would know about the existence of a buried box at Sankore. But that question is not of relevance.

"Is it not odd that after almost six hundred years, two men claiming to be descendants of Ibn Batuta come to our Sankore Mosque and present letters of introduction, asking for documents that we did not know existed? And all this happens in the space of a few days! There is something peculiar here, but we will not allow ourselves to be taken advantage of and made fools of!

"And do not try to be violent here," he wagged his index finger angrily at Boughaid Arroub, his eyes red. "This is a madrassah, a place for learning. We are not fools. All my slaves are armed and others will be summoned in seconds! In this holy place, all who visit must be humble and be calm and respectful."

I intervened.

"Haji, we are sorry. We did not intend to upset you. Now you see, this matter is very serious. We are the keepers of the heritage of Ibn Batuta. This man here is indeed the descendant of Ibn Batuta. We will do our best to prove it to you."

Haji Mohammad Yahya Wangari, who seemed the most calm and thoughtful of the three, intervened.

"Whether you prove it or not, the question really is, why? How will it help you or us? What difference does it make to you or to us?"

"Haji, as the letter has said, we have come to request you for whatever Ibn Batuta left behind in your safekeeping."

The three looked at each other again.

"Well, my question is still valid. It makes no difference to anyone whether you are who you say you are. The mistake committed in good faith by the Imam of the mosque so many years ago has come back to trouble us. The fact is that we do not have what you seek. The previous claimant also possessed what he said was proof, and what we, as men of God and as teachers, believed was true. He took away a box of documents that Ibn Batuta had indeed left behind here."

We were utterly shocked.

"How could you do that?" screamed Boughaid Arroub, extremely agitated. "That man was an imposter! You have betrayed the trust of Ibn Batuta!"

"We have done no such thing. We are not worldly men. If a man comes to us with proof of something, we are not equipped with more than simple ways to see if he is telling the truth. Do not reach for your daggers and swords! We are not frightened!"

Al-Kaburi raised his hands, gesturing for calm.

"Brothers. Let us be calm. Let us try to understand each other. A man comes to our mosque and says he is the descendant of Ibn Batuta. He brings us proof that is convincing to us. True, Haji Toumani Kouyate was initially suspicious. However, even he was eventually convinced that the man was telling us the truth. We helped this man, Yakub Beg, find what he wanted. We did not ask him what was inside as it was not our business. We were custodians, no more, no less. Then Yaqub Beg left, saying he was to go to Yaounde and he even invited us to Bukhara.

"Let us say that he was an imposter. Let us say that you, sir,"—he nodded at Koya—"you, are the real descendant of Ibn Batuta. We do not have any means to determine if that is true. The letter you have shown us is as convincing as the one Yaqub Beg showed us. Even if we believe you, the problem is that we cannot help you. Yaqub Beg is gone with the box that you seek. Perhaps it contains matters of great importance. But we cannot take responsibility for it beyond a point."

The Master was surprisingly calm. "Haji, I understand what

you are saying. Let us confirm this—you say that a box was found and it was taken away by this man called Yaqub Beg."

"Yes."

"Did he look inside?"

"Yes, briefly. He even showed us a paper that was nothing but some kind of shopping list, clearly in the hand of Ibn Batuta. Then he shut the box again and left."

"And was he was satisfied by what he saw inside?"

"As I said, there were a number of documents. He just went through a few of them quickly. He did not say anything. I have no idea if there was something specific he was looking for."

"I see. When did he leave with the box and where did he say he was going?"

"Two days ago. He said he was going to Yaounde to visit a friend and then to take a ship to return to Tangier and then back to Bukhara."

The Master spoke to us in a low whisper.

"There is no point in getting these men upset. They are simple *marabouts*. They have been fooled by Yaqub Beg, this so-called Father. The best thing to do is to chase him and find him, don't you agree?"

We reluctantly agreed that it made sense.

"So let us leave quietly and then make inquiries. Such a large caravan could not have left without being noticed. If we think carefully, we should be able to catch up with them."

"I agree," said Boughaid Arroub, looking sullen.

The Master turned to the three Hajis, who looked very serious and grim. He bowed. "We are very sorry for this situation. We sincerely believe Yaqub Beg was an imposter and he has tricked you into parting with some very valuable manuscripts. But you are not at fault, and it was not your responsibility to verify the matter beyond what you did. I am indeed the descendant of Ibn Batuta, but at this moment, nothing will be achieved by explaining the facts and proving it to you. Once we track down and retrieve the box, I shall return and discuss the matter."

The three men nodded, but without any enthusiasm.

We got up and bowed to the *marabouts* and walked out of the mosque.

We walked silently to the *arabadiou*, lost in our thoughts. Had hundreds of years converged to this single moment of loss? The matter was very upsetting. But somehow, the calm demeanour of the Master made us feel better.

We spoke to the Negroes at the *abaradiou* again. They said that some members of the other group had returned to Tangier via Taghaza, and the rest had gone east toward Gao. They had not paid attention to any specific member of the caravan though they did remember a tall, slim Tuareg who was always accompanied by a shorter, stouter Tuareg, who they thought was his slave.

We sat in a circle on our haunches and drew maps on the sand with long twigs.

"I do not think they have returned to Tangier. It was just a simple trick. They must have known we were following. Only very experienced Tuaregs would travel in a very small band across the desert. The Father is not a Tuareg. It would have been too risky for him to travel with a very small group. I am sure he went east with the bigger group."

"If we chase them, we may never catch up. They are Tuaregs and know the desert. They would also guess we are following."

"The river bends south after Bourem here."

"So anyone going east might follow the river going south to Niamey and beyond."

"But if we cross the river just south of Timbuktu, we could then go east and catch them at Gao, could we not?" asked the Master.

"Yes, that is a good idea."

"Yes, we can save time. They might not expect that."

"Of course, there is a small risk. What if they are NOT going to Yaounde?" asked the Master, keenly.

"Then they would be going east, and would follow a path to the south of Lake Chad. But that area is hostile. He might then travel to the Nile."

"That is possible," nodded the Master. "I suggest that we cross the Niger and go east. If we catch them at Gao, fine. If not, then we travel east from Gao."

"We may not be able to do that, Master," Boughaid Arroub demurred. "The desert there is very harsh. Some say even harsher than what we just experienced. Let us remember that we are not Tuaregs. Only our guides are. They may not travel further east than…say, Tamanrasset. They would need a reason, which we do not have yet."

"Well, let us start and think of possibilities along the way. It may be better for us to simply follow them as they have the complete map. Let them lead us to the treasure. I am sure that is where they wish to go. The Father is a very shrewd man, according to our Paris advisor. He always has many options for action. Nothing is done without a reason." The Master had suddenly transformed into a natural leader after reaching Timbuktu, with a tendency toward firm action. We were happy; this was very necessary.

There was no time to waste. Our caravan began immediately. We moved relatively quickly down to Kabara, an access point to the Niger River, with the intention of crossing it and travelling to Gao.

Inside Sankore Mosque, there was a tense silence as the three Hajis considered the events of the day and of the past few days.

"Let us discuss this tomorrow, after we have slept over the matter," mumbled Haji Al-Kaburi in a low voice.

The others did not respond. They got up and left the room. The mint tea had lost its flavour, in any case.

From Timbuktu to Tamanrasset

As we moved toward Kidal, I felt a little more at ease. Everything had gone with relative smoothness, and though we had faced tense moments, we had emerged unscathed. We were aware that we were being pursued, but did not feel discomfited. Our Tuareg friends were with us and, in fact, we had added several more at Bourem. The journey to Kidal and beyond to Tamanrasset was through terrain that was firmly theirs and that they knew intimately.

But I was quite confused. I could understand the need to mislead our pursuers and be on the move. And yet, this refusal by Holmes to trace a path back to Rome was inexplicable. Why then had he spent so much time in Tangier? Had he not himself agreed to take up the assignment? Was it not, somehow, an ethical violation?

As always, Holmes could feel the presence of Professor Moriarty in the hostile environment of the Sahara. The man had perhaps barely moved from the chair in his study somewhere in an anonymous apartment in Paris. But through his vast network, and despite the nonexistent means of communication, he had ensured that pressure was being relentlessly applied on us. He wanted what Holmes had. And he intended to get it. I felt like an onlooker to a game of chess, played across deserts and countries, with others acting as proxies for Professor Moriarty. I was dissatisfied by my own involvement; but I was consoled by the fact that Holmes reiterated many times that he felt so much more at ease whenever I gave him company.

But where were we going now? Why this abrupt change in direction, from a presumed flight to the south where we would, I had thought, board a ship and return to England to a more salubrious climate with the pleasant advantage of British mores? Instead, we were now moving northeast, and from what I could gather, would thereafter continue to the east across brutal deserts and roving bandits. When I asked him how long it might take, his answer was cryptic: "Months." What must my wife be thinking? I worried. Holmes read my mind and said, "Give Mrs. Watson credit, my dear fellow. Her intelligence is acute, and she knows you are with me." His answer reassured me but confused me a little more. Was there a subtle hint in what he had said? I could not put my finger on it.

The deserts of the Sahel do not lend themselves to the beauty of poetry in the first instance. Shakespeare might have been at a loss for words to see endless shifting sands, a hot sun that did not tire of extending itself day after day, and acacia trees of no interest to anyone except our beatific camels who were quite satisfied moving over dune after dune without a break.

The caravan proceeded with new energy. I had become accustomed to the rhythmic movements and the personality of my camel, which, on a whim, I named Freddy, a matter that amused the group. Somehow Freddy always sensed when I was tired and would stop and allow himself to be brought down to the level of the desert. I often fed him acacia, some millets, and anything edible that I had. It was a curious and satisfying bond. It was a small lesson on how all creatures depend on each other for survival in a land that otherwise is merciless and does not yield to prayers.

The men sang beautiful poems they called *tisiway*. Holmes had a fine baritone and joined them. These interludes broke the monotonous journey. The Tuaregs who had joined us at

Bourem were particularly musical. An old man, Amaha Ag Barha, turned out to be a blacksmith with a gift for storytelling. Due to his Inaden caste, he was always at the periphery of the group, but respected at the same time. A couple of men were, in fact, slaves but they seemed to behave quite like the others. These social dynamics were mystifying, but I saw that Holmes took everything in his stride and did not pass any judgment.

"How strange the Tuareg society is, Holmes! Everyone is born into a profession! These castes are mystifying!" I remarked.

"If we were to take our Tuareg friends to England, might they not find our ways absurd, Watson?" asked Holmes, needlessly caustic, I thought. "Kings and queens, altogether absurdly complex protocols involving dukes, earls, and lords. Understatements. Double negatives. Stiff upper lips. Raised eyebrows. Tea and crumpets. Clubs. Cricket. How odd it would seem to the Tuaregs!"

"No doubt for a moment an outsider would be surprised. But I am sure they would grow to appreciate the superior logic and adapt to it."

The sun was in my eyes and so I was unable to discern the expression on Holmes' countenance as he turned abruptly in my direction. He did not say anything; perhaps he appreciated the validity of my argument.

I befriended Amaha Ag Barha along the way and we tried to communicate with each other. Other friends translated his tales and I was extremely impressed by his ability to relate a story with such energy and animation.[23] He was a master storyteller who used very few words, supplemented with modulated words,

---

[23] Of late, the modern editor—female, as only to be expected—gratuitously offers advice to writers underlining a newly invented phrase, "show, don't tell." It means, in an extremely roundabout way, that elaborate details are needed, rather than to make a simple point and let it stand on its own and let the reader make an effort to exercise his imagination. It appears that the modern reader today wants explicit information and is not interested in the exhausting exercise of visualization. When confronted with such a demand by the writer, he is likely to sulk and complain in a letter to the newspaper editor, appropriating to himself the qualities of an outstanding literary critic. I differ firmly. The modern reader is lazy, I regret to say (except for you, dear reader; you are a rare exception).

music, and mime, to convey the richness of a tale. The Tuareg culture does not encourage verbosity, which I must appreciate. Their own written script, Tifinagh, is noted for its brevity and is learned in a way entirely different from the way we learn the alphabet. That is, children pick it up by imitation and through games in a markedly informal manner, and there is no concept of a classroom. I mention this because I understood its merit while communicating with Amaha Ag Barha. Over the long distance between Bourem and Abalessa, he must have recounted about twenty stories of considerable merit. I have translated them and propose to submit them to a high quality publisher, of which there are so few, to bring attention to the admirable literature of the Tuaregs, a project that received Holmes' enthusiastic blessings. I have included one such tale in the appendix, ambitiously called *Poems in Sand*; I hope you find it of interest. I personally found its lyrical quality fascinating.

We continued onward to Kidal. The journey was under two hundred miles. We expected to travel at a moderately rapid speed of about thirty to thirty-five miles per day, as we were not loaded and our camels were relatively fresh. At Kidal, we would again load up for the journey to Tamanrasset.

Kidal was known for Tuareg music and art, we discovered. Holmes and I enjoyed the journey to Kidal and spent the entire day there listening to various musicians.

"A significantly advanced conceptualization of the value of rhythm and melody, Watson," Holmes commented. "I find their *imzad* to be of particular interest. Observe the parallels to the violin. I shall now make an attempt to learn from them."

"You should teach them, too, Holmes," I said, disapproving of his putting this rustic—though admittedly attractive—music on a pedestal.

"To me, at the moment, I must assert that their music is superior, Watson. Say no more," Holmes snapped.

At Kidal, Holmes and the local *imzad* maestro Omar Ag Oumbadougou performed an excellent duet for a large crowd of Tuaregs from various clans like the Kel Ahaggar and the Kel Adagh. They laughed and clapped and shouted. On Holmes' advice, I did the same, though I felt that music should be listened to quietly and respectfully. I must confess it was a delightful auditory and visual sensation, though extremely alien. The men and women swayed and clapped, expressing their appreciation loudly and without inhibition at various points. Others musicians joined with the *tende*, a percussion instrument and an *ajouag*, a flute. The ululation of the female singers provided a most unusual musical interjection that was first quite alarming and then suddenly most apt.

Omar Ag Oumbadougou and Holmes exchanged instruments and tried to play them, much to the amusement of the onlookers. Holmes had indeed fully immersed himself into the culture of the Tuaregs, and they in turn were deeply appreciative of his sincere attempts.

The conflicts with the French threatened to disturb the Tuareg culture, Holmes said. It had the unusual effect of stimulating their outstanding musical gifts even further. I made a note of a charming melody that the Tuaregs sang.[24]

Matadjem yinmixan sarhremt yaratan Tojawan alrhalem, taterarawan	*Why this hate between you that you teach your children The world looks at you. It is beyond your understanding*
War toliham id"koufar war toli- ham d"araban Tomanam istiwsaten tidit tindarawan	*You who resemble neither a westerner nor an Arab Your faith in the tribes blinds you to the truth*
Wada al assawka iyalah walaiyen dowan adahar D"Imidinet taflist is wadek atekdar	*Even if God were to send a blessing down for you to share With a friend, they would only betray you*

But it was soon time to leave. The caravan departed from Kidal with hundreds of Tuaregs bidding us good-bye and wishing

[24] Lyrics of a contemporary song by the Tuareg group Tinariwen

us well. We were now on our way to the grave of Tin Hanan, whom the Tuaregs called "the Mother of us all." Of course, we had not forgotten that there was every possibility of the Guardians following us, but we felt safer somehow, deep in Tuareg territory. Hasso Ag Akotey had left instructions with the elders in Kidal town to distract and delay any caravan with Tuareg guides who inquired about us.

Kidal to Tamanrasset was to be a gruelling journey, almost four times the distance between Bourem and Kidal. This time, many families had joined the caravan, so we could not expect to move as fast. The Tuaregs had prepared carefully but I could sense a palpable tension. There were two reasons—one, they expected bandit raids. And, two, more positively, they were looking forward to see the grave of Tin Hanan. It was essentially a dangerous pilgrimage.

Holmes, Hasso Ag Akotey, some other senior Imajaghan Ahaggar Tuaregs, and I sat around a campsite one night.

"We wish to visit Abalessa and the grave of Tin Hanan, to pay our respects," said Holmes solemnly, in Tamasheq. "We seek your permission."

The Tuaregs are not talkative. The circumspect man commands greater regard in their society. Only fools are given to excessive talk, is the belief.

Hasso Ag Akotey knew Holmes' plan in detail of course, but it was important for the rest to understand who these travellers were and what their mission was. He kept his counsel.

"She is our Mother," said one of the Tuaregs briefly, looking at the sand. It was an important statement, perhaps not original. He was simply emphasizing once again how sacred the place was.

"Yes. I hold her in great regard."

"Only Tuaregs are allowed," said another, looking at his feet.

Holmes paused. It was a delicate point. The statement was not a challenge. Holmes was being encouraged to help them decide in his favour.

"I shall go only as far as you allow me. I have come from far away. I am an outsider but I hope you will accept me as a

Tuareg, though I was not born one. I wish to be blessed by the *tamenukalt*, the leader. I seek your permission."

At this point, Hasso spoke in a low voice about Holmes and how he had helped him in Tangier against the tricks of the hated French. There were nods and grunts of appreciation. They were already aware of these facts. No one spoke. Then there were some low whispers.

Hasso turned toward us shortly. "They will tell you tomorrow after discussing the matter."

We stood up and left the group. They wished to discuss the matter privately.

Early next morning, we continued toward Tamanrasset. We were on guard against bandits, though the size of the caravan had become unwieldy with the addition of many women and children. The size of a caravan did not guarantee safety. The right men had to be assigned as scouts and equipped with weapons. The most valuable goods had to be placed at a precise location within the caravan. We had to think about where the women and children were to be in the sequence.

We stopped at various points for one reason or the other. During the afternoon halts and just before we rested at night, Holmes went about practising his Tamasheq while I spoke with Amaha Ag Barha, the storyteller. Holmes proved to be very popular with the children, playing their games and puzzles with enthusiasm. The Tuaregs found the matter amusing.

One day, we passed through a hilly area with no particular distinctive feature, except that the path had a number of ups and downs. It was very picturesque and I could imagine some of our painters in London and Paris being quite content to paint the vistas of endless sands studded with mesas and unexpected rocky outcrops. The camels moved at a steady clip. We were an hour away from stopping to rest before the heat of the sun became unbearable. Holmes and I were in the second half of the caravan. The chatter and laughter of children provided a most pleasant diversion. The camel in front had three children seated on it and they made faces at Freddy and me, just as little children do. Freddy was the picture of equanimity. I smiled and waved at the children who responded with shrill shouts of excitement. Their games continued for hours.

No one anticipated the attack.

From behind a hilly outcrop, a large number of bandits on horses and camels suddenly came dashing out as one large unit, swords raised, shouting in the most fearsome and bloodcurdling manner. Since the first half of our caravan had just turned around a bend that was also at a downward incline, they were at a disadvantage and could not easily swing back to join the rest of the caravan. Further, a lot of the heavier loads were on the camels in the front, making their job even tougher. The latter half, in which Holmes and I were situated, was, in effect, left to our own devices against a group of ferocious, armed bandits who additionally had the element of surprise. Holmes and I had only primitive revolvers. And, seated on camels, we could not have aimed and fired at anyone with the constantly moving targets.

We tried our best to group together with the camels in an outward-facing circle and women and children pushed into the centre. But time was not on our side. The Tuaregs took out their spears and swords and assumed a defensive posture as the bandits came swooping along. In no time at all, two Tuaregs were killed and another seriously injured. Fear and panic gripped most of the caravan, while the first half tried to return to our aid. In the melee, we lost our places. Agitated camels dashed about, separating families. The sounds of shots being fired, the yelling of men and the screaming of the women, the dust and sand—everything created chaos in a manner I had not experienced even in battles in Afghanistan.

All of a sudden, a Tuareg from our midst suddenly dashed out with a sword, yelling in the most bloodthirsty manner. Through a sudden gap, he directed his camel at the chief of the bandits who happened to be slightly behind his team, directing the raid. Before the bandits could respond to the maverick Tuareg's single-man attack, the chief's horse panicked at the sight of the camel running straight at him. It turned, neighing in fear, and ran in the opposite direction, with the Tuareg's camel in hot pursuit.

The unexpected turn of events caused a brief period of confusion, with the bandits not knowing whether to continue their attack or rescue their chief. For a few critical moments, they lost their confidence. Meanwhile, the rest of the Tuaregs had regrouped, having climbed back up the incline and now had the advantage of a flat terrain from which to mount a counterattack.

Three bandits were cut down in fierce combat and two more were knocked off their steeds. The tide had turned in minutes. The bandits pulled back and fled, heading back toward the protective rocky outcrop from whence they had emerged. The bandit chief and the chasing Tuareg were nowhere in sight.

The caravan regrouped, with screaming women, crying children, and shouting men adding to the chaos. Suddenly, a woman shouted, pointing.

We looked and saw the missing Tuareg returning slowly to the caravan. He appeared to be seriously injured; he was clutching his right upper arm with one hand and his stomach with the other, and was leaning forward in his saddle in a position suggesting acute distress.

I realized to my utter horror that the Tuareg was none other than Holmes, and that he was severely wounded.

As he approached, the Tuaregs surrounded him and the camel with great cries of joy. As far as they were concerned, this man was a hero, and indeed he was. Holmes had taken the battle to the chief of the bandits, an act of incredible boldness against all odds.

They helped a barely conscious Holmes down from the camel and brought him to me. I quickly stripped away the cloth at the upper arm where he was bleeding. There was a bullet in his abdomen, too, which could potentially have been more serious.

"He fired at me with a rifle at rather close quarters, my dear fellow," mumbled Holmes, looking at me with a wan smile. "He escaped, unfortunately. Now, are you all right, Watson?"

"Not a word from you, my dear Holmes!" I cried, utterly shaken. "Not a word! The wounds appear to be deep! I shall have to remove the bullets immediately—you have lost a lot of blood!"

"How are the children? And check on my violin, my dear Watson. A most temperamental instrument unused to bloodshed and chaos. We must hurry on, time is of the essen—"

Holmes fainted dead away in my arms; the Tuaregs collectively cried out in alarm. I took him to the shade under a large boulder and set him down on a sheet. The Tuaregs boiled some water for me and I took out my instruments. I was able to remove the bullets from his arm and abdomen, and then clean and dress the wounds.

I stood up and looked down at our hero. Sherlock Holmes was still unconscious. It would have been good to give him blood but we lacked the ability to do this in the middle of the Sahel.

We took stock of our situation.

We had lost two Tuaregs. Two more had been injured, but not seriously so. We bandaged them as well. Three bandits had been killed and two had been captured. Both had suffered wounds, which I attended to, before returning them to the custody of the Tuaregs.

This development put the entire caravan under stress. It was one thing to be delayed but quite another to take a few bodies along, as well as captives and a few injured men.

There was an oasis about five miles farther. We repaired to it and consolidated our position, ensuring that we had enough water, and that the camels were fed.

Hasso Ag Akotey called for a meeting of the senior members of the Tuaregs. It was agreed that the bodies would be buried at the oasis and the captured bandits handed over to someone in Tamanrasset, perhaps to be executed. And as for Holmes, it was very clear that he had once again demonstrated the most extraordinary bravery and saved a very large caravan. No one could recall such a feat of raw courage.

"He is one of us!"

"He gave blood for us!"

"He saved the lives of our children!"

"What is there to discuss about whether he can visit the grave of our Mother?"

"How can we refuse such a request? What purpose would it serve?"

The admiration for Holmes' act[25] ensured that we would see the Tomb of Tin Hanan, which he had set his heart on doing. He was still unconscious; I injected some morphine to help him endure the pain.

After I concluded that the wounds were extremely serious, we decided that it was important to stay at the oasis for two or three days to help Holmes recover.

Holmes developed a fever and went in and out of consciousness, mumbling to himself. The women in the caravan insisted on tending to him, fanning him, keeping the children away, and making sure he was very comfortable. I feared at times that we would lose him. His condition was certainly grave, and better medical facilities were necessary but simply not available. I may say with some modesty that my experience in treating war wounds in Afghanistan came in handy.

In a lucid moment Holmes requested that some of the Tuaregs play their music for him. Two young men brought out their *imzad*s and played for long hours. It was a moving sight: a sick man listening quietly to the traditional music of the Tuaregs in the heart of the Sahara.

I hope the following minor digression will be excused: I have, of course, always believed in the therapeutic impact of music. I recall a case, never published, I called "The Silent Musician," in which Holmes had investigated, on the request of the German ambassador, the disappearance of the first violinist of the Philharmonic orchestra of a German city, only to discover that the man was spending long hours tending to his sick and sinking fiancée, who responded only to his music. The matter ended

---

[25] Several years later, we heard from a source that the Ahaggar Tuaregs had composed a musical poem extolling the virtues of Sherlock Holmes. At the time of writing, we had not received confirmation from our Tuareg sources, due to continuing conflicts in that area.

tragically. The case was too sensitive and private to be brought to the notice of the public who, in any case, are long accustomed to relish the sadness of others and to revel in their misfortunes.

With a combination of the most tender of care, music, and modern and traditional medicine, Holmes showed signs of recovery by the second day. He was conscious and asking questions by the late afternoon.

On the fourth day, once Holmes was able to stagger to his feet and had consumed vast amounts of millets and goat cheese, the caravan resumed its journey to Tamanrasset. From there to Abalessa, to the tomb, was a short distance that could be covered in two days.

The caravan moved on, subdued perhaps, but confident. Soon the camels fell into a rhythm and the sounds of happy children filled the Tinariwen again. The spirit of Tin Hanan was caressing their hair, claimed Amaha Ag Barha with a smile, and there was no doubt that it had a role to play in bringing Sherlock Holmes practically from the deathbed.

Freddy moved very calmly along to Abalessa, not showing any signs of stress.

The Grave of Tin Hanan

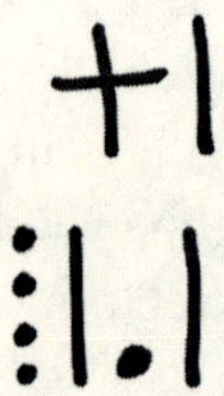

Our songs sung in the Tinariwen
O Mother, listen to them, for they are yours
Our stories told in the Tinariwen
O Mother, listen to them, for they are yours
Our children who play in the Tinariwen
O Mother, watch over them, for they are yours
We are brothers, from Tindouf to Tamanrasset
We are sisters, from Timbuktu to Tlemcen
Watch over us, O Mother of us all

Much has been written through the ages about those with natural authority who altered the destinies of entire peoples. A single man or woman may change some basic way of thinking of thousands by the power of his or her words or actions. Secret societies, countries, political movements, music genres—everything can shift, either gradually or abruptly, simply because of their charismatic power.

Holmes had theorized that the average citizen sought someone to follow because he had a fundamental need for order. The citizen wished to believe that there is a *reason* for his existence and that *something* would finally happen that would explain the very mystery of existence. These are matters for philosophical debate, and I must confess that my qualifications here are less than adequate to say something of deep import backed by sound arguments made by others, except in the area of medicine, where I have strong opinions by virtue of my training. I am otherwise content to listen to people argue, and prefer to express an opinion only if one is sought.

But I have strayed into debate when what I really wished to emphasize was that the desire to be led is a powerful force in society. Even the leader often has no clarity and does not know where to go and what to do, but the pressure of expectations and a willingness to take risks propel him forward. Let us not talk about quasi-religious figures; let us limit ourselves to political figures.

The extent of the influence on the Tuaregs of a woman who lived more than fifteen hundred years ago was difficult to comprehend. There was barely an aspect of day-to-day life that had not been touched by her omniscient presence. The complex social stratification that gave particular importance to women was noted by Holmes. "In no other society, Watson, have I seen such deference to a woman, whether to her opinion or to her presence. This must be applauded," he said.[26]

The excitement within the caravan grew steadily as we approached Tamanrasset, a small town, quite like many others. Yet this town was the base from which a person might travel to the grave of Queen Tin Hanan, respectfully referred to as the Mother of us all. The story that has come down has been that she and a servant travelled from the Tifilalt area of Morocco across the Sahara and established the rough boundaries of the Tuareg nation. She gave them a language and a sense of identity. In our

[26] As can only be expected, Holmes did write a monograph on the matter and presented it to the Royal Society. Indeed, for dramatic effect, he went dressed as a Tuareg, which disconcerted a number of scholars. To complicate matters, he insisted on playing the *imzad*, an unprecedented event that led to the formation of an inquiry committee to consider disciplinary action. Thankfully, and most unusually, the members themselves developed an interest in the instrument and took lessons from Holmes. The matter was dropped. Today, the disciplinary committee travels from city to city in the British Empire performing Tuareg music, a most astonishing sight.

countries, we have similar persons. If you are an American, you are required to think highly of what are called— with considerable hyperbole, I might add—"the Founding Fathers" to whom you bestow great attributes, when in fact they might have been ordinary men who just happened to live at an extraordinary time.

The Ahaggar Tuaregs were particularly attached to the memory of the queen and jealously guarded her grave. They had generously agreed to allow Holmes and me to visit Abalessa. On the way, I listened carefully to the wonderful storyteller and my new friend, Amaha Ag Barha, as he told me in his unique animated way all about Tin Hanan. These tales captivated my imagination, and I thought about them while resting at night, with my back on the blanket on the sand, with the gentle breathing of my fellow travellers the only reminder of life close by, and of my mission. I looked at the brilliant starlit sky, the same that had looked on benignly through the centuries as countless caravans and travellers crossed the Sahara. This time was the time to imagine, and not to worry about writing, style, voices, editors, readers, the machinations of modern man and the fundamental inconsequence of individual lives, except of those who live on simply because of the magnificence of what they did. I felt proud that my friend Sherlock Holmes would always be one such man. A century from now, people would remember this man with the greatest regard.

I dreamt that I was looking on as Tin Hanan and her maid, Takamat, started from the oasis of Tifilalt toward Taghaza, quite like us. I travelled back in time more than fourteen hundred years. Perhaps it had been safe enough then for two women to travel across the ocean of sand.

> *Listen to the songs without words, O Friends, for they say the most. The melodies of the Tinariwen gently settle on the sand, which itself sways to the beat of the heart of the Mother of us all. The dunes shift and move with the music that swirls around the lame Queen as she moves steadily onward. The mission is clear, for she was born with knowledge of her destiny.*

"Tamenukalt, what is your mission?" asks Takamat silently.

The sand hisses and stops moving. The wind halts too for it wishes to listen. But the camels continue, for they already know.

"To unite. My people, those whom I love, they run as if blind, to whichever oasis seems tempting, fighting like children for little toys. I shall unite them."

Her voice has gentle authority. The shadow of the Queen shimmers; the future awaits. The beats of the unheard desert drums continue, the sound pushing through the music-mad sands.

"How must I help you?" Takamat asks.

The wind stops again to listen to what the Queen will say. Time passes, for she speaks in silence, and only when she wishes. And then she says:

"You shall know when you must. And I shall say not a word."

The wind sighs with happiness and moves on to tell the acacia and the mountains of the beginning of something wonderful.

And the women move toward Taghaza, where the salt blocks are hacked out by men who have no name or hope and merely breathe till they die, with nothing to cherish, no one to love, and no memories that shall mix with the salt.

She, Tin Hanan, sees the Kel Tamasheq wander aimlessly through the desert from oases, finding ways to differ, finding ways to quarrel, not knowing they are brothers, not knowing they are sisters.

And she brings them together, from the Haggar Mountains to Tunisia to Tlemcen to Timbuktu, these boys, these men, who no matter how old, needed a mother to tell them about themselves. And she was that mother.

"Here, O Queen, is the music you said you would give them," says Takamat, handing Tin Hanan a fistful of sand.

And Tin Hanan throws the sand over the heads of the veiled men, who accept the wonderful gift and come together as one, bound by the wisps of music that come from the heart of the earth. At the center of the music is the walk of the camel, who gives us our very life.

"And these beautiful daughters. What shall you wish of them?"

"They shall show their faces to the sun, and with their beauty to guide them, the men shall travel fearlessly across the Tinariwen, who shall protect them and their children who shall trace stories on the sands. They shall never cover their faces, for beauty veiled is a crime against nature. They shall wear silver and everything the Tinariwen gives on its own."

"Is this our land, then, O Queen?"

"Yes, it is but not in the way of those who dig the earth and hurt her. We shall stay but only till the earth permits. We are free and we shall go wherever we choose, never forgetting who we are. We do not own the land and must not stay for too long anywhere."

And so Tin Hanan travels across the Tinariwen, holding close the men and women who make up the Imuhagh, teaching them their language, how they must conduct themselves, how they must sing. Oh, those songs are magnificent! Each song travels unaided over the Tinariwen, finally nestling on a pillow of sand.

If the million stars are the sand in the firmament of the night sky, then the million specks of sand are stars embedded in the Tinariwen. And as long as they caress the skin of the children, we shall live on.

And as the Kel Tamasheq discover themselves, and as Tin Hanan ages, limping graciously toward the void that is the fate of everyone, the ether of a culture like none other spreads like a blanket across the Tinariwen. None can shake these people, none can change them.

So it shall be as long as the Kel Tamasheq respect the memory of Tin Hanan, the Mother of us all, and her grave, at Abalessa in the Hoggar Mountains.

I drifted into a most pleasant state of rest. It was, of course, my hyperactive and creative mind that imagined that the desert had suddenly been suffused with the sweet smell of oleander.

We continued the long journey to Tamanrasset again, and despite our worries, finally reached the ancient town. The caravan was received with great joy, as an advance party had already told the inhabitants about us and related events. Despite our entreaties, Holmes was much feted and a great fuss was made about him.

"We must move on, Watson, my good fellow," whispered the weak and ill Holmes, as I sat next to him. "The longer we wait anywhere, the greater the chance of the Guardians catching up. Moreover, I am most keen to return to London. I have not entirely forgotten the issue of the manuscript and several other pending cases that await my attention. The Duke of Grafton had asked me to look into the peculiar case of the missing books from his personal library, which were always returned with the last four pages torn out. I have my conjectures, but must verify a few facts."

He continued, now in a fevered, disconnected rambling.

"The ostrich must be allowed to wander at will in Piccadilly Circus. How did we overlook the casket of wine that was sent by Richard Darwin from Australia? Avast! Avast! It is time for the whaling boats to weigh anchor! Why in the world is that sailor wearing blue boots? I think I must ask Mrs. Hudson to turn down the heat; it is altogether too hot in this room. What has that woman done with my violin? Always meddling, though undoubtedly with the best of intentions. I think there is a cobra in our soup, Watson. Does it wish to listen to me play the violin, perhaps? A fine specimen, indeed! What would

Lestrade at Scotland Yard have to say? A reliable man with little imagination more concerned with Santa Claus and chocolates than criminal detection…"

The women in the camp were extremely taken by Holmes and tended to him with a mixture of authority and deep emotional concern. His delirium affected them greatly and I saw many of them praying. The men were kept at a distance; I was the exception.

After a day of rest, when Holmes' fever broke, we readied ourselves to travel to Abalessa. A party was chosen to accompany us on the relatively safe two-day trip.

We said good-bye to our friends at Tamanrasset and started again. Amaha Ag Barha and I hugged each other, something I am not as a rule comfortable with, but which seemed perfectly appropriate at the time. There was a great feeling of excitement. Holmes was positively impacted and was quite garrulous, asking the Tuareg in front of him all manner of questions about the queen. It had nothing to do with the manuscript that had guided our actions through all these days but there was no possibility of us not taking this important diversion.

In the meanwhile, I had not fully understood why Holmes wished to travel to the lower Nile Valley instead of finding a way to return to London. In fact, an even quicker way might have been to move north to the city of Algiers and find a ship. There was something in the Nile Valley that Holmes needed to address. Yet I wondered how a wounded and weakened Holmes would survive many more weeks of constant travel through the most unimaginably hostile terrain.

We finally reached the Abalessa oasis, northwest to Tamanrasset, after meandering through the Hoggar Mountains.

The sight of the large mound of earth, perhaps a crumbling fortress, had a profound effect on our Tuareg Imazhigen friends, who fell silent, overcome with emotion. Returning to their cultural moorings had allowed them to discard the mask of cold indifference, already enhanced by their *tagelmusts*. But now, at this place, there was nothing to hide, nothing to be wary of.

The men of mystery showed themselves to be wrought of sentiment like men elsewhere. Somehow, their indigo dresses looked breathtakingly beautiful at that moment, standing out against the brownish-yellow sands that rolled away into the distance. There was a great visual harmony—it was *just right.*

We stopped for a considerable period simply looking on at what was perhaps the defining structure of the Tuareg culture....

Tin Hanan, the Mother of us all.

Yes, this is where she was buried, undisturbed, for so many hundreds of years. Rain, heat, the cold of the nights, time, the mad movements of men rushing about outside searching for transient happiness and power—nothing had disturbed this strange, isolated place. It was a profound moment at a sacred spot that deserved its remoteness and solitude. Perhaps Holmes and I were the first Englishmen ever to visit Abalessa.

We dismounted from our camels and went up the hill. It was a quiet day, and unusually pleasant. The odd lizard watched us from the shrubs. I could practically hear the overwhelming silence, occasionally punctuated by the calls of a few busy birds. The whole experience was most pleasing.

We walked about the old crumbling edifice, which was roughly circular. One could even argue that there was no tangible edifice. There was just rubble, placed there deliberately, in a vain attempt it seemed, to shield the tomb from curious eyes. Its walls were twelve to fifteen feet high and the diameter would have been about seventy-five to eighty feet. There was evidently no way to enter.

"How do you know this is your queen's tomb?" I asked Hasso.

He shrugged. "Our stories say it is so. I believe it."

"I wonder why no one has attempted to excavate this place, Holmes," I remarked.

Holmes was looking upwards at the top of the rubble. "Some things are best kept undisturbed, Watson. The dead must be respected. We would be outraged if Tuareg archaeologists endeavoured to dig up the Royal Burial Ground in Frogmore asserting their desire to add to the world's knowledge about our kings and queens. In any case, what do you hope to find within? Gold? Jewels? How unimaginably boring that would be." Holmes appeared tired.

"Who can say, Holmes? A few thousand miles away, our archaeologists are unearthing treasures in the Nile Valley. Pyramids! Pharaohs! Quite enchanting! Well, this does not appear to be archaeologically significant to my untrained eyes, but it doubtless has historical merit."

"Some secrets are best kept, Watson,"[27] said Holmes, quietly, his eyes far away.

We spent some more time examining the ruins. There was no way to know what lay inside. Our hosts would have been offended if we had tried to move the stones. Yet, I could not help feeling a pull from within. It was a hair-raising sensation.

We descended and again turned to look at that mass of haphazardly accumulated stones. I felt that magnetic pull again. For a moment, I felt like rushing back and removing the stones.

"So near yet so far from a fantastic discovery, Holmes."

"You seem unnaturally excited, Watson." Holmes was leaning against a large rock, smoking his pipe. The Tuaregs were at a distance immersed in a discussion, preparing for the return journey.

"Indeed, Holmes. A wall separates us from the remains of the defining symbols of the Tuaregs, our good friends. Yet, we must defer to the accumulated aura of awe around this edifice and not question this adoration. Ah, well, I find myself at a loss for words, but there is certainly something within that calls out. Perhaps it is the heat...what has happened Holmes?"

Holmes had suddenly stood up and taken his pipe out of his mouth. He was staring, stupefied, at Tin Hanan's grave.

---

[27] Several years after this event—in the year 1926, to be precise—the archaeologist Byron Khun de Prorok did the unthinkable and inexcusable. He entered the tomb and carried away the skeleton of Tin Hanan. It is presently in a museum in Algiers. Legend has it that the event of the desecration was marked by an unusual storm. The reader is advised to investigate the matter independently.

"What a fool I've been, what an absolute, complete fool!" he said in a low, intense voice, trembling with excitement.

"Explain yourself, Holmes! I do not understand."

"You scintillate, Watson, you absolutely scintillate!" Holmes' eyes were shining. No one might have guessed that this was a man just recently returned from death's door.

I was flattered. "Well, thank you, Holmes. But what precisely did I say?"

"It has long been my feeling, Watson, that you always complete the painting with an incisive observation. Two words you used: "not question"—ah! Everything suddenly fell into place! That vague unease that I have felt for so long—it vanished in a moment! We stare at a problem or situation for so long that we fail to notice the most obvious. We think there is something cloaked when it is in plain sight. Thank you, Watson! I must someday compliment Mrs. Watson for agreeing to a state of matrimony with you, Watson, though I had some reservations!"

I felt flattered but something he had said confused me, though I could not put my finger on it. The moment passed.

"The path forward, Watson. I can see it with absolute clarity! We must move on quickly now!"

The Tuaregs had come up to us. It was time to go, they said. I reluctantly turned and looked back at the grave of the Tuareg queen. My hyperactive mind still imagined that someone was calling me from within. I was amused with my sense of the dramatic, but grateful that I had this opportunity to at least visit. Moreover, it appeared that a casual comment I had made had evoked strong positive emotions from Holmes; it was gratifying.

"You did the same thing on at least three occasions, Watson, though you are possibly unaware." Holmes smiled as we began our journey back to Tamanrasset.

I felt very pleased with myself.

"The forgeries of the Dutch Masters—you had admired the new lacquered frames at the Cambridge exhibition. And then the episode of the alleged kidnapping of the son of the Ambassador of Austria—you had been effusive about the elegant clothes of second secretary's wife. Both of those casual observations helped me make rapid conclusions."

"Indeed, Holmes?"

"Yes, Watson. One, that your mind is always somewhere else, far away from the central issue. But this very act of irresponsibility helps bring tremendous contrast to my own line of thinking, which in both cases was overly focused on what I thought were indisputable facts. I allowed discipline to constrain rather than liberate. And that, Watson, is your special gift, the ability to ask the simplest of questions, to make the most inconsequential observations, which suddenly brings me back to the fundamentals."

"I—"

"No, no, Watson, say no more. In this case too, I suddenly found myself challenging assumptions that I had made. I am annoyed with myself for having made those assumptions in the first place. Tut! But thank you, Watson, thank you, my dear fellow!"

"But what is the discovery, Holmes? I am most curious."

"At the opportune time, Watson, at the opportune time! Else your future readers will grumble about the story. Let us hold their attention for several more pages."

"Holmes, you do me an injustice!" I cried. "Do you believe I am here merely to pick up the pieces of a story in order for it to be published? I am here on your express request!"

"Do not be agitated, Watson, my good man! The remark was in jest. I do not care a whit for your mediocre readers!" Holmes chuckled and turned away. I followed him on Freddy, feeling a mixture of outrage, pleasure, and confusion.

At Tamanrasset, Holmes and Hasso discussed the plan, looking at the map. Holmes asked for a post office and dispatched a wire and a letter. I posted a letter to my wife assuring her that we were well.

We were soon off on an indescribably grim journey to the lower Nile Valley in Sudan. Destination: Khartoum.

To Khartoum

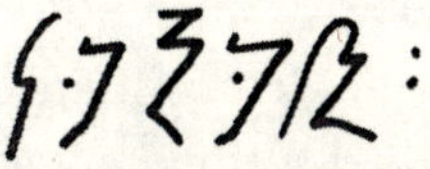

A theory has occasionally been advanced that adverse conditions truly test the mettle of a man. A primordial need to survive may overwhelm reason and bring us down to the levels of animals, which thrive on following their instincts (or so we believe). How does a man find the power to detach himself from extreme physical distress and still conduct himself with great dignity and fortitude?

In the numerous situations of a grim nature that Holmes and I had been thrown into together, I always found that Holmes managed to find ways to turn a challenge into an advantage. The extraordinarily harsh journey to Khartoum would have easily felled a lesser man—and I confess that there were times when I simply lost the will to live—but Holmes' brain never ceased tracing new paths of logic. We might as well have been actors in Dante's *Inferno*; it would have been a kindness to have had a sign at the beginning of the stretch after Tamanrasset that said *"Lasciate ogne speranza, voi ch'intrate"* or "Abandon all hope, ye who enter here."

We were a group of forty. The original set had been largely dispersed and this new group, with the exception of Hasso Ag Akotey and a few others, was drawn from Tuaregs who were connected in some way with the region, which was obviously desirable as they knew the contours and topography. There was concern expressed by a few about our ability to withstand the rigours of the journey ahead, but Hasso pointed out that we had managed to successfully travel for more than fifty days from Morocco to Timbuktu and must be given credit. After careful planning and loading of the camels, we set forth.

Waves and waves of the most intense sand-peppered hot winds blew across the caravan after we descended from the Hoggar Mountains. What can I say about the intense feeling of thirst we experienced? The caravan had planned a journey to the southeast through what is currently called Bornu[28] before entering Sudan. While there were assurances of many oases along the way, each mile travelled seemed an accomplishment. Even the Tuaregs claimed to feel a drag; the camels were unhappy and moved with effort and persuasion. Holmes' condition did not make things easier, though to his credit, he asked for no special treatment. He was visibly weak pretending to be otherwise, smoking a pipe while riding high on his mount.

The journey was considerably slower than at any time before. There were at least two incidents when men were bitten by scorpions. Here were men quite accustomed to the hidden dangers of the desert and yet they too had lowered their guard. Or perhaps their instincts were not as responsive for reasons that puzzled them.

Camels complained of problems with hooves; precious water mysteriously spilled into the sand; food did not cook well. There were occasional bouts of stomach problems. One man suddenly fell off his camel for no apparent cause, something that had never happened. He could not say what had happened; it was bewildering. One moment he was on the camel, the next he was facedown on the sand.

And many insisted that they could hear Tin Hanan calling for them, asking that they return to Abalessa. They whispered

---

[28] Modern Niger

about omens. For them, the Tinariwen was alive, it had a soul, it had stories, and it had advice to give.

I did not react, but I was no longer convinced that my allegedly rational mind had clear answers that could dismiss such ramblings. I remembered distinctly that ghostly pull from within the tomb of Tin Hanan at Abalessa. Holmes would have approved of my new liberal thinking, bereft of British cultural calcification, of course, but oddly, this was precisely when his gentle leadership pulled along the caravan.

We sat around a campsite one night.

"Perhaps we should return to Tamanrasset and consult an oracle." Hasso was quietly brusque. He stared at the fire.

Holmes did not respond.

He had long since understood that verbalizing was not necessary in the ways Tuaregs communicated. Often, silence articulated messages more effectively. And actions spoke even better.

Hasso poked at the dying fire with a long stick and threw in a few twigs. Holmes took another stick and did the same. The embers burst into flames again. A gentle crackling and hissing broke the silence of the night.

Holmes took out his violin and the Tuaregs waited for him to begin. He played a slow tune of the most haunting potency, one that I had not heard before. In the ghostly night, with stars looking on and the sand responding, with veiled men gathered about him, Holmes playing a wonderful piece of Tuareg music had an eerie effect. The violin caressed, it smiled, it listened. The tune had a life of its own. It spoke of courage and never giving up. It spoke of grit and determination.[29]

Holmes had responded to Hasso's remark. After a long silence, the Tuaregs dispersed quietly.

---

[29] Readers in Southampton or Glasgow may remark that this is not the John Watson they have been used to reading. Perhaps. Yet, I assert that travel is a great liberator, and I am not reticent in admitting that this journey added much to my worldview. I felt a light embarrassment that my views in the past may have been construed as overly conservative.

The next morning we continued, with new determination, spurred on by the Tuaregs' own music, delivered by the magical fingers of my good friend, Sherlock Holmes. The unrelenting heat was suddenly bearable and we were less susceptible to seeing evil designs in the most inconsequential of things.

By and by, we reached Bilma, another important oasis town, also a part of the Trans-Saharan salt trade routes. We rested for a while. Hasso, Holmes, and I discussed the plan.

"Hasso has explained that it is better we seek the help of the khalifa in Khartoum, Watson."

"And why?" The matter was quite puzzling to me.

"In the hostile terrain in the Nile cataracts, being under the protection of the khalifa is best, he feels. We have no friends there. To have strangers searching for something in his empire would not go well. Their system of spies is excellent, he says.

"I understand that Herbert Kitchener is the *Sirdar* of the Anglo-Egyptian army and the British Empire has interests in the Sudan. Lord Dufferin had sent me a message before we left Tangier that the khalifa came across as a man of moods who keeps his tactics close to chest. Kitchener apparently repelled the khalifa's Ansar troops at Tushkah—when was it? Yes, 1889, which has him simmering. There has been some bad blood in his dealings with Ethiopia too, and Lord Dufferin requested that I meet the man himself and then convey my impressions to the Foreign Office. Hardly a reasonable assignment, given the uncertainties of this mission and my standing, or rather, the lack of it. I have myself read the English translation of the report of Father Joseph Ohrwalder about the situation in Sudan, and it does not make for pleasant reading. We are dealing with some very tough people. It has been months since we left Tangier. Much must have changed. At any rate, Lord Dufferin expects me to introduce myself as Father Bąkiewicz. All rather extreme. But we may well get some mileage with such an identity. Someone with a British background, such as you, may be frowned upon. You may be executed, Watson. I hope that prospect does not unduly alarm you. You will not be aware of any discomfort after the execution, except for a momentary feeling akin to the prick of a needle, I am informed by knowledgeable sources."

"I shall endeavour to learn Polish quickly to avoid such a fate, Holmes. You will recall that I have lately been your slave in Timbuktu. To be your Polish assistant now appears a simple matter."

"You disappoint me, Watson, but I can understand, I can understand." Holmes puffed at his pipe.

"Once we gain the confidence of the khalifa—if we can—we must find a way to visit the Lost Valley. Of that I shall say nothing more for some time, Watson."

Khartoum was still very far way. The crossing of the desert would take several weeks; indeed the Darfur area in western Sudan was rumoured to hold the skeletons of thousands of unfortunate slaves being marched north by Arab slave-traders during centuries past.

And soon we entered the deserts of Bornu—later, Chad—south of the Tibesti Mountains and then the great Djourab depression. The landscape would certainly have appealed to anyone with artistic sensibilities, but the caravan was cognisant of the very hard path ahead. Days and nights of relentless terrible heat, sandstorms that changed direction abruptly, disorientation, unexpected injuries to the animals—again whispers grew about the Djinn of the desert and how they seemed intent on pushing us back.

Desert horned vipers, scorpions—all endeavoured to associate with our caravan. The descent into the Djourab depression was akin to reaching Hell. The air was sometimes still, dry and hot, making it difficult to breathe. There was a suffocation that made it impossible to think clearly. Even the effort of thinking seemed tortuous and unnecessary. And yet, mysteriously, it seemed as though a thin layer of violent wind attacked the feet of the camels and those who chose to walk. There was sand and dust everywhere. Dust this time because the Tinariwen was mixed with patches of soil with unimpressive scrubs and bush. The Bodélé depression was apparently the source for this and I later discovered it fed the Sahel, just below the borders of the Tinariwen. We were used to sand, and could shake it off regularly but the white dust had the additional property of staying on us and making us feel grimy and dirty. Oh, the excruciating misery of that trip!

The camels again showed signs of discomfort and unease. One or two seemed positively nervous, and that affected the caravan. We lost a man during this section. I was woken one morning with the request that I attend to someone who was gasping for breath. I rushed to his tent, and found that his symptoms were similar to asphyxiation. The poor man suffered greatly and despite my best efforts, he slipped into unconsciousness and finally died. It was the combination of heat, poor quality air, and dust that had felled him.

We buried him near an oasis at the edge of the Bodélé. The mood was very sombre. The omens seemed to have a basis, I imagined. There was a deep silence. Conversations had come to a noticeable halt in a group of men who were normally not talkative at the best of times.

"No, Watson, there is no option now. The map shows that we are near the Darfur, Sudan's western region. If we brave it across the Ennedi Mountains coming up and continue for a few more weeks, we shall succeed." His manner betrayed a slight unease.

In a culture in which voicing discomfort was rare, and courage was expected at every turn, there was no option but to move ahead, especially since the matter had apparently been conclusively settled a couple of weeks prior. Yet there could be no doubt that a dragging soup of reluctance tugged at our feet, making our progress appear to be in slow motion. The white dust swirled, often reducing visibility, unnerving even the most placid camels in the caravan.

We forged on, as men possessed, numb, wondering if such inhuman conditions were real. I knew that most of the men had not travelled this route before, instead having gone straight down south to Lake Chad and then headed east. Foolhardy hardly described us. But going to Lake Chad had been deemed too risky and would have added time to our journey, which we could not afford.

Days merged into weeks. We crossed the Ennedi Mountains and moved through paths rarely frequented by men. In a few canyons, we found shade and water and observed the rare dwarf crocodiles not found anywhere else. We rested for two days, gearing up for the last long march to Khartoum. Bodélé had been harrowing and most challenging. I would venture to say that it was only our collective determination that took us through. The remoteness, the serene, savage beauty of the land, the unexpected sandstorms—none of us had experienced anything similar. There was no question of travelling again via the Djourab back to Tamarasset, and I knew that our Tuareg friends agreed.

Some weeks later, we were in the Darfur region, yet another oven, witness to the ghostly screams of tortured souls, slaves who had died unknown, their graves unmarked. We reached Kobbei, a dying transit town, once on the Darb el Arba'in, a prominent slave-trading route, particularly notorious as a favourite of the Arab traders.

At Kobbei, we chanced upon another small caravan of Tuaregs who were westward bound, though they proposed to go to N'Djamena to the south. About ten of our party decided to return with this group owing to ill health and other reasons. We were now about thirty, set to go east to Khartoum.

Thirty is not a large number but after replenishing our supplies, we were emboldened to strike out across the Western Darfur desert, on our last leg of an excruciatingly hostile journey. The Jebel Marrah volcanic massif was at a distance looking at us impassively. There was a healthier mix of grassland and then the desert. Our Tuareg friends did not travel on this route often.

It would be germane to mention here that Hasso Ag Akotey had expressly wished to help us. Though we did compensate the Tuaregs for their expenses as much as we could, their commitment to our mission was driven by loyalty and a deep love for Holmes, whom they still called "Father," even though Hasso knew that was not his real name. The months of travel had created very strong bonds of friendship between them and us. Our visit to Abalessa—and the incident of the attack by the bandits—and subsequent display of respect to their queen's grave had only added to their list of our praiseworthy attributes.

The caravan moved on due east over several days. We were at the edge of the Sahel for the most part and while the journey was not easy, it was certainly much better than the harrowing travel just prior. The collective mood of the caravan became more relaxed. We had endured a most singular journey, one that had taken a toll on even the toughest Tuareg. To have emerged unscathed seemed almost a badge of courage. The men were singing often and the camels moved at a comfortable pace.

Holmes was always reviewing several papers he had with him whenever we set up overnight camps. It appeared that we had the manuscript that promised eternal life, a concept that was as far away from logic and science that I could imagine. Preposterous! What did Holmes really wish to do? Why was he of the belief that he had stumbled upon something of value subsequent to my innocuous comment at Abalessa?

Soon, after a monotonous and uneventful journey, touching upon places like Al-Fahir, Al Nuhud, and Al-Ubayyid, the unmistakable signs of a large river valley became obvious. We saw many more birds and large clusters of desert flora. And the number of villages and people increased. We were able to halt often, as water became more abundant. We reached the banks of the White Nile at a small town called Kusti. A great mental milestone had been reached. We had travelled across the Sahara, from Tangier to Tifilalt to Taghaza to Timbuktu to Kidal to Abalessa to Gilma to Kusti—and that was not counting the arid mountains, the horrors of Bodélé, the bandit attack, the hallucinations. And all this with the spectre of the Guardians chasing us, determined to cut us off and claim what they felt was theirs. Timbuktu seemed an entire world away. I wondered if we had actually experienced those events at the Sankore Mosque and the journey on the Niger River.

Our caravan was soon on a well-worn path north to Khartoum. Now we were faced with the problem, hopefully easily solved, of getting an audience with the khalifa. Would he meet us? Would he entertain our request for permission to visit the Secret Valley, wherever it was? I did not question Holmes—I knew he had a clear idea of what he was looking for. He would ask me for help when he thought it appropriate.

Young Freddy seemed pleased to be travelling north by the side of the Nile. He, too, had seen the Sahara in its entirety and magnificence, and given me quiet companionship and protection. I would not have survived without him.

The khalifa and the Valley

I now come to perhaps a key point in my narrative.

The knowledgeable reader with a good memory would recall the reports that emerged from Egypt and Sudan, in *The Times* and other newspapers of the day. Despite every effort made by the Foreign Office to arm-twist the Press, rumours and innuendoes did get occasionally published. They were cloaked in mysterious language, but it was easy to see beyond obfuscation. A little background—the fussy may call it a digression—will be important to the scholar. An examination of the footnote on this page[30] will be invaluable.

---

[30] With Western Africa firmly in the grip of the French, it was necessary for the British to consolidate their position in the area close to the Suez Canal. I recall my good friend Charles McKenzie, who had important responsibilities at the Foreign Office, travelling frequently to Cairo for confabulations. He never spoke much about it and neither did I ask, as it would not have been good form. But I knew that he had much to do with the Convention of Constantinople, which gave control of the Suez Canal to us, thereby providing significant leverage in world political and economic matters. I would go so far as to say he was one of the unsung heroes of that event, which, even if notionally, was a courteous agreement between us and the French, given that we had at least a 44 percent stake in the Suez since 1882.

The role of Sherlock Holmes in the quiet backroom machinations behind the Convention of Constantinople is unlikely ever to be revealed, though I am in full possession of the facts. The public today thirsts for sordid crime and punishment, and so the quiet victories achieved by others in furthering the interests of the country are rarely acknowledged, or even understood. There is the apparent and there is the cloaked. Only very foolish men find satisfaction in exposing what is best kept under wraps. I have chosen to not speak about this matter; let it be buried quietly.

The alert reader will observe that I speak of an event predating our arrival into Khartoum. Indeed, my reference thus far has been to the Constantinople matter, not the matters that brought us to Morocco and subsequently to Khartoum in the manner described in several previous pages. By this you may infer, quite correctly, that Holmes was entirely abreast of the affairs of this region for many years. It was just a curious, completely separate matter that had brought him (and me) to the Sudan. I am quite sure that even Lord Dufferin was unaware of Holmes' unspoken advantage.

I have spoken briefly of the khalifa before. His name was Abdallahi ibn Muhammad and he was certainly quite adept in the matters of state, having seized power after the death of his predecessor, the magnetic religious preacher, the Mahdi, also known as Muhammad Ahmad ibn as Sayyid Abd Allah. His ability to challenge the French and the British and, in parallel, take care of domestic intrigue, was a matter to be admired, even if the result was not favourable enough for us. It was always helpful then to keep watch on his actions and have multiple sources of information so as to derive a consistent conclusion.

But yet, without understanding the subject, a story is necessarily incomplete. We had arrived at the gates of Khartoum at a time that could be described as tense. The British feared that the khalifa might attack the Suez Canal and seize control of commerce, a prospect that was unthinkable. In that sense, the alliance between the European powers was strong; Egypt, Ethiopia, the headwaters of the Nile, the Suez, French interests in Central

Africa, British interests in Kenya and Tanganyika—this heady cocktail of issues required strong intelligence on the ground. Sherlock Holmes was not naïve; his brother, Mycroft, would have prevailed on him to act on behalf of the British Empire.

Some years later, I was privy to a largely silent conversation between the brilliant brothers at the surly Diogenes Club.

We sat quietly in Mycroft's presence. He was reading a large volume on Shakespeare's plays. After some ten minutes, he spoke.

"Khartoum."

"Yes."

"As inferred?"

"Mere logic."

A raised eyebrow, a shift in the seat, a page turned.

"The…?"

An imperceptible nod.

"Moriarty?"

"The obvious."

A relaxed slump in the seat. A gentle half-smile.

"You were right," said Sherlock Holmes.

"I always am."

Mycroft's eyes opened briefly and he raised an eyebrow in my direction while looking at his brother.

Holmes nodded briefly again.

Mycroft reopened his Shakespeare.

The interview was over and we both left the oppressive atmosphere of the club that frowned on even the slightest whisper.

The corpulent Mycroft and the athletic Sherlock—two brothers with vastly different temperaments but the same razor-sharp minds.

After camping at a spot just outside Khartoum, we rested and then set out to the city. We decided not to take Hasso because we were unsure of the attitude of the khalifa to the Tuaregs. It was best to go as Europeans. I had already been informed by Holmes that he had rechristened me and my new name was now to be Tadeusz Bór-Komorowski and I was to be his secretary. I am embarrassed to say that I could barely pronounce my own name.

After suitable inquiries, we finally reached the palace, a modest structure in Omdurman, just northwest and adjacent to Khartoum, across the Nile. It was well guarded, as we expected, but otherwise a simple affair. Sherlock Holmes was dressed in his priestly habit. His commanding presence allowed him to approach anyone and get answers immediately.

After some initial inquiries we were escorted into the presence of one of his chief aides, Uthman Shaykh Al-Din, who was also one of the khalifa's sons. He was dressed in white, in the custom of the region. After some initial pleasantries and introductions, while sipping some tea and sampling some dates, spoke (in Arabic).

"Where is this Poland, Father Bąkiewicz?"

"It is in the north of Europe, Your Excellency. An exceedingly cold place."

"Far away from the lands of the British and French?"

"Indeed. We have nothing in common."

"That is good. We are not fond of them. They are not trustworthy people. Always interfering and telling us what to do and how to live. For them, money is everything."

A few surrounding assistants shook their heads and clicked their tongues, disgusted by the British and French.

We, too, nodded in approval, though we were embarrassed by the rather harsh opinion they seemed to carry of us.

"What brings you here, Father Bąkiewicz?"

"Your Excellency, we seek permission to visit the area near Meroe. I am an archaeologist and very interested in the history of your ancient civilization."

"What is an archaeologist?" he frowned.

"He digs for history, Your Excellency. He tries to understand how people lived, what they wore, what kinds of houses they constructed, what they ate, how they wrote, and so on."

"Hmm. I see." Uthman seemed unresponsive. "I have heard of such men, yes. It seems a waste of time, but I shall need to think about it. Do you have men?"

"Yes, Your Excellency. We have a team of Tuaregs."

His face hardened and he shook his head. "We do not trust the Tuaregs. This cannot be permitted."

My heart sank.

Father Bąkiewicz sidestepped the issue by suddenly showing interest in a piece of art nearby. "Ah, Your Excellency, a remarkable painting!"

Uthman Shaykh Al-Din's face relaxed visibly.

"Yes, in Sudan, we are very fond of painting and art. That was created by someone I know in the south."

"May I look at it?

"Certainly!"

Father Bąkiewicz stood up and went to the painting, looking at it very carefully and with considerable interest.

"It seems to be some kind of a hunt."

"That is correct." Uthman Shaykh Al-Din was pleased.

"Very lifelike. Remarkable! Look at the colours, Tadeusz!"

I remembered that I was Tadeusz and made appropriate cries of appreciation.

"Yes. The khalifa himself likes art, though few know that about him," Uthman observed, with a hint of pride.

"Those who appreciate art certainly think at a higher level! We seek an audience with the khalifa, Your Excellency. We would like to personally present our respects to him."

"Ah, yes. Let me see what I can do. Hmm, well…today will not be possible. Would you come here tomorrow morning? We expect him back from a trip then."

Meanwhile, more tea was brought in. I was reminded uncomfortably of my tense experience at the Sankore Mosque.

We bid Uthman Shaykh Al-Din good-bye and walked back to our camp.

"A close shave there, Holmes."

"Every man keeps his interests and passions within reach, Watson. The way to a man's heart and achieving our objective is to determine what his likings are. That is invariably his Achilles' heel. Though of course, we are not seeking to exploit him in anyway. It is simply a practical negotiation tactic."

"Astute, Holmes. Let us see what tomorrow brings."

"I am hopeful, Watson. And with you as Tadeusz, how can I fail?"

I looked at him sharply, but Holmes' face was inscrutable.

The next day brought us to the office of Uthman Shaykh Al-Din again. He was a striking man, quite fit and energetic, of medium height. He beamed at us.

"Welcome, my friends. I have good news. I have been able to convince the khalifa to give you fifteen minutes. You may ask him whatever you wish."

"We are deeply grateful, Your Excellency!"

And without further ado, we were escorted into a large room, in the presence of the khalifa, with a number of courtiers spread across the room.

Khalifa Abdallahi ibn Muhammad was certainly a charismatic individual. His eyes were cold, not betraying his thoughts in the slightest. He was dressed in a white *jallabiya*, with a grand turban, and looked impressive and every bit a ruler.

We bowed respectfully. He nodded imperceptibly and glanced briefly at Uthman.

After the introductions, we sat quietly on a rug waiting for permission to speak.

After a while, the khalifa spoke. "Uthman says you wish to meet me to seek permission for something."

"Yes, Your Excellency. We are from Poland. I am a scholar of history and wish to learn about your great country." Father Bąkiewicz' Polish accent was quite remarkable.

"Hmm." The khalifa took a date from a plate nearby and popped it in his mouth.

He chewed with great deliberation. He looked long at Father Bąkiewicz with expressionless eyes.

"But are you not a man of God? Why do you do this?" he said.

"You, too, are a man of God, Your Excellency. Yet you are interested in providing a good government for your people. We know you respect knowledge. Did not the Prophet, Peace Be

Upon Him, say that all men should seek knowledge even if we have to go to China?"

The khalifa nodded gravely. It had hit home.

"What exactly will you do?" he asked, popping in another date.

"I wish to visit the area near Jebel Barkal."

"Yes, once upon a time, there were great things there. But no one remembers now. What will you do once you reach that place?"

"I will search for the buildings of the King Aryamani who lived more than two thousand years ago. I wish to write about the matter."

The khalifa thought for a long time. He beckoned to Uthman Shaykh Al-Din and the two spoke in low voices

"I give you permission but on several conditions. One: that my guards will go with you. Two: that you will not take anything from there without my permission. Three: that you will tell me what you have learned. And four: that you will help me with a strange problem I have just encountered."

"Of course, Your Excellency. That is completely agreeable. It is your land and your country's heritage. I shall certainly do as you suggest. But I do not understand your fourth comment."

The khalifa spoke slowly. "Someone who studies the past and makes inferences must have a logical mind. And I can sense you are an intelligent man. I require the services of men of strength, culture, and wisdom, wherever they may be from. I have long understood that I do not know everything and that it is wise to look for those who might impart new knowledge."

Father Bąkiewicz bowed. "I thank you for your compliments. I shall do my humble best to assist you."

The khalifa stood up. So did the entire court. He beckoned to us and we followed him as he went into another room.

Uthman closed the doors and asked us to sit. The two Sudanese men in their large billowing dresses and hard faces made an arresting sight.

"I hope you have consulted a doctor, Your Excellency," said Father Bąkiewicz. "Travel causes one to be careless with food, and the effects linger long, unfortunately. Please rest for a few days."

"Yes, the palace physician has given—but wait! How did you know I am unwell and have travelled recently? Are you a spy?" The khalifa jerked up, his eyes round with astonishment. Uthman looked flabbergasted.

Father Bąkiewicz smiled. "The fact that you were consuming a considerable number of dates did not escape my attention, Your Excellency. I am aware that dates are considered very effective for stomach disorders. Your face seems dull, if you will excuse the remark, suggesting that you are quite tired. And outside your palace, I observed a number of steeds who, judging from their state of exhaustion, had possibly just brought you in from a sojourn outside Khartoum. Surely, there is not such a mystery."

The two Sudanese men looked agape at Holmes and then at each other.

"Excellent, excellent. You are precisely the kind of man I am looking for! My judgment was right!" cried the khalifa.

"A small matter, Your Excellency. Please do let me know how I may help."

The khalifa took a deep breath. "The matter is very sensitive." He spoke slowly.

"We certainly appreciate that. Nothing will ever be revealed unless you wish it."

"I do not know why I am telling you this. It is rare for me to trust anyone so easily. But because I am the successor of the Mahdi, perhaps I have been blessed with divine insights." Uthman nodded in assent, and made appreciative sounds.

"The situation is as follows. We are presently severely challenged to our southeast by the Ethiopians. To our north, the Egyptians are playing games and the dirty, untrustworthy British, French, and Italians are working with them. God is on our side, which of course is the side of all that is just and correct."

Father Bąkiewicz nodded politely. I looked at my shoes; I was British.

"I have been the target of three recent assassination attempts. In one case, an attempt to poison—of course, my taster died. In another case, an assassin managed to slip through every layer of security and shot at me from that niche—that one over there. Unfortunately for him, the gun was defective and misfired, causing him injury. He would have been executed anyway, but the wounds were fatal and he died before we could interrogate him. And lastly, on this very trip, I was fired upon by a group of bandits at a town called Haya in the Nubian Desert, near the Red Sea Hills. This is very surprising because the Beja chiefs of Haya are completely loyal to me. So we believe they were not bandits but trained assassins. They escaped. But one of my men was killed."

Father Bąkiewicz sat back in his chair, eyes closed, listening intently.

"I am of the opinion that the British and French are behind this but I have no proof. I need advice."

Father Bąkiewicz opened his eyes and looked far into the distance. He was lost in thought for a few moments.

"Please proceed. What else can you tell me? You will have to be open with me, Your Majesty, if you wish me to be of assistance."

The khalifa did not repond. He exchanged glances with Uthman.

"Are you sure, Your Excellency, that you have not omitted some matter, believing it to be minor? Are you facing, for example, any kind of internal revolt?"

The khalifa hesitated.

"A revolt? No, that is not the case."

"And everything is peaceful in the provinces? Darfur? Kordofan? Sawākin? Juba? And here in Khartoum?" Holmes looked at the khalifa keenly and then at Uthman.

"Well, it is not possible to ensure happiness for all," said Uthman vaguely, his eyes shifting to the drapes of the window. "You certainly are aware of Sudan," he added, his voice betraying reluctant admiration.

"Why do you suspect the British and French?"

"Well, first, they are Europeans. Everything they do has a motive. Yes, you are one, but are a man of God, so I trust you. They have laid claim on the Suez, from Sinai to Aden. The Suez has always belonged to us. They simply lay claim on whatever interests them and then say it belongs to them because no one else has laid claim in a way that they accept. An admirably convenient habit. We must learn how to do the same." He snorted.

"I am the only ruler who can challenge them. The rest are slaves—in Egypt, Ethiopia, and elsewhere. They are upset with me for having defeated King Yohannes of Ethiopia some years ago. A long list of grievances. But I do not care. God is with us."

The khalifa suddenly stood up and strode about the room restlessly, clutching his stomach.

"But in any case, I have not told you what the problem is. I can certainly get more guards and improve my personal security. The Mulazimiyya soldiers are very good and will protect me well. You cannot help me there. But what I need to do is find out who is behind these attacks. How do the attackers seem to know where I am going and when?"

Father Bąkiewicz raised an eyebrow. He had already settled in well in his chair, the tips of his fingers together.

"You suspect someone in the court or perhaps the household?"

"That is correct. But it is not possible to directly confront anyone without proof. The matter is very delicate. The loyalty of no one should be either assumed or suspected."

The khalifa grimaced, rubbing his stomach.

"I used to worry only about the north and the east. But I am sure the Frenchmen will move upward from below the Nile's origin, from Congo. In other words, there is pressure from practically all sides. If, at this time, I am unable to manage internal problems well, we are finished. Outwardly, I must give the impression that we are united and powerful." The man was in the grip of significant tension—physical and mental.

Uthman excused himself, citing another engagement.

Father Bąkiewicz spoke. "And what, Your Excellency, are the issues that are uppermost in your mind?"

"Since the Suez Canal opened some twenty-five years ago, the economy of Sudan has been affected. I have some very specific plans to reclaim control, which I cannot reveal."

"It is not possible to help anyone, Your Excellency, who does not want to give information." Father Bąkiewicz shook his head. "I am only a man of God and cannot guess."

The khalifa looked down for some time, thinking. Then he raised his head.

"The issues that occupy my mind, Father, are the following: The problem of the Suez—now that the Suez Canal is working, the economy of Sawākin[31] is affected. Ships that previously unloaded at Sawākin for an overland journey now have no need; they continue straight up north. The new ships that travel to India have no need to stop at Sawākin, and continue to Aden. Thus, our economy is affected.

"Next, the problem in Darfur is acute. The Mahdi had tried to reduce the slave trade via Bahr el Ghazal but did not realize the economic impact of lost tax revenue. I am restoring it—the slave trade—to some extent but it is not easy. There are some problems with the social fabric there now. The Dinkas are usually a source for slaves. Now they are restless. There is talk of possible rebellion. I must crush it for the sake of our economy.

"Third, I am worried about one of my sons, Omar, who is Uthman's older brother from my first wife. He is not a strong boy, mentally. To be a ruler, one must be harsh and restless and only occasionally kind. Some function in the opposite manner, but I believe that people respect the ruler who is tough and clear. Omar is kind and soft, perhaps an unfortunate trait inherited from his mother.

"Those are the things that consume me these days, Father."

There was an awkward silence. The khalifa helped himself to another date, chewing carefully. Presently, he spat out the pit.

---

[31] Sawākin was replaced by Port Sudan some years later.

"What is your view, Father?"

Father Bąkiewicz reflected.

"I can think of more than a dozen possibilities. Could the issues be linked? And what is the name of your son? Omar?"

"How could the issues be linked?" The khalifa was puzzled. "Yes, my son's name is Omar."

"May I have the pleasure of meeting him?"

"Fine. Let me summon him," said the khalifa.

The khalifa shouted out to an attendant, who came in and then departed quickly.

The conversation strayed toward art and Father Bąkiewicz' perspectives were much appreciated. The khalifa's interest in colour and shape was unusual, and he talked about colour radiating energy of various kinds. And about various Sudanese schools of art. I found the discussion ironic to some extent—a warlord discussing fine art with such passion and interest with a Polish "man of God."

The attendant came back to say that Omar had not been found.

"Where is he?"

"Some say he may have gone to Khartoum." The attendant spoke in a whisper, looking away nervously.

The khalifa reacted in the most extraordinary way.

He got up in a rage and shouted. "Again? What is wrong with this fool? I told him to stay here and listen to my report about my trip! How will he learn if he keeps going away? Fool! Imbecile!" He threw a ceramic tea cup violently at the wall. It broke into several pieces with a loud crash.

Father Bąkiewicz and I watched the khalifa. His behaviour was most extraordinary. Presently, the khalifa caught himself.

"Please visit my chief of security, Ismail El Kachief. He will help you."

He said something to the attendant, who gestured to us to accompany him.

We stepped into the next room where we met Ismail El Kachief. He was a tall, unsmiling man with cold eyes. We walked together to his office a little way away.

"And what precisely is this slavery issue in Bahr El Ghazal, Ismail?" Father Bąkiewicz asked as we sat down again.

"Do you know about our slave trade?" the chief asked, observing Father Bąkiewicz carefully.

"No."

"We have a long history of slave trade between sub-Saharan Africa all the way through to Egypt. The source has lately been Bahr El Ghazal, where there are many Dinkas, whom we use as slaves. They are filthy people with no intelligence. Traders catch them and take them to Egypt through Darfur. It was previously an important source of taxation for us till the Mahdi, the khalifa's predecessor, unfortunately put an end to it."

"I see."

"The revenues through taxes were significant, though of course, many slaves died on their way to the North. The loss might have been manageable had it not been for the Suez Canal problem, which in turn caused a problem at Sawākin and reduced the revenues of the kingdom even further."

"What is your opinion about the assassination attempts?" asked Father Bąkiewicz.

"I regret that my staff is not very competent. You must know the history of Sudan to understand what has happened. In any case, internal politics are extremely complicated here and it is difficult to get reliable intelligence. I occasionally wonder if my police give me intelligence or are loyal to someone else."

"I see. But yet, it cannot be that you do not have an opinion."

"Correct. I do."

"And?"

"I think it could be the work of Omar, the son of the khalifa." The chief spoke slowly.

Father Bąkiewicz waited for the chief to elaborate.

"Other than me, Uthman, and Omar, there is no real way that anyone in the palace would know about the movements of the khalifa."

"And, what is more, over the past year, Omar has vanished for long periods and refuses to explain where he goes. I have tried following him but he always slips away. He invariably goes in the direction of Khartoum. I believe he meets his men there and gives them instructions."

"But why would the son of the khalifa seek to overthrow his own father? Would he not succeed him naturally?"

"Ambitious sons do not wait for their fathers to die," said the chief curtly. "In any case, though Omar is the eldest, the khalifa has younger sons from other wives. Uthman also is a son and he is seen as a successor because he has intelligence, strength, and the characteristics of a ruler. The khalifa trusts him the most, though perhaps he wishes that Omar would mature and become his successor. But given the political situation, we need a hard person as a king. This is the khalifa's view. I am merely repeating it. I know that Omar is aware of the fact that he may not be the khalifa's successor."

"I see. You conjecture, I think, that the drying up of revenues from the slave trade and from Sawākin is creating internal instability and stoking disaffection in the people and that Omar is trying to take advantage of the matter."

"Yes," nodded Ismail El Kachief.

"Surely it would be an easy matter to detain him."

"It may seem so, but it is not. He is usually with his brothers or friends, and his father is fond of him. We do not have adequate proof—in fact, technically, we have none. We only have whispers. Why did he travel to Darfur alone last month and the month before? Why does he travel to Khartoum so often without warning? Why did he travel to Jeddah and Mecca without informing us? He has no answer when we ask him directly. He refuses to answer. The assassination attempts have come immediately after these visits."

"To travel to Mecca, he must go through Sawākin, is that correct?"

"Yes. And Haya is on the way. Which is why we are suspicious since another attempt happened there very recently."

"We shall be glad to assist you if you think we would be useful."

"The khalifa has ordered it," shrugged the chief. The meeting was over.

As we moved out, Father Bąkiewicz spoke. "Will you keep us informed of any new development? We plan to be here for a day or so. Here is the location." He scribbled the area where we had camped on a piece of paper. The chief agreed.

◇◇◇

"An interesting conjecture, Holmes. The son of the khalifa is suspected!"

"Interesting, but very thin, very thin, indeed. We have not seen the slightest proof. Moreover, we have not met this young man. Does he indeed have the temperament needed to plot against his own father while functioning in his palace? Yes? No? There is more to this than meets the eye, Watson. Did you not find something peculiar in that last interview? No? Ah, nevermind. Let us make inquiries. Hasso would be a good source."

We reached our camp and Holmes discussed the case with Hasso, who promised to gather some information about the matter.

"Is it not surprising that the khalifa has entrusted us with so much information and wants us to help him in such a sensitive matter, Holmes?" I asked.

"Quite so, Watson. As usual, you scintillate! But I suspect he has a number of other indirect motives."

"Such as?"

"He may not even be interested in having us solve this problem. He may just wish to observe our sincerity before allowing us to proceed to Napata. Or it may be better for everyone to see that an outsider is helping solve the issue. He is possibly suspicious of everyone he deals with. It would send a message. Or he is playing into the hands of some advisors who would like to keep him occupied. A son is always a blind spot for a father. You do recall the case of Sussex vampire—how difficult it is for a father to believe his much-loved son is capable of any error."

"Astute observations, Holmes."

Hasso returned.

"All that I could learn was that Omar is known to be a dreamy youth with an artistic temperament. While he, like his mother, is the khalifa's favorite, he is unlikely to ever become his successor. He is mostly preoccupied with writing poetry and singing songs. He has quite a talent for it. There is a belief that he really does not want to be the khalifa after his father."

Holmes frowned. "That is puzzling. And yet, the chief guided us in his direction, as if he wants us to implicate the khalifa's son. To me, that suggests that the real culprits are known but no one wants to confront them. Is the khalifa's son a convenient scapegoat? It does not make sense. And yet, we cannot rule it out. Some of the most vicious murderers I have known have been gentle, anaemic men of great sensitivity, perfectly happy to spend the afternoons in meadows writing poetry. No, I do not have enough to proceed in that direction. But there is enough circumstantial evidence, we are informed, to assume that the son meets his fellow conspirators in Khartoum."

The next day brought no news. We travelled to Omdurman but Uthman and the khalifa were busy. The chief of security was also preoccupied. We returned to Khartoum and walked about the old town with Hasso and a couple of Tuaregs.

In the late evening, a messenger arrived from the chief, summoning us urgently back to the khalifa's residence.

Ismail El Kachief looked tense. "We think we have found the house where Omar goes. Can you keep a watch on it? No one will suspect you."

We agreed readily and returned to Khartoum yet again. The escort took us to an old and poor area of the city, through winding little streets. At a corner, he spoke with Hasso.

"You may find him in the third house on the next street. I will not come, as someone may have seen me earlier."

Khartoum at night did not feel safe. The streets were dark and narrow. There were no gas lights as in London and the buildings themselves were small and packed. There was an unpleasant smell everywhere and the heat, while not extreme, was still enough to make us uncomfortable.

Suddenly, we heard the most beautiful singing from one of the windows of the watched house. It was a male voice, not very loud but distinct and melodious. The song was laden with emotion, though we did not know what he was singing. I would venture to say that it was haunting and deeply moving. It left a profound impression on all of us. We looked at each other in the dark.

After about fifteen minutes, the door to the house opened.

In the moonlight, we could see a slim young man emerge, slightly bent. He wore traditional Sudanese attire and his manner suggested that he was preoccupied.

He walked by us, quite lost in thought. He was followed by two tough-looking men who had been standing unobtrusively just outside the house.

Father Bąkiewicz and the messenger followed him at a safe distance. In due course, the man did cross the Nile and entered Omdurman and finally the residence of the khalifa.

He was clearly Omar, the son of the khalifa.

On Father Bąkiewicz' instructions, Hasso and I stayed behind and watched the small house from which Omar had emerged. Nothing happened for two hours. We returned to our camp.

This series of events recurred on two subsequent nights. During the day, it was observed that the street was very busy, though there were the two sturdy men always at the door.

"An accomplished young man, would you not say, Watson?" asked Holmes perfunctorily, strumming his violin in our tent one night.

"Yes, indeed," said I. "What ails him? I find the story of the attempted assassinations being engineered by this man quite plausible. His behaviour is secretive and he refuses to explain his travels. Why do we not enter the house and find out what is going on? What of the two bodyguards—they certainly look dubious. Could it be a safe house for the assassins, Holmes?"

"A fertile imagination, Watson. You expect to meet veiled men with daggers and poisons, jumping out of shadows, do you?"

"If we believe that he is some kind of mastermind, then that is possible. He does not give answers and he was seen travelling alone to Darfur, which is in ferment. Then he travels to Haya and Sawākin and even Jeddah. He again gives no explanations. Meanwhile, his father faces assassination attempts. And his own chief of security casts doubts."

"Capital! Capital!" Holmes clapped his hands in appreciation. "I almost see Lestrade whispering in your ear, Watson!"

I felt pleased, though there was something in Holmes' manner that was odd.

On the fourth day, Ismail El Kachief himself came to our camp in the afternoon.

"We shall have to act today, I am afraid. Once again, an assassination attempt has been thwarted. An adder was found coiled in the personal effects of the khalifa. The attendant has been arrested but claims innocence. It is time to detain Omar. I cannot take any further risk."

Father Bąkiewicz was disturbed. "I am not convinced, Ismail El Kachief, but you have to do your duty. Let us catch Omar in the act, then, perhaps tonight."

About ten of us gathered in a tiny building opposite the house where Omar was expected to visit and sing.

The night was unusually chill and the stars shone from the sky with particular intensity. By about nine-thirty, Omar was seen entering the street and then the building. His white billowing robes marked a ghostly presence in the dark night. The two guards who had been lingering in the shadows sprang to attention and stood at the door.

We waited for him to enter. It was agreed that we would enter the house when he started to sing, perhaps to catch him at his weakest moment.

Nothing happened. There was no singing for almost an hour. And then began a quiet and distinct sobbing. A man was in deep distress.

"Now!" cried Father Bąkiewicz.

We rushed forward, overpowering the surprised guards who were quickly subdued. Then we broke open the door and went in, pushing aside a protesting old man who happened to be in the way just behind the door. We came upon a most remarkable scene in the flickering candlelight.

A young woman lay on a modest bed, her eyes closed, covered with a sheet up to her shoulders. She was of the Negro race and possessed an ethereal beauty that had remained during her last moments. On the floor sat Omar, his forehead pressed against the frame of the bed, his body heaving with sorrow, weeping bitterly. I rushed forward and searched for a pulse. There was none. I examined her pupils. She had just died.

Ismail El Kachief had the grace to hold himself back. We had burst rudely into the scene of a deeply private mourning but we left quietly, mortified. We left Omar to grieve for the woman and stood just outside the door.

Ismail came out momentarily, his face sombre. He left two guards behind with instructions to escort Omar back to the palace, walking at a respectful distance.

Readers will recall that Holmes and I have stumbled more than once. The assigning of a dark motive to a person's behaviour comes easily because we tend to assume the worst. We then embark on a train of related action that appears to be logical. And yet, the explanations may be completely different. Holmes always had the grace to accept that he was capable of making errors of judgment because of long years of always assuming the worst of human behaviour.[32]

From being asked to believe that Omar was a potential mastermind of a palace coup to discovering that he was actually visiting a young woman who was on her deathbed was deeply upsetting.

Holmes said, much later, that he did harbour such a suspicion, but at that time, he did not have enough to go on. Be that as it may, it was an absolutely mortifying error in judgment.

---

[32] The reader will recall two remarkable tales—"The Adventure of the Missing Three-Quarter" and 'The Adventure of the Yellow Face"—which might be distantly related in some way to this vignette. Specifically, they alluded to a very human dimension that had been grossly overlooked as we plunged into unravelling extremely unusual problems.

A day later, we sat with Omar and the old man, trying to understand this peculiar tale. Uthman also joined us, though Father Bąkiewicz had requested he avoid speaking. Omar was in mourning.

The old gentleman sat quietly, looking down at his prayer beads. He was thin, perhaps about seventy, and weatherbeaten and frail, not looking quite typical of the robust stately Sudanese men we had encountered thus far.

"Who was she?" asked Father Bąkiewicz. His manner was most kindly.

"Amani," whispered the young man. "And now she is gone. Gone." Omar buried his face in a cloth and wept again.

"Who are you?" Father Bąkiewicz turned to the old man.

"Ibrahim. I am Omar's slave. I did no wrong."

"We never said you did," responded Father Bąkiewicz gently. "Tell us about Amani."

"I am a Dinka," said Ibrahim. "So was she. She was my niece. Omar loved her but could not marry her. That is why he visited her secretly."

Father Bąkiewicz raised an eyebrow and looked at Uthman.

"Marrying Dinka slaves is forbidden," Uthman explained. His tone was matter-of-fact.

Ibrahim continued. "This boy, Omar, is a great poet and musician, yes, very great. He met my niece on a visit to Bahr El Ghazal where he had come to buy some slaves. She too was to be sold. He purchased her but fell in love with her and decided not to treat her as a slave. He purchased me, too, to look after her. They were both fond of music. She taught him many songs."

"What was her ailment?"

The old man was silent for a period. He spoke with some difficulty. "She died of grief."

"But why? Was Omar not there?"

He shook his head. "It was not about Omar."

"Then?"

"Her parents had been taken to a slave market in Darfur. When Omar purchased Amani, her parents had already been sold off. She begged him to find them and purchase them, too. He tried very hard, the poor boy, very hard. He went to Darfur, Kordofan, even Cairo, I think. He went to Sawākin, too. He tried to find her parents for more than a year. He finally did."

"And?" prompted Father Bąkiewicz gently.

"They had been sold to an Arab family and taken first to Jeddah and then elsewhere inside Arabia. Omar went to Jeddah and traced them. Unfortunately they had both been killed by their master for some mistake the master thought they had committed. He came back to her with the news. She was grief-stricken and could not be consoled. He sang to her, the poor boy, but she could not bear the loss. I explained to her many times that this was our fate as slaves. We cannot hope to live like free men. It is our destiny to be slaves and suffer in every possible way. We belong to our masters, not to each other. We teach this to our children so that they do not develop bonds of love with their parents. But she, Amani, she clung on to hope. And finally, when Omar brought her the news, she simply died of a broken heart. She loved her parents very much."

Omar had moved to the far side of the room and sat on the floor with his back against the wall. His eyes were glazed.

Uthman sat next to him.

"Brother, come with me," he said, his voice unexpectedly gentle.

Omar did not stir.

"Brother, come with me," Uthman repeated.

Then he said something most unfortunate.

"She was only a slave, brother."

Omar turned slowly and stared hard at his younger brother.

I saw a true man. A man who deserved to be the next khalifa.

Uthman lowered his eyes.

The old man spoke. "Let me read this poem that Omar wrote for Amani. He sang it to her in her ear just before she died."

"You can read?" Uthman was surprised.

"Yes. I learned secretly." The old man was almost apologetic; perhaps it was not quite right for a slave to be literate.

The old man took out a sheet of paper. He cleared his throat and read out the poem in Arabic. The rough translation is here:

Amani, I tried.
I looked. I searched.

I saw you in Badr El Ghazal, Amani
You sat with your brothers
And your sisters.
And your father
And your mother.

Waiting for a buyer.
Waiting, waiting.

When I saw, I knew.
And so did you.
Fate had brought me to you
Coins were handed over
My heart beat fast. How could I buy love?

I shall be back to take her, I said.
In a week. Only seven days.
I shall be back to take her.
And her family

I returned a day late.
The owner had sold your father
And your mother

They had been taken away
On that hellish journey
to the north.

The slave trader apologized.
"There are so many more," he said.

"Of far better quality.
Younger, healthier.
You may have them free
For you are the khalifa's son."

I took you away
And removed the wooden collar
Burying it deep in the sand.
Only then was I able to hold you close.

I have tried to find them, Amani,
I went to the slave markets in Egypt
I travelled to Haya.
Some said they had been seen
In a ship to Jeddah
They walked endlessly to Unaizah
Chained together in the hot sun.
And I rushed to find them
To buy them back.
Again a day late.
Here is proof, Amani
Do you see?
The wooden collar your father wore
While he was alive.

From the heavens they now watch
From there they send music
For you to sing, Amani
For you to sing.
Sing to me, Amani
Sing to me.

The translation, while perhaps adequate, does not capture the beauty of the old man's recitation in a high, thin voice in his language. Omar sat with his face in his hand, tears streaming down. Uthman sat with him, holding his brother by the shoulder gently.

We stood up and walked away slowly. Hasso was also quite moved.

"Watson, a favour, please." Holmes' eyes were unusually bright.

"Of course, Holmes."

"If ever you find me strutting about, mocking at love and related foolishness, just whisper the words Omar and Amani."

"Yes, Holmes."

The next day, we visited the khalifa's residence again. He spoke to us privately, out of earshot of Uthman.

He was quite subdued but appreciative of our assistance in a very personal matter.

"Well, my son is back. I feel sorry for him, but such matters are not permitted, so perhaps it is just as well. We are faced with many problems and cannot afford these kinds of distractions. I will groom him for something else."

"But we have not really solved your problem, Your Excellency."

"That is true. You have addressed one of the three matters I had spoken off. But it was a very important matter. I am thankful."

"My suggestion," said Father Bąkiewicz, seizing the moment, "is to carry forward the slave-trade ban. The economic effect will be compensated by the loyalty of a large population. I also suggest that you look into the assassination matter from a different perspective. The manner in which Omar was sought to be implicated suggests that your enemies are circling closer and closer."

"Meaning?"

"Are you prepared for an honest answer that may wound you?" asked Father Bąkiewicz.

"For the honour of the country, I must face the truth, no matter how harsh," the khalifa replied.

"The son who deserves to be your successor is Omar, Your Excellency."

"What? But he is an artist and poet. He cannot be my successor! Uthman must be my successor." The khalifa was aghast. "Why do you say this? And what does this have to do with the assassination attempts?"

"In matters concerning families, an outsider's view is unwelcome but sometimes necessary," said Father Bąkiewicz.

He turned to me.

"Tadeusz, do you remember that I mentioned I was puzzled by what Ismail El-Kachief had said? I was struck by two things. One, that he was not displaying the objectivity that he ought to have, given his position. He deliberately tried to influence us. And you, Tadeusz, were regrettably influenced. He spoke highly of Uthman and his abilities but he himself gave us the first clue that all was not well. He said that an ambitious son does not wait! Knowing that the khalifa was very fond of Omar, Uthman was, I believe, uneasy. What if the khalifa, in a weak moment, decided to anoint him his successor? Thus the slightly clumsy attempts to paint a picture of Omar as a weak, bumbling son with an artistic temperament.

"And yet, when I looked at the evidence, I saw little evidence of him being weak. Simply being a musician is not a disqualification. For that matter, you, the khalifa, like art and you cannot be considered a weak ruler. A crude attempt was being made to influence us.

"Only Uthman, Omar, and Ismail were in a position to know the plans of the khalifa. We imagined that *one* of them could be the person. But in fact, it was *both* Uthman and Ismail who were conspiring to disturb you.

"They kept you constantly on your toes, with four attempted assassinations. But how could it be that *all* were conveniently thwarted? A snake, poison, a back-firing revolver, a botched attack in Haya—every time an error? The probability is slim, unless we conclude that the attempts were deliberately botched. This created a sense of danger and consolidated the position of Ismail El-Kacheif, which made you depend more and more on him, who, I am sure, spoke often on the need to be a ruthless king, suggesting again and again that Uthman was the natural choice. Therefore, in contrast, Omar looked weak and insipid, consumed by love and music.

"I therefore recommend that you consider a new chief of security, and send Uthman to the front as a commander of soldiers. You need a leader of men, someone who unites and not someone who divides."

The khalifa looked long and hard at Father Bąkiewicz.

"You are making a very serious allegation."

The khalifa stroked his moustache slowly.

"And yet your points are correct. Only a very brave man would have spoken to me in such a manner. I shall think about it carefully. I am indebted to you. In the meanwhile, you may leave for Jebel Barkal as you planned. Come back soon."

We bowed and left the khalifa's residence.

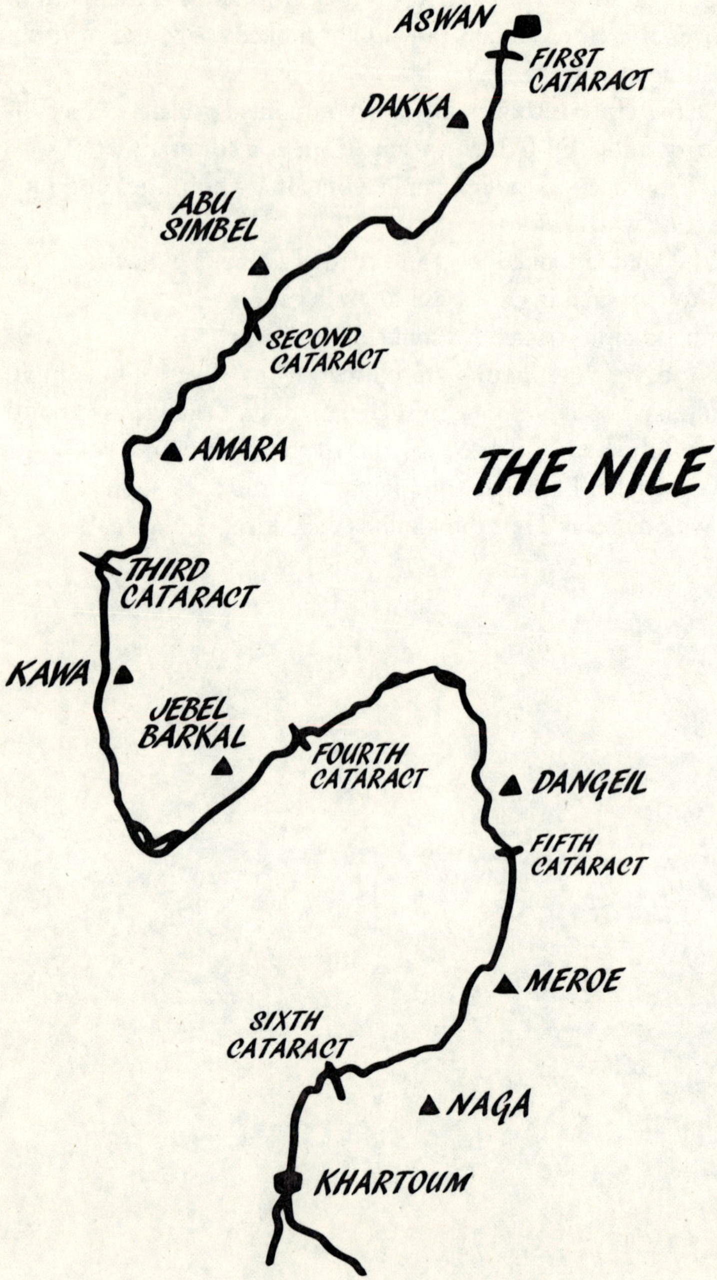
THE NILE
ASWAN
FIRST CATARACT
DAKKA
ABU SIMBEL
SECOND CATARACT
AMARA
THIRD CATARACT
KAWA
JEBEL BARKAL
FOURTH CATARACT
DANGEIL
FIFTH CATARACT
MEROE
SIXTH CATARACT
NAGA
KHARTOUM

The Valley

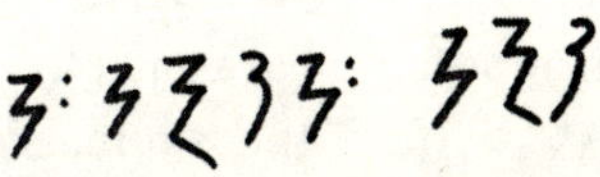

The circumstances that led to the arrest of Baron Stafford[33] and his partners in crime are only superficially known to the members of the public. When the news broke in 1889, I recall the sense of consternation and bewilderment that was experienced by whomever was more than notionally acquainted with the few facts that somehow managed to appear in the news. Indeed, were they facts at all or just red herrings? Yes, certainly a valid point. It was Holmes who so cleverly solved the mystery.

Here was an upstanding member of the landed gentry, possessing a formidable reputation, who brought the problem to our notice himself, providing information and participating actively, and apparently sincerely, in the investigation of the shocking murders of three foreigners (a Spaniard, a German, and an Italian) in Birmingham in a single day. We were overcome with shock and revulsion when Holmes found that it was the baron himself who was involved. I never published that story because crucial sensitivities were involved; the prime minister himself called me in for a quiet chat and explained that the diplomatic relations between Britain and a number of European

[33] Name changed

states could have been irreparably affected if the case received publicity beyond what had already been printed.

The reader may find it puzzling that I make a reference here to a completely unconnected case at this point in the narrative. There is a reason. On reflecting upon many past cases, Holmes and I concluded that in the overwhelming majority, the matter could have been easily solved with the gift of hindsight. That is, had we the luxury of time, it might have been very easy to arrive at the end by simply sitting in a club and ruminating, quite like Mycroft at the Diogenes. But in some, the twist, as in the case of Baron Stafford, was not obvious and it was only on account of an accidental remark that a new train of thought was triggered. It was at a disreputable bar that Holmes overheard two men speak of the case. One of them remarked on the fact that the baron had ordered a large number of expensive Cuban cigars from his shop. This very innocuous remark electrified Holmes… and the rest we know. I am forced to be somewhat opaque here but you will understand my predicament given my constraints.

The attentive will recall Holmes' near-violent and euphoric reaction at Abalessa. I had said something quite casually and he saw something there of great import. You will shortly see the connection.

After our more recent adventure in Khartoum, we set out to Jebel Barkal, near the city of Napata. The group was of modest size: Holmes and I, fifteen Tuareg men led by Hasso, and four members of the khalifa's personal guards. Twenty-one in all.

The actual destination was in Holmes' mind. He had memorized the location of the valley and knew how to get there. But Jebel Barkal was the base camp. He said vaguely that the actual location was not far away, but did not say in which direction or where exactly.

We moved north of Omdurman, after saying good-bye to the khalifa, promising to return soon. The short journey was quite comfortable; we were equipped well and were secure. Conditions were optimal; Holmes, Hasso, and I were quite excited. This was the final leg. Events that would presumably unfold shortly would tell us whether or not the journey was a success. Could the whole thing have been an elaborate hoax? What if the map was simply incorrect? What if there was nothing to be found? We would soon know.

We passed Wadi Seidna and then cut across the desert to Kurti, instead of following the Nile. At Kurti, we crossed the river. It was in the afternoon of the second day that we reached Jebel Barkal, not far from the Fourth Cataract. We set off immediately in a ______-______ly direction. Holmes said that the destination was not more than ___ miles away.[34] We soon reached a little nameless village. Just beyond were some nondescript hills. It seemed promising.

Hasso spoke with a local villager.

"Salaam. Can you help us? Where is ______?"

The man looked steadily at Hasso and then at the soldiers.

"Why do you want to know?"

Before Hasso could respond, the man waved in the direction of the hills, perhaps a distance of three miles.

"There in those hills. Those hills are called ______. There are ghosts there. Do not go. It is prohibited. Those who go never return."

Then he moved on swiftly.

The mood suddenly changed. The men became noticeably nervous as the horses and camels walked on toward the hills. There was a narrow path, not very distinct, suggesting that there was some regular movement between the village and the hills. But soon, the path disappeared, though the entrance to the valley, while narrow, was distinct, marked by stacked rocks.

Holmes and I dismounted a quarter-mile before the hills, as did the Tuaregs and the Sudanese soldiers.

It was agreed that the Tuaregs would stay at that spot and follow after a while. We would proceed only with the soldiers.

"If we do not return in a few hours, please come into the valley to find us. Force may be necessary. I do anticipate trouble."

---

[34] I am forced to obfuscate for reasons of security.

Hasso nodded.

The six of us proceeded on foot to the marked entrance. As we approached, we saw a sign in Arabic.

٢- ال لخدت نودب نذإ الإو فـوس لتقت

One of the soldiers said that it was a warning: *Do not enter without permission, or you will be killed.*

"But we are soldiers of the khalifa and this place belongs to him. That warning cannot apply to us," he said, dismissively. "We shall go in as ordered."

The others nodded. We walked into the valley.

Sheer rock rose vertically on both sides of the narrow entrance, blocking out sunlight. It was a few minutes before the path widened and the rocks vanished behind us. As we turned a corner, we saw a small grassland—an oasis and a valley spreading out for some distance. It looked like any other place.

We stopped and took in the sight.

And then, from behind us came an unfamiliar, grating voice.

"Mr. Sherlock Holmes, I presume."

We spun around as a group, with the soldiers drawing their weapons instinctively.

Facing us, with rifles drawn, were six men spread over the surrounding hills. They had been camouflaged, it appeared. It was a perfect trap.

The man who spoke was rather old and lean. His hair was white; he was balding too. He was seated on a large flat rock. There was something cadaverous about him, something rather sinister. I was reminded of a vulture.

"I would really suggest the immediate application of logic, Mr. Holmes," he said, in a thin querulous voice, sounding weary.

Holmes' reaction was surprising.

He smiled.

He spoke out in Arabic to the guards. "Please drop your weapons. There are too many of them."

The men did so, looking confused.

"As expected, Professor Moriarty." Holmes bowed briefly.

"Oh, I knew that you knew I would come."

"I would have been disappointed if not. We finally meet. A rare sojourn away from Paris?"

"Yes. Important enough, would you not agree?"

"Of course. But I am disappointed. Surely what you desire is illogical."

"On the contrary. Your lack of desire is illogical."

"About Rome—well done."

"You took a long time to realize that. I was most disappointed. Yes, by all means, do have a smoke."

The soldiers had come forward and snatched away the weapons of the Sudanese soldiers, who were asked to sit down on their haunches. I noticed that they were Europeans.

"*Grazie*," said Holmes pleasantly to one of the soldiers who took away his personal effects. He had settled on a rock and was busy cleaning his pipe and searching for his tobacco pouch. I was utterly bewildered by his behaviour.

He finally lit his pipe. "And where is your man in the Vatican?" asked Holmes, evidently delighted by this meeting.

"Coincidentally, a well-timed question. Our tents are pitched a quarter-mile away. He has been summoned from his siesta. Here he is."

We saw a small man walking across to us from a distance.

"Ah, Father Ciasca, we meet again! Quite some distance from Rome. A pleasure." Holmes was most cordial.

The curator of the Vatican Secret Archives came up, catching his breath. "Ah, Mr. Holmes. The pleasure is mine," he beamed.

"The weather is most challenging," he complained, his voice betraying some weakness. He wiped his forehead with a handkerchief.

"Do sit. Perhaps one of your soldiers will bring you some water." Holmes was most solicitous, despite being constrained in his movements because of several rifles pointed at him.

"*Grazie, grazie*," said Father Ciasca, as someone brought a simple functional chair from somewhere.

I could make nothing of this strange conversation.

"I see that your friend, the lugubrious Watson, appears confused by this conversation. Quite right on your part to not discuss this matter with him, quite right." Professor Moriarty chuckled malevolently.

"He is smarter than you give him credit for," Holmes responded, pulling at his pipe. "Indeed, his mind is superior to mine, though his humility forces him not to acknowledge it. A wonderful trait, humility."

"If you insist. Let us not waste time. Please hand over the complete manuscript."

"But tell me," said Holmes, ignoring the request. "Tell me for my own edification—when did you come and why the soldiers?"

"We were here a few days ago and found the valley through some sensible triangulation," said Professor Moriarty. "Your copy of the map sent from Timbuktu helped. I was quite sure you would try to mislead Father Ciasca, but you disappointed and sent him the precise copy—perhaps a mistake. Only of the map. Not of the completed chant. Quite shrewd, quite shrewd.

"The Pope wants to safeguard the manuscript. But we have other plans. Ciasca obtained permission from the Pope to take along these guards and bring us here and obtain the secret. But of course, we have no intention of giving it to him."

Holmes replied, "Of course, that is understood. But I really wish to know how it would help you. Do you really believe this rubbish?"

"Rubbish, Holmes? Rubbish? I have seen enough to never discount the outrageous. We were involved in the case of the shamans of the Sumatran head-hunters, were we not, Holmes? Have you forgotten the zombies? You may never admit that I got the better of you then. But let me not digress.

"As far as this is concerned, the probability of this being true is enough reason to acquire it. My plan is simple. The finest and the best of men must have access to time. If they are constrained by the fear of death, their minds will be distracted. The weak, sick, and unproductive are not required beyond their normal lifespan."

"You wish to play God?" Holmes pulled at his pipe.

"I am disappointed again, Holmes. How can a man of your intelligence believe in or talk of God? Utter nonsense. Surely a musician, a scientist, a leader of men, an artist—surely they need more than a mere lifetime to truly excel! True brilliance in any field emerges after the age of seventy, at which point ambition has diminished as have other faculties! What a genius needs then are extra years! As many as he wants! Can you imagine? Do you realize what power means? To determine who should live and who should not—and not a drop of blood spilt! I—yes, I— will decide who those persons should be! I shall decide who is not worth living.

"However, I do not wish to debate since I am quite aware you have considered precisely these matters. So let us come to the point. Where is it?" Professor Moriarty waved his cane impatiently.

"I do not have it." Holmes tapped his pipe gently against a nearby rock.

Moriarty sighed. "Did I overestimate you then, Holmes? My interest in coming here from Paris was really to meet you and examine your frontal lobes at close quarters. I have always appreciated your reasonably logical mind and from time to time considered you a worthy adversary. But you never fail to disappoint." He clucked disapprovingly, glaring at Holmes.

"I can only repeat what I said. I do not have the document. You are wasting your time."

"I see. And where is it?"

"Of that I have no idea. I appear to have lost it."

"How remarkably convenient. And yet you have travelled all this way based purely on your memory of the map."

"Yes. As have you."

"And why would you bother coming all the way to this valley if you had no purpose?"

"Sightseeing."

Professor Moriarty glowered at Holmes.

"I see. You delight in mocking me. Well, you will certainly have more than enough time to enjoy the attractions of this valley. Perhaps eternity."

He gestured to Father Ciasca, who in turn spoke to the Italian soldiers. A few of them systematically searched the persons of the khalifa's soldiers, and then of Holmes and me. They took out whatever they found and placed it on a stone ledge. They then emptied our bags in the same way.

Father Ciasca and Professor Moriarty went through the material on the ledge for some time. Meanwhile, Holmes continued smoking his pipe, and looked at me with expressionless eyes. My head was swimming. I could make nothing of this; it made no sense, least of all the conversations and the presence of these men.

Presently, the two men returned and sat down.

"I know you have not lost it. You are best advised to hand it over. I find violence quite repelling. But when necessary, I do know what to do." Professor Moriarty's voice was freezing.

"Yes, I too dislike torture. It is the mind that is the toughest to crack, as I know you will agree. I have read your remarkable monograph on psychological torture in *The Annals of Historical Research*."

"Flattering. I knew you would see through my identity as professor of history at Grenoble."

"I noticed your adverse remarks about the Chinese method of a thousand cuts. I am not sure I completely agree with some of your views, but they do have merit."

The academic digression was perplexing.

"As I said, bloodletting as a means to extract information and damage a person's sense of self-worth is primitive and entirely unnecessary. The battles to be won must be in the mind. A man must willingly hand over secrets. I would be surprised if you disagreed."

"Quite so. Nevertheless, the fact is that I really do not have what you seek. The rest is up to you. And these men, these Italian soldiers—a quaint but practical choice."

Moriarty waved his cane in the air dismissively. "Tch, tch! Not from the official Italian army, Holmes, but a secret group charged with protecting the Pope. No, not the Swiss Guards. So obviously, given the importance of the task, quite necessary."

Sherlock Holmes refilled his pipe and lit it. "How long has Father Ciasca been working for you?"

"For longer than he realizes."

"I had my suspicions. An ill-formed image. But he played his part very well."

"I choose only the best. You might have been useful. But you have a distorted sense of right and wrong. Much too late to do anything about it." Moriarty glowered.

"Every capital, every government. I congratulate you." Holmes' effusive admiration was puzzling.

"Only you know. But we digress."

"Do we? Are you sure you have thought of all possibilities? I still do not understand the logic of what you wish to do. This is delicate, but given your age and condition, what is the use?" Holmes looked positively concerned.

"That is the difference between you and me, Holmes. I am as aware as you of mortality. If you think I am driven by a selfish need to keep myself alive forever, you are quite wrong. It is the need to keep only the right persons alive. That is immortality, Holmes, not just endless shallow breathing. The others can live out their pathetic lives like fireflies. Bah!" Professor Moriarty spat out his contempt for the men and women who had no distinctive characteristic.

Unaccountably, I felt a chill down my spine. There was no doubt that this man represented lethal evil.

"Father Ciasca, why?" Holmes turned toward the representative of the Holy See.

"You know, my dear friend. You know." Father Ciasca smiled wanly.

"Just to be used. Hmm. I am not pleased with myself, no, not at all. But thanks to Watson, that realization did come to me. The letter I wrote to you from Timbuktu—do you think it was a gross error in judgment? Or perhaps just a way to draw you out?"

"There is no harm in accepting that we—Professor Moriarty and I—lack your physical strength and social abilities. In any case, this was the assigned mission. You were to return to Rome via Tangier. But instead, you disappeared. We were alarmed when you did not send us a copy of the complete manuscript from Timbuktu. Perhaps a desire to double-cross us and take possession of the secret yourself."

Holmes laughed. "Do you really believe the secret is simply sitting here waiting to be discovered and used?"

Professor Moriarty interjected. "I am not in a hurry. Let us carry on inside. We arrived only yesterday. Let us move further down to where we have camped. There are signs of habitation a few miles further we are told."

The Italian soldiers pulled up the Sudanese guards and made them walk single file, with us walking behind. The day was hot and we felt uncomfortable. I had not comprehended the staccato conversation full of strange allusions. I wanted to speak urgently with Holmes but there was no immediate opportunity.

We reached the camp, from which we had a clear view further on. Already, there were hints of the dusk. A few birds were announcing their plans to return to their nests.

"Do you observe a few settlements there, Holmes?" Professor Moriarty asked, pointing.

We could see a thin wisp of smoke at a distance.

"Yes. Clearly. About five miles away, I should think."

"Now, who might live there, given that this is a prohibited area?"

"But of course."

"Which means you know what I am thinking."

"Yes."

Was it my imagination or were Professor Moriarty and Sherlock Holmes the best of friends?

The Italians led us to a clearing where they had started up a few fires to cook dinner. The cuisine was excellent, as could be expected. Over pasta and wine, Professor Moriarty and Holmes discussed various unrelated matters with an odd bonhomie. Trigonometry, the Pole Star, the Bay of Biscay, Pondicherry, pyrites, the murder of a French notable's wife, and so on. They did not touch upon the problem at hand.

After dinner, Moriarty stood in front of Holmes.

"Sleep over it. Tomorrow we conclude our mission. It is best to cooperate," he said.

"You make a convincing argument. Regrettably, I have nothing new to add," Holmes replied.

Moriarty turned on his heels and left. We were escorted to our primitive tents, guarded by the Italians.

◇◇◇

"I can say with absolute certainty that I know what is to happen soon." Holmes was lying on his back, making a rude pillow of his hands, and smoking a cigarette.

"What, Holmes?"

"I do not mean to keep you on tenterhooks. But even these open tents have ears. Professor Moriarty and Father Ciasca are making a mistake."

"What is happening here, Holmes?" I cried. "How is Father Ciasca here? Was he not the same person who sent you to Morocco and then to Timbuktu?"

"Yes, Watson. You are right. It was this that I anticipated when you made that remark at Abalessa. I simply did not guess till that point that Father Ciasca was involved. It was an extraordinarily perfect cover. In my mind it was one of those things you take for granted, like the air we breathe without thinking of. A senior Vatican official working for Professor Moriarty? But I am prepared. And you get every credit, my dear fellow, for deflating my ego and removing the blinders from my eyes at the right time.

"But what these men do not understand," Holmes whispered in my ear, "is that—"

At that point, there was a loud shouting as the sounds of a large number of galloping horses swept the camp. Holmes and I stared at each other and jumped out of the tent.

Hasso Ag Akotey and the Tuaregs had moved in silently behind the Italians and in a swift manoeuvre, seized the guns, and taken over the camp without a shot being fired. The Italians had relaxed their guard and had not realized that we had left the Tuaregs behind.

The tables had turned in minutes. Our captors were now our prisoners. The Sudanese and Tuaregs were now in charge.

Hasso walked quickly up to us with a beaming smile. Holmes and he hugged each other.

"Father, we followed after two hours, as you said. We watched everything from the rocks over there."

"The ever-reliable Hasso! I knew you were close by. That is what I was telling Watson here. I was not the least bit concerned." Holmes clapped Hasso's shoulders.

Professor Moriarty, Father Ciasca, and the Italian guards were herded together by the Tuaregs and the Sudanese soldiers—who were certainly agitated and not keen to be calm and forgiving—in the center of a clearing, with a long rope tying them all together. They were then forced to sit down on the ground. The bonfires from the evening meal gave us light as did the moon. The hills added to a rather picturesque sight. We walked across to them.

Professor Moriarty glowered, his hands tied behind him. Father Ciasca was silent as well, but more out of fear.

"I am surprised this never occurred to you," observed Holmes with the hint of a smile.

There was no reply.

That night, however, Holmes again fell sick. The old injuries and lack of rest once again caught up with him. A fever raged and the normally energetic Holmes was forced to acknowledge the power of nature. I tended to him through the night, applying damp towels to his brow.

Sometime after midnight, I heard the shuffle of feet just outside the tent. I asked the person to come in.

The curtains parted to reveal a striking Tuareg woman.

I was considerably surprised since there had been no Tuareg woman with us on the journey. Not being able to speak the language, I was unable to communicate at all. She had with her a bowl of water and some small pouches—perhaps of medicine—and a few pieces of cloth.

I understood that she wished to tend to Holmes. I put up a restraining hand and shook my head. She ignored me, and to my chagrin, gently pushed me aside. She then sat next to the fevered Holmes and made him comfortable. I could see she was a very experienced nurse of some kind, moving Holmes carefully and correctly so that he was comfortable. Hasso had obviously sent her. It was kind of him.

I watched as she created an even more comfortable bed. As the hours dragged on, Holmes once again slipped into delirium.

"A fine river, the Joliba! What would Mycroft say about the crocodiles? Watson, what a fine man, ever ready to help...If only he used his head a little more...Rainfall in the Sahara? Now where is my cocaine? I wish to travel to Taghaza, my good man. I shall live there. Balmy, soothing climes, would you not say? Ha ha ha!"

I was considerably troubled by this relapse but took comfort in seeing the Tuareg lady take care of him with such attention. He needed nursing more than medical assistance.

In the morning, I stepped out of the tent and mentioned to the Tuaregs and the Sudanese that Holmes was not well. They expressed concern but I told them as best as I could that Holmes was in competent hands, though I did not discuss the matter further.

It looked as though we were unlikely to make any progress for the day. Professor Moriarty had been tied very firmly to a stake in the ground in the shade of a large hill.

"Holmes is ill, eh?" he snarled venomously. "Doesn't look good, doesn't look good. And who is tending to him? Dr. John Watson from Harley Street!" he mocked. I ignored him

I returned to the tent. The woman was sitting by Holmes. She glanced at me briefly and returned her attentions to Holmes.

The Tuareg woman is handsome, if I may be permitted to say. The colour of the skin varies, tending to be dark. The face is usually tattooed. Though there is no veil, a cloth usually covers the hair. There is extensive use of ornamentation, particular silver. The design of the jewelry is seldom found, I am given to understand. I noticed a particularly attractive silver bracelet.

This nurse assigned to Holmes by Hasso was certainly quite remarkable. I refrain, as a rule, from looking at a lady in too bold a manner and so observed her countenance furtively from time to time. I would venture to say that she was most charming with commendable features. She possessed immense confidence and never asked me for any help. She helped Holmes up regularly, and fed him or coaxed him to have the medicines she had brought. Holmes was not a difficult patient. He drifted in and out of sleep and his fever did not break for several hours. The constant attention given by the Tuareg nurse to Holmes was quite moving.

She rarely turned in my direction and did not speak a word. It was not possible for me to express my gratitude to her. I was grateful to Hasso, too, for the kind gesture of assigning such a competent nurse to me.

By the evening, Holmes' health had indeed turned for the better. The fever broke conclusively but the nurse's attention was so impeccable that Holmes looked fresh. That aquiline nose, those sharp features, that intelligent countenance—had I not known better, I might have said Holmes was just enjoying a light late afternoon nap.

And just as abruptly as she had entered, she collected her materials and slipped out of the tent very quietly.

◇◇◇

"I feel like a new man, Watson. Your ministrations made the difference. I am indebted," said Holmes the next day. He did indeed look rejuvenated.

"It was not I, Holmes," said I, amused by his incorrect inference. "Hasso had assigned a Tuareg nurse to you. I was most impressed by her abilities. Please do thank him when you get an opportunity."

"Indeed?" Holmes frowned, but did not comment further. We prepared for the journey further into the valley.

It was decided that only Holmes, Hasso, and I would walk toward the settlement.

We had barely travelled for twenty minutes when we came across a group of people walking slowly toward us.

Something about their clothes, their gait, and their countenances struck us as unusual. Holmes gestured to us to stop. We were, after all, intruders. As they neared, he bowed respectfully and we followed suit.

The men and women looked strange and quite out of place. I have to confess I experienced extreme unease in their presence, though they carried no weapons and seemed quite peaceful. But their clothes, their demeanour, their physique—everything was unusual.

The seventh man stood out. He was rather old, with a white beard and a feeble gait, using a stick to balance himself. But he was someone from a different time. He was certainly European. I felt I was looking on at a medieval play.

He bowed gently to Holmes. The two men looked steadily at each other, smiling.

There was no obvious threat from any in the group. Through sign language and much laughter, the old man indicated that he would like to walk back to our camp with us.

The six inhabitants of the valley walked about the campsite, looking at the intruders. They showed particular interest in the Sudanese, who resembled them. There was an attempt to communicate but their languages seemed mutually incomprehensible.

The old man seated himself on a rough rock and looked about with a pleasant smile. Then he beckoned to Holmes. After a few trials, they found French a common language to communicate in.

Some ten minutes later, Holmes asked that Father Ciasca be brought forward as well.

The old man addressed Father Ciasca, speaking in a pleasant voice in a language that sounded like Italian but had a peculiar, unfamiliar inflection. I gathered he was introducing himself.

Father Ciasca's face was drained of all blood. He stared at the man, his eyes wide with horror and shock.

Holmes looked at me and smiled. "Watson, do you know who this gentleman is?"

"I confess you have me at a disadvantage, Holmes."

"Allow me to introduce you to Marco Polo, Citizen of Venice." He bowed with dramatic flair.

I cannot quite describe my feelings when I heard this. I am a man of modern science, and every sense of rationality protests when confronted with "evidence" of matters that defy natural laws. Marco Polo? A man dead since the year 1325 now alive in a secret valley near the Fourth Cataract of the Nile in 1893?

The reader will find this aspect of the story absolutely outrageous and possibly even insulting to his intelligence. I must heartily agree that I too found it impossible to believe Holmes. He did have a dry sense of humour, but this was plainly in extremely poor taste. I was forced to protest.

"Holmes, this is an outrage! We are the best of friends, but this is not an occasion for such levity," I cried out in consternation.

"There is nothing amusing about the matter, my dear Watson. This gentleman with the odd Italian accent is indeed Marco Polo."

"Marco Polo is dead, Holmes! Dead! He died in 1325 and was buried in a church in Venice. You told me so yourself! I greatly fear that the sun has affected you. No, it is a combination of sunstroke and the ill effects of the injury you suffered. This is—"

Holmes interrupted me. "I did tell you he was buried in Venice, Watson, because that is what I believed was the case. But the facts are otherwise. And in the meanwhile, observe that Father Ciasca is quite disturbed."

Indeed, Father Ciasca was hysterical, speaking loudly and rapidly, addressing the old man in Italian, who looked at him with a curious, glazed look. The translation of the conversation, as best Holmes and I could recall:

"I seek forgiveness! The greatest citizen of Venice! Alive! Yes! Not dead! Alive! Alive! Five hundred and fifty years after he was buried—he has risen! Do my eyes betray me now? But no, this is he, Marco Polo, the great traveller himself! Do not punish me! I did not know you were alive, Signore!" Father Ciasca was in a state of extreme agitation.

The signore responded in a soft, quavering voice. I could make nothing of it. I had the surreal feeling I was watching a performance of Shakespeare's *The Merchant of Venice*.

"Ah, my son, there is nothing to apologize for. I am so happy to speak in my own tongue. So much time has passed. Centuries, perhaps? You speak Italian in a very strange way, my son. Or perhaps my hearing is not very good."

"But how is it, sire, that you are alive and are here?"

Marco Polo spoke in a most grandfatherly manner. "Do you wish me to tell you why I am here, my son? I shall try. But I am old and weak and may forget parts. Unfortunately I cannot die, so I only have eternity to regret my rash act.

"Know then, my son, that I visited the Pope in Rome—I have forgotten his name, alas—and told him quite clearly that I had in my possession the secret to eternal life and that I wished him to decide what should be done with it. Should we destroy it forever, keep it secret, or hand it over to humanity? There were many philosophical and religious questions that needed to be answered, I believed.

"I spoke of the circumstances of China, of the Zamorin, and so on. But then I saw that he was not interested—no one pays attention to the old, my son—and thought I was talking nonsense. I concluded that I would have to do something about the matter myself.

"I returned to Venice and thought about the matter carefully.

"I decided that I would go to the place mentioned in the map and find out the truth, no matter how hard it might be. What did I have to lose? At best or at worst my life. Had I not enjoyed a full life? How could Marco Polo not travel himself? What was the point of giving away the secret to people who doubt and lack humility?

"I then searched for an old man who might look like me and who was perhaps dying. It was quite easy. A forgotten man lay dying in a village nearby, his life ebbing away. His name was Alberto, I recall. He had no one to call his own and no one would mourn his passing. He agreed to die as Marco Polo as he would be guaranteed a proper burial. I took him home and made him Marco Polo. We had a good chuckle, two old men, finding the idea amusing. We looked in the mirror and laughed at ourselves and thought it would be a great joke. I think he saw beyond the mirror into the other world. He looked forward to dying soon and was happy that we looked so similar. Perhaps all old men look the same at the end. But the old are happy in a different way—the journey is to end. So many years of endless activity, all ultimately pointless. Exhaustion. Emotion. Frustrations. Disappointments. Surges of extreme happiness and sadness. For what?

"I hid in a house nearby and watched Alberto slowly die. A priest was called. He asked Alberto to confess and accept that my stories were false. But what was he to confess to? Those were not his stories in any case. He refused, quite rightly. And he died shortly.

"I saw my own funeral from a distance. The priests argued about burying me as they felt I had not confessed to lying. It was all quite amusing. Finally, Alberto was buried and there was a great fuss about him. I am sure he would have enjoyed the joke.

"I then left for this very place, accompanied by two sturdy servants whom I had sworn to secrecy.

"We travelled to Rome and Sicily and Alexandria. Then we travelled down the Nile. It was not very difficult, though, of course, it was very hot. It was only a problem because of my age and sickness, but I surprisingly became better and better. The climate suited me. After many weeks, we reached the Fourth Cataract of the Nile and found Napata.

"I found the valley. Though no one had heard of it, it was not difficult to find because the location in the map had been precise.

"We entered the valley, yes, this very one, my son. It was quite like this. Did you come by a village? Yes, it was there then, too, though there were perhaps fewer than ten huts then. Is it bigger now? I never leave this place, so I do not know. None of us do.

"We reached this place, yes, this very one. These six men and women were there and, let me tell you, my son, they looked exactly like this when I met them first. You seem shocked; do not be.

"They confronted me and asked me to leave immediately. Since I was older—I simply looked older but, as you will see, it is *they* who are much older, my son!— they were considerate and allowed me to rest. They made it clear that we should leave soon.

"But I showed them what I had copied on a piece of paper from memory. They became very respectful. They were able to read the script well and, in fact, had an exact copy with them which they showed me later. It was the chant as prescribed by the priests of their king.

"There are instructions for the chant as you know. They must be spoken in a certain way, at a certain time, at a certain place in the valley. Yes, that man there, Signore Holmes, he understands perfectly.

"We had to wait a while more. In the meanwhile, I dismissed my servants and asked them to return to Venice. I do not know if they reached the city.

"We waited for a few weeks, during which time, I befriended the six men and women. Without a common language, it was initially quite difficult to communicate but we managed well enough. Of course, I now speak their language quite well. They showed me the sacred spot where they themselves had performed the ceremony, my son."

"What ceremony?" asked Father Ciasca.

"Ah, I have jumped ahead! How old do you think these men and women are, my son?" Marco Polo pointed at the others.

"Their age? Let me see, they all seem to be in their twenties, do they not?"

"No. They are about two thousand years old," he smiled.

"Two thousand? That is impossible, sire!" Father Ciasca was horrified.

"Unfortunately, it is true, my son. You yourself have come searching for eternal life. The secret was found two thousand years ago by the priests of their king and they were the only group of citizens that the king insisted should test the chant. They were sent into the valley and forbidden to return. They shall live forever."[35]

"Forever? How can it be, sire?"

"You ask that question, my son, but again, I repeat, you are here because you want to find out how to also live forever. You do not want to die. Am I right? If you are willing to believe such a thing, then why should you be surprised that someone else is already doomed to live forever? It is a horrible curse, my son. Pity them, for only fire or some other disaster will destroy their bodies. Pity me! How old do you think I am? More than five hundred years ago I cheated death in Venice but now have to see day and night dissolving into each other forever. What benefit could you possibly see? What power could possibly accrue from living forever?"

Father Ciasca looked suitably contrite.

Marco Polo sighed. He seemed overwhelmed by sadness. "I could blame my time for wanting to find out whether it was truly possible to live forever. A very stupid and dangerous gamble. I cannot blame these men and women, as their king ordered them to live forever. But you, my son, have you not learned from our mistakes? What is it, 1893? What is the meaning of progress if you seek that which will destroy by keeping alive? I weep for you."

"Who is that evil man?" asked Marco Polo, pointing at Professor Moriarty standing at a distance. "I know he is not to be trusted."

Father Ciasca started to respond, but Marco Polo raised his hand. "I understand. He wants the chant and wants to live

---

[35] The reader is referred to the appendix.

forever. We know what to do. This is not the first time this has happened. It is fine.

"It is time for all of you to go, my sons. You must not stay here. They will make a soup for all of you and prepare bread as part of their banquet for visitors who stray into the valley by mistake. You must have it and go. Never come back."

"And you, sire?"

Marco Polo smiled sadly. He shook his head. "I am cursed. I must stay here. Forever."

"You, sir," he beckoned to Sherlock Holmes, speaking in French. "Let us go for a walk while they prepare the meal. I wish to show you something."

Marco Polo and Holmes walked slowly away toward a grove. Meanwhile, the inhabitants went back to their village and returned with food. After a couple of hours, with the meal ready and Marco Polo and Holmes having returned after their long, private confabulation, we were asked to sit down at a rough table made of stone. We were served some exotic fare—brown rice, fish, some vegetables, and some excellent soup. They insisted that we have plenty of vegetable soup saying it would give us energy and keep us in good spirits till we reached our destination. I did not like the taste somehow and had only a spoonful. The rest consumed vast quantities, swearing by the fragrance.

Holmes and I said good-bye to Marco Polo. I realized that I was experiencing something remarkable, something that no one would believe when I reported. I will have to live with taunts and derision, perhaps.

Then we mounted our horses and camels and bid good-bye. Already, the heavy food and the stress of the previous days had made us sluggish.

We waved at the seven inhabitants of the valley. Marco Polo waved back, smiling sadly, I thought.

It had been a remarkable experience.

I recall that we somehow made our way out of the valley. We were led by one of the inhabitants who returned after taking us as far as the village.

All of us were overtaken by sleep.

◇◇◇

When I woke, I found that the animals had taken us to an area near the Nile. There was not a soul in sight. Everyone else was still asleep on their steeds and camels, which were standing quietly. Who had led us there? I could not tell where we were; the place seemed entirely unfamiliar.

I realized that we had been drugged. I had only consumed a very small amount of the soup and that was probably why I was still in command of my senses and had been the first to awaken.

It took almost a complete day for the rest of the group to become conscious. I saw that everyone, including Holmes and Professor Moriarty, was considerably disoriented.

"Where are we now, Watson?" asked Holmes, holding his head in his hands.

"I do not know, Holmes. All I recall is that we were led out of the valley."

"What are you raving about, man?" Holmes was irritated.

"I believe we were drugged in the Valley, Holmes. That is why you are so sleepy and disoriented."

Indeed, everyone was still staggering in a pitiable way, holding their heads and stomachs and moaning. It was an unnerving sight.

Professor Moriarty, Father Ciasca, and the guards were in a similar condition. They had walked with great difficulty to the Nile and washed their faces. Then they came back and collapsed in a heap near their horses.

"Holmes? Is that you? Yes, it is Holmes! You will pay for this!" shrieked Professor Moriarty before going into paroxysms of pain.

"And why must I be given credit for this, whatever it is?" inquired Sherlock Holmes, observing his adversary writhing in agony.

"You are behind this! I am sure of it!"

"Not at all. I myself am severely inconvenienced. My last recollection is of us leaving the valley, sent off by Marco Polo. I see that we are without any of our belongings. An unfortunate situation."

"*Mama mia*! The pain! My head!" Father Ciasca moaned in pain.

I was quite puzzled to witness this extraordinary behaviour. Many grown men were walking about unsteadily, moaning and screaming, holding various parts of their bodies. Other than a very slight headache, I was quite fine and had none of the symptoms of the others.

"I suggest that I tend to all of you," I said.

Holmes and I gathered all the men and made them sit down on the ground. Then I looked at Holmes with growing concern. He looked pale and weak. Was it my imagination or were his eyes dull? He seemed utterly fatigued, a mere shell of the upstanding, alert man I knew so well.

Meanwhile, all the rest were still in acute discomfort. The entire group would need time to recover. I guessed it would be a good two days of care and nourishment. I managed quite well, given that someone had thoughtfully provided us with minimal provisions. It was a crude hospital, with no facilities at all, except a doctor (me) and access to the Nile. At a distance, I could see some crocodiles staring thoughtfully at us. I ensured that we made a nice barrier between us and the rest of the raw wilderness. We had no idea where we were, except that we were collectively ill but not, apparently, likely to die.

By the end of the second day, everyone was able to converse. Professor Moriarty, Father Ciasca, and the Italians were isolated and still watched; trusting them was impossible. The evil within Professor Moriarty remained. He had been thwarted by a power greater than he could manage. I finally had time to sit back and think.

I recall standing still for a while, completely dazed. Holmes was watching me quietly from a distance. He was leaning against a large rock.

"Holmes!" I cried. "The matter is most extraordinary! It is beyond fantastic!"

"Indeed, Watson? You surprise me. When have I seen you last in such a mood?"

"It is singular, Holmes! Did we actually meet Marco Polo? Were we hallucinating, Holmes?" I was very agitated.

"Watson, if there was ever anyone who needed medication urgently, I believe it would be you. Come to your senses, man! Of course it was Marco Polo himself! Let us take stock: One, we have evidently been drugged and sent away. Two, we are here in the middle of nowhere, with nothing except our clothes on. And three, we have the pleasure of Professor Moriarty and Father Ciasca's company."

"Holmes, we were saved by Marco Polo! Who would believe us in London, Holmes? What would we say?"

Holmes had pulled out his pipe. He filled it with tobacco and lit it.

"Marco Polo did you say, Watson? Ah, but of course! Mr. Marco Polo from Venice, Italy? It is rumoured that he moved on to better climes almost half a millennium ago. But you now say he is in the vicinity, saving people in distress. This comes as a surprise or a shock depending on your perspective. I must report to the Royal College of Surgeons that a fine colleague has been the victim of a sunstroke. Tut. A charming tale, Watson. I am just joking, my dear fellow, forgive me, an excusable liberty, I would hope! I quite agree that it would be difficult to convince anyone, including your wife, a lady of the finest intelligence, that we could have met Marco Polo! But I see possibilities in this exotic tale! Shakespeare should feel uneasy about his position. Next you will say there was a mysterious woman who—"

"But there was, Holmes, there was! A woman looked after you for a day!" I cried.

Holmes clicked his tongue in exasperation. "Really, you babble like a brook today, Watson. Amusing in itself but after a point…"

Sherlock Holmes made a gesture of impatience and put his hand in his trouser pocket.

His face changed. He slowly brought out a bracelet.

"What kind of prank is this, Watson?" Holmes was annoyed.

"Am I capable of such a strange prank, Holmes?" I cried.

Holmes paused and considered the matter. "Yes, you are right, Watson. You are right. You could not have done this."

Something in the way he said it annoyed me.

"For the life of me, Watson, I have no recollection of having kept this bracelet in my trouser pocket. This is preposterous."

"Let me see it," I said, and examined the bracelet.

"That is exactly the same bracelet that she was wearing!" I gasped. "This is proof, Holmes!"

"Watson, my good fellow!"

"You will have to believe me, Holmes. A woman tended to you. She must have given you this bracelet as a gift and put it in your pocket!"

Holmes looked at the bracelet closely.

"Hmm. Unusual workmanship and material. Silver, traces of gold perhaps, unusual stones, amethyst certainly. I would hazard it is hundreds of years old, though one can see that it is of Tuareg origin. You will undoubtedly recall my monograph on the jewellery of the Kazakhs. I presented it to my friends in a tightly knit forum of scholars who have extensive knowledge and interest in the matter. But this is fascinating, Watson, fascinating."

Holmes put down the bracelet. He scratched his chin thoughtfully.

"I digress. I am inclined to consider your wild proposition a little more carefully now, Watson.

In the meanwhile, it appeared that the group was now restive and ready to move on. We gathered around Holmes, as he beckoned to everyone. The mood was sombre.

"My friends. We must now move on. We do not know where we are and how it happened that we have reached here. Please speak up if you have any ideas."

One of the Tuaregs spoke.

"These two men have something to do with it, I am quite sure. Let us put them to death."

The others nodded in vigorous assent. Professor Moriarty and Father Ciasca had not achieved any level of popularity with the men. One the Tuaregs took out a long sword and moved closer to Professor Moriarty. To his credit, he did not flinch. Father Ciasca, on the other hand, turned pale and hid behind Professor Moriarty, cringing like a little boy behind his father.

Hasso commanded the man to stop. "Wait, nothing must be done in haste. This is not the time to take decisions other than on matters of survival. What is your suggestion, Father?"

Holmes beckoned to Hasso and spoke briefly to him. He nodded in response.

He spoke out loudly in Tamasheq to his friends. "The Father suggests that we follow the Nile south. We shall probably reach Khartoum soon and then we can think better. We shall take the Italian guards with us to Khartoum as prisoners and decide their fate there. As far as these two evil men are concerned, he suggests that two of us take them along the Nile in the northern direction."

Holmes translated for my benefit.

I was shocked. I hissed in a loud whisper. "Holmes! How can you just let Professor Moriarty go? He is wanted by so many for so many crimes! You must apprehend him."

Holmes spoke in a quiet undertone in my ears. "Watson, please think. The probability of both of them surviving a trek back toward Cairo walking along the Nile is slim. Cobras, crocodiles, hostile locals, no money, sand, baking heat that they are not used to. Do they look fit? No.

"If they do survive, which is quite unlikely, they would return without what it was that they were looking for. We are still ahead. They do not have the chant. And to your point about Professor Moriarty being 'wanted.' I regret to inform you that he is *not* wanted as no crime—not one—has been ascribed to him directly. In fact, he is a perfectly respectable law-abiding citizen. Of course, I do know the reality. But without proof, what can anyone do? Neither the Sûreté nor Scotland Yard believe he is responsible for the many outrageous scandals that *we* know have his imprint. And on what grounds and authority may I apprehend someone in Sudan and transport him to London?"

I nodded reluctantly. "You have a point, Holmes."

"I always do, Watson, I always do.

"However, this is indeed an opportune time to discuss certain matters with Professor Moriarty before we depart. We may never see him again. He will be either in a grave near the tomb of a Pharaoh or will be back in Paris, planning further outrages."

We announced the plan to our party. The Tuaregs appreciated the novelty of the idea. Two men were assigned to take Professor Moriarty and Father Ciasca about ten miles to the north along the Nile and to leave them there with absolutely nothing but their clothes and food for just a day. Professor Moriarty did not respond. Father Ciasca did not seem to understand and had a puzzled look. He asked for a cigarette which was given him.

Holmes called Father Ciasca aside.

"Ah, Father, you do anticipate difficulty in returning to the Holy See, perhaps?"

Father Ciasca appeared to be surprised.

"Yes, Signore Holmes, the Pope will be disappointed."

Holmes puffed at his pipe.

"Do I refer to that or to something else? Do you think the police might await your arrival?"

Father Ciasca tilted his head quizzically.

"I see that you are left-handed."

Father Ciasca glanced down at his left hand.

"The Italian police await you in Rome, Father Ciasca."

"Why should they? I have committed no crime." Father Ciasca was indignant.

"Indeed? Well, they will have a different view. They will charge you, Father Ciasca, with the murder of Antonio Rozzi in his office at the museum in Venice."

I was unprepared for this blandly delivered statement.

For a fraction of a moment, Father Ciasca's eyes hardened.

"I deny it. You have no proof." His voice was rather melodious.

Holmes raised an eyebrow.

"Let us stop this pretence of being a holy man on a mission, shall we, Father? I am quite sure that you visited his office, with the intent of persuading him to part with the translation of the manuscript. I know this because I did ask the guards if they recalled who had visited Antonio Rozzi over the past few days, and your name came up, though I did not know you then. I believe he refused to give it to you, because, after all, he had given it to me. I know you opposed the Pope consulting Lord Dufferin; in fact, Antonio Rozzi told me so. And, my dear sir, when you smoke cigarettes, holding them with the fingers of your left hand, you certainly suggest that you are left-handed. But I have better proof. The fact that Rozzi was hit on the left side of his head and he fell forward. Perhaps you were pretending to look at the view from his office window and surprised him from behind. Most cowardly. And then the luxury of a cigarette while in his office. Complacence! I know that ash—and that flavour! Perique tobacco from Louisiana, an absolute rarity! I recognized it in Antonio Rozzi's office. It is no coincidence that you smoke cigarettes with that tobacco, as I have been observing. Have you read my monograph on tobacco ashes? No? Tut. In any case, I took the precaution of writing from Tamanrasset to my friend Lestrade about my conjectures, and he in turn, would have certainly informed the Italian authorities and the Vatican. I guarantee that you are expected."

We turned away from Father Ciasca. His face was expressionless.

As the groups prepared, Sherlock Holmes invited Professor Moriarty for a stroll along the verdant banks of the Nile. I watched from afar as the two adversaries conversed as old friends.

I spoke to Holmes later and this is the paraphrasing of the conversation that he said took place.

> *We walked down to the Nile. It was Professor Moriarty who began the conversation.*
>
> *"I compliment you, Holmes. Your solution is most brilliant. I shall soon be dead by my own hands, in a manner of speaking."*

"You certainly see that I am challenging you."

Moriarty waved his cane in the air impatiently.

"A challenge? This is hardly a sporting duel. Only a young fool would consider it so! I believe your logic is outstanding. It is in fact an unequal battle. You send two men of indifferent health into an unknown territory. I am not afraid. But I am not stupid either. We lack the strength and the resourcefulness to survive in such conditions. I would venture to say that it is similarly logical to conclude that you have won and that I have lost. There is no chance at all that I shall reach Paris. Yes, death is certain and is absolutely guaranteed. The game is over. I congratulate you."

Holmes smiled. "Had I been in your place I would not say anything that conclusive. But be that as it may, I wonder if we may discuss a few situations in the past where we have been adversaries?"

"By all means."

"The case of the Amsterdam Dutch masters. The tall nun in the cloister…?"

"Obviously. She is excellent. One of my best."

"The kidnapping of the Italian chef at Café Gondola in Brussels?"

"It was Lafarge, as you guessed."

"But the matter at Geneva?"

"A distraction by Phillips. It was intelligent of you to travel to Basel, but everyone had left by the time you reached. You were late."

"What was the point of the blackmail of the member of Parliament? I knew he was the thief."

"We knew about his interests in the South Africa mines. That was the only point you overlooked?"

"I did not. I did send someone to Johannesburg to institute inquiries."

"Creditable. Well, that was a draw then."

"Perhaps I won, because it was a draw. But if I may ask, who told you about the manuscript? The Guardians?"

"Of course. Be logical, man."

"The Royal Family. Who? I shall guess ______."

"Correct, and the ______."

"Creditable. I commend you. I disagree with your objectives but your penetration has been more than I guessed."

"That is why I am who I am and you are who you are."

"Brave words."

"I won many battles. This important one, I lost. And so the war."

"Why this?"

"Humanity is insufferable. They must be controlled, manipulated."

"They are already."

"I knew you would agree."

"Not completely. Men with free will roam the streets."

"Fireflies."

"The streets are lit, however dim."

"Mere poetry."

"But human. Well, I see your escorts are ready. I must bid you good-bye."

"I may soon be part of sand but sand is eternal. That is eternal life perhaps, eh, Holmes?"

"Yes, for once I agree. That which we feel has no life actually endures, watching life and death. Good-bye, Professor Moriarty."

"Good-bye, Sherlock Holmes."

He walked away shakily, using his cane. He still seemed confident and in command.

Professor Moriarty then mounted his horse with the help of a couple of men, as did Father Ciasca. The Tuareg escorts waited for a signal from Holmes. They were ready to go. Father Ciasca had suddenly become quite pious and had clasped his hands and closed his eyes. He head was turned toward the sky and he was muttering a prayer, it appeared.

Holmes waved at the departing men.

Professor Moriarty halted briefly and pointed his cane at Holmes.

"And Holmes, some information as a farewell gift..." he shouted.

"Yes?"

"The president of____ is my man. I know you do not know."

He kicked the sides of his horse and the small team moved on. There was something harshly beautiful about the scene. Three Tuaregs leading two men to their death, moving single-file through the sands with the Nile's shadow enveloping them. At a distance some pyramids added a charming touch. I almost smelled frankincense.

◇◇◇

We returned to Khartoum from an inexplicable and singular journey. From the point where we bid good-bye to Professor Moriarty so that he could proceed on his final journey (certainly a phrase with more than one meaning!), we simply followed the bends of the Nile. After a few days, we suddenly found ourselves close to Omdurman. Holmes maintained a stoic silence throughout. We were subdued, unsure about how to explain the events to the khalifa or anyone else.

We reached the court of the khalifa at Omdurman and presented ourselves. The khalifa was very pleased to see to us return. It appeared that he was very preoccupied with several issues of statecraft, not the least being the question of the Italians hectoring him from Eritrea.

"Did you find what you were looking for?" he asked, though not with a great deal of interest.

"Yes, Your Excellency," said Father Bąkiewicz. "But we decided that the place is sacred for the Sudanese and we should not proceed. The core of your culture should be kept undisturbed. We had an encounter with some bandits but we prevailed, and in fact, brought back some prisoners."

"Well, I am glad you finished your little adventure. I must consult you on some pressing matters."

To our relief, the khalifa did not show much more interest in our trip to Napata, as he really wanted to speak to Holmes about the problems he was facing from his adversaries beyond the borders of Sudan. We learned that he was busy assembling his soldiers and the four assigned to us were immediately sent away to the Eritrean border, where all were killed almost immediately in a one of the endless skirmishes being reported from there.

The captured Italian soldiers were taken away and, given the general atmosphere of hostility toward the country, were summarily executed. Perhaps Father Ciasca was luckier than he realized.

"By the way," said the khalifa, "at about the time you left for Napata, we apprehended some spies who came on a boat to Sawākin and were moving into Sudan. We executed all of them except two men—an Indian man and his Moroccan lieutenant. Perhaps you can meet them. I do not understand what they want. Maybe they would be of some use before I put them to death."

Father Bąkiewicz had to perforce spend a number of days in close consultation with the khalifa, who had taken a strong liking for him. The khalifa did not hide his equally strong dislike for the British and the Italians and his determination to throw them out of Egypt by appealing to the religious sentiments of the masses—he was, in any case, in a state of jihad, first declared by the Mahdi. Father Bąkiewicz found himself in a piquant position, and so offered specific advice only when asked. But it was he who gave the khalifa a brilliant stratagem vis-à-vis Ethiopia, which I am still unable to speak of as I have been sworn to secrecy. The fact that the stratagem proved unnecessary later is irrelevant; a certain key assumption proved invalid. But its strength and clarity endeared Father Bąkiewicz to the khalifa even more.

Father Bąkiewicz and I were finally able to meet the two prisoners that the khalifa had referred to earlier.

The new chief of security, whose name I do not recollect, escorted us to a dungeon in a building close to the khalifa's palace in Omdurman.

I still shudder when I recall the stinking horror of that place, filled with men doomed to rot for years. Windowless cells, unsanitary conditions to the extreme, no access to water, unending torture by the guards—I could not have imagined a more ghastly place. But Father Bąkiewicz did not turn a hair.

In a dark cell behind bars, sat Thalassery Vatoot Mohammad Koya, the descendant of the great traveller Ibn Batuta. With him was Boughaid Arroub, his lieutenant.

"Koya? I am Father Bąkiewicz. And this is my colleague Tadeusz Bór-Komorowski."

The man looked at us dully from the dark cell. I was almost gagging with the unendurable stench of the place.

"I am sorry to see you here," said Father Bąkiewicz. "I know who you are."

"And I know who you are. But what does it matter?" said Koya in a low flat voice. "All is lost. I look forward to my death. They have killed everyone except us."

"Was all this worth it?"Father Bąkiewicz asked gently.

"Had I known my ultimate fate, no. I should have lived my life as a spice merchant in the Malabar. I should not have come searching for treasure. I thought I would see Mecca on my way back to my country. I will not. I have a wife and a sister. I have a son I have not seen. And never will." The man's despair was deeply moving. My eyes had adjusted to the darkness and I could see two extremely emaciated men, well on their way to certain death.

Father Bąkiewicz was silent for an extended period. Perhaps he was struggling with emotion. I certainly was.

"How is it that you are here?" he asked.

"Boughaid," said Koya wearily, gesturing to his companion and asking him to respond.

"After we missed you at Timbuktu, we went to Gao, hoping to trap you there. But you were cleverer than us and went away toward Kidal. We had no ability to travel there, so we decided to travel south to the sea and then take a ship down to the Horn of Africa and then up again to Aden and Alexandria. We got off at Sawākin. Unfortunately for us, the khalifa's soldiers apprehended us as we started moving inward and suspected us of being spies. We had no opportunity to explain. We seemed very alien. All were killed except the two of us. We have been here for several days. I hope to die very soon. Can you request the khalifa to have me executed immediately? Can you?" The man was distraught.

"I am very sorry."

"Koya, let me also tell you that what you seek does not exist. It is a waste of time." said Father Bąkiewicz.

I could not tell if the man inside shrugged his shoulders. In the dark silence, I could only hear laboured breathing; a particular cadence that I knew so well. My heart sank.

"I no longer seek it. I never knew what it was when I set out to look." Koya's voice was a whisper. It was clear that the act of speech was draining him of whatever little physical strength he had left.

"Wait!" said Father Bąkiewicz, with considerable feeling. "I shall try to help you."

We left that hell and returned to the khalifa's palace. Father Bąkiewicz sought an audience and was immediately granted one.

"Your Excellency. The men you hold are not spies."

"Who? Oh, those two men. Why do you say so?" inquired the khalifa.

"He is a spice merchant from India. The other man is his guard. It has been a terrible misunderstanding. They meant no harm."

The khalifa turned to his new chief of security (whose name escapes me). "What do you say?"

"It is possible," he shrugged. "It is true that we have not found anything on them. But that does not mean they are not guilty. I would prefer to interrogate them for some more days."

"Your Excellency, your reputation as a fair and compassionate ruler is well-known," said Father Bąkiewicz. "This is the time to win more friends. I repeat: these two men mean no harm. I appeal to you to release them. I will personally escort them outside your kingdom and shall be their guarantor."

"Hmm." The khalifa deliberated silently.

"My attentions are needed elsewhere," he eventually said. "If you are willing to take personal responsibility, then it is fine. Ismail, what do you feel?" he asked the chief of security.

"Yes, Your Excellency. But when are you leaving, Father?"

"With the khalifa's permission, immediately."

The khalifa protested. "Immediately? No, I need your advice! You must stay!"

I held my breath.

"Your Excellency, I am flattered. But we have already taken advantage of your hospitality. I shall be your ambassador and speak about your compassion and wisdom. It is time for us to return to Poland and resume our work. I request your permission to leave. We shall always be in debt."

The khalifa seemed visibly affected.

"I cannot hold an advisor against his will. Can you not stay for one more week and then leave? Will you return next year, perhaps?"

Father Bąkiewicz bowed. "I accept, Your Excellency."

I was able to breathe again.

"But please release those two men. I shall tend to them. They need to regain their strength to leave." Father Bąkiewicz was gently persistent.

The khalifa nodded. "You have a good heart and head, Father. You would have been a good advisor to my son. I agree."

The two men were indeed released and brought to the Tuareg camp to the south of the city. Suffice to say that they were in a pitiable state and it took two complete days of my medical attention to bring them back to a condition where they could stand unaided. Hasso kept them under close guard as he was still suspicious of them; it was not necessary in my opinion, but I kept my counsel.

Father Bąkiewicz spent the week with the khalifa at Omdurman.

It was finally time to say good-bye. It was agreed that Father Bąkiewicz would return at the same time the next year if his health permitted.

The khalifa gave us several gifts, which I need not enumerate. Father Bąkiewicz (Holmes) donated everything to the British

Museum on our return. But the gift that Father Bąkiewicz always treasured was a small poem written by his son and presented to him personally. There had been limited interaction with Omar, but I gather he knew that Father Bąkiewicz understood his personal tragedy and had influenced the khalifa in some way.

Since the average reader of my work tends to be impatient with poetry, preferring the morbid, I shall not supply the translation, but I may say that the words were extremely moving, touching upon humanity, friendship, justice, love, and duty. That poem is now amongst Father Bąkiewicz' most valued possessions and I have observed him refer to it silently many times, especially at times when a problem was particularly complex.

After an elaborate send-off at Omdurman, we set out to Sawākin. Though Father Bąkiewicz urged Hasso and the other Tuaregs to return to the Hogger Mountains, they insisted on escorting us till Sawākin. Under the escort of the khalifa's guards, we travelled to Haya and Sawākin. There was still some trouble with the Italians and even the British, but we finally reached the border of the town in the early hours. We had to continue on our own to the actual port with just a couple of guards as per previous agreement with the administrators of Sawākin town.

The parting was extremely moving. Even for the reticent Tuaregs, it was an emotionally laden moment. Was Father Bąkiewicz not one of their own? Had I, his assistant, not helped them many times with ailments? It was difficult for us to express our feelings. So many months together had created a bond of love and respect.

"Good-bye," said Holmes.

"Till we meet again," replied Hasso.

It was a magnificent sight. The silhouettes of two proud and tough Tuareg men looking steadily at each other with the rising sun in the east as a backdrop. The cries of a few gulls punctuated a salty silence.

They clasped hands tightly knowing that words were unnecessary. We said good-bye to each of the Tuaregs. Meeting again was unlikely.

We had dismounted from our camels, which were to return with the Tuaregs. I patted Freddy—he had been a silent and good-natured friend.

The Tuaregs turned and began the journey west. Who knew what their destination was? Perhaps Abalessa? Perhaps Timbuktu? Perhaps Sijilmasa? Though they did not sing this time, I could hear their songs, speaking of their Tinariwen and the beloved Queen Tin Hanan.

As they slipped into the desert, Holmes suddenly found the bracelet in his pocket. He removed it and instinctively called out to Hasso. But he was out of earshot.

"It belongs to them, Watson," said Holmes, dismayed.

"No, Holmes. It belongs to you. Who do you think gave it to you?"

Holmes turned and looked at me, his eyes comprehending.

"Would anyone believe it?"

"No. But do you care?" I replied.

That bracelet is amongst his prized possessions. Perhaps the most.

The four of us and the khalifa's escorts went to Sawākin.

We then boarded a ship to take us to Jeddah.

And from there, we were to travel to Mecca.

مكة المكرمة

Mecca

Holmes, Koya, Boughaid, and I travelled across the Red Sea from Sawākin to Jeddah. It was only after the ship left Sawākin that the two wretched men in our liberal custody were able to breathe easily. I felt sorry for the young man. His misadventure had been harrowing, to put it mildly. I was acutely aware that the descendant of one the world's greatest travellers was with us. But he had never bargained for the fact that Ibn Batuta's missives would cause so much turmoil across so many lands more than five hundred years after his death. Now Thalassery Vatoot Mohammad Koya wished only to return to India. He had no interest in eternal life.

Koya did not want to lose the opportunity to visit Mecca. And the descendant of Ibn Batuta fulfilled his desire. He was ecstatic that he would be able to complete his religious duty as a Muslim, under the benign protection of Father Bąkiewicz, a man whom he might have killed had he an opportunity. Instead, the Father had saved his life. The matter was perplexing.

After the rituals at the Kaaba, Koya turned to Boughaid Arroub. "We must now part. I shall go home."

"Yes, master," said Boughaid Arroub, looking down at his feet.

"I am not your master anymore. Are we not all equal in the eyes of Allah? Have we not so proclaimed right now? Go, I release you from any further obligation to the descendants of Ibn Batuta."

"How can that be, master? We live for you," whispered Boughaid Arroub.

"No longer. Here is a letter in my hand that I have prepared. I insist on it."

"How shall we now live, master?"

"Halt your activities immediately. In this letter, I have declared that the Guardians of the Letter no longer exist. And this letter gives you authority to sell the mansion and divide the proceeds amongst yourselves. Take up a peaceful trade and live on. This is my order." Koya spoke with commendable firmness.

Boughaid Arroub took the letters with shaking hands.

Koya turned to Sherlock Holmes. "And you, sir, I thank you. I am liberated in many ways. You saved my life. And I am grateful for your advice about what steps I needed to take regarding the Guardians. It is absolutely correct." Koya spoke quietly but with feeling. "I shall return home now and never leave it again. We shall not meet. But I shall always think of you."

He clasped Holmes' hand and then mine. Then he merged with the crowd of pilgrims and was gone forever.

Boughaid Arroub watched the retreating back of the descendant of Ibn Batuta. Then he bowed to us and slowly walked away in a different direction.

Epilogue

The return to London was in disguise, of course. It would not do to travel otherwise.

After the initial hysterics of Mrs. Hudson were concluded, Holmes and I visited the Foreign Office and met Ian Felton, our contact there, who was to take us to meet the minister.

"Welcome, gentlemen," the affable young man beamed. "An honour. Mr. Holmes himself! And Dr. Watson! Outstanding work, if I may say so, outstanding!"

"Thank you," said I.

"If you can give me your report, I shall arrange for it to be copied and—"

"That will not be necessary. Perhaps we could meet the minister now."

"Of course, of course," Felton was flustered. "This way, gentlemen."

We were escorted to a meeting room.

We entered to find the minister standing and in conversation with two other men. One was Lord Dufferin. The other had his back toward us. It was that person who spoke first without turning.

"Mr. Sherlock Holmes." His voice was deep. "Your services to this nation—I acknowledge them with gratitude."

"Mr. Prime Minister," Holmes bowed.

After a round of handshakes, we sat down and exchanged pleasantries.

"Your report then," inquired the minister tentatively.

Holmes proffered an envelope to the minister, who gave it to the prime minister, unopened.

It took some sixty minutes before the report was read by all three men.

"Commendable," said the prime minister. "An excellent analysis of the khalifa's views of the Italians and the French."

"Yet, oddly, you make no mention of what he thinks of us and his plans." Lord Dufferin was puzzled.

"I am perfectly aware of what they are," said Holmes calmly.

"Well?" inquired the minister.

"I cannot tell you."

There was a stunned silence in the room.

"And why is that?" asked Lord Dufferin, angrily.

"There are two important reasons. One: that I was not an instrument of the Crown and the intent of this mission was something entirely different. And two: the khalifa trusted me. I cannot break that trust."

"You were masquerading as a Polish priest! You speak of trust?" Lord Dufferin was most annoyed.

"No. The objective of my visit was different. I did not mislead him with a devious intent."

"But, Mr. Sherlock Holmes, as a subject of the British Empire, surely your loyalty toward the Crown outweighs any feelings you may have had toward a renegade native potentate!" The minister was flustered.

"I repeat what I said. That was not my mission to begin with. I am not committing any act of treason by not revealing what the khalifa confided in me. I am simply not acting on the information he gave me. To do the contrary would not be cricket, would it?" Holmes directly addressed the prime minister. "Is the information I gave not valuable? I have explained his perspectives. I have spoken about the way he runs his kingdom and who his confidantes are. And about his views on the French, Germans, and Italians. That should be more than enough for you to formulate your own strategy. I cannot betray the khalifa's trust. He thought I was not British and confided in me in that spirit.

"And even more importantly, I have spoken about the situation in Mecca, where I predict the Al-Saud family will unite the tribes and create a confederation. I see the possibility of the Americans getting involved there as well."

The prime minister got up from his chair abruptly and went to the window. He stood there for a few minutes.

"This business of the Vatican and its infiltration by Professor Moriarty. That alarms me," he said. "Lord Dufferin, perhaps you should pay greater attention there."

Lord Dufferin's face turned crimson. "I…I…yes, Mr. Prime Minister."

"Your report is brilliant, Holmes. I also agree that you are not in our direct pay and have no obligation to reveal the khalifa's plans to us. It would not be cricket. It is an honourable stand and I applaud it.

"Now, General Herbert Kitchener is doing a fair job in Cairo, perhaps this will be food for thought."

"I know a better man, Mr. Prime Minister," smiled the minister. "By looking at the report, I expect him to easily infer the khalifa's plans for us. And he is in our pay."

"Whom do you speak of?" inquired the prime minister.

"Mycroft Holmes."

◇◇◇

Sherlock Holmes cradled his violin, puffing at the pipe hanging from his mouth. The scene was most comforting and one that I had been witness to countless times. The man sat with his chin sunk in the chest, blue smoke enveloping him. He strummed absently on his violin with his left hand.

It was difficult to believe that we had spent so much time in the Sahara, chasing a mirage in a manner of speaking. Morocco, the Vatican, the Tuaregs, the salt mines of Taghaza, the Joliba, Tin Hanan, Darfur, the khalifa, Omar, Marco Polo, the secret valley, the shadow of Ibn Batuta, and of course Timbuktu. Had it happened? For three years, the world's greatest consulting detective had simply vanished in pursuit of—what?

"So, Watson, your mind is on our trip, I gather," said Holmes.

"Indeed."

"The twitches of your face, those vacant eyes, those wrists turning helplessly. Yes, you wonder why. Quite fair. Endless danger. Quite so."

"You never did tell me where the complete manuscript was, Holmes."

"I erred, Watson," said Holmes. "Here it is."

He handed over his violin to me.

I was considerably surprised. "What do you mean, Holmes?"

"It is inside the violin, Watson. Look."

I peered through the S-holes into the body of the violin. There was something in the shadows within.

"May I look at it, Holmes?"

"Of course, my good man. You will not understand a word, of course."

He gently prised out the folded manuscript from the violin with a forceps and laid it out on the table. He smoothened out the sheet. It was a rather small manuscript.

We stood and gazed at something of immeasurable value. The two halves had been put together very carefully. They had spent hundreds of years apart—one in Venice and the other in Timbuktu.

"I had left the violin behind when we left Omdurman for the secret valley, Watson. I anticipated trouble. And we did face certain challenges. I was speaking the absolute truth when I told Professor Moriarty that I did not have it." Holmes puffed at his pipe.

"What will you do with this now, Holmes?"

He glanced at the far wall and raised an eyebrow seeking my approval.

I nodded.

Holmes set aside his pipe and violin, and took the manuscript to the fireplace.

As it crackled and burnt, it released a strange blue smoke, which wafted to the ceiling. It then disappeared into the dark night.

"I went with Marco Polo to that spot, Watson. It was quite intriguing. The area has an inexplicably disturbed magnetic field."

Something struck me. "Holmes! Did you…?"

Sherlock Holmes lifted his violin. He began playing a Tuareg tune.

Poems in Sand

Amaha Ag Barha[36]

What are we but mere drifting sand in the vast desert of time and space? Who shall tell me why we are born, whom we are to serve and to whom we shall reveal love?

I have travelled in the deserts of the Sahara, the Tinariwen, and where people have seen emptiness, I have seen the ghosts of children playing with the dreams of those long departed, whose skeletons have become sand. I have seen men walk alone in a silent caravan, with no real destiny except perhaps the silent welcome of a lonely wife, who was now quiet as the winds on which the eagles soar. With them, their camels have walked, contemptuous of existence, their wooden bells ringing out in the dead of night, reminding the ghosts watching from behind dunes, that they are not intruders, but vehicles for the tormented ambitions of weak men.

Many years ago, I cloaked my face with my *tagelmust* and began one such journey, unannounced, as was my custom, but only after invoking the blessings of those who seek only to love. Love would surround me as a slowly whirling cloak, and protect

[36] He was the old Tuareg storyteller Holmes and I met while travelling to Abalassa from Timbuktu. He sang this story-poem with the accompaniment of the tambour.

me from the cruel hot winds of the Tinariwen. I held the hand of kind wishes and set out from Sijilmasa to Abalessa to visit the grave of Tin Hanan, the mother of us, the Tuaregs, the Kel Tamajaq. I carried dates and incense as a courier for another man, who envied me my deep longing for solitude.

During the day, I walked. At night, I walked too, for the moon and stars shone in the clear sky and asked me not to rest but to understand eternal beauty and the true benediction of the mother of us all, Tin Hanan.

Two days from the town of Tindouf, as the sun sank in a pool of red, I came across three men, resting with their camels. We greeted each other solemnly and I inquired if I might rest nearby as well. They insisted that I share their food and we exchanged stories and searched for common acquaintances. We were surprised that the names of people in familiar towns were not familiar to either of us. I inquired about Moctar Ag Souca of Sijilmasa but they knew not of him, though they said their family was from Sijilmasa. They inquired if I knew of Iskaw Ag Intahana from Tamanrasset, but I did not know of him even though I had spent many waking moments there.

The stars shone in great brilliance that night. I looked at the moon for its blessings. And the camels looked at each other with half-closed eyes. One of the men took out an *anzad* and played tunes sprinkled from the heaven. The tunes were created then, stroked by starlight, and ravished the nearby sands without touching them. From deep within the sands came the beats of the *tende*. The night winds calmed down and stopped to listen. The others sang, asking that fellow-men know of love and loneliness, and that music bring rest to the troubled mind. Such was the gentleness in their music. I listened, with my head resting against the side of my camel, and his heart and mine came together, to the beat of the dark night. I wrote poems in the sand, with words I had not heard of before. And I saw the sand embrace them and take them down, down, down, to the hearts of poets who were lost for so many years in the desert. The men sang my poems, and the words now crept over the dunes and slipped away into the night. I slept, dreamlessly. But no, there was light. The light of love from ghosts who had listened to the music and held it in their hands.

When I awoke, it was the time of the dawn and the men had gone. For the first time, I saw the tracks of camels leading away, and the sand not erasing them. From the far distance, I heard the *Anzad* and the *tende*, and I knew that I was not to go toward the music.

I walked toward Abalessa, alone, with the bells of my camel, subdued, but caressing, now with the fragrance of love. For soon I would be at the grave of Tin Hanan, the Mother of Us All.

Hail Ar-y-mni, Ruler of Kush, who rules the three worlds
Hail Ar-y-mni, Ruler of Kush, to whom the animals bow
Hail Ar-y-mni, Ruler of Kush, to whom the plants bow
Hail Ar-y-mni, Ruler of Kush, for whom the winds cease
Hail Ar-y-mni, Ruler of Kush, for whom the Nile stops
Hail Ar-y-mni, Ruler of Kush, whom even the God Amun praises

We, the priests of Amanap, the one who is at Meroe, bow to you
We pray for your everlasting health and happiness
Hear us, O Ar-y-mni, Ruler of Kush, hear us, your oracles
Hear us, in the name of your father and his father

Here, as you ordered, is the sacred chant
Only you may chant, or the one you permit
At dawn, on the twenty second day of the months of Hathour or Bashans
Invoke first the Gods *mkh-lh-li, mkh-lh-li, mkh-lh-li*
A thousand times, ask for their benediction
And only when you are at the valley where we dare not enter
Beyond Jebel Barkal of the city of Napata
And where no man can hear your prayers
And which we have marked on this copper plate
So that you may travel alone, guided by Osiris
And where only you, O Ar-y-mni, or those you choose, may speak to Isis.
There call the Gods, *mkh-lh-li, mkh-lh-li, mkh-lh-li*
Then say the following a thousand times

Wos h ol-te
Lk ol-ne
Me net
Ar ste
Enep-l ato b lo-l
Qore Ar-y-mni
Ant Amnp ty-l Bedewi
Apedemk ty-l Aborepte
Tr-n tn to
Šo b-e Qene šo be-te
Wosi-ne Shore i-ne. Ty wi-ne
Kho-a lte šo be
Arini tene-a šo be
Yo m·Osale-te-te, šo be
Tr-n tn to
Yo m Omotrun-te, šo be
Tr-n tn to
Yo m· Pirko-te šo b wine
Tr-n tn to
Yo m·Klasko-te šo b wine
Net-te net-te
Tr-n tn to
Yi-ne Tel-n Yi-ne Tel-n
Art Ra. Art Wos-ne. Art Šore i-ne.
Net-te. Net—te

[37]

---

[37] O Isis the Great
Now behold greatness
We bow in reverence
Mother of Horus
The bestowal of abundant water
From the King Ar-y-mni
From the priest of Amanap, that lives at Meroe
Apedemak who is at Aborep
He goes to be reborn the light
Give abundant life, creator, give abundant life
Isis the Good. Osiris the eternal. To live forever

While lighting a fire of the wood of the lu'ju tree
In which you must pour myrrh
In which you must pour frankincense
And send the smoke to the heavens

Thus you shall be blessed by Nephthys
Thus you shall receive life from Amun-Ra
Thus you shall receive the blessings of Isis
And from all the Gods
Your flesh will not decay
Death shall not dare approach
And you shall live forever
This we say is the truth

Hail Ar-y-mni, Ruler of Kush, who rules the three worlds
Hail Ar-y-mni, Ruler of Kush, who rules the three worlds
Hail Ar-y-mni, Ruler of Kush, who rules the three worlds

I, Ar-y-mni, Ruler of Kush, received the secret chant from the priests of Amanap at Meroe[38] in my inner court.

When the soul transmigrates, give abundant life
Glowing manifestation to be reborn, give abundant life
To The North, give abundant life
Raise to be born the light
In the direction of the South, give abundant eternal life
Raise to be born the light
To The East, give abundant eternal life
Raise to be born the light
To The West, give abundant eternal life
I bow in reverence, I bow in reverence
Raise to be born the light, raise to be born the light
Eternal strength, eternal strength
Praise Ra, Praise Isis the good, Praise Osiris the eternal
I bow in reverence, I bow in reverence

[38] The ancient city of Meroe lies between the fifth and sixth cataract of the Nile Valley, about two hundred miles northeast of Khartoum. It is inhabited by ghosts, say the legends.

I thought long and hard about the matter.

My pyramid-grave is ready. In some time, I too shall be summoned by the Gods. When I was younger, I had commanded the priests to derive the secret for eternal life.

But now, I do not seek it.

When those whom I have loved have gone away, of what use is a life without death? My mother, my brother, my sister, my fifth wife, my son—they are alive in my memory, but I yearn to meet them, wherever they are, rather than stay alive. I loved them greatly. No, far better that my priests prepare me for the after-world like others before me, where I shall find solace with those I loved. Already I see that my grave contains all that I hold dear and all that I shall need for the afterlife. Of what use now is this collection of flesh and bones in which I think, in which I feel, to which my people bend forward?

I came to a conclusion. I decided to accept the copper plate from the priests. Then I read the chant silently and was convinced that my decision was right. I do not wish to live forever in this body.

On my bidding, the priests were taken away and put to death immediately.

I did not wish to destroy the copper plate however, as I recognized that the secrets revealed by the Gods to my priests could not be disrespected. Who can say how Kush and I would be cursed by Amanrap?

But I was curious. I selected three men and three women who my priests said were blessed, without any physical defect and of high intelligence. I made a copy of the copper plate on papyrus. I then commanded them to take the papyrus copy and go to the valley and chant the incantation. I ordered them to spend the rest of their lives there and not to ever return to Meroe, on pain of death. I gave them enough to live for a year without discomfort—food, wood, cloth, seeds to plant for crops, mules, and more. They were to continue forever there, but not to beget children. There is only a single narrow path into the valley and none dares enter because of bad omens. The valley is about ten days southwest of Napata.[39] Even camels hesitate to walk in the sands of that region, which hiss with the angry words of demons and annoyed gods.

They were to send back a mule on the path once they finished the chants. My guards were to wait outside and to bring the mule back to me. This happened a year after I sent them inside. I assume that the incantation has worked. I ordered that all references to the valley be removed from my court records. All those who knew about what I had done were also put to death. These included the guards who I had sent to the mouth of the Secret Valley.

I wrapped and sealed the copper plate in the skin of an antelope that had been treated by the smoke of frankincense, and kept it with me, waiting for the time when I could dispose it off.

I decided to send it with many other gifts to my friend, the ruler of Asmara when I heard that he proposed to send a group of ambassadors to the rulers of lands to the east. They would go, he had said, to Persia, to Nineveh, to Bactria, to India, to China and to other such lands that we have not heard of. I wrote to him, in Greek, complimenting him on his wisdom and vision, and requested that he should ask his ambassadors to give as tribute the copper plate, unopened, to the very last land they would visit. In strange lands with different cultures and languages, the copper plate would just be seen as a tribute from a distant king and stored in the treasury. I too have several such gifts and tributes from the kings of many lands that I have never looked at and have no use for.

I received a letter—written in Greek—from my friend in Asmara. He thanked me for my gifts and promised to honour my request. The ambassadors were soon to leave. No one knew

---

[39] I have deliberately provided incorrect information about the chant and the location, for the safety and well-being of my eager and devoted readers, who may otherwise feel compelled to visit the site to find the valley. I can understand their disappointment but hope I shall be excused.

when they would return, he said. Perhaps after five years, perhaps ten. Perhaps never.

And now I wait for my time when I shall enter my pyramid, prepared for the afterlife. The *shawabties* have been prepared. Nephthys shall protect me. Anubis shall be by my side.

Then I, Ar-y-mni, Ruler of Kush, shall meet those I loved when they were alive.

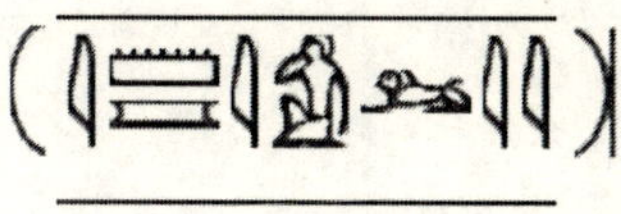

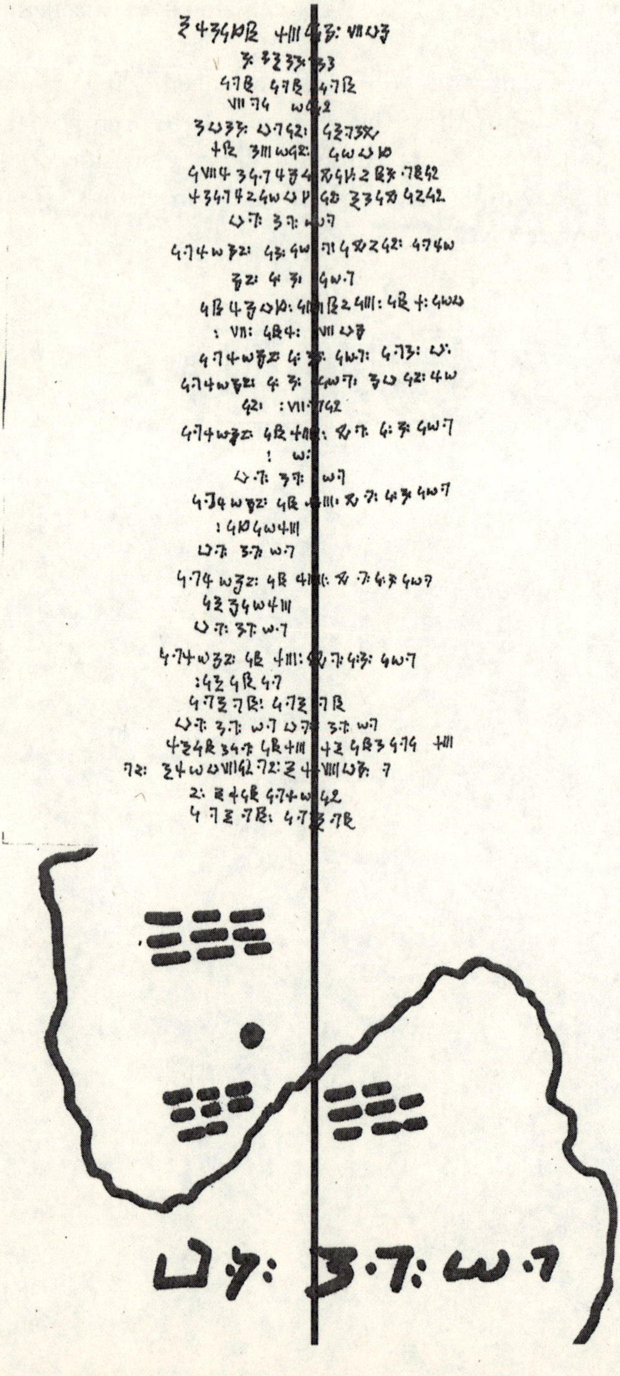

Acknowledgments

Writing this book has been a wonderful journey.

The persona of Sherlock Holmes lends itself to countless possibilities. My previous book took him to Japan. This one spans historical figures, geographies, and cultures. Researching old civilizations, learning the basics of unfamiliar languages, trying to adhere to an authentic treatment of Holmes and Watson while creating a plot; it's been very challenging but I've enjoyed the experience.

This book would not have been possible without the support of many. I would like to thank the following.

- Roger Johnson, the scholarly editor of *The Sherlock Holmes Journal*, for his kind Foreword. If there's anyone who knows the world of Sherlock Holmes, it is he.

- Barbara Peters, the editor at Poisoned Pen Press, who approved of the idea and encouraged me. I consider myself very fortunate that she gave time to this project.

- Diane DiBiase was my fellow-conspirator from the beginning and gave me excellent feedback and suggestions along the way. I came to rely on her well-grounded opinions.

- Sudarshana Ghosh and Vidya Nayak read my drafts along the way and gave me many suggestions, most of which I incorporated in my work-in-progress.

- The complex matter of the Meroitic language needed the suggestions of experts. I was fortunate to get some advice from Dr. Clyde Winters and of Dr. Alex de Voogt of the American Museum of Natural History, both experts in Meroitic.

- Tareq Al-Garawy guided me on the Arabic. I am grateful.

- Amit Fenn helped with the Meroitic writing.

Vasudev Murthy
Bangalore
June 2015

About the Author

Vasudev Murthy was born in Delhi and has meandered around the world with lengthy stopovers in Tallahassee and Dallas. His books span a variety of interests, from Indian classical music to crime fiction, humor, and business management. A violinist and animal rights activist, Vasudev lives with his family and five snoring dogs in Bangalore, India, where he runs a consulting firm.

http://vmurthy.blogspot.com/

JAICO PUBLISHING HOUSE

Elevate Your Life. Transform Your World.

ESTABLISHED IN 1946, Jaico Publishing House is home to world-transforming authors such as Sri Sri Paramahansa Yogananda, Osho, the Dalai Lama, Sri Sri Ravi Shankar, Sadhguru, Robin Sharma, Deepak Chopra, Jack Canfield, Eknath Easwaran, Devdutt Pattanaik, Khushwant Singh, John Maxwell, Brian Tracy, and Stephen Hawking.

Our late founder Mr. Jaman Shah first established Jaico as a book distribution company. Sensing that independence was around the corner, he aptly named his company Jaico ('Jai' means victory in Hindi). In order to service the significant demand for affordable books in a developing nation, Mr. Shah initiated Jaico's own publications. Jaico was India's first publisher of paperback books in the English language.

While self-help, religion and philosophy, mind/body/spirit, and business titles form the cornerstone of our non-fiction list, we publish an exciting range of travel, current affairs, biography, and popular science books as well. Our renewed focus on popular fiction is evident in our new titles by a host of fresh young talent from India and abroad. Jaico's recently established translations division translates selected English content into nine regional languages.

Jaico distributes its own titles. With its headquarters in Mumbai, Jaico has branches in Ahmedabad, Bangalore, Chennai, Delhi, Hyderabad, and Kolkata.

SINCE 1946